Thomas Berger:

"A great writer. There's no doubt about it."
—*Los Angeles Times*

"A master of fiction with a sense of the comic bordering on genius."
"Our most entertaining and thoughtful slapstick satirist."
—*Playboy*

Vital Parts:

"As funny and pertinent as anything Berger has yet written . . . as tart as it is true."
—John Barkham,
The New York Post

"Massively humorous and immensely mature. . . . It reads like some kind of masterpiece."
—John Hollander, *Harper's*

Other SIGNET Titles You Will Enjoy

☐ **THE UNIVERSAL BASEBALL ASSOCIATION, INC. J. HENRY WAUGH, PROP. by Robert Coover.** A book about baseball, life and an accountant named J. Henry Waugh, who devises a dice-run baseball game that becomes an obsession.
(#T3890—75¢)

☐ **FLASHMAN by George MacDonald Fraser.** Here's the top selling hardcover book which fooled reviewers and readers alike into thinking this fantastic story was based on the life of a real man. But indeed it is entirely the work of novelist George MacDonald Fraser. Flashman is a ne'er-do-well with an uncanny ability for survival, who buys his way into a regiment of Lancers, goes to India and Afghanistan where he becomes involved in the uprising which signalled the beginning of the end of the British Empire. (#Q4264—95¢)

☐ **THE DANCE OF GENGHIS COHN by Romain Gary.** Romain Gary, author of the bestselling **The Ski Bum** and **The Roots of Heaven** has written a sardonically irreverent and brilliant allegory which centers around Schatz, a "de-Nazified" ex S.S. officer, who is haunted by the **dybbuk** of Genghis Cohn, comedian on the Yiddish burlesque circuit.
(#Q3929—95¢)

☐ **MOVE! by Joel Lieber.** Meet Hiram Jaffe—playwright, pornographer, professional dog-walker, relapsed Jew and practicing Zoroastrian in this "Haunting, mysterious novel of slapstick and painful wisdom."—**Saturday Review.** Soon to be a major motion picture starring Elliot Gould and Paula Prentiss. (#T3870—75¢)

VITAL PARTS

A *Novel by*

THOMAS BERGER

Ⓢ
A SIGNET BOOK from
NEW AMERICAN LIBRARY
TIMES MIRROR

SIGNET TRADEMARK REG. U.S. PAT. OFF. AND FOREIGN COUNTRIES
REGISTERED TRADEMARK—MARCA REGISTRADA
HECHO EN CHICAGO, U.S.A.

SIGNET, SIGNET CLASSICS, SIGNETTE, MENTOR AND PLUME BOOKS
are published by The New American Library, Inc.,
1301 Avenue of the Americas, New York, New York 10019

FIRST PRINTING, DECEMBER, 1970

PRINTED IN THE UNITED STATES OF AMERICA

– 1 –

Reinhart unwrapped himself from the terry-cloth robe and hung it on the back of the bathroom door by means of the embroidered label (BIGGIE'S, FOR A LOT O' GUY, trademark of a mail-order house specializing in the needs of the outsized), so obliterating the fun-house image of his gross nudity in the full-length mirror thereupon.

He padded to the toilet, planted his great hams on the turquoise cozy which covered the lid, supported his chins in his palms, and proceeded to review certain events of the day, beginning with the lunch-hour incident in the men's room of Gino's Restaurant.

Standing at one of the porcelain receptacles, he had read, on the wall just above the chromium flush-button, a ball-penned exhortation: MAKE LOVE NOT WAR AND MAKE IT WITH ME, signed "Chuck." "P. S. If you're interested, leave your number."

Reinhart had glanced in a nervous circuit and seen only some matter-of-fact gent running a faucet over his glasses, shaking off the excess, and applying paper towel for the final polish. Having fitted the black plastic temple pieces, wide as tongue depressors, onto his ears, the stranger gave Reinhart a keen, stern look. Reinhart decided to punch him in the mouth if he turned out to be an importunate "Chuck." But what if the guy was in turn entertaining suspicions of Reinhart?

The eyeglassed man caught himself in the act of leaving, and halfway through the door threw his head back at an odd angle and asked: "Don't we know one another?"

Oh-oh, Reinhart thought instantly, being trapped by his preparations, *here it comes*, yet found, self-hatefully, that far from assuming a hostile righteousness, he felt weak and guilty.

The putative fag took two backward steps, clearing the doorway. "Sure," said he, "you're Reinhart. Bob Sweet: we went to high school together."

After a couple of drinks Sweet insisted on buying him lunch. Reinhart had eaten no breakfast. He was a sporadic weight-watcher, and took advantage of opportunities that came his way, such as bottom-of-the-morning nausea. He was soon drunk on two Bloody Marys. Staring at Sweet's smooth countenance he remembered the acne of school days. No trace of it remained, yet time was, Sweet had been famous for his pimples. Reinhart fell unbearably sad, and ordered another gore-colored drink. Sweet was talking of business. Reinhart had long since seen his youthful dream of a synthesis of commerce and culture go down the same drain as his build. Sweet was apparently a successful moneymaker, had a trim figure, and would have choked on his porterhouse at an allusion to the *Divine Comedy*. Which in fact Reinhart himself had not looked into in the more than twenty years since leaving college. Yet neither was Reinhart solvent. So if laugh there was, it wasn't on Sweet.

Sweet said: "It's just by chance you find me here today." As if Reinhart had been looking for him; yet that was the style of the successful businessman. "It's sheer luck," Sweet went on. "Choked carb on my Comanche. Otherwise I would have been lunching in New York." Then, correctly suspecting Reinhart did not get his drift, he said: "My airplane."

"Yes," Reinhart thickly replied. "The congestion at our airports is deplorable. Sometimes you are in a holding pattern for longer than the flight took."

"No." Sweet pointed with the bloodstained tip of his steak knife. "You haven't got the picture. I'm not talking about the commercial carriers. I own my own aircraft."

"You *are* doing well," said Reinhart. "Your own plane."

"Excuse me," Sweet said. "It's always 'airplane' or 'aircraft.' Listen to the pilot next time you're up."

For some reason the correction stung Reinhart, though it was understandable that any art or craft had its own jargon. And Sweet, whose businessman's radar was tuned to detect the surface emotions of any vis-à-vis while his own features maintained a strategic, seemingly oblivious confidence, moved quickly to assuage the smart: "Nothing personal."

It was just the wrong thing to say, though in fact Reinhart appreciated the sentiment behind it. He certainly would not have preferred that Sweet be inconsiderate. Yet Sweet's very exercise of what might be termed a polite delicacy succeeded in reminding Reinhart of a much more serious matter than the discrepancy between Sweet's worldly achievements and his own.

Glowering over the crust of his chicken potpie, from the starter-hole in which a pea peeped at him like a frog's protuberant eye, he said: "Sweetie," the old school name coming involuntarily to his lips, "Sweetie, I tell you this. There isn't anything that isn't personal."

"My God," said Sweet, "nobody's called me that in years. We're getting old, Reinhart."

Reinhart blinded the imaginary batrachian with his fork and got a bit of alleged chicken as well, carried it to the hopper of his mouth, dumped it there, chewed, and swallowed this needless reminder that Gino's really wasn't big on anything but steak, and that happened to be too tough for Reinhart's removable bridge.

Reinhart's memory of Sweetie now came along in detail, dragged along, as it were, by the name. Not only had Sweet held the class championship in acne, and thus was popularly accused of being a fanatical masturbator, but Sandy O'Connell, a smaller boy, had in some altercation at a water fountain struck him in the chest and Sweetie, who must have been about fourteen, bent over and sobbed like a girl. After that he was for years the frequent target of feints to the sternal region, though certainly not by Reinhart, in whom physical victims always incited more disgust than sadism. If he had been asked, Well, what's a frail guy to do, he would have answered, Build yourself up, as I did. Those were the days when Reinhart never questioned the American principle of self-improvement, for the simple reason that it worked for him. Get yourself a set of barbells from York, Pennsylvania, use them regularly, and in several years you can be a monolith of muscle. Then take no exercise for several decades and let the heat of life melt you into a lump of fat.

"Excuse me?" Sweet was asking. Reinhart gathered from this that "Reinhart" had said something aloud, as he was wont to do when drink separated the selves. At neighborhood parties "Reinhart" had been known to wander out to the kitchen and fondle the hostess' behind, while Reinhart sat quietly in the corner of the living-room sofa wearing a thin, supercilious smile which distinguished him from the surrounding drones who talked of lawns and baseball, or, if the other sex, offspring, vacation prospects, and national figures who appalled them.

"I was pursuing a train of thought," he said now to Sweet, a portmanteau phrase he had heard in some English movie once and since carried for this kind of occasion, which was far from infrequent.

"Acne," said Sweet. "You said the word 'acne.' You were thinking of me as a kid." He lifted a piece of steak and feinted at Reinhart with its striated redness. "No, don't apologize. I don't mind in the least. I'll go you one better: I was the most wretched youth the world has ever known. I couldn't bear to look in a mirror. And I was yellow as a lemon. You remember how you and the other guys used to beat me up."

Reinhart protested. "I never touched you." Nor had anyone else except Sandy O'Connell, unless it was in private and that would have been utterly out of character for those schoolboys, for whom harassment of a weakling was exclusively the theme for public demonstrations and not therefore serious.

"Listen," Sweet cried jovially, "you don't forget those things if you're on the receiving end." He vigorously toothed his morsel of meat with excellent white choppers that were obviously his own. "But have no fear I want to settle accounts at this late date." Saying this, he was host to another emotion than bonhomie, and his eyes flickered across Reinhart's scalp, which after all these years was yet crew-cut, but thick, by God thick still, that was one thing he had not lost, and because he had been fair the gradual graying had not upset the balance of color.

Reinhart gave him a halfhearted hard look. "Think you could take me now?"

Sweet turned genial again. "You could jail me if I laid a finger on you. I come under the law's provision for prizefighters. I won my black belt last year in kung fu."

Reinhart nodded and finished his third Bloody Mary, no longer tasting the Tabasco sauce as such; it seemed pure sulfuric acid.

"That's a Chinese school of karate," Sweet explained, "outlawed in some places. Your body is a lethal weapon." He showed Reinhart a hand. "This will disintegrate a brick."

Reinhart leaned forward to inspect it, and caught himself with his own soft paws lest he keep going for a faceful of potpie. "I don't see a ridge of callus."

Sweet snorted. "TV stuff! Built up with putty on pansy actors. My master has hands like a woman, yet can break five one-inch boards simultaneously with his thumb."

"Listen, Sweet," Reinhart said loudly, and then broke into a huge, idiotic grin. He was dimly conscious that nearby diners, attracted by the noise, now turned away at this facial show of harmlessness. They would, however, soon know revulsion when he rose and vomited on the floor. Thus he would have evoked from utter strangers three distinct emotions. He still had a certain power, if mean and within the reach of any stray dog. The thought encouraged him to hang in there a while yet and milk his wretchedness for Sweetie alone.

"Listen," he repeated, "and I must admit I don't recall your first name. I can't keep saying Sweetie because you don't have acne any more and you are rich and tough and own your own airplane—"

"Bob," said Sweet, who sat stanchly concrete behind a swirling screen of Reinhart's sudden doubts that this colloquy was real.

"Mine's Carl now, though my parents named me Carlo, but my wife, whom you might remember as Genevieve Raven, she's younger than us and never lived here when small but worked for Claude Humbold, the realtor, after the war, she never liked the name Carlo, said it sounded queer . . ."

"OK, Carl," Sweet said, grinning derisively. There was a time when Reinhart could hold his liquor, could be drunk as a skunk and never let on, and friends would attest to this next day. Sweet, who had begun as a middle-aged anonymity in the men's room, looked younger and younger. He wore a uniform tan; his conspicuous glasses were stylish and did not signify infirmity. When Sweetie and Reinhart were young, specs gave a boy a pansy look. Reinhart had almost forgotten that. He kept coming back to the touchstone of his youth and rubbing things on it to see whether they were precious.

"Bob," he said sloppily, "you don't have to pull that karotty stuff on me—"

Sweet interrupted. "I hate to do it again, Carl, but it's 'ka-ra-tay,' all syllables evenly stressed and a little trill on the *r* if you can manage it. *Kara*—empty. *Te*—hand. 'Karotty' is TV-talk."

"Well, Bob, that's appropriate," Reinhart said quietly. "That's all I've got, Bob. That's the only excitement and color in my life—television. And don't worry. Even if you were still pimpled little skinny Sweetie you could take me with one hand now. You could also buy me from petty cash."

Now that Sweet received the unconditional surrender, he was as benevolent as was his country with its fallen enemies. He said sympathetically: "Don't you think you should get some food into your stomach? Why don't I have that mess hauled away and get you a steak instead?"

"Bob, I couldn't chew it. I have to mince my meat before I can get it down. My teeth are in bad shape."

"Good red meat," said Sweet, swallowing the last of his, which in fact was largely a yellow gristle which it did not help Reinhart's digestion to see being milled behind Sweet's flashing incisors. "Good red meat never hurt anybody."

"You married, Bob?"

"I was," said Sweet, attacking the salad, which glistened with oil. "I may do it again when I get old."

Even in self-pity Reinhart lied about his age, a habit of several years' standing. "I *am* old. I'm forty."

For a moment Sweet was taken in by Reinhart's desolation. "That's funny," he said, frowning behind the horn rims. "You and I were in the same class, yet I'll be forty-five in November."

Reinhart was beyond embarrassment at the moment. "All right, forty-four then. What does it matter? I'm finished, pal. I'm a living corpse." He snapped his fingers at the passing waitress. "Hey, you, bring me another."

She skidded, backed up, and stated evenly: "I don't have to take that sort of a thing, sir. You can request but don't demand like I was your servant."

Worse, she was not the hard-pressed hag of his own age which, not having inspected her earlier, he assumed she would be. She was young, and had a lovely hard pair, and though she remonstrated with him he was to her only a rude abstraction. "I'm a human being," she said redundantly.

He tried to smile, saying: "I'm not."

She was even more winsome with her lip curled. He took a swinish delight in the exchange, and as she marched indignantly away, he sneered for Sweet's benefit and muttered: "Snotty bitch."

"Get hold of yourself, Carl," his host said sharply. "There's no profit in that."

A heavy hand touched Reinhart's shoulder. He turned his head to look at it and saw a thick growth of swarthy hair amidst which flickered the gold of an almost hidden ring. Far above loomed the Mafia face, blue with close-shaved beard, of Gino, whose restaurant this was.

With a thug's courtesy, Gino said: "I wanna speak to yuh in private, *sir*."

"Sure, Gino." Reinhart was proud to be singled out by the proprietor of a popular establishment. In these parts influential people sucked up to restaurateurs, maître d's, and bartenders. It was a prestige-making thing to address such worthies by name and hear your own in return. Though having run up a modest bill, Reinhart had not yet got on the top terms with Gino, but now was apparently the time. And just when he had seemingly reached bottom. He excused himself to Sweet, already regretting he had bared his soul to the pimply schoolmate reborn.

He followed the thickset figure and managed to keep erect while threading through the tables, from almost every one of which some diner hailed Gino. Reinhart recognized many of these people. He had lived his life in the region, and most of the local businessmen ate lunch here. He nodded at certain faces, said a word to others, touched a shoulder now and again. The responses were not enthusiastic. They were a think-small, provincial lot, else they would have been in New York or Chicago, but no doubt they were perceptive enough to catch the assurance behind Reinhart's superficial amenities, for he was on his way up again after a series of descents which would have ruined a weaker spirit.

Gino's office was full of cold from a whirring window air-conditioner. Gino was shorter than Reinhart but as wide and not fat at all where it counted. He stood very close, breathing cigar fumes and a piquant memory of his famed spaghetti sauce.

He said: "It isn't easy to get good waitresses nowadays and they don't come no better than June. If you was not in the company of that gentleman I would kick your stinking teeth out, you lousy slob. I don't want to never see you in my place again."

Reinhart held his temper manfully. "There's been a misunderstanding, Gino. The young lady didn't catch what I said. There's a lot of noise out there—"

Gino's eyes closed slowly and did not open until he had finished saying: "Any man who talks dirty to a woman is a filthy skunk, period." Then his lids rolled swiftly up with an almost audible clangor. "Now you getchurass out of here."

"Tell you what I'll do," Reinhart persisted. "I'll write a nice tip on the bill."

Gino, who had seen Reinhart on countless noontimes,

had greeted him on entrance and detained his parting with an oily expression of trust that he had enjoyed the meal, now professed to be dumbfounded. "You sign here? I never seen you before in my life, you bum." He seized the chest of Reinhart's wash-and-wear suit and forced him into a chair. "Don't make a move, you." He fisted one of his two telephones and shook it at Reinhart's face, then snarled his pegteeth into the mouthpiece.

"Name's Carl Reinhart, for God's sake," cried the man who had put a signature to that effect on scores of lunch checks.

Gino slammed the instrument home. *"Reinhart!* So you are Reinhart, the biggest deadbeat on the list." He laughed in a savage scream. "Reinhart, Jesus Christ, Reinhart." Wonderingly he addressed a glossy leather-bound photograph on his desk—Reinhart was behind it, so could not see its subject—"He owes me a hunnert and eighty-three dollars. The collection agents can't find him. Where is he? *In my fucking restaurant, eating my fucking food, signing more of my fucking checks!"* Gino's face was a mélange of several colors and his voice that of a machine which wanted grease.

"You'll get every penny of it," said Reinhart. "My guest is Mr. Robert Sweet, the well-known tycoon. We are discussing a deal that will be very profitable to me in the near future."

Gino's breathing obscured the racket of the air-conditioner. He grasped a bronze paperweight, done in the form of an alligator or crocodile, and broke it into two more or less equal portions. At length he said, as if to himself: "So I kill him and go up for murder. Am I *really* better off?" Again he closed his eyes, and he whispered hoarsely: "You don't take another bite, see? You don't take a sip of ice water or wipe your hands on my napkin. You don't grab a toothpick or after-dinner mint on the way out. And you leave in five minutes flat."

Reinhart gathered himself together. "All right, Gino," he said. "If you want to be that way, I'll spare myself a lot of heartburn." As he passed through the doorway, one half of the bronze crocodile or alligator dented the frame, very near his right shoulder, with the force of a bullet.

Back at the table he said to Sweet, who he saw with relief had finished the meal, "I'm terribly sorry, but a call just came in reminding me of a one forty-five appointment and it is past that already."

While Sweet, as promised, took care of the bill, Rein-

hart revisited the toilet and, choosing one urinal to the
right of "Chuck's," inscribed upon the clean wall above:
GINO IS A CROOKED GUINEA. The phraseology, somewhat
out of date and thoroughly contrary to Reinhart's soul—
his best friend in the Army had been an Italian-
American, and as irony would have it, Reinhart had once
joined him in beating up a guy who called him a guinea—
the epithet was chosen with a sense of what would wound
Gino most to find on his own toilet wall, revenge being
futile unless it strikes bone.

Just as Reinhart finished, another customer checked
into the stall next door and, reading "Chuck's" message,
stared at Reinhart's disappearing ball-pen and assumed,
you could tell from his steely irises, that Reinhart was the
Phantom Faggot.

It would have been useless to explain. Reinhart joined
Sweet on the square mile of asphalt outside, the apron of
a gigantic shopping center which trapped and intensified,
by solar reflection off the white and pastel-colored
façades, the tropical heat of July in southern Ohio, to
which was added the thermal exhausts of a thousand cars
as well as the steamy exhalations of countless cooked
consumers.

Sweet glanced at his black-faced Omega, of which
Reinhart wore a fifteen-dollar plagiarism. "The work on
my aircraft should be finished by now, so I'll go straight
out to the hangars." He wore a beautiful pearl-gray suit
of some zephyrweight material, with working buttonholes
at the wrists, which Reinhart had read, in the woman's-
mag reminiscences of a former flunky in the grande luxe
hotels of Switzerland, was the true test of a tailor-made
garment.

The encounter with Gino and the suffocating heat of
outdoors had begun to sweat Reinhart towards sobriety.
Already there were blackened areas of damp beneath his
armpits, which cooled briefly, nastily, if he lifted his upper
extremities. Therefore he put his hand out to Sweet, while
keeping the elbow close in.

"Bob, I can't say how much I have enjoyed this. Let's
do it again soon."

Sweet's hand was forceful yet fleeting. He was clearly a
man who could not waste time on nugatory routine.

"It's a pity we were only getting around to the core of
things when that phone call pulled you away," said he.
"Carl, I have my sentimental side too. This shopping
center depresses me when I think of the fields that were

here when we were kids. But things change every sixty
seconds in life. I am myself no longer the little mess I
was, so if the landscape is lost, the gain is mine. You have
to think of things that way or you'll be drowned by the
changes of time. Someone's always losing, and someone
else is winning. There is no standing still for anybody."

Sobering, Reinhart wished again he had not been so
candid. He said: "I've had my ups and downs. There's a
kind of rhythm to that too. I drink too much once in a
while and lose my sense of proportion. Thanks again,
Bob, and I'll see you around." If he had had an automobile, he would have jumped in it and gunned off. But his
own vehicle had been repossessed and Genevieve used the
other one.

"Wait a minute," said Sweet. "Let's exchange cards. I'd
drop you someplace but you obviously didn't walk here—"

But he had, at least from the bus stop. "As it happens,
my Cad is in the shop. An associate dropped me off here.
I was going to catch a cab back."

"Then that settles it," Sweet stated. "We'll have a few
minutes more together." He stared at his watch again and
then across the vast parking lot towards the roaring
highway.

Reinhart wondered why the tycoon tarried. He asked:
"Where is your wagon?" Amid the multicolored hundreds
ranked on the plain, through the aisles between which
women pushed steel-mesh shopping carts, followed by
sturdy, tanned children sucking on Good Humors or chewing wilted pizza slices of flecked yellow on blood-red.
Men trundled power mowers, aluminum wheelbarrows,
golf carts, and miniature snowplows on which there was a
preseason special, virtually a giveaway, a "loss leader"
with which to lure customers to blow their wads on other
items. Reinhart was painfully familiar with this tactic,
having once given it a fling at a gas station he owned.

A husky clerk, good-natured mesomorphic type with
melon-clumped biceps, toted a color-TV set from a nearby appliance shop to the purchaser's station wagon, capacious as a city bus of yore. Farther along, another store
enjoyed a run on air-conditioners, stereo hi-fi's, bathing
suits, and whole salamis, to judge from the huge signs
which obscured their show windows and the overburdened
clients who staggered out the self-opening doors.

Sweet said cryptically: "He'll be here in a minute." He
nodded his head generally at the mass of consumers and
their goods. "Look at that, Carl. That's money in motion,

where we used to play cowboys and Indians." Sweet replaced his glasses with sun lenses in the same type of frame. A slight balding could be taken, on the other hand, as a high, powerful forehead; each temple wore a splash of gray.

A young mother, plodding along in self-righteous oblivion with two grocery bags and two small children, the type who invariably plowed Reinhart down, yet respectfully circumvented Sweet, dropping a few oranges in the shift of line. Reinhart retrieved them, and the woman thanked Sweet, who had not even noticed the incident.

Reinhart panted from the effort of bending, and momentarily he seemed to be looking through the dark portion of a photographic negative.

Sweet asked impatiently: "Is there a helicopter service out here?"

"I don't think so," Reinhart said. "That is just a little private airport."

Sweet clapped Reinhart's shoulder. "Call 'em up for me, will you? Somebody should have a chopper he can send over here. I must get to New York without delay."

Reinhart might have acted on the request, even braving Gino's again, for the thrilling extravagance of it, the whirlybird clattering down on the blacktop like a deus ex machina to carry off his friend to a financial Olympus, while he, the faithful retainer, stood earthbound in a storm of flying candy wrappers and supermarket checkout slips.

Instead, a silver-gray limousine, with deep maroon fenders, chose that moment to glide through the vulgarity and stop silently before them.

"Good God," Reinhart blurted. His snobbish anticipation had been tuned too low, to Caddie or Continental or Imperial. "Is that a Rolls?"

"Bentley," Sweet answered curtly while stiff-arming Reinhart's attempt to open the door for him. The reason for this appeared when the uniformed chauffeur, an elderly man who was none too spry, came anxiously around the trunk to furnish the service.

In the air-cooled back seat Sweet explained: "You can't get a young man or Negro to drive for you nowadays. And just as well. Allison is too old to run around in the car while I'm away, and he doesn't try to drag at lights."

His buttocks deep in luxury, smelling the bouquet of glove leather, Reinhart sought to compensate for the instinctive slavishness with which he had grasped the door

handle. "Yes," said he, "you can't get any kind of personal service these days. Everybody thinks he's too good for
it—any kind of punk or moron."

"That's all right," Sweet said forcefully. "I don't knock
it when I think it's the same state of affairs in which I
have prospered. You have to be elastic. You can't get a
kid to cut your lawn, so you buy a power mower and do
the job yourself. OK, take that one step further: you
retail mowers in a seller's market. Everybody needs one."

"I see," said Reinhart.

"Just one example," said Sweet. There was a glass
partition between them and the chauffeur, and below that
a polished walnut panel with several discreet little doors,
one of which Sweet opened to reveal a telephone. Within
a thrice he was talking with New York: "Charlie said his
aunt is sick and can't go to Rome, but there's always the
Pyramids or even Grand Teton National Park, but cigars
are available." Or something on that order. Reinhart
gathered it was a sort of code by which Sweet ordered
the buying and selling of securities, or perhaps communi-
cated with industrial spies. He was big, oh was he big.

When Sweet hung up he said to Reinhart: "Where can
I drop you, Carl? Your office is in the old business
district? Hey, you remember Molly Kruger's candy store?
She can't still be there."

"Dead long since," Reinhart said. He found that Sweet,
who had left town to make a fortune, was basically much
more nostalgic about the landmarks of the old days than
he himself. That was a curious difference between them.
He yearned for his bygone personal powers; Sweet for
architecture and landscape.

"You can let me out on the corner of Allen, if you
remember it, then keep straight on to the superhighway
entrance, which feeds right out of Main."

"Right by the American Legion home," said Sweet.

"That's gone, too, I'm afraid. The First National built
there. A drive-in bank. I don't think they can handle you
if you show up on foot."

Sweet grimaced sadly and stared through his closed
window. "Well, at least this area hasn't changed much."
Dark-skinned persons were going about their business on
the sidewalks in front of discount jewelries and television
shops of the old kind. "The West Side still all colored?"
He turned to Reinhart. "There's a new market, Carl.
Especially in consumer goods. Always was good, but

getting better. The Negro is a bigger per capita spender than the white man."

"In the mood they're in these days, they don't want white enterprise."

"Nonsense. Don't be taken in by windy propaganda and PR baloney. Money is money, is colorless and sexless and doesn't give a damn for age. Shrewd men are making a bundle from the so-called youth revolution. But others are doing even better in the geriatric area."

Reinhart nodded. "Yes, my mother lives in Senior City and they shake her down for plenty."

"But the real revolution," said Sweet, "has been, and continues to be, in science. You wouldn't believe some of the things that are possible." Suddenly he was studying Reinhart in a stock-taking manner, as if—how preposterous; Reinhart should not have drunk so much at lunch nor insulted the waitress nor played high-and-mighty with Gino—as if he were a surgeon, no, a mortician estimating how large the coffin need be. But by this stage in his life Reinhart was accustomed to the perversity of his imagination, in which the truly sinister seldom appeared as such, whereas benevolence or even indifference evoked suspicion.

"Do you have extensive interests in technology?" Reinhart asked, because he knew that was one place where the loot was.

Sweet's inspection had reached his scalp. "I see you still swear by the crew cut."

Now Reinhart was gratified, because it was a personal observation and Sweet had not made many. "I'd feel like a phony if I changed after all these years. The way I see it—"

Sweet cut him off. "Excuse me, Carl, but we'll be there in a few minutes. Forgive me if I go straight to the heart of the matter. I used to hate you when we were kids, I'll admit. You were big and I was small. You used to push me around."

Reinhart protested. "No, Bob, never. I tell you that was—"

"No, no." Sweet shook his head. "It's over and done. *Time never returns.* The only reality is now. And you've convinced yourself that you are on your way out."

"You don't know the half of it."

Sweet's hand was impatient. "I can guess. You know, for one thing, you could still look pretty formidable if you stood up straight. You haven't lost a hair and you don't need glasses. A little dental work and you'd be set. Then put on a clean shirt and have your suit pressed. That wash-and-wear material really does need an iron, whatever the ads say. Don't believe what you read in print: that's for the mob. There are those who say and those who listen. Be sure you're never among the latter. Don't believe the current crap to the effect that the punks are aristocrats because of their youth alone and that the middle-aged are senile. That's the old shell game. There are the same sixty minutes in every hour for everybody. Don't take the 'generation gap' seriously unless you can make money from it. Suckers come in all ages."

He rapped on the partition and the silver-haired driver eased the car into the curb. "We're here," Sweet said to Reinhart, who in desperation tried to scramble out. No good to hear gung-ho talk from a man who had made it. The Sunday supplements always printed inspirational messages from statesmen, industrial giants, and show-biz celebrities. But if you thought about it, as Reinhart had, it stood to reason that successful personages had no motive to raise the level of nonentities. These statements were mere boasts, their purpose to maintain rather than alter a status quo in which the subject continued to amass money and glory and force while the object, a fat unshaven Reinhart, dunking his pastry in Sunday coffee, hopelessly read empty slogans.

Sweet seized his forearm with a Japanese-trained weapon-hand. "One moment. Call me sentimental—"

"Jesus," said Reinhart, "you're hurting me." That was a girl's line; but true.

Sweet loosened him slightly but did not let go. "You depress me," he said. "You're part of my past, after all. And we have reversed positions in thirty years. Look," he cried urgently, "is your pride too weak to let me help you?"

It was. Reinhart pulled away. "I'm doing all right in my own small way. It might not mean much to you, up top, but I have a nice little business, a home, and a fine family."

"You are on the verge of bankruptcy," Sweet said without expression. "And your kids are at the age when they are giving you hell. And your wife—"

"Please," Reinhart warned, "I'll have to hit you if you insult my wife." Then of course he quickly fashioned a flabby grin at the thought of his defenseless honor. "And you might kill me with a karate chop."

But Sweet was not amused. "While we waited for the car you were staring like a sex maniac at teen-aged girls."

Now there was no shame left to hide, and Reinhart ceased to strain against Sweet's grasp. "How about my coming along with you to New York?" he asked obsequiously. "Have you got a driver there? I work cheap."

"Don't dodge the issue with fake humility," said Sweet, releasing him. "And if there's anything my ego doesn't need, it's an old schoolmate working for me as a flunky. I don't mean that at all. . . . But why teen-agers? You are in the grip of some sort of fantasy, Carl. They are terrible pieces of tail. They are hard-fleshed and selfish and dry. They are—"

"Please," said Reinhart, who was discomfited by smutty talk.

Sweet said: "There is no more useless a thing on which to squander yourself than sex. Even drinking is better, because at least it can be pursued alone."

"What do you think a lech is for me, if not alone?" Reinhart did not say this in self-pity; he was striving for precise nomenclature. Sweet had begun to seem like some wizard or genie, especially since concealing his eyes behind the sunglasses. Were Reinhart to imagine a god, Sweet would certainly have been a feasible candidate for the role, a man of his own age and background, but apparently omnipotent and all-knowing. Reinhart was proprietary about his deities, like those Mexicans who locate the Virgin in Guadalupe. He could not remember ogling young girls at the shopping center, though long familiar with his disincarnate preoccupation with female teen-agers, which by now must have become subliminal, contaminating him secretly while his unsuspecting consciousness grappled with surface reality.

"I meant with dignity," said Sweet. "Of all the crazes sex is worst because it is dependent on other human beings, and if it gets bad enough, it can't be satisfied even with them. In the end it becomes completely inhuman. For Christ sake, what is it, finally, but the swelling of tissues? I wager to say you do not have any particular girl in mind, but rather the whole breed—in fact, preferring the total stranger, the anonymous pair of knockers and round behind bobbing through the park."

"Expanse of spirit in a waste of shame," Reinhart remembered.

"Why shame?" cried Sweet. "I take it you don't molest children. If they're big enough, they're old enough. The shame is that you are not getting any. The shame of the rich is felt only by the poor. Shame in oneself is an excuse for failure. When applied to others it is merely a form of envy."

Reinhart said wistfully, "I suppose you get all the teen-agers you want?"

Sweet's reply was harsh. "Age is the last thing I consider in a woman. Quite rightly, they all lie about it anyway. I have yet to get an erection from figures on a birth certificate. But if I have a choice, I steer away from the inexperienced. I haven't time to train a girl."

"Well, that's just it," said Reinhart urgently. "They all fuck like rabbits nowadays."

"Bullshit. Don't you believe it. I warn you, don't take your sense of reality from the communications media or your will will be paralyzed and your head stuffed with trash that is utterly arbitrary. There is the actual and there is the representation. They have almost nothing in common, except insofar as people begin to act according to what they hear, but they can almost never pull it off properly. Most teen-agers are still sitting alone fingering themselves."

"Your passion is money," said Reinhart with an air of discovery.

"If so," Sweet said pleasantly, "it's not its accumulation in cash. What I am trying to explain to you is that I don't worship statistics. I hire accountants for that. Only losers think in numbers. There is no such thing."

"Then what is your secret?"

Sweet said: "You know the old thing Morgan said when asked how much it costs to keep a yacht?"

Reinhart of course was a walking chrestomathy. " 'If you have to ask, you can't afford one.' "

"How does that make you feel?"

"Like shit."

"That was the idea," Sweet said. "Now one way to avoid that feeling is to abandon all desire in a positive fashion. A monk is not a failure."

"Unfortunately, I am not religious."

"Neither are many of them. That has nothing to do with it. We are talking about respective strategies. . . . Carl, you're doing it again. You're a hard case." Sweet laughed and tapped the back of Reinhart's hand with the steel rod of his finger.

Over Sweet's shoulder Reinhart was watching a young girl cross the street. She wore a sailor-striped jersey and no brassiere. The hem of her skirt reached scarcely below the delta, her hair to her shoulders and beyond; her eyes confident that traffic would part for her crossing, which of course it did very soon, defying Reinhart's prayer that she would be run down. One face of Reinhart's lech was murderous.

Sweet pressed a switch that caused the window to lower itself silently. "Miss," he called. "Over here, please."

Reinhart's heart whirred like an outmoded air-conditioner. "Don't, Bob, please don't do anything embarrassing." For he knew he would be blamed.

Ignoring him, Sweet waited for the girl to arrive. When she did, and hung her moonface, draped in hair, at eye level, her chest receding, her breasts pendulous as cheeses in an Italian grocery, he said: "I'm lost. I'm looking for the local airfield."

She did something with her tongue. "That's twenty miles away, across the river." She ritualistically acknowledged the absurdity of it, with batwinged shoulders.

"You're not thinking," Sweet said coldly. "Obviously I don't want the commercial airport." Her dark-rimmed eyes wandered through the interior, passing across Reinhart as though he were an empty seat. She looked about fifteen. "I fly my own airplane," Sweet went on. "It's at the private field. If your ears are pierced you should never go without earrings."

She touched her right lobe; both were in fact concealed by the amber fall of hair, so Reinhart assumed Sweet was faking.

"What's your name?" Sweet asked accusingly. Then in a sudden move he smiled in frank warmth. "No," he said, "don't tell me. I'll try to guess it from some of the things about you. You have Susan hair, long and fine and full of light. But your face is definitely Debby: pussycat nose. Your eyes, well, very exotic, Spanish I would say, like a girl's I knew once in Old Mexico, very Rosarita. . . ."

She seemed interested. Of course Reinhart's taste would inhibit him from trying anything of this sort. He had never been glib with girls even when he was young, except perhaps when writing letters, but to look into a face and tell it fantastic rubbish had never been his game. Surely a girl knew she was attractive. Why would it not suffice to make a simple statement of want? Reinhart stubbornly adhered to his principle, though in fact he was well aware of its practical deficiency. Even years ago, when it stood to reason he must have possessed certain

minimal charms, he had not scored as well as many
stunted, downright grotesque contemporaries. At college
the beauty queens were often pinned to troglodytes, prematurely balding or greasy forelocked, emaciates or lards,
peering through bull's-eyes mounted above pimpled
cheeks. Many big Army assmen had bad breath and body
odor and the manners of mobsters.

But all no doubt with golden tongues—and didn't care
where they put them, according to the envious. But Reinhart was not one meanly to libel the winners. Nobody
began a relationship with a genital kiss. A flow of language must precede, which properly made its point by
having no literal sense. But that too was wrong. In the
service Reinhart had known monosyllabic brutes who said
little more to pickups than, "Let's knock one off," and
did.

Useless to chew it all again, the same gall-flavored
paraffin for thirty years. At his present age it was perverted to desire minor female persons and any attempt to
feed such a hunger was criminal.

He was brought from the reverie by a joyful intelligence that, ha-*ha!* the teen-ager was not buying Sweet's
line after all.

She had smiled and smirked and, finally, winced. She
backed off two steps.

"You're putting me on."

"Sure I am," Sweet brazenly admitted. "You make me
nervous. You're driving me crazy with your body. It's the
wildest thing I've seen in this crummy little town."

She shook her head as if to clear it. "God, the way you
talk. Aren't you kind of old for this?"

"I'm seventy-four," Sweet said. "It's not against the law
to worship beauty, is it? Listen, I am on my way to New
York to do something about the conditions in the ghetto.
We are the richest country in the world, yet permit some
of our citizens to live like animals." He seemed to speak
with real passion. Reinhart was astounded, having taken
Sweet as a ruthless capitalist. "Too many older people
prefer to ignore this state of affairs. They grill their steaks
and suck their martinis and complain about their kids.
But if the kids aren't the hope of this country, then there
is no hope. I predict an explosion unless people like you
and me do something."

The girl was frowning. She had come back to lean on
the windowsill, her breasts on her forearm. Reinhart
projected his mind's eye into the street, became an imagi-

nary sewer worker in a manhole, saw all of her delicious behind encased in the sheerest doveskin.

Sweet said: "You know the militant blacks are right. The kids are right. Something must be done, and *now*. What is your thinking on this crisis?"

"Well," she said, "I want to do anything I can to—"

Sweet grasped her wrist, making a depression in the jersey between her knockers, his thumb against one, little finger crooked on the other. "Bless you. You carry with you the hope of our time. I'll be back in two days to organize a youth rally in this area. I'll need your help. We'll have top acid-rock groups, strobe lights, electronic environments, posters, everybody with his own thing, and telling it like it is. The ball field, Monday. Come early. You're a pussycat." He smoothly opened his hand and massagingly encircled her left breast. "Now wish me good luck in New York." He kissed her generous uncolored mouth and ran the window up.

It was of note to Reinhart that she nodded through the glass and walked around the hood in apparent self-possession. He watched until she turned the corner and disappeared. She never looked back. Her stride was full-juiced, on sturdy tan thighs bare almost to the cheeks.

Sweet said: "Do you know she put her tongue down my throat, the little twat? Well, there you are, Carl. You can knock that off if you want to represent yourself as my advance man for the rally. If that's your taste. Though why it should be, I don't know. Maybe you are attracted by the illegality of it."

Reinhart said: "You could be put in prison for what you did."

"No," said Sweet. "*You* could."

Reinhart had not recognized the girl, but might well know her name. No doubt the offspring of some other old schoolfellow, one who had stayed locally like himself to spawn a family, and was held in contempt by the adolescent members, feared Negroes, and was driven to impotent madness by rock music and the threat of a youth takeover.

"What gets me," said Reinhart, "is that you really sounded sincere."

"Oh, I might have been, except about wanting to screw her. I told you there was money in Negroes. There's more in youth. I know a man who made a half-million last year in posters, buttons, psychedelic clock faces, and the rest of the garbage they buy. Being a father you must be aware that their allowances are more than a salaried man earned all week when we were kids."

"Yes indeed," Reinhart said fervently, touching reality's base for once. "But Bob, forgive me for the question. Don't you have to be pretty callous to play it your way?"

"Callous," Sweet repeated quickly. Yet he did not seem offended. "No, far from it. Nor hypocritical. If I were colored, I would be militant. If I were young, I wouldn't trust anybody over thirty. I would scream when my own ox was gored, or even pretend it was when it was not. *I would get mine.* I am what I am, and expect others to be the same."

"You're a Claude Humbold with class," said Reinhart. "He's the real-estate man I worked for years ago, except his ideas were ahead of their time. For example he predicted that meadow and woods would be a perfect location for a supermarket, but nobody bit in his day. He's been in California for years."

Sweet was not interested in former personalities. He impatiently reminded Reinhart of the waiting airplane. "I have lingered here," he said, "for this sentimental motive. I have thrown you a few ideas in retailing because you seem to be a local sort of man who might feasibly operate on that level. But you haven't been eager to field them."

"Maybe I've tried it," said Reinhart. "Maybe I went into television too late in the early days, a few months before the market was saturated for black-and-white and color had not yet been developed. Maybe I tried other things on the eve of various recessions, which I couldn't weather because of lack of capital. Maybe I had—"

Sweet shook his head. "Let's drop all profitless precedents. What do you have right now?"

"The last thing I tried," said Reinhart, "was a gas station on old state route 215. That whole thing is now bypassed by the superhighway. I didn't get a dozen customers in a week."

Up front the old chauffeur looked asleep. Reinhart suddenly wished him dead, in which event Sweet would have to consider him, Reinhart, for the job. He was now reluctant to leave his powerful ex-schoolmate.

"Look, Bob, if you are serious about helping me, maybe you have a place in your organization."

"That's the trouble," Sweet told him. "I function essentially alone, except for lawyers and accountants. I don't have a plant to my name or even much of an office force. I have to work quickly, often, and in a certain secrecy."

He removed his sunglasses and nibbled on a temple piece, his shrewd dark surveillance on Reinhart's beseeching gray-blue eyes. "What I had in mind was, frankly, a loan."

"No," Reinhart avowed, "I never borrow money from an individual." He didn't count his mother as such. His sincerity made him breathless for a moment and he stopped to pant. "All I ask is to be allowed to earn an honest living."

Sweet threw back his head all at once and poured a glance down over his forceful chin. Reinhart was larger then he but sitting in a crumpled fashion.

"OK," Sweet said. "Give me a call when I get back." He wrote a number on a serrated quarter-leaf from a pocket secretary bound in glistening lizard. He gave it to Reinhart with one hand and clasped him with the other. "Two days should wrap it up."

"You won't regret this, Bob." Reinhart dared not say more, on pain of offending Sweet and disgusting himself, on reflection, with maudlin whining. He left the car but, unlike the teen-ager, remained at the curb, big hands in twisted pockets, sweating again in the sudden heat and inner expectation.

The exquisite automobile diminished down Main Street and flowed left at the light into the superhighway access road, disappearing behind the concrete wall, already fissured, of the ramp.

Bentley, eh. Reinhart was vaguely troubled by the two-tone effect. Was it not a bit vulgar? His would be monochrome, all silver-gray.

The teen-ager returned. "Hi there," said Reinhart.

"Hi," she answered heedlessly and crossed the street.

Reinhart did not have an office in the old business district, being temporarily at liberty, but Genevieve worked there as manager of a dress shop. He did not want her to see him at large. The best place to go was, ironically, home: empty, quiet, cool, and dark on a merciless day in July. "Shall I compare thee to a summer's day?/Thou art so lovely and so temperate." Imagine saying that to a modern adolescent and of a hot afternoon in Ohio.

At home Reinhart showered, took a long nap, and then prepared dinner for hardworking Gen and the rest of the family: baked pork butt, if the truth be known, with string beans. *Bien sûr*, he was no Carême, but he did more than warm tinfoil platters of frozen food. He toyed with the idea of opening a restaurant and killing Gino's business. Gen was tired and surly at dinner, his daughter stuffed herself idiotically, and his son did not come home.

All this had preceded Reinhart's evening visit to the bathroom, ostensibly to take another shower, for the kitchen was not air-conditioned nor equipped with an automatic dishwasher, and he was again self-soaked.

He now rose from his seat on the closed toilet, ritualistically tripping the flush lever. It was one of those habitual series of movements which in forty years had become integrated into the life process.

Reinhart's safe, so to speak, was at the bottom of the laundry hamper, a pink, iridescent, woven product of a company called Pearlwick. The treasure secreted therein was a pair of Japanese 7 x 35 binoculars. Up to the shoulder in soiled underwear, he groped for them, brought them up through fathoms of clinging garments, freed the right eyepiece from a persistent bra-strap, then stood these Siamese twins on the always convenient toilet cover.

For once the ballcock did not stick and the flush ended in the all's-well gasp followed by a plink and a distant gurgle, signaling that it was OK to run water elsewhere without prejudice, and he opened the cold-water tap in the bathtub, full-throat, leaving the disengaged plug where it was.

Just as he had not authentically used the toilet, neither would he employ the tub except as another auditory red herring. Reinhart's true purpose in occupying this room at this time was to watch his neighbors' daughter undress in the house next door. The girl was not quite seventeen years of age, by record, but she was built like twice that, and in any primitive tribe would have been a multimother long since. At least twice in recent months Reinhart had caught her visually in brassiere and bikini briefs, and once she had obviously been on the point of unhooking the former when a burst of ill wind had clatteringly reminded her of the open Venetian blind—through which Reinhart had watched a composite figure of many horizontal divisions—and with a single, indolent twitch of the wrist she blacked him out.

Reinhart had known the girl since she was a newborn piece of protoplasm, virtually hairless over her cute little testy red piglet face, pink prehensile feet clutching the air. After all, that had been less than seventeen years ago. "She looks like Eisenhower," her dad observed in a mock-rueful way, he and Reinhart being for Stevenson. Then several regimes flashed by in speeded-up newsreels, and this kid burgeoned from spindly child to succulent woman like one of those collapsed life rafts which at the pull of a cord inflate before your eyes to plump maturity. So much for the passing of years after you reach thirty.

Patience is essential for the sniper, the burglar, the Peeping Tom, but its exercise often caused Reinhart to anticipate failure as a means of killing time. Imagining success might turn out to be a mockery, whereas if you counted on losing you lost nothing further if proved right and were happy if erroneous. The economy of the emotions could never be allowed to go laissez-faire.

He would probably never see Sweet again. Surely the phone number was bogus. Or he would, with his gift for self-damage, lose it. Gen would burn up the note, or tear it into confetti and flush it away. If he reached him, Sweet, like the rich dipsomaniac in *City Lights*, who took Charlie Chaplin home every night but threw him out every morning, would disclaim all acquaintance.

More immediately, as he crouched at the slit of window, binoculars resting on the sooty sill, surveying the empty rectangle of yellow light next door, he expected to see nothing of the girl, perhaps not even her clothed figure—this sometimes happened; she didn't get to bed on time, and he eventually had to honor family protests and void the bathroom—and yet be caught in the fruitless act by wife or son or random policeman.

Having laid waste to the future, he would next begin a count of past injustices. Time hangs heavy on the voyeur waiting at his post. Reinhart was on the verge of reliving in spirit the ugly encounter with Gino when he recognized that the girl next door had not only materialized but had, bending and shifting from one leg to the other, whisked off her underpants and now stood, squarely in the frame of the window, shaking them at him and smiling shamelessly.

– 2 –

To think, Reinhart thought, that this young girl, the daughter of respectability and hard work and enlightened attitudes—both her parents were college graduates—that this young minx had turned whore. In moral outrage he lowered the glasses.

The Swedes, he had read, had evolved a theory that would encourage the natural complements to get together legally: voyeurs and exhibitionists, fags and friends, the yins and yangs of sexual peculiarities, thus satisfying one another and no longer troubling the routine society of bulls and cows who mate in bovine orthodoxy. But what of the weirdo who had once importuned Reinhart, years ago, in a public street and with a young woman on his arm—Reinhart, that is; the queer was alone but well dressed. This fellow's urge was obviously for scandal, not flesh. But why did Reinhart think of inversion while watching the body of a luscious object of heterosexual craving?

Because he understood instantaneously that he wanted only to look and in secret. He did not want her to know that he knew. And that cast of mind of course was deviate.

So he froze. He might have died from a sudden heart attack while trying to close the window against a chill draft which had threatened his old bones. But how explain the binoculars still clutched in his rigid hand? Satellite tracking. Practice for viewing a moonshot. . . . The simple fact was that no excuse would be credible. This truth made him free, and he raised the glasses again.

He now discerned that nothing was expected of him, he was still in safe hiding, the girl indeed smiled towards him but not at him, seeing nothing but the usual solipsist image of her own youth, vigor, and beauty, mirrored in the blankness of everybody else.

She pitched her pants offstage, a movement which

caused her firm parts to tremble hardly at all. Reinhart's own trunk had been more tremulous when he tossed his socks aside. In all primary and secondary respects she was full grown, yet not a centimeter, a milligram beyond. She robustly straddled the apex of ripeness. By comparison even the early twenties were already the road to rot.

Reinhart thought his heart might break, but he felt no desire whatever. There was nothing this girl could have done for him but what she was doing, and of that she could not be told, not only by reason of law, social humiliation, and other ugly, essentially irrelevant possibilities, but because self-consciousness would corrupt this glorious and unreflective bestiality. A young girl who thought she knew something was unbearable. She was at her best in a silent movie, and teenlike she was moving though standing still. Life is short, but Reinhart's glasses were long enough even to characterize the dimpled navel in her golden belly. It was mauve. A dot of mole marked her left collarbone, which was no doubt usually revealed in her garb for the summertime streets, yet was the sort of thing that Reinhart saw in nudity, for he was no priapic ape with wet lips and pumping hand.

He did not dwell on the forbidden trio, the funny face of two sore eyes and Vandyke beard so often mocked by lavatory cartoonists. Rather he examined the little shadows of her nostrils, the cupids who grinned in her knees, the extraordinary hips which were at once full and flat, round but self-contained, robust yet in communication of nerve and muscle with even remote extremities, the blunt, dancing fingers, say, which had lately hurled away the wisp of undergarment and now seemed to be talking in the fluency of the deaf-and-dumb alphabet.

Versatile Time had scarcely moved a second in reality while Reinhart's inner clock, deranged, had sped on: the panties were still aloft but beyond his frame. She watched them descend on bed or dresser or floor, to her left. Then looked right, at the interior of what he saw outside as the obscure corner of the house with the darker perpendicular of the drainpipe and a black clump of something at the point where it entered the ground. This latter phenomenon stirred now and proved itself, through sinister undulations against the pale siding, as a stalking cat, and was dismissed from consideration.

The glasses climbed the wall. Another reason for running cold water into the tub was that no steam developed to befog the binoculars: one of the petty but real problems

of the Peeping Tom. Sometimes the heat of the July face
was enough to do it. Reinhart was a massive sweater, and
kept handy a square of what the commercials termed
"bathroom tissue" should the lenses need swabbing. He
used it now to wipe his under-eyes.

The figment of his surveillance was moving her plump
lips, and teen-agers weren't much for gum any more. Also
her vision seemed more or less directed now, still into the
corner, which, he quickly estimated, was large enough to
hold a bed. A chum was staying over. They talked of
boys, records, clothes, rot. They brazenly undressed in
front of one another, having been reared to find nudity no
shame. A bare-boob scene was now de rigueur in commercial movies, and Reinhart had caught a flash of pubic
hair in some mannered treatment of contemporary London. Worse, bare dongs adorned the Broadway stage,
according to the newsweekly to which he trial-subscribed.

A mild enough manifestation of the change in mores,
when a staggering percentage of California high-school
girls were pregnant. Yet Reinhart sniffed with a blue
nose, by chance smelling the chemical bouquet of the
Jonny Mop pads used to clean the johnny bowl. His
attitudes had been fixed in another era, a lovely time of
hypocrisy when it was a triumph to overwhelm the modesty of which a female was the natural exemplar. For
young girls to assume the locker-room insouciance of
jockstrap-doffing, crotch-scratching, nail-inspecting athletes would always to him seem heretical.

He had been made that way by wise elders masked as
idiots and/or charlatans, the delightful irony of his own
youth having been that one defied the established morality
with the sense that he would inevitably grow up to impose
it someday on another generation. If there were satisfac-
tions in aging, paramount among them surely was re-
straining the young who came after. Except for the human
beings who perished in childhood, this policy was as fair
as life would allow and a gain over the practice of lions,
say, who shoved the superannuated away from the kill
and the mangy old beast, once Lord of the jungle, chewed
his yellow gums for a while and died.

Simba Reinhart shook his mane, then spat out in his
hand the three-tusked bridge for which he still owed his
dentist, another old schoolfellow, who owned two Cadillacs and recently had sacked his old wife for a new one
met at a convention in Atlantic City, no doubt by means
of a five-spot slipped to the bellboy. Reinhart knew a

hooker when he saw one, or thought he did, until last week, in the city, when hustled, while buying a newspaper, by a nondescript woman attached, by a braided-leather leash, to a panting spaniel. "Would you like to come home with me and help me wash my cocker?" she asked. Of course, she could have been merely one of the cranks who, along with able-bodied panhandlers, self-righteous freaks, and winos, were taking over downtown.

As painful as were the thoughts inspired by the girl's bare body, when she with a jolly lope suddenly left his frame of vision, Reinhart was at once desolated and had his first intimations of sexual desire, typically anachronistic. He also noticed the dental bridge in his palm, and wondered how it got there. He forced it back into the break in the upper-right fence, and felt an exquisite pressure-pain, as if pumpkin seeds had been hammered through the interstices of his remaining natural teeth.

The end of the show. He was not one to linger till the scrubwomen slopped in and turned up the gum-encrusted seats. He had seen what he had come in quest of so many times, and knew the strange feeling which accompanies complete achievement of any kind: the loss of a future. The unseen roommate had probably undressed while he sat head in hands reviewing his day. Yet another ten seconds would not hurt. He had no prospects but TV. The light was still on across the way. Perhaps the guest had perched her little rump on the bed-edge to unroll her knee-high stockings, the ghosts of the teenyboppers' wintertime boots—little Prussian martinets that they were—and lifted roseate haunches to free the weave from roughened heel and hooking toe, and before his count was done, would appear in the frame to rip off the rest of what she wore, skimpy ribbons at bosom and vee, and flex her pelt at him in turn. She might be the other kind, not the stocky, full, fruity species of the neighbor's daughter, but the tall, attenuated, languid teeny, pubesced but lemon-breasted, boyish-hipped, lean in flank, with long, pointed feet and tawny hair, tendrils of which curled into the hollow of her prominent clavicles. Slim, if you like, but deeper in the side view and with buttocks like twin mandolins.

Reinhart, who would gulp any wine and swallow any food he could manage to chew, was a connoisseur in these matters. Ten seconds came and went without incident, and true to the vow he left his post. For a moment the crick in his sacroiliac made him walk like a goose. As with most bathroom windows the sill was four feet above the floor; he had had to prop himself on the wrists of the hands holding the binoculars.

The tub was now three-quarters full of cold water. He turned off the faucet, and with the noise gone, heard the querulous end of a speech from the hall outside.

". . . consideration for others." He recognized it as his wife's, and supplied the missing words *You haven't any*. That she had been talking for some time he might assume. She was attracted to obscuring conditions of sound.

He immediately pulled the plug and as the water left the tub—drop by drop, owing to some obstruction in the drain—he shouted back: "One minute!"

The unjust feature of this situation was that another complete bathroom divided the children's bedrooms in the northwards projection of the house, a facility that was seldom used even by those for whom it had been provided and never by anyone in an emergency. As a very young child, Reinhart's daughter, inclined towards car-sickness, excess weeping, and odd phobias, had professed to be upset by certain irregularities in the enamel of that tub, which indeed was a factory "second" supplied at a favorable price by the scab plumber who did the work. "It has pimples that scratch my bottom!" was the anguished assertion of Reinhart's secondborn. His son of course stated no reasons whatever for the boycott; even as a little blackguard of eight or ten he was motivated by an undifferentiated malignancy towards his dad. To get him to eat a certain food Reinhart had only to pretend a personal dislike for it, else the child would have died of malnutrition.

At puberty the boy had made a devastating change, taking up Reinhart's precise tastes and corrupting them subtly. He would watch certain of his father's television favorites with the sound turned off, if he commanded the set. If eating deep-fried chicken, the lad would peel off and discard the golden crust. He might also borrow a necktie of Reinhart's and knot it strangely, so that it would never again hang true. At sixteen, when he got his driver's license, he began to do mysterious damage to the car, some of which the keenest mechanic could not identify and correct: at the least, maddening birdlike squeaks which no tightening or greasing would eradicate; at worst, inexplicable seizures in the differential, abrasions down to metal of new brake bands, and so on. Yet not only did he drive circumspectly when under his father's surveillance, which was to be expected—Reinhart himself had so performed as a youth, but once away from Dad gunned and braked the guts out of

the '38 Chevvy—but one time when Blaine could not possibly have known he was being watched, Reinhart emerged
from a highwayside café to which he had been lifted by an
acquaintance, to see his son tool past at a speed less than
the limit and slow to a conservative stop at the nearby
crossroads.

No doubt the trouble had begun two weeks after
Blaine's conception when Genevieve on the first day of
her missing period insisted that if it was to be a boy he
must be named for her father, one of the few unmitigated
scoundrels Reinhart had ever known, perhaps the only,
surely the worst.

Reinhart now withdrew from behind the toilet a
plumber's suction cup, the kind that, less the stick, was
used in the old days of real musicianship to mute a
trumpet—the time of Goodman, Basie, the Dorseys, long
before the current long-locked, costumed, electronic-
toned androgynes had begun the voyage down the Fal-
lopian tubes—and plunged it into the tub water with an
enormous gobble of air fleeing hyperhydration. With four
or five thrusts he caused the drain to disgorge, as he
suspected, an octopus of hair, the origin of which was
obvious. Gen and his daughter were dark. Reinhart's own
gray-blond locks were regularly clipped short at the bar-
bershop. Blaine was very fair, in fact of so light a hue
that nature furnished it only to albinos, of which company
he was not a member. This pale mess was a hank from
his coiffure, which was not only bleached but shoulder-
length.

Very like, indeed, the lovely mane of the houseguest of
the girl next door, who as luck would have it was standing
in the window, her graceful back to Reinhart, when he
picked up the glasses for a valedictory focus before returning the instrument to its bed of laundry. Magically
enough, she confirmed his fanciful projection, exceeded it,
really, because no imagination is so vivid as the actuality
of young flesh: the damask of the supple skin, the pearly
summit of her upthrust hip on which rested the upended
tulip of her right hand as asymmetrically she stood
beneath her shower of gold, slender arm akimbo, innocent of sinew or distension. Quite tall she was and of a
glorious grace even in stasis. When she moved, with a
subtle rearrangement of her globèd bottom and soft
lavender shadows below, bisected by light's wanton yellow
finger, pointing up between the slim thighs, when her hair
shimmered, her slender shoulders rose and fell in some

transitory teeny mirth, Reinhart discarded all control and
exhorted the Devil to make her turn. It was little enough
in exchange for a soul, even Reinhart's, which was something of a retread.

But the Devil replied, Wait a while, she is so beautiful—
Verweile doch, sie ist so schön, in his native tongue—
and anyway, hell, like any other public housing facility,
had a long and hopeless waiting list; you would probably
die before you made it. But Reinhart persisted, offering in
support his forty-four years as sinner, and reluctantly an
invisible but massive diabolic hand reached up from the
cellar of the house next door and turned the girl as if she
were a figurine. And transformed her sex as well, so that
at 180 degrees she proved to be his son.

"You have hounded that boy since he was born," said
Genevieve, to whom time had dealt a better hand than to
Reinhart, though true enough she was his junior by several years. Short and apparently threatening to turn plump
in her early twenties, she had instead acquired several
inches of height—which may have been an optical illusion—and lost ten pounds of her youthful weight by the
end of the first decade of their marriage. Now, twenty-
two anniversaries after the fact, Gen was sharp-featured,
spare-figured, and leather-skinned, to put it one way, but
handsome, svelte, and flawlessly tanned, to put it the
other. Which was to say she had made much the same
progress as Reinhart had in the order of familiar resemblance; both of them had begun as run-offs of their
respective mothers (Reinhart's being muscular) and
moved in middle life to favor their fathers.

Gen sat in the corner of the couch, in her usual cloud
of smoke. Yet semiannual X-rays showed her lungs were
clean, whereas Reinhart's chest often ached though he
had given up cigarettes years since.

From his chair Reinhart said: "Look here, this is not
the subject for argument, Genevieve. What I am talking
about is law. That girl is underage, and Blaine was twenty-one last February." A cold bleak day, the yard spotted
with clumps of dirty snow, a bucketful of which Reinhart
had gathered to chill an eight-dollar bottle of champagne
to salute the new manhood, but Blaine did not come
home until the next morning, having had his own party
with hyena friends who raved on hashish and amplified
music, obscenely mutilated an effigy of the President of

the United States, then buggered one another till dawn (for all Reinhart knew).

Until tonight he had never seen a jot of evidence that the boy was not queer. He still found it hard to believe that a girl would accept the sexual attentions of a male whose hair was not only longer than hers but finer, whose body was softer, and whose wardrobe at least as gaudy.

But the legal question was serious. Reinhart in his time had been a frequent law-bender but never a candid breaker of ordinances however unjust. When he himself had enjoyed the favors of an underaged girl it had been in the context of Occupation Berlin, where codes were as yet unformulated.

Gen spat smoke at him. "All right, Mr. Cop," she said through the blue stream. "Get your billyclub and pound the child's head to a bloody jelly, like the pigs did to the youngsters at Columbia who were appealing for a better life. The human body is a beautiful thing, only we have made it filthy with our stinking hypocrisy."

"Genevieve, please don't widen the scope of this discussion. I don't want to get enmired in social theories while my son is naked and in the room of the girl next door with her parents away on vacation. She is a minor person."

"Well, he isn't," said Gen. "Therefore you have no responsibility for him."

"Aw, Gen, Gen."

"I am sure," said Genevieve, as always imperfectly crushing the cigarette butt in the ashtray so that it would smolder and stink for some time to come, "I am sure there is some reasonable explanation if he is there at all, which frankly I don't place any credentials in." She had her own way with idiom. "Blaine told me definitely when he left he was heading for the Heliotrope Thing."

This discothèque occupied the disused movie house in which Reinhart had spent every Sunday afternoon as a boy, watching never-resolved serials and main features in which the cowboy did not kiss a girl, did not even, in the earliest years, sing songs. Later Reinhart had owned a piece of this theater, served as manager, helped to close its doors forever.

"Will you at least then," he asked his wife now, "go and look? Why should I tell such a vile lie?"

"Because you hate Blaine," Genevieve said flatly. "You hate all young people. Youth is hated in this country. Their idols are always shot. No, I will not go and peep through the window like a dirty perver. I am going to bed now, as I have a job to get up and go to every morning, and if I did not, we would be on relief."

Gen had developed the stride of a horsewoman or anyway the type used by a bygone generation of film actresses with square shoulders and jodhpured legs, a little black fox-hunting derby atop their heads and married to a man who wore a houndstooth jacket and hairline moustache. Gen's locks had got darker through the years— though Reinhart had never actually caught her dyeing them—and were pulled back into a flat doughnut at the nape. The tension served to keep her face smooth as a drumskin. She cultivated a timeless look that defied estimates of age and was relative to her companions: often she made the nearby young seem callow and those whose years matched her own, elder. And from Blaine, perhaps partly for her own uses though she doted on him, she had picked up the lie that America persecuted its youth, the country in which a teen-ager's allowance might well exceed the wages paid a European for laboring all week, not to mention the income of adult Africans and the child prostitutes of Hong Kong.

However she in no way played fast with the truth when she spoke of her job. Indeed she had one, and without it the Reinharts, at least for the moment, might have been a statistic on the roster of snouts in the public trough. Because of the reversal of roles signified by this state of affairs, Reinhart could not be too harsh with her. Bread-winner Gen deserved to come home to serenity and a hot meal, slippers, and pipe if she wanted them. Until he got going again in business he must speak softly.

Therefore he pulled in the horns which were unseemly on a parasite and blew a kiss at her departing back. He must face this crisis alone. He had a certain history of extremities, as who did not at his age; however, a precedent was lacking in this case. It takes no long deliberation to defend your life from an assailant who would destroy or mutilate it. Had Blaine and/or the neighbor's daughter jumped Reinhart in a dark alley he would instinctively have fought like a tiger. But bare-assed and in bed together they were a much more formidable enemy, and his own position was badly eroded owing on the one hand to the incessant castration of having a son like Blaine, and on the other to his own voyeuristic lech for the girl.

He who as a radiant young man had gone to fight the

Nazis was now just another dirty old fascist. Reinhart had volunteered for the Army. Blaine was deferred as a college student and threatened to flee to Canada if the immunity was revoked and he was called to the colors. Reinhart half believed "we" should get out of S.E. Asia and with the remaining half-opinion, compounded of TV pictures of Vietcong atrocities, a historical sense of America's world mission created initially by Adolf Hitler's unopposed rise to tyrannical power, and the strident selfish objection of punks who served no cause but nihilism, favored the use of the hydrogen weapon. In less nervous moments he knew the latter of course as the expression of empty bombast, which he allowed himself since in no event was he ever consulted by White House or Pentagon.

He was wont, in heat, to tell Blaine: "Christ, I had to go to a much bigger war. The Japs held the Pacific and the Krauts all of Europe except plucky little England, who swore to fight on the beaches and in the fields until the New World came to redress—"

"Shi-i-i-i-t," said Blaine, in his poisonous, effeminate style of drawing out one-syllabled obscenities. "Why should I be a sucker just because you were?"

And if Genevieve were in attendance, as she always tried to be lest Reinhart become physical with her darling—women and undersized, infirm, and nonviolent kinds of men tended to imply that Reinhart because of his size alone would answer reason with force; thugs like Gino on the other hand enjoyed a conviction that he would respond to their threats with pusillanimous cajolery: both in fact were right, Reinhart being a realist—if Gen were nearby she might at this juncture say. "He's got you there, Carl, ha-HA."

The cruel feature of this was that never could Reinhart have been described as a superpatriot. Indeed, in his youth he had been much more cynical than Blaine. However, if he pointed this out to his son, Blaine would suddenly turn into that flabbiest of philosophers, the young idealist.

Would swing his hair behind his right ear and squeeze his eyes into slits and then release the lids so as to flutter the long lashes while the blue irises swam in self-induced fury and pain and simulated compassion. "You still *are* a cynic about the poor and the blacks and youth and everything that represents change from the rotten system which has made you what you are."

"The system! What the hell have I ever got from it but debts? Am I a rich exploiter of the deprived? And don't tell me anything about Negroes. Before you were born I had a colored friend whom I helped out of several scrapes. For which incidentally I can't remember being thanked. I have been pro-Negro all my life, and in a time when it was not exactly popular."

Blaine wrinkled his long, skinny nose, an appendage the model for which could be found nowhere else on either side of the family. Reinhart might have been suspicious of Gen had Blaine been born so; but in fact as a baby the boy had shown a marked facial resemblance to Reinhart and his nose had actually been modest till puberty. Reinhart's own now was somewhat porcine.

"If I have ever called you fascist, I am sorry," Blaine said. "You are far worse. You are a liberal, Northern style. The Southern type wears a sheet."

Then, as Reinhart lifted his fists in chagrin, Blaine quailed as if about to be struck.

Which indeed put the thought into Reinhart's head and not for the first time that day or this life. But he had never laid a hand on Blaine in twenty-one years. Blaine was legally a man. Reinhart could not get over that. Today, when the young clamored for power as never before, they nevertheless refused to grow up. In spirit a spoiled infant, Blaine was physically far from being a child. There were black shadows under his eyes and bird-tracks in the corners. As an Olympic swimmer he would have been an old man. Without his exaggerated growth of hair he might look thirty; with it he could be seen, through wincing eyes, as a homely woman fighting middle age.

Yet there he was, over in the house next door, impugning the morals of a luscious minor. Reinhart had a dreadful thought, remembering an incident from a pornographic eight-page cartoon book of thirty years ago: a potbellied, balding dad finds young son in garage putting blocks to teen-aged girl, routs son, and climbs on maiden himself. A perfect situation for the unscrupulous, like that of the corrupt cop bursting in on a prostitute and her client. But the only way Reinhart could have managed it, and perhaps not even then, was if the initiative were taken by the girl: "If you won't tell, I'll—" Hardly likely in a shameless bitch who cared so little about publicity as not even to draw the blinds.

He lurched through the hall and into the darkened

bedroom, hurting the tender instep of his bare foot on a
nasty shoe Genevieve had discarded just inside the door,
by blind touch found his street clothes in a chair, and
climbed into shirt, trousers, and sockless brogans. Gen
was at length established as a dark breathing lump in the
oversized bed, bought originally so as to accommodate his
large figure but from which he had since been banished
on charges of snoring, striking out with brutal fists while
his consciousness was lost in dreams, muttering loathsome
words, and being unemployed. For some time he had
taken his nightly repose upon a studio couch against the
windows.

Dressed and back in the living room, his hand on the
knob of the front door that projected one, in this tract
house, directly into the yard, vestibules and front porches
being now as obsolete as he, he hesitated. What would be
the use? A rhetorical question on which his self-dialogues
so often concluded. Try to borrow more money from
Maw, apply for a job with Hal, make a pass at Elaine,
attempt to converse with Gen, ask the bank for more
time, expect the plumber to be prompt, even anticipate
that a ham sandwich would be made with fresh bread and
lean meat. What was the use?

You are only beaten if you think so, said Thomas
Edison or George Washington or Satchel Paige, as popularly quoted. *But I think so* said Reinhart. I can't invent a
phonograph or lead armies or pitch a sinker. I am just a
guy who regardless of what he thought at twenty knows
at forty-four only that he will die. It is now grotesque to
talk of anything else, especially suicide, which no real
loser ever commits because it would deny him the years
of pain he so richly deserves.

He threw the lever freeing the brass bar which sealed
the door against the entry of militant Negroes bent on
massacring white households who had never done them
wrong, and stepped out. Too late he saw another person
preparing to enter, a girl shorter than he but, in a context
relative to her own height and age, quite as stout, so
sturdy in fact that their collision was a standoff from
which each recoiled in an equal degree.

"Sorry, Winona," he said and backstepped inside.

"Hi, Daddy," said she, from a perspiring pumpkin-face
under the proscenium of high wet bangs and skimpy side
curtains of her Buster Brown coiffure.

"How was the picture?"

She breathed out heavily and ran a chubby finger

through the channel between temple and ear. "Not as good as *The Dead, the Maimed, and the Ravished*. But not bad."

"Isn't it funny they make those Westerns nowadays in Italy?" Reinhart observed, trying to make his mood seem light.

"Italy?" Her soft brown eyes watered. "Are you making fun of me?"

"Now there's no need to cry about that, Winona. They do it for economic reasons, I understand. Italian extras don't cost so much."

She was already in full sob. "But it's supposed to be *Texas*. Oh, that just ruins it." Winona was sixteen years old. With fallen shoulders she went to the couch and dumped herself into the corner spot earlier vacated by Gen, throwing her fat red thighs wide and clasping both chins.

Reinhart reminded her of all the trouble in the world and what was worth tears and what not and gradually she peeped waterily up at him. "You see, darling," he explained. "Even if it had been shot in present-day Texas it would be fictional, because cowboys don't carry guns any more. It's imaginary, anyway. As long as it's believable on its own terms nothing else matters." But she was not yet quite mollified, so he sat down next to her and put his heavy arm around her thick waist. She smelled of clean sweat, rather pleasantly, something like ginger in fact, but no doubt it added to her many social difficulties and he would have liked to find a way to tell her about it without reinciting a despair so hairtrigger as to be set off by disillusionment over a trashy movie.

Winona rubbed her nose. She said: "Just as you begin to like something, you find it is not what you thought it was."

Reinhart stretched his left arm along the top of the sofa, "Yes, dear," said he. "You begin to discover that at your age. And some people never get beyond it." Meaning himself, for one. But the great thing about having a sympathetic child was that by projecting oneself into him or her one could look at universal difficulties in an equilibrium between intimacy and distance. For example, Winona could be considered as himself as a pudgy female of sixteen. At the same time, she was not he but an independent entity. He did not actually bleed if she were wounded, but of course he would willingly have taken any blows directed at her.

On the other hand he could understand why people might want to abuse her: with very little effort they could elicit an expression of pain, succeeding which they naturally found her presence an unbearable reminder of the meanness they had hoped to discharge and forget about. This kept Winona in a state of imbalance. Those companions who tormented and then escaped from her today would welcome her back tomorrow for another episode of the same.

A human condition to which she no doubt referred in her latest comment on the failure of reality and appearance to jibe. This was no new observation.

"Did your friends give you the slip again?" Reinhart asked gently.

"You guessed it." However, Winona had by now returned to her usual phlegmatic state, which was the mask of pride. On her own initiative she complained only of seeing her principles mocked in the area of false animation, like movies, or gross materiality, like cheeseburgers and pizza. Until baited she would never mention her living contemporaries.

"You want to talk about it?" asked Reinhart.

She shrugged, which meant that her father felt the shifting of some seventy-five pounds of her upper body.

"It might help," he said. Or simply recall unpleasantness: one never really knows the soul of another, even one's own offspring. Perhaps in bringing up the subject he was merely joining Winona's persecutors.

She dropped her wet head on his shoulder. "When I came out of the ladies' room they were gone."

Reinhart threw his own legs out upon the carpet to match Winona's position, and looking at his sockless shoes, he said: "They've done that before, haven't they?"

"They *always* do it."

She had her tiresome side. Reinhart raised his voice. "Well, hell, Winona, then you should be prepared. Those who can't remember history are condemned to repeat it. Are you the only one who goes to the bathroom after the picture? You better train yourself to hold it."

She pulled away and said indignantly: "I always get a Coke from the machine on the way in, or a black cherry except that's usually empty I don't know why, because nobody much likes it but me. Beth has Seven-Up and Carol drinks Tab, and sometimes Dodie won't have anything, but generally they all drink as much as I do and really we all go to the ladies' afterward but they take the booths first and I have to wait and—"

"OK," said Reinhart. Somehow Winona had, in a day when other teen-aged girls had the sophistication of courtesans in the Age of Pericles, got herself into a crowd of creeps with nothing better to do postcinematically than practice toilet one-upmanship. But something good came of this in a selfish way: when he thought of Winona and her crowd he could never remember his lust for teenagers.

"OK," he repeated. "You have a problem. The first thing to do is to identify it. Once that is done you can set about solving it. One, you don't have to give up your soft drink. Two, the john must be visited. Three, you don't want to get involved in a vulgar race for a booth, which would be undignified in a young lady." Also, with her bulk she couldn't run fast; he left that unsaid.

She writhed against his arm. "Ummm. Daddy, this is embarrassing."

"Not to me, Winona," he said quickly. "I see it as an exercise in tactics. Remember how you always beat me at checkers?" Because he let her. "You distract me by sacrificing one of your pieces, thus getting me into a position where you can jump three of mine. Now what I suggest is that before the picture is over, you get up and go to the toilet."

"What's that got to do with checkers?"

"I didn't mean literally. I meant a similar use of the unexpected."

"And miss part of the picture?" Winona wailed.

"Think of it this way," said Reinhart. "You're giving up one thing to get a better."

"You don't know *them*. No matter when it was they would say it was the best part."

Winona had managed to carry losing to a rarefied height of proficiency that Reinhart himself seldom could attain.

"What does it matter what they say?"

"Then why," howled Winona, "have them as friends?" She began to weep again, he saw from the southeast corner of his eye, looking down her cheeks which were also still running with sweat.

"A good question, dear. Friends who are not friendly are not worth much." Reinhart thought bitterly of various inert if not treacherous types for whom he had once entertained affection: few enough, actually, but he was attempting a vicarious projection into his daughter's frame of life. "You are lucky to have discovered that this early. We all die alone, Winona, though we are accompanied when we come into the world. Living is a process of developing independence."

"Easy for you to say," Winona said, settling against him like a bag of sand. "You are big and strong and popular and successful."

There were resplendent joys in having a daughter. At that moment Reinhart shook off the mortal coil: he had spent only half his years, in this era of improved medicine. He could still be anything he wanted, as at twenty. He could even realize Winona's fantastic opinion of him.

But why bother when, for no reason except that he had helped to conceive her, he already wore the crown? Reinhart loved this chubby child who, defying her epoch, refused to mature. He loved her for that, of course, and for her troubles, and for her resemblance to him, and because he had known her all her life, and because she loved him. But several of these same motives, or others of equal substance, also informed his feeling towards Blaine, and Gen too for that matter. He had enough cause to loathe his wife and son, perhaps, but he loved them. The difference was that Winona uniquely refused to confirm his self-hatred.

She deserved to hear him say: "Well, it hasn't always been easy. Daddy has had his knocks like everybody else." She made some comfortable puppy-sound. "The main thing is not to quit, dear, not to lose your hope. Something wonderful may happen at any time, and you should be ready for it." His arm was going to sleep at its broken-wing angle. For years he had worshiped the god of benevolent chance, who had repaid him in such bad fortune that the ringing of a telephone was often a knell and he could not bear to open his mail immediately.

But now he cleaned off his ancient faith for presentation to his daughter, as one might take from the attic an old Flexible Flyer sled with which one had once broken his collarbone, apply new varnish, and pass it on to a young heir. Blaine, who had from the age of twelve onwards an invincible sense of self-possession, had never given him an opportunity to do that.

Subtly disengaging his sleeping arm, Reinhart noticed that Winona was also snoozing. So secure did she feel with her old dad. Her best features were a flawless skin that, though perspiring, did not show a pore, and long, fine lashes, now stuck to her moist lower lids by the sandman. "Does he really come and sprinkle your eyes, Daddy?" Not so many years ago she still asked that, and not before her first menses would she tolerate a Christmas Eve at which Reinhart did not steal in in a Santa suit (into which the last few times there had been no room for both his natural gut and a pillow) and laugh Ho-ho-ho while stuffing her capacious stocking.

She awakened, though, as he levered himself up, freeing the couch of two hundred and sixty-five pounds—he had about a hundred on her when it came to weight—and asked, in terrified suspicion: "Where are you going, Poppy?" She had always called him that at bedtime.

No longer could he seriously consider going next door and accosting Blaine and the girl. By making him feel superior, Winona also invariably weakened his moral resolve. Were he what she thought he was, he should have a lackey do his dirty work. Failing that, forget about it. Anyway, by now Blaine had surely emptied himself, impregnating the girl, and would run off scot-free while her father shot Reinhart: in the head, quickly, was his prayer.

"I thought I might have a little snack," Reinhart said, lumbering towards the kitchen, soon followed by her amble, and the two of them with greedy efficiency transferred many comestibles from the refrigerator to Formica tabletop and proceeded to wade in. Winona polished off a quart of homogenized milk and two and a half peanut-butter-and-pickle sandwiches while Reinhart cooked for each of them a one-eyed man, an egg fried into a hole in a slice of white bread. He washed his down with two sixteen-ounce cans of beer.

Winona loyally stuck by him while he washed the skillet, going to sleep again at the table, with a milk-moustache. Looking at her sweet, guileless face, Reinhart remembered how in earlier years she would trot to meet him at the door when he came home, and he would pick her up high and swing her around and require at that moment no further justification for life. He wished he could still carry her to bed. As it stood she was burden enough merely to steer down the hall. A large rag-doll buffoon lay on her pillow. "G'night, Poppy," she murmured as he kissed her forehead. "I love you."

"Likewise, dear," said Reinhart. "Now remember to take off your dress and put your pajamas on before hitting the sack." More than once she had lazily slept all night in her street clothes.

"Promise me," she muttered, but firmly, "you won't watch TV now." Another of her peculiarities, a form of paranoia or merely jealousy: she was troubled by the reception of television into a house where she lay sleeping. At breakfast he did not dare talk of postbedtime viewing to Winona, though one of his joys was to watch late-night showings of ancient movies, made in the time when he was young, and then tell the plots to somebody. Winona was the only member of the household who would tolerate the paraphrasing of a screenplay—but not one from a picture transmitted after she was in bed.

So he lied, bade her good night for the fourth or fifth time—they had an old game the winner of which said it last—and repaired straightaway to the den or study or office, originally termed in the prospectus as a "utility or service room," a walk-in closet somewhere between the kitchen and the furnace room in this cellarless house. Reinhart used it as his business HQ. A scarred filing cabinet held the records of several enterprises that had run into the sand, beginning with the real-estate firm he had taken over when the former owner, Claude Humbold, had emigrated to Encino, California. Claude claimed he couldn't stay in the black if prudish types occupied town hall, his specialty being the elasticization of zoning laws, vending gracious old buildings in prime residential areas to builders who promptly broke them up with a huge iron ball and erected motels, char-broil steak restaurants, and drive-in movies.

While the set warmed up—a tiny six-inch Sony on which he still owed many payments; it sat on Claude's old desk, which had had to be disassembled and re-erected to get it in the room—Reinhart swung back in the swivel chair and perused the schedule. Alas, he had seen the two movies: Joan Crawford, playing a female impersonator married to a softy named Craig, and one of those Hercules films starring a cast of weightlifters who reminded him unpleasantly of his own fiberless lard.

The screen developed a picture of several gnomes sitting on doll furniture. They were less grotesque but more grainy when he leaned over the desk and put his eyes against the glass. One man, seated behind a desk, was conversing with people arranged along a sofa, a young woman bare from the waist down though with her legs crossed so nothing could be seen but haunches, a recognizable actor who played villains, and nearest to the host, an individual in heavy-rimmed glasses and sideburns with a touch of gray: Reinhart's host at lunch, Bob Sweet.

The host said: "Bob, may I call you Bob? We want to hear more of this incredible process of yours after Jody's song."

Jody rose from the couch and turned out to be wearing a short skirt which now fell just past her groin. She gave a serviceable rendition of a Broadway show tune, which Reinhart listened to intermittently, dying to get on to Sweet.

At last, after three endless commercials, the host resumed.

"Now, Bob, what is this about freezing dead men? Are you putting me on?"

"No, Mr. Alp," said Bob Sweet, "this is no joke. Cryonics is a serious science."

"Now have I got it right?" asked Alp, joining his brushy eyebrows. "I didn't have time for more than a glance backstage at the notes taken by a member of my staff, and he was probably drunk as usual." Alp smirked, and the audience guffawed as a single entity.

"Simply," Sweet said, "it is this: if a body is frozen within a certain time after what is known as clinical death—the cessation of heartbeats and brainwaves—but before any cellular degeneration sets in, it can be maintained in that state of suspended animation interminably."

The camera pulled back to show the returned Jody's naked thighs. Alp pointed at them and wisecracked: "Even a body like that?"

Sweet said soberly: "Any body."

Alp's face grew disingenuously bland. "Well, that's your theory anyhoo. Why? Explain it to the folks."

"Excuse me?"

"To freeze," said Alp, between puffs of a cigarette, "a human body. The purpose of it. I gather it's not for weirdo kicks but a contribution of a serious nature."

"Yes, indeed. It begins with the proposition that medicine has made more advances in the past fifty years than in all the preceding centuries. Think of how man in the Dark Ages was helpless against the plague, which decimated whole populations. All of us can remember that only a few years ago polio was a dreaded scourge. Perhaps a cure for cancer is just around the corner, yet people are still dying every day from it. Suppose such a victim, instead of being declared lifeless and lowered into the ground—from which there is no return—is quick-frozen and stored in a facility until the day when science has arrived at a cancer cure. At which time he is thawed

out, his tissues still in serviceable condition except for
those ravaged by the disease. He is brought to life and
treated with the new therapy—"

Under his nimbus of smoke, Alp said: "Hold on. How
easy you say that. 'Brought to life.' Well, that's the rub.
What makes you think that basic trick can be pulled off?
And without it, like they say, you ain't got nothin' for
nobody nohow." He mugged at the camera.

Sweet smiled calmly. "Fish can be frozen solidly into a
block of lake ice, chopped out, thawed, and they swim
again. This happens in nature, in fact, every winter. In
laboratories chicken hearts, eels, certain insects, and human and animal semen—may I say that on the air?—"

The camera went to Alp, who said: "Sure, the censors
will think it's sailors."

This persistent wiseacre stuff annoyed Reinhart, who
grumbled into his tiny screen.

"Many types of organic material have been tested,"
Sweet continued, "and there is more than enough evidence to the effect that life by no means ends at the
moment a heart stops beating or lungs take in no more
air. Of course we do not yet know enough about these
matters. But this is the point. If we can preserve a body
against decay and degeneration, we have time in which to
look for cures for the ailments that caused this temporary
death"—he put up his hand to ward off Alp's incipient
iteration—"*and* the means for revival from the frozen
state."

"Aha," said Alp.

"I'll go so far as to admit that if we froze a body today
we could not revive it next week. I'm not so sure about
the next century."

"You're not?"

"After another hundred years of research? Who knows
what will be possible. Or why stop there? After a thousand years. There is no necessary reason why, once frozen
perfectly—at temperatures nearing absolute zero, which
is considerably colder than the familiar home freezer.
Minus four hundred and fifty-nine degrees Fahrenheit,
actually."

"Wow," gloated Alp. "That would chill your beer."

Sweet said: "The refrigeration methods are ready now.
Liquid nitrogen is almost two hundred minus zero Centigrade, and liquid helium even colder."

"We live in a fabulous time," Alp said, his pointed chin
hovering over the fat knot of his tie as if ready to spear it

as he lowered his forehead at the camera. "Eternal life, eh? That is a fantastic concept that bowls you over with its ramifications. Frankly I don't know that it is desirable. Wasn't it some sage, Chinese probably, who said that the only justification for life is that it eventually comes to an end?"

"It's a matter of personal choice," said Sweet. "But you seldom find anybody who if conscious at the moment of death would not choose life if he could. Frankly, I can imagine a time when your heirs might be charged with homicide if they did not have your body frozen."

Alongside him, Jody, the chanteuse, gasped, and in pulling back to catch her expression, the camera also picked up the actor, who played badmen but was in life of course a social meliorist. "I dunno," he said in necessarily the same voice in which he represented conscienceless brutes. "If we could make living men good and loving and nonaggressive, maybe we should preserve them. But merely to prolong hate— Maybe a committee of leading individuals could be formed—social leaders, clergymen, and so on—to rule on who should be saved. Because there wouldn't be literally room for everybody I don't imagine?"

For a very long time, perhaps three hundred seconds, Reinhart had lingered in a fascinated disregard of himself and the applicable pity. But this expression of the ethics of the ant-world called him back to order. If common good were the gauge, Reinhart would never be spared. The actor expected to be frozen as a reward for his piety. But what about a power failure. The local lights flickered every time the heavens broke wind.

"It is not my place," Sweet said, good for him, "to go into the moral questions here. Surely they are complex. Nor can any of us who are working in this field make an absolute promise of success. But think of it this way: what does a corpse have to lose? As things stand, he is dead. If he is frozen and never revived in the future, he has not lost anything."

"By golly," said Alp, looking through the camera into his viewers' millions of homes, in some of which it was statistically likely that certain persons were dying, as well as others making love, chewing food, quarreling, itching, suffering nonlethally, and even being inert; alone in his little corner of America, a shy clerk played with himself while watching Jody's thighs; a furious crank began another denunciatory letter to Alp: "Dear Commie Fuck-face . . ." The universal brotherhood of the mortal; there is no other kind.

"It makes you think," said Alp. "It is frightening, it is thrilling. I have a feeling we haven't really scratched the surface of this topic, and our time is already gone. Can you come back again, Bob? By the way, what's your part in this? You're not an M.D., are ya?"

"No, I am not, Jack. You might call me a publicist, for want of a better word."

"Going to make a bundle out of it?"

Sweet was not offended. Reinhart knew that Alp often spoke in this mock-provocative style.

"I'm a retired businessman. I arrived at the conclusion that money isn't enough—"

"Having made enough of it to afford that sentiment," Alp noted. "I'm kidding, folks. Mr. Sweet is a true philan-thropist. He has endowed this Cryon Foundation, and not a person makes a penny out of it. He is dedicated, he is committed, and I for one think he is a groovy individual in a day when so many of us have hangups and are uptight." Alp sighed. "Now we're going to get a lot of cards and letters. You have stirred up a beehive, I'm sure. Please don't write directly to me, folks, don't do it!" To Sweet: "You have an address where people can write for information?"

Reinhart sat in what used to be called deep-brown study while the program was succeeded by the final news reports, a short inspirational message from a sardonic-looking man of the cloth, a rendition of the music accom-panying Francis Scott Key's unsingable doggerel, and a dead screen giving off the hum of a capricious tube.

It was a dirty racket to exploit man's natural desire for everlasting life. Also an extraordinarily bold one if an-nounced on national TV. Sweet's game was one of infinite magnitude. Of course it must be a swindle. No man could seriously take on eternity. The theme staggered the imagi-nation, and for relief Reinhart fled into a memory of his father's attitude towards death. Himself an insurance man by profession, Reinhart's dad had been fully covered. One of his many policies paid the expenses of his own funeral; since the age of twenty-one Dad had been buying his coffin in installments. During the Dark Ages, Reinhart had read, certain orders of extremist monks slept every night in the wooden box in which they would eventually be buried.

A grisly subject, but one with which we must all come

to terms. As a merciless kid one sang a ditty: *Your eyes
fall in, your teeth fall out, worms crawl over your nose
and mouth*. What Sweet projected were refrigerated cata-
combs, frozen bodies stacked like ice-cube trays.

No, of course it was a complete fraud. . . . What
interested Reinhart was not eternal life itself. The one of
which he had lived forty-four years was often unbearable
enough as it was. A mere continuation would be no
answer. But a second chance, another start, was most
attractive. Sweet had spoken of a *thousand* years hence.
The mind could not accept that. But suppose one died of
some simple accident—self-inflicted, to put it starkly:
severed his aorta with an ordinary paring knife found in
any kitchen. Heart transplants were still a dodgy affair.
The recipient who was shown smiling at the TV camera
two days later usually died quietly on the third. But
another twenty years should perfect the process, maybe
less. One day in July 1988 a clerk pulls open a drawer in
the *R* section of the massive file cabinet wherein lies
Reinhart in the sleep of ice. The surgeons plug a new
ticker into his chest, thaw out the lot, and send him on his
way, no younger than he was but, more importantly, no
older, having eaten the cake of suicide and yet possessing
the fact of renewed life.

Reinhart did not actually believe in one iota of this
fantasy. But neither did he believe in the reality of his
son, who at this moment materialized in the doorway to
the study. Though facing the wall above the desk, Reinhart detected this presence by an involuntary rising of his
hackles.

He spun around in the chair. Blaine wore a vest of
sheepskin, hair out, over an otherwise naked body. Far
below his pinched navel was the waistband of the gang-
ster-striped pants, which flared at the ankles but at the
bulge of the crotch were snug as bathing trunks. He stood
in reversed-cowhide boots, and a wide-brimmed flop hat,
derivative of Greta Garbo's, finished him off at the top,
from under which his pale locks flowed to splash onto his
narrow shoulders.

Reinhart was never prepared to see Blaine after an
absence. He was infuriated anew at every audience. It
occurred to him now that were he to go through the
series he had fancifully projected, his brand-new heart
would explode at the first sight of Blaine, who could be
relied on not to have changed meanwhile except in inci-

dentals. Whatever his own prospects, Reinhart had no
hope whatever for Blaine's.

However, his son's appearance upset him so violently
that he forgot for the moment what Blaine had been up
to next door, and asked his usual hostile, monosyllabic
query: "Well?"

Blaine stared at his father through pale eyes and under
the hatbrim. His right hip was slung high, caressing the
doorframe. His languid lily hand rose to toy with a flaxen
lock. His left thumb hooked into his belt buckle, not a
proper one but an arrangement of two harness rings. He
looked like some kind of swishy gunfighter, star of the
Pansy Spat at the OK Corral. He continued to stare, in
arrogant confidence that he was a master of timing.

Reinhart at last fired one round. "Have you got something to say, or are you waiting for me to focus the
camera?" Sarcasm was never Reinhart's forte. He always
managed to delude himself with it. That cocky little
blackguard, he thought now, actually thinking I would
want to photograph his costume.

Finally Blaine said: "I threaten you merely by standing
here. That's fantastic, isn't it? Merely by living, I give off
lethal rays."

This argument was an old story to Reinhart. He had
heard it from Blaine before, and Gen, and in print from
journalists who were sycophants of anybody with enough
bullshit to fill a column.

"I'm trembling with fear," he answered. "You might
strangle me with one of your silken strands."

Blaine grinned, showing the tips of both gray canines.
It was also switched-on, with-it, and revolutionary not to
clean one's teeth—a blow at the middle-class bacteria
which cause caries.

He probably stank too, but Reinhart had not for a long
time got close enough to him to tell. How that girl next
door could stand him— All at once Reinhart remembered, and cerebral blood swamped his reason and, spill-
ing over his forehead, flowed down his cheeks just
beneath the skin.

"You look," said Blaine, "like you're going to spit
catsup."

Reinhart's speech began as a distant belch, like the
initial disturbance deep within the volcano's core, hearing
which the Pompeiians might have saved themselves. But
Blaine stood his ground, impervious to lava as to common
decency. Again and again Reinhart had erupted on him

without effect, and now Vesuvius was tired. So he turned back into a fat, sad old father.

"Son," he said, "let's start all over. Hell, it's not too late. You just became a man a few months ago. A good time for a new beginning for us both." In this mood of philosophical benevolence his memory swooped back over two decades and plucked up an apposite experience of his own young manhood. "I don't know that I have ever mentioned being with the first Occupation troops in Berlin."

"Not so far today, anyhow," said Blaine, rubbing his sunken chest self-lasciviously.

Reinhart declined the provocation. "OK, I guess I have bored you with it too much. My fault," he hastened to add. "I understand now the old World War I veterans who bored me in my time. Being in a war has an effect on you."

"I'm sure it does," said Blaine. "It makes you into an animal."

"All right, I know your feelings on the subject, and I'm not going to argue about it. I'll just say it might interest you to hear I'm no militarist, but there are times when a man must fight to defend him—"

"Oh, pigshit," said Blaine in weary impatience. He suddenly slid down along the doorframe and sat on the floor. He was very limber, his sole physical gift.

Again Reinhart rose above the situation, managing even to smile. His face felt much cooler already. "All right." He decided against wryly tossing up his hands, a movement Blaine might interpret as aggressive. "One day you'll be where I am and I'll be dead." Or perhaps only frozen, but that must at the moment remain his secret. "What I want to say now is when I was in Berlin, I was just twenty-one years old."

"Only yesterday," Blaine said pseudo-pleasantly, his knees at an angle and his face, with hat, between them.

"It seems like it. . . . I had a German girl. . . . She was sixteen." He went on quickly: "She was a sort of little whore. It was her idea, really."

With a smearing movement Blaine pushed his hatbrim back from ear to ear. In the better light Reinhart believed he saw the origins of a new moustache on the long white upper lip, and approved; it would diminish the girlish effect of the hair. He should have had a quiet, reasonable, nostalgic little talk like this long since. He sensed the beginnings of a new relationship with Blaine.

"*What* was her idea?" Blaine asked, already less nasty. He seemed truly puzzled, wrinkling his parsnip nose. "Why 'really'?"

Reinhart was shy. He had not talked directly of sex to Blaine since the boy was ten and he had given him the lecture Gen had suggested on returning from a PTA roundtable discussion. "Well sir," Reinhart had said then, to this towheaded tyke, who also had a button nose, "babies don't actually just appear in the hospital, Blainey. It starts before that when—" "Yeah," little Blaine interrupted in his soprano, "when the father inserts his penis in the mother's vagina and ejaculates seminal fluid containing thousands of tiny sperm," and so on. It had been rather amusing, at that.

Reinhart now searched his vocabulary for an up-to-date idiom. "Making out" was one he had read in magazine think-pieces on the young, but it sounded awfully hokey, like the "sleeping with" of his era. In Hollywood, he knew on the authority of the biographer of a tragic movie queen, they said "ball." "I balled her, baby," an actor told his agent, or vice versa.

"I mean," Reinhart said, grinning nervously, "we had relations."

Blaine tilted his hatbrim down again, and clasping his legs under the knees, rocked back and forth, hooting. "So you *fucked* her, man. What does that prove?"

"Why you dirty little—" Reinhart caught himself. In all justice the offending term had been continually upon his lips when he was a soldier. Of course he would never have spoken it to his own dad. But he had heard the colonel, a man older than his father, employ it habitually. What's in a word?

"You're not making it easy on me," he said.

"If you do it," Blaine stated, "you call it by its right name. Your generation is only delicate about terms."

This was not the time to defend hypocrisy, which Reinhart happened to believe was far from deplorable. With it the Victorians had made the family an impregnable institution while managing also to have lots of jollies in private, so well concealed that only in recent years had the academic busybodies sniffed them out. Somewhere near the summit of values Reinhart put privacy, and he had learned through crude experience as well as refined ratiocination that almost the only way to get it was to be hypocritical.

Still he retained his temper, but he said to Blaine:

"You know, my only real difference with you, if we subtract the exterior things like hairstyle and clothes—I wore a zoot suit with fourteen-inch pegged cuffs and a hat with a rolled brim, my first year in college, and a duck's-ass haircut—my essential argument is that you are completely within the mainstream of conformity."

"Yeah," Blaine said, "I know that trick too. When the other side has shown up your values as immoral, cruel, and false, you then project your sins onto them. You can't beat the Vietcong, so you claim they have committed all your crimes."

"No, my dear Blaine, I do not mean that," Reinhart said levelly. "I don't refer to the superficialities of politics or the sociological shit you take as divine sanction for refusing to exist authentically. I accept and confirm your criticisms of the status quo, which is rife with injustice and bad taste. If you read history with both eyes you will know that has always been so. Greeks of the Golden Age kept slaves and many of the most eminent statesmen and philosophers reserved their highest passion for other males. In the Elizabethan era, those who had what today would be the highest-priced theater seats, stood eating, drinking, and fist-fighting during the performance of Shakespeare's noblest tragedies. In the street outside, dung, urine, and garbage were knee-high, which is why you will find in *Romeo and Juliet* the first fight between young men of the Montagues and Capulets is over who must walk in the crap."

Blaine joined his long white fingers around his calves. "We're really not interested in the past. You can have it. You can cuddle it, feel it up, go down on it, and pretend you and it love each other. You deserve one another. We're not just going to let you kill the future. If you try, we will kill you."

" 'We,' " said Reinhart. "The hyena speaking of his pack. Never for God's sake foul your mouth with 'I.' The irony of my position is that 'you' plural is the same word as 'you' singular. I am presumably part of the mass 'you' for purposes of denunciation, yet I have seldom shared in the advantages. I belong to the 'you' past thirty and therefore physically beyond the prime, tending as a class to graying, weak eyesight, disintegrating gums, discoloration of skin, excessive weight, and shortness of breath. But I have never had the money and power which compensate for those failings. I don't own a swimming pool in which you can float around and get tan and then dry off and revile me for conspicuous consumption. I have never lectured you on the positive virtues of Puritan morality, the American flag, the Presbyterian faith, the Republican party, the sanctity of mothers, the middle class, or the white race."

"Straw men of your generation," Blaine said. "We never considered them seriously. Our enemy is liberal, agnostic, rationalistic, moral relativists, 'men of goodwill,' 'common decency,' 'humanitarianism,' and all those frauds."

There you had it, a recognizable quotation from *Mein Kampf*. It would, however, be uncritical to take Blaine as Hitlerian.

Reinhart therefore nonabusively pointed to a similar position taken, with horrible consequences, by the German Communists, of whom he had learned only after serving in Occupation Berlin and returning to college. "Like you they believed the society was rotten from the ground up. Of course it was, and is, and will always be." Part of Reinhart's rationale was anarchistic. "They encouraged the Nazis to pull it down, intending themselves to take over when all lay in ruins. But they were themselves soon wrecked. The rule of life seems to be that people are always ruined by the fulfillment rather than the denial of their hopes." In the light of this principle, Reinhart could feel better about himself.

"Communists," said Blaine, "are part of your world and your era. They are at worst morally disgusting and at best awful bores. And they are always old men."

"I thought you worshiped Ché Guevara?"

"I told you before that once the Cuban revolution had been achieved and institutionalized, he left the country. What better evidence that he was not a Communist in your sense, a bureaucratic bully, but rather the eternal revolutionary. Don't talk to me about Robespierre and the Terror and the inevitable appearance of a Napoleon or Stalin or the change in a Castro. That's your style of politics, getting back to normalcy and a serene life in the suburbs. The real revolution never ends. You ask what we would substitute for your structures. You can't dig that our thinking is not structural. We don't want another Congress where those old fuckers sit around and jerk each other off."

Reinhart could not help it. With the best will in the world he nevertheless found that kind of talk erected his short hairs.

"I'll say this for you, Blaine," he said soberly. "You are

a very successful provoker, to be which it takes fantastic effrontery combined with a contempt for the literal meaning of words. In short, the politician's demagogic gift. That, conjoined with your adman's sense of publicity, makes you a classic American from the central tradition: a superconspicuous, loudmouthed vulgarian whose exhibitionism is yet strangely impersonal. You proclaim nothing for your self, and everything for your crowd. Or maybe it would be accurate to say your crowd is your self. That principle was enunciated on the founding of this country, in Franklin's pun to the effect that unless we hang together, we will hang separately."

Blaine was moving his head, and hat, from side to side in a regular movement like that of the escapement in a watch.

"Also," Reinhart went on, "your mystique is precisely the same as that of the American businessman, who initiates new enterprises on the profits of the old, reinvests his dividends, never takes his winnings and goes home, but rather assumes more obligations, greater risks, in an ever-increasing momentum, with ever-expanding expectations. The flux is all. . . . I have never been able to manage that myself, as you know."

"Yes, Father," Blaine said, still ticking off the seconds which if continued would in the aggregate be a life.

"My own criticism of Franklin," Reinhart pointed out, "is that we will all hang separately anyway, in the end. Thus I find all social thinking limited, ultimately false if you like. 'There are many unpleasant ways to die and you are far more likely to have an unpleasant form of death than an easy and painless one.' I read that once years ago and have never been able to forget it."

Blaine winced, threw his hands out behind him, over the threshold, and leaned on them, shoulders squeezing his neck.

"Well," he said, "you can't use that excuse any more. They can freeze people now at the moment of death, cold-store them for years like steaks, and thaw them out in some future time when a cure has been perfected for what ailed them."

So he would even take that away from Reinhart, "that" being not only the process, which Reinhart romantically assumed was his alone though broadcast on national TV, much as other madmen get a crush on an actress and are devastated by the information that she is married, but also what Blaine was quite right in calling his excuse.

"How," he cried indignantly, "do you know about that?"

Blaine made a passionless murmur. He said: "I voluntarily exposed myself to the preceding abuse of my intelligence. You ought to wonder why. I did not come here merely to backstroke in the vat of tepid piss wherein you habitually float while deliberating philosophically. I need some money, and I ask you to give it to me."

"I won't give you a penny until you answer my simple question. Is that thing about freezing the dead general knowledge?" It could be. Reinhart's fund of same was only sporadically replenished nowadays. His usual television fare was old movies. He frequently missed the daily encyclopedia of catastrophes, more and more humanly remote, which had replaced the old newspaper of the man-bites-dog era of journalism. And his dentist's magazines were so ancient as to show features of the hula-hoop craze.

"The Jack Alp Show," Blaine stated. "Tonight. It just went off, if you have to know. You were probably watching Andy Hardy. 'Gee, Dad, all I wanted was a little hug but she blew me, and it was great! Wow! Wooee!' 'We had better have a man-to-man talk, son.'" Blaine said the latter in a deep, artificial voice that sounded nothing like the late Lewis Stone's in the sentimental yet, for all that, virile role of the just Judge. Though it came to Reinhart that he himself and his pals, a quarter-century before, had derided those pictures in much the same idiom, except that today's oral images were then anal for some reason not easily isolated. The difference was that none of those guys, including himself, had ever yet had a piece. Thus their mockery had a harmless, infantile purity to it, and the ugliness was funny.

Reinhart suspected this interview would end with his throwing Blaine through a closed window, which even in his present condition he could do with the left hand, but first he had to reach another conclusion.

"Were you watching television next door?"

"Yes I was."

"You were also walking around naked in Julie's room."

"Right again." Blaine's grin would have been radiant had his teeth been clean.

"You admit it?"

"I admit anything," said Blaine. "Whatever you can dream up, I've done it." He stared for a while at his father. "And so have you."

"What does that mean?" asked Reinhart. "What in the world."

"The German teen-ager, dig? And what, twenty years later, are you doing looking into Julie's window?"

He had the goods on Reinhart, as Reinhart somehow suspected all along he would. The irresponsible have a permanent one-up on those who feel obligations. Even when he himself was young, Reinhart belonged to the latter company. It was true that the little Kraut had in effect seduced him; she had been more or less a tart, definitely a shameless liar, and no doubt the offspring of Nazis. Still, by one definition he had been a man and she a schoolgirl. He would have been a criminal almost anywhere in the United States. On the other hand, she had been nine-tenths full grown, whereas many outright children sold themselves to GIs, especially in Italy. Julie, next door, was already bigger than her mother in breast and hip, and all he did was look at her.

"My conscience is clean," Reinhart said. "But more importantly, it is I who support you. With all your talk about revolution you understand nothing about power. Frankly, *I* don't have to justify myself to you. That is the realistic truth. You are a parasite."

Blaine came to his feet in an impressive, fluid movement, almost balletic, without the use of hands. Of course he did not weigh much. Still, in the old weightlifting days Reinhart could not have done that without a visible effort and the audible expelling of breath by which the athlete increases his power. Everything came easy to Blaine, at least everything he tried. The rest he apparently let alone. He was a brilliant student yet was seldom found with book in hand. He seemed effeminate, but the girls took to him, called him on the phone, whistled at him in the street. Until tonight Reinhart had told himself these were expressions of the fond, proprietary amusement which females of his own age showed towards the nonthreatening antics of mincing Southern celebrities and awkward puppy dogs.

Blaine said, while rising: "No, Mother supports us both, or all three counting Baby Whale."

Reinhart was ready for this. "Then why beg off me?"

Blaine threw his mouth open. The beginning moustache looked like a dirty lip. "To bug you, man. To drive you out of your skull."

Reinhart said: "It takes a load off my mind, anyway.

Until I saw you over there with her, I always thought you were a dirty little faggot."

Blaine inhaled, laughing. "To your generation that's the ultimate horror, isn't it?" He cocked a hand on his hip. "You're all uptight about that, and carry billyclubs and guns like extra cocks to demonstrate your virility. Well, maybe I am. Or perhaps I'm bisexed. The gross sexual distinctions are disappearing. Love is where you find it. Perhaps I was trying on Julie's clothes." He performed a bump and grind with his snakelike trunk. "My idea of a groovy experience is to be ravished by the unshaven driver of an interstate truck, up on that shelf behind the seat where they sleep when the co-driver takes the wheel. Or to be buggered by the nightstick of a huge apelike cop, his bad breath in my ear—"

He neatly dodged his father's massive fist, which bruised itself on the doorjamb and brought down some plaster dust from overhead. Once again Reinhart had been successfully baited.

Actually he had been aware of Blaine's purpose throughout, had knowingly followed the script. In a strange way he believed he owed it to Blaine. It was the only form of love the boy would tolerate from him. And it had to be performed seriously. He must as a finale try genuinely to strike Blaine with a killing blow. Blaine would have detected any pulling of the punch or false aim. He respected only the true impulse of viciousness, and, underneath it all, Reinhart respected him for his adherence to the principle. Blaine played a ruthless game. He was a pacifist when asked to go to war, an advocate of violent demonstrations for Negroes and college students, a believer in free love for anyone under thirty and repression for those older; he had contempt for money and those who earned it but demanded to be given as much as he needed; he dressed and comported himself flagrantly so as to attract attention, yet getting it he derided and/or denounced his audience.

He was, in short, altogether human and absolutely normal. There was no mistaking his commitment to injustice, to incessant provocation, to maximum publicity, illogic, malice, attachment to his own crowd and frightened hatred of any other, his solipsism, his nightmares, his sadism, or his relationship to his father. You wouldn't find him tormenting a stranger. He loved his old dad.

And vice versa. And if Reinhart was being ironic when he made that reflection, he was neither more nor less so

when, having waited an hour for Blaine to get to sleep, he
stole into his son's room with a little penlight and found
the pile of discarded clothing on a bedside chair. As it
happened, Reinhart, despite his financial difficulties, always managed to maintain a little cache of loot which he
kept between the pages of a *World Almanac* for the year
1953. Before leaving his study this night he withdrew a fin
from it, leaving three dollar-notes.

The clothes stank of perspiration, as he had supposed.
Oddly enough, the pants had no pockets. Blaine and his
ilk liked snug hips. So Reinhart pushed the folded bill into
a little kangaroo-niche in the vest. Blaine slept soundly, in
the regular breathing of an impeccable soul. He always
had. Reinhart remembered him well as a baby.

With no more illumination than the dime-sized spot of
the penlight and no finer instrument than a pair of Japa-
nese-made desk shears, Reinhart cut his son's hair to
within approximately two inches of the scalp. During the
operation Blaine murmured occasionally, and when Reinhart gently lifted his head off the pillow and bent it
forward to get at the back, the boy burbled like an
infant, giving Reinhart an intimate feeling he had not had
in years.

Before retiring, Reinhart flushed the shorn locks down
the toilet, took two Sominex, and eventually was hummed
to sleep on his narrow couch under the window by a duet
of mosquitoes to whom his corpus would furnish late
dinner.

— 4 —

Reinhart entered an elevator in the Bloor Building, in the city, a skyscraper that might have been commonplace in New York but was the highest edifice hereabouts, and was projected, with funny ears, to the twenty-seventh floor. His fund of odd information as usual came in handy: he knew that the familiar nightmare of the elevator-rider, given the nod in many films and TV episodes, had no base in reality. The cab never came unhooked and plunged to the bottom of the shaft; because of many safety devices this could not happen.

But here was his floor. He found the number and opened a frosty-paned door labeled CRYON FOUNDATION.

"I believe I spoke to you earlier on the phone," he stated to the young woman who sat behind a kidney-shaped desk of crystal-clear plastic. Her telephone was of a rusty hue that Reinhart had not known was one of the options. She wore outsize metal-rimmed glasses which he doubted were prescription. Her hair was a sort of mane of tan intermixed with black. The bosom of her dress, puffy and colored in pastel streaks, defied the eye to tell whether flesh was immediately underlying, or air, padding, or whatnot. Time was when Reinhart knew exactly what an office girl had beneath her blouse: an impeccably white brassiere, fastened over the groove of her spine with two or possibly three metal hooks sewn into strained elastic.

"I understand your hangup," she said. "It takes more than a deep breath to plunge into something like this. Has the death already occurred or is it in the works?"

"As I told you on the telephone—but perhaps it was difficult to hear: I was in one of those lousy outdoor booths, which was filthy, and furthermore it was so ravaged by vandals that frankly I didn't expect to get through at all." It also stank of piss and the glass walls were covered with obscenities written with a wide-tipped laundry marker in green ink and various phone numbers accompanied by sundry promises of a sexual nature. Some years before Reinhart in a desperate moment had dialed one such combination of digits, lifted off the plaster flanking a coin phone in a bar, and got the Public Library.

"The point is," he went on, "that I am a personal friend of Mr. Bob Sweet's. He wrote down the number for me himself." Reinhart held up the leaf from Sweet's lizard notebook.

"Excuse me?" She had a large, pale, fashionable mouth and big white teeth.

"Well, I'd like to see him if he's in."

"He isn't." She cocked her head and, smirking, pronounced an impersonally cute "Really."

"May I wait?" He sat down in a half acorn upholstered in lemon Naugahyde and mounted on cat's-cradles of chromium wire. Ordinarily he would have lingered for the invitation, but he now suddenly felt adrift on a wave of impuissance. The scene at breakfast had been frightful: Blaine with his ravaged head, looking like a wet bird, Genevieve's swordplay with the breadknife, Winona's howls. Pretty strong stuff.

"Mr. Sweet's in New York for the *Jack Alp Show*," said the girl. "I don't know when to expect him."

"Yes, I saw it."

"I gather the presentation piqued your curiosity as to what was entailed," she said in an unreal pronunciation, or perhaps Reinhart heard her faultily as he found himself staring up her generous naked haunches all the way to the bare crotch, which, unless he had gone blind or mad, was smooth as one as a youngster imagined a girl's to be, without orifice or beard.

"Sir," she suddenly cried with impatience posing as compassion, "aren't you well? Can I get you a glass of water?"

Reinhart made a croaking sound which the girl took as assent and she rose and strode through a plastic-rosewood door to some inner sanctum. She was tall and hefty. The minimal skirt, of a stubborn stuff which remembered the crumpling it had undergone from the seat of the chair, stayed halfway up her posterior. A crackless behind showed Reinhart that what he had taken as nudity was panty-hose in the color of Caucasian flesh.

The same garment on a Negro female would not have misled him, though no doubt he might have been accused of racism on some other pretext—he had already picked up a magazine and, leafing urgently past an article written by an eighteen-year-old philosopher, entitled "Why Do You Hate Us?" had come upon another, labeled "Here's Why We Hate You," by a writer identified as "a black" or perhaps it was "A. Black," written without capitals to be pretentious. Further along were the cartoons, peopled by "hippies," speaking in such terms as "turn on," "freak out," etc. Prepositions were in fashion. Up with this I shall not put, Reinhart said Churchillianly to himself, dropping the periodical onto its fellows on a coffee table of leaden, solid slate. His dentist's old mags were full of "beatniks" and other vanished phenomena.

The big girl returned with a measure of water in a disposable cup made of hardened, dead-white foam which had no weight when emptied, for Reinhart though not thirsty drained it considerably.

She said, hanging her breasts over him, "My father gets those attacks." Girls her age, anywhere from twenty-five to forty-three, often pretended he was old enough to have sired them.

"Thank you," Reinhart answered curtly. "As it happened I lunched with Mr. Sweet yesterday and rode partway to the airport with him. We are old pals from high school."

"Is that right? Well."

Reinhart decided to be avuncular, having nothing else going for him. "And don't say you thought he was a lot younger. I'm not yet a candidate for your freezer." Now he could see her big nipples, the pinkish swirls in the multicolored dress being transparent.

She shrugged, reclaimed the weightless cup, and, having let it fall, which took ever so long, into a wastebasket of woven strips of Philippine mahogany, sat down again at the desk. Now, with his informed sight, Reinhart noticed that her crotch sagged slightly. He had known a very large nurse when in the Army. Today she must be most of the distance towards fifty, having been a few, then meaningless, years older than he. Nowadays he lusted only for teen-agers, but if this receptionist threw herself at him he would catch her. Time enough for that, though, when Sweet hired him.

"I suppose we will be colleagues soon," said Reinhart. "I imagine I will be joining Mr. Sweet in the firm."

She peered dramatically at an immense watch on a purple patent-leather band around her wrist. "It's lunchtime, and I have to go out now. Was there anything further? I have to lock the office, you see."

"Are you alone here?" Reinhart regretted having put the question when he saw her suspicious, even frightened, glance. He smiled to allay any fears that he might be a potential rapist, but felt his treacherous face assume a leer.

"People keep coming in," she said quickly, staring at the door. "We're just getting under way. We aren't really organized yet. We don't even keep any petty cash on hand." She grew shrill. "And certainly no stamps. We have a Pitney-Bowes postage machine in back." Her hair fell across her glasses on both sides, and she whiplashed her neck to throw it back.

Reinhart lifted himself. "I'm leaving too." He would have liked a quiet moment to examine his wallet and see if he possessed the wherewithal to buy her lunch. She probably ate copiously; her figure did not suggest the old office-girl's old standby, tuna on toast.

"Have several things to do first," said she, presenting no interstices in which he could put a toe, and went to the outer door and held it open. "I'll send you our brochure. It answers all possible questions." She was a good five feet ten, he estimated now they were both erect.

He reached her and stopped. "Nice to meet you, Miss—" The corridor was thronged with noontime traffic. Some young-executive or office-boy types—you could no longer tell—sauntered by in pinched-waisted summer suits and feathery sideburns. One was saying, "A wedge of Stilton and a pint of nut-brown ale. That's lunch to me. But where can you get it in this burg?" You fraud, thought Reinhart, who had lately read an article on cheeses of the world, Stilton is scooped out with a spoon. But he saw the girl eyeing them with obvious admiration.

Her attention cruised reluctantly back to him, and her mouth clamped together. She forthwith abandoned all pretense of courtesy.

"This way out, man." She threw a brawny thumb over her shoulder. The crowd made her nervy.

"You didn't seem to hear me say I would soon be working with Bob. . . . But that's all right," he added quickly, in response to her expression, which now signified open maleficence. "I'll let Bob tell you himself when he gets back. Please inform him that Reinhart, Carl Reinhart, was in."

She shuddered in revulsion and closed the door behind

him. No, he had checked his fly before entering; he had shaved, washed, and deodorized himself that morning. It was simply that women ignored him nowadays and if he tried to assert himself, acted like this girl or the waitress at Gino's. The only thing that kept him from turning fag was his detestation of men. People were so rotten that why anybody would want to be frozen in order to preserve himself as a human being—the elevator opened its jaws, swallowed him, and he descended its esophagus.

The strange, almost eerie coincidence was that he had also first met Genevieve, in a similarly unpleasant fashion, on entering an office of which she was the lone functionary. But he had then been twenty-two, which term of years if doubled brought him to his current pass. Now, at forty-four, he had been thrown out of his own home.

Gen had threatened to put the police on him if he showed up there again. He had not anticipated that she would react so violently to the rape of Blaine's locks.

"After all," he pointed out, "it will grow back."

Blaine was still hysterical and, wrapped around his mother, his half-plucked chicken-head against her neck, sobbed into the collar of her housecoat. Her fanatical face, which an infusion of bad blood had turned swarthy as the traditional portraits of Savonarola, stared over him.

She said: "I'll see you prosecuted for battery." She was a lawyer's daughter—to be precise, a disbarred lawyer's daughter, but she knew her terms. "That's just for starters. I'll ask Daddy to consult the statutes with reference to sexual perversions. There are deviates who snip hair from people in crowds—"

Reinhart hoped to conceal his fear behind a blustering show of indignation. "Genevieve, you know damn well why I took that measure. Enough is too much. That boy has embarrassed me continually in recent years, and I have reason to believe he does it deliberately. Sheer malice. He admitted as much last night, after we had another set-to."

Blaine howled an imprecation into his mother's collarbone.

"There, there, dear," said she tenderly. "I'm going to fix his wagon one for all." Gen managed somehow always to warp a cliché.

"This is disgusting," said Reinhart. "He's twenty-one years old. At that age I was in the Occupation of Berlin. If I ever tried hanging on my mother and blubbering about my troubles, she'd have punched me in the mouth."

"That's where your insanity comes from, your mother. She's a crazy old lady." This was not complete nonsense, but had no relevance to the situation. "But not even she would have approached her child with a lethal instrument."

"Wrong!" crowed Reinhart. "Many a time when I annoyed her while she prepared meals she would throw the knife at me, usually a little paring knife, true, but more than once the big carver used by chefs. But come off this stuff about edged weapons. A scissors, a pair of library shears, and none too sharp at that." He snickered. "That's why the job is not so hot. He's lucky I didn't charge him. Barbers get two-fifty nowadays."

Gen picked up a glass of orange juice that Reinhart had just squeezed and had her son make a mouth and poured some in. Reinhart kept his back against the kitchen counter.

Winona chose this moment to waddle into the kitchen, in the sort of charwoman outfit she wore to a school otherwise attended by go-go girls. Even Reinhart thought the skirt too long, though he sympathized with her intent to hide her fat limbs.

"Hi," she said in the glee aroused by an imminent meal. "Oh, I hope it's waffles, I do hope it is. I have my heart set on maple syrup and lots of butter. I think I dreamed of waffles."

"Leave the room, Winona," Genevieve said harshly.

Winona had not yet seen anything untoward. She was looking for food, not people. Now, without an interest in the motive behind the command, she blurted out a great cry of desolation and her eyes streamed. She addressed the ceiling: "Without breakfast! Ohhhh-oooo-ahhhh."

This however brought Blaine briefly out of his act—which it was at least in part; his own eyes were quite dry.

He snarled: "Get out, Fat-ass."

Reinhart showed him a fist. "I won't tolerate that kind of talk to your sister."

This was when Genevieve picked up the breadknife, a serrated-blade instrument that would deliver a cut with deckle edges, a kind of saw, really.

She threatened him in a quiet way that was definitely sinister. Her voice was so low that he had to lean towards her to hear it.

"Make your move," she said. "I'm just praying for the opportunity."

"Talk of legality," Reinhart pointed out. "What you're doing constitutes assault, I believe."

"Just put me in court, with my size alongside of yours," Gen asserted, no doubt fashioning her combat style from those movies, already long outmoded, in which juvenile delinquents belonging to criminal gangs menaced solid citizens. What had become of leather jackets, motorcycles, and switchblades? Already stuffed into the garbage can of history.

Squealing like the rabbit Reinhart shot imperfectly, twenty years before, and then lost his stomach for hunting, leaving the small game to the mutilation of unsentimental hawks and ferrets, Winona propelled her flesh from the kitchen. This bothered Reinhart most.

He said: "How can you be so cruel?"

"Hypocrisy won't stand you in good stead any more," Genevieve cried. "You introduced violence into this house, and now you can lie in it."

Blaine cackled. Were his hair still long he would have resembled a witch. As it was he recalled for his father an old animated character called Woody Woodpecker, the mention of which like so many other bits of lore, would mean nothing to this generation. Woody was always being blown up by dynamite or TNT and reassembling without hurt. How harmless the culture used to be.

Blaine said: "Up against the wall!"

"You little fraud," said Reinhart. "I'd have some respect for you if you held the knife, and even more if you used it against a real enemy. But your game is to threaten only those who wish you well, only those who in affection have placed you in a position where you can be a threat, those who abolished child-labor, those who let their children choose their own careers and pay them enormous allowances, get them the best in medical care and warm clothing and—"

Blaine said: "Why don't you die?"

"Excuse me," said Reinhart. He really did not mind Gen's knifeplay that much. In twenty-odd years of marriage he had seen her fury a thousand times and more. In recent manifestations it had crested more quickly because the general level of her ill will was so high that only a flash flood could distinguish itself from the mean. By the same token it soon subsided, not having far to fall. At any moment she would return to the familiar state of cold contempt. Then, if he made a success in business, which he still intermittently expected to do, he could rely on her to be the feasible wife she had been long ago. Or so he told himself. At moments of extremity Reinhart could be very cavalier about time.

He did not believe she would actually cut him, that is, or if she did, it would only be a nick. Perhaps if it bled sufficiently she might even be contrite. It was something he could hold over her in the future—now, ease off, you remember that time with the breadknife, etc.

Blaine's suggestion, however, was something else. A truism of Reinhart's day held that sons were normally psychic murderers of their male parent on the one hand and mother-lovers on the other, reflecting a quaint Austro-Jewish theory that, however, had once been revolutionary. Reinhart used to catch himself in slips of the pen regarding his own father, of whom he could not consciously have been fonder. He could also recall having said, "Darn you, Daddy," once at the age of eight when having been led to a drugstore for a malted milk he found it closed. Dad said: "Well, Carlo, I didn't know." And being already of a reflective nature, little Reinhart said: "OK, I'm sorry." "No offense taken, Carlo," answered Dad. Reinhart remembered this because he had never before heard that turn of phrase: where would you take a fence? When he repeated it to a schoolmate, he got punched on his vaccination.

"Excuse me," he said now to Blaine. "What I really can't stand about you is something that unfortunately I can't trim with a pair of shears. That is your outlandish rhetoric. You don't know what dying is, and as far as I can see, you've scrupulously avoided any form of violence, even the contact sports. College rioters often howl their praises of Ché and Ho Chi Minh, professional killers, but snivel and whimper when the cops hit them with nightsticks—just as you used to do when some years back I tried to show you some of the jujitsu we learned in Army basic training. And I of course was only trying to teach you some self-defense. But even in just learning it you get hit once in a while and are dumped on your prat."

Reinhart shook his head. "Christ, Blaine, you are old enough to get a sense of reality. Not everything can go your way."

Much of this reasonable turn applied to his own needs. It is no joke to be told to die, even allowing for youth, passion, and the fashions in idiom by which a man could be termed a crypto-Nazi merely for shaving off his sideburns, a genocide because he deplores a mob, and a bully for questioning the credentials of folksinger-statesmen. Though it did occur to him that he might have thrown Blaine too hard occasionally. But the young have rubber bones. "Here's another one," Reinhart would say, and with left foot and right wrist quickly floor him. Indeed, Reinhart had never before been able properly to accomplish these judo maneuvers and certainly never tried them when involved in bar-fights as a soldier. And he had never been in combat. He suspected they were pretty useless except to beat up a son.

At this point Winona reentered smiling, obsessively pretending it was the first time or having weakmindedly forgotten the earlier scene. "Good morning!" she said brightly, and all three of them, Reinhart included, shouted at her.

"I'm going to kill myself," she screamed and retired again, sobbing from the vast empty cavern of her stomach.

Reinhart said to Blaine: "All right, for the purpose of peace-making, I apologize. I'm sorry I cut your hair, I regret having been rough in playing with you as a little boy. But I'll tell you something: you can't ever get your father back for his flaws. The traditional way is to get your revenge on your own son, and you will certainly want to, I'll tell you that. Besides, I slipped you five bucks last night."

Blaine put his hair against his mother's shoulder. He was wearing his gangster pants and a soiled strap-undershirt, filthy bare feet with evident toe-jams, but preposterously enough it looked as if he had shaved his armpits, though not his skinny jowls.

Carving several slices of air, Gen said: "Now hear this. It is too late for apologetics. We've got you on the run. I intend to call the police cruiser unless you're out of here pronto."

"I can't be thrown out of my own house," Reinhart observed, throwing in the authority of Robert Frost, " 'Home is where when you come they have to let you in.' " But in point of fact, his name was not on the deed. The down payment and most of the subsequent payments on the mortgage had been from Genevieve's own funds. Thus it had been just for her to insist on exclusive ownership.

Gen sneered, so sure of her power now that she tossed the knife aside. "You're finished, Carl. Can't you see that?

I mean, really. For some years now you've been living on sheer sentiment and habit. If you were a dog the ASPCA would have put you out of your misery long ago. I am not a calloused person, as you well know. I was willing for years to feed and house you, but I can't endure attacks on my children. You are sick, and have become a menace to yourself as well as others. I suggest, in all kindness, that you turn yourself in to some public facility."

Reinhart sensed this was some hideous dream, but he could not come to.

"Can I call time out, to collect my thoughts? What you propose may have a certain justification from your perspective, yet all things being relative—"

And Blaine, the nonviolent champion of civil rights versus the pig-police, shouted: "Don't try reason. Call the cops."

Genevieve made a wry smile. "There you have it, Carl. The clarion call of youth. They simply will not put up with the nonsense any more. Maybe it's the result of being brought up on television. You just can't fool that camera lens."

Reinhart got his second wind. He began in the nostalgic vein. "When I was Blaine's age the world seemed to be run by guys the age I am now and I thought them complete frauds. I have never had reason to change my mind. Now the balance of power has altered. I know you and he find it politic to pretend you are victims, but statistics show that women control most of the money in America and young people are dominant in the population and certainly the mass media.

"Somehow I have always missed the advantage, and this has probably warped me with jealousy. Ever since I was born I have had to listen incessantly to someone else's propaganda, and not only an account of the superiorities, but, what is worse, their pains, for which they have always contrived to make me responsible. As a youth I was a pleasure-loving punk, as an adult I am a bully, as a white man a former slaveholder, as a member of the middle class an all-purpose exploiter. When in good shape I was thought to be stupid and insensitive, and now as overweight and with short breath, I am considered ugly and moribund."

Reinhart in fact stopped here for a moment to catch air. He knew his face was purple though not in the least royal.

He resumed: "But did you ever think of this: How the hell could you ever have got along without me?" Yet he did not want to leave it there; a still stronger statement was needed; these were ruthless people: Gen, Blaine, and everybody else. So Reinhart stood very straight and said: "Long reflection on this state of affairs has led me to an inescapable conclusion: *You can all go fuck yourself.*"

(Or should it have been "-selves"?)

In practice great lines never go unanswered, as on the stage and in historical accounts of Oscar Wilde's snotty repartee. When sounded in life they are quickly obscured by abusive responses from unimpressed listeners. The defense against which is of course an edited memory.

Thus the rush of the opening doors of the grounded elevator in the Bloor Building obscured Gen's and Blaine's shrieking, mouth-foaming, pathological ripostes, which in *their* reminiscences no doubt figured as the final blows which sent Reinhart packing. He did pack thereafter, filling an old valise with, mainly, soiled underwear, took the bus downtown, and checked into a YMCA full of seemingly the exact fairies he had encountered in one twenty-five years before and in another town altogether. Then to the Bloor Building and Sweet's office.

Until Sweet reappeared Reinhart must find a way to survive. Now that he was not under the secretary's pressure he could remember quite clearly the precise amount of his funds. Twelve dollars constituted the billfolded wad, with another sixty-three cents swinging in the cool nylon pocket to the left of his genitals. Naturally, before leaving home he had emptied the secret depository in the *World Almanac*. A sudden sharp turn, caused by the inexorably departing crowd in the lobby—large men and small are buffeted by the mean herd—motivated the small change to smite him in what astrology charts nicely called the reins, passion's seat. The blunt and brutal mini-blow was not altogether unpleasant. Nowadays incongruity was almost the only stimulation Reinhart could recognize.

He stepped into a telephone booth. The bell rang ten times at the other end before a sleepy but cigarette-harsh contralto answered.

Reinhart said nervously: "Hi, Gloria. This is your old pal Biggie." Hookers preferred that a customer did not use his right name. Theirs was a stern code comprising many such details, hence Reinhart's unease. Nothing was more unsettling than to be taken to task by a harlot for a failure of protocol. For example, Gloria was not to be phoned before high noon on weekdays and four P.M. on the sabbath, and never at all on national holidays.

She made a kind of *mmmpppfff* sound. "Jesus, I was dreaming. What time is it? What year is it?"

"Thursday. Have I called at an inconvenient time?"

"Happy Thursday," she said. "Who'd you say you were?"

"Biggie, you know." It had been convenient to take the name off his bathrobe.

"Oh yeah. I haven't seen you for a while. Have I?"

Surely it was an honest question. A tart with a keen memory would probably go mad. As it happened, Gloria was right this time, but she always asked the same question, once even when, having missed an initialed tie clasp, he phoned her ten minutes after leaving. He later discovered he had not worn it that day. This incident was from the era when he believed whores, because their work was illegal, were perforce criminals who would swipe your possessions. He was to learn that Gloria, the soul of honesty who kept a lost-and-found bureau drawer full of forgotten watches, articles of clothing—odd socks!—and assorted male jewelry, much of which she would have been within her right to dispose of, after thirty days, by auction, like a public checkroom, Gloria was frequently cheated by her customers and always by the cops. Clients sometimes paid her in queer money or bills folded in a trick way so as to seem double in value, ransacked her purse when she went to wash, had made off with a gold bracelet, a silver religious medal, many an earring, and underwear thefts were routine. Cops threatened to arrest her unless she provided a freebie, and occasionally did so anyway after zipping up their flies.

"I was thinking of coming over," said Reinhart. "If you are not engaged."

"If it's noon I'm already late for the hairdresser," Gloria said in her normal tone now, which was one of happy expectation. She was wont even to complain in that voice, which Reinhart had learned to identify as a feature of her professional role, like her now old-fashioned bouffant which the beauty shop would reinforce. It felt like a helmet. Her body felt like an inflated dummy. Copulating with her lacked the intimacy of one's own hand. Making the appointment was the sexy thing, being invariably suspenseful. Perhaps Gloria understood that. Once you cornered her she would do anything for a fee, but until then she would be more coy than any virgin.

Reinhart's need for bought sex being always a rare flower that died within an hour or two after bloom, he was often frustrated by Gloria's shenanigans. Screw your pedicure, your cat's shots, your drycleaner's pickup, your mother's (!) visit, he would think, though never aloud. Must I make a date with you as if for the junior prom? But he would, he usually had to. You could not buy Gloria on the moment. But Reinhart often could not perform in a sequel utterly lacking in romance. Worse, Gloria was extremely sensitive to any failure of what she regarded as her art. If it went unrequited, she grew more vigorous. Masochists, he supposed, must have found her competent, but her energy to him was but spadework that buried his desire ever deeper. "Play hard to get, will you, Biggie?" "Maybe I'm turning queer." But enough of this bantering exchange, gutter-rolling in shame, and he might indeed finally acquire the adequacy of sheer humiliation, which like any other profound feeling has its curious strength. Carlo Reinhart, bare, supine, and in the bed of a common drab: Sir, you are an unmitigated scoundrel, a total cad. Signed, your Amour-Propre.

"Gloria, we're old friends, are we not?"

"You know it, Big. I think about yours a lot."

She aspirated dramatically, as she did, on some sort of schedule, during the act. Before he had got used to this bit of stage business Reinhart had believed, in alarm, that she suffered from a respiratory disorder, TB, say, against which there was no practical contraceptive. "Ooo, baby . . ." her voice soaked into the wire.

"Look, what I was wondering was—well, I'm stuck and can't get to the bank before closing time. Would you take a check?"

He swore he could smell the cheekful of cigarette smoke she belched at the mouthpiece, but it was surely some stale leaving of the last booth-user. Gloria said: "Would that be wise, Biggie? Your name is probably printed on your checks, right? I wouldn't want that responsibility, doll."

"Oh, I trust you."

"It isn't *me*, Big. It's if I get busted and they print your name in the paper. It's when the canceled check comes through and your old lady sees the endorsement."

Pretty farfetched. He divined that Gloria's real objection was much more serious. She wanted no document that confirmed his existence as a person. She dealt solely in human parts, never whole entities. She sold her snatch but not her soul, and she wanted no communion with his. It was, if you thought about it, the only means by which a whore could manage. Freud in his day could not bear the eyes of patients; hence began the practice of recumbent sufferer, analyst sitting behind, listening calmly to accounts that exceeded even Gloria's adventures, being noncommercial. Any fool knew the consequences of love were far worse than those of money. Which in fact was why Reinhart had for some time found it less troublesome to drain himself into Gloria than to claim his legal rights from Genevieve.

"In view of your inconvenience," he said, "I could of course be more generous."

"What is your usual present?" sweetly asked Gloria, who was euphemistic about all phases of her operation. Plain-talking Blaine would have believed her a mealy-mouthed Nice Nelly.

Reinhart cleared the lump in his throat. "Twenty-five," he said, and all by himself he colored. In the code of his young manhood anybody who paid was a sorry specimen. He remembered that whenever it came to figures. What punks believe is ever confounded by experience, which in time turns brave men into cowards, satyrs into eunuchs, sons into fathers, and even transforms Juliet into her withered, blathering Nurse.

"What were you thinking of upping it to, Big?"

"Well, say another ten." She grunted speculatively, and Reinhart bared his breast. "The only detail is, Gloria, if you would accept a predated check. I mean, hang onto it a few days and then march right down to the bank and get cold cash, good as gold . . ."

She murmured: "Biggie, Biggie, Big—" and suddenly changed into the dial tone.

What could you expect from a rotten hooker?

WHO RAN, the sampler said,

> TO HELP ME WHEN I FELL,
> AND WOULD SOME PRETTY STORY TELL,
> OR KISS THE PLACE TO MAKE IT WELL?
> MY MOTHER.

Oddly enough, Maw, like Gen, had gotten more sinewy over the years. In her case this was especially strange considering the high-carbohydrate diet on which she sub-

sisted. His gift box of candy was already half gone to
empty brown-paper cups, of which he was personally
responsible for only three or four. He and she, in
matching chairs of Swedish modern, flanked a legged
square of teak which held the candy box as well as a
plastic rose in a green glass vase, and an ashtray holding a
morsel of discarded chewing gum rolled into a perfect
gray pea. The sampler was not embroidered old-style but
rather simulated on or in Lucite and hung on a peach-
colored wall above an orange sofa upon a blue rug. The
sun illuminated all of this, as well as the putting green just
outside the glass doors and the bent bald heads or baseball caps thereupon. In the other direction one could see
spry oldsters swatting Ping-Pong balls across nets in the
rec room.

This was the West Lounge of Senior City, a colony for
the superannuated but modern as a motel. Maw lived
there and swore by it.

In fact, at the moment she was repeating her favorite
notion that had Dad survived to accompany her, he would
not now be underground.

"No, siree," she said. "The man would not have expired. Grass cut by the help, and if your drains clog the
house plumber comes with his suction cup. Maintenance
drove your dad up the wall. I saw the light when he was
gone. Gave our junk to the Goodwill and sold the old
homestead to one of Them. Imagine our old home full of
howling Africans."

"I don't know," Reinhart said. "I haven't been by there
in ages."

"Well, don't you go," said Maw, "unless you want to be
picking banjo strings out of your head." To her, Negroes
were still song-and-dance men, yet strangely malignant on
that score alone. Reinhart would not seek to set her
straight at this time when his purpose was to shake her
down for some money. He was interested to reflect that
while vis-à-vis Blaine he as it were wore a swastika,
when with Maw he tended to fly the hammer-and-sickle.
Yet Maw and Blaine were on good terms.

"How's my grandson?" Maw asked, biting into a
caramel, right through the cellophane.

"That's in part what I wanted to talk to you about,"
Reinhart said dolefully.

A spry old chap wearing a flowered shirt and chartreuse
trousers doffed his sporty straw at them as he made for the
glass doors.

"Lively old devil," said Maw. "He'll be dead in a year."

"Blaine, I'm afraid," Reinhart began, "is—"

"He stole ten dollars off me at supper last night."

"Blaine?"

"That Mr. Rumford, going there." She leered at the carpet. "This place is full of criminals." She seized Reinhart's wrist. "He'll give you the eye and say things to turn your head, but will lift your roll." She produced her tongue at the old man's back.

Reinhart said. "You should report him, Maw."

"To who, Carlo? To who? You see, that's the problem. They hang together. He gives them a kickback in the front office. They are in cahoots with him and vice versa. This is a terrible place, a next of thieves. It's awful of you to keep your old mom here."

"Thought you said it was just great," Reinhart lightly noted. Maw had little but paranoia to occupy her these days.

"Now don't you put words in my mouth, Carlo. If you was the loving son you pretend to be you would defend your old mother instead of letting a lot of old coots give her the business."

At last Reinhart pointed out that she should not eat the transparent covering on the caramel. He had intended to let this matter go; it was probably harmless stuff and Maw had excellent false teeth, of much better quality than his own bridge.

Maw was in fact loaded, Dad having been an insurance man who was his own best client, and she had also made a bundle on the sale of the house, in addition to which an eccentric cousin of hers had been found three weeks dead amid stacks of newspapers dating from 1911 and every peanut-butter jar he had emptied in fifty years. His will though had been legally up to the minute, and left forty-five thousand dollars to Maw, whom he had not seen since February 27, 1923, at which time she however had a kind word for his devoted collie. The source of his money remained mysterious. After watching a certain TV program Maw had more or less decided it had been blackmail.

In a quite graceful action Maw now spat out both plates and picked cellophane fragments from the interstices. "It doesn't surprise me one iota, Carlo," she said with some slurring. "There have been many attempts at poisoning." She clapped the teeth back in. "I often give a bit of my lunch to that parrot in the dining room and he

will say a filthy word. That bird will die one day from
arsenic meant for me." She hurled herself from the chair,
adroitly as a gymnast. "Which reminds me of teatime,
though you can just as well take coffee. You are welcome
to come along and fill your fat gut."

Maw made off in an athletic lope which Reinhart was
hard put to match. The bright corridor was crowded with
oldsters dressed in pastel colors. Maw steered ruthlessly
through them, crying more than once, "Watch your wallet, Carlo!" But far from taking offense, the throng made
noises that would suggest her popularity, friendly cackles
and wheezes and some still booming voices as well. "Hi,
bud," said one pink old, hale old, glabrous head to Reinhart. "When did you check in? Glad to have you aboard.
Pinochle's my game." He threw out a hand.

Reinhart tried to make a joke of it, as he had when a
small kid in his neighborhood asked Gen where her father
was, meaning him, but the man soon dropped his hand
and, turning to an eighty-year-old, blue-haired demimon-
daine tripping alongside, said in a blaring sotto voce:
"Getting older all the time, ain't they?" To which she
replied, inclining the ear without the hearing aid: "Yes, it
will be fall soon and there's another year down the
commode."

Maw seemed not to have noted this exchange, but
when they were seated at the little table in the dining
room, under one of the Muzak grilles emitting Broadway
show tunes, she said: "Most of those women are prostitutes, among who she is the worst, and that dirty old man
is her pimp."

"Getting back to Blaine, Maw—"

"I'll say this, Carlo, he's more of a man than you ever
was. I'm going to give you a check for him, because if I
know you you keep that boy on a short leash financially.
You always were stingy as a boy. I used to say to your
dad, 'The hinges on that one's purse have gone to rust.' A
person would give you a penny and you'd bank it. You
have a nice bundle by now, eh?" She made a knowing
grimace and punched his arm with a fist of granite.
"Pulling down six percent per annum, though the kids
dress in rags."

A young brown girl appeared, saying, "Well, what will
it be today, Molly?" She was dressed as a waitress and
her manner was derisive-maternal, indeed rather like
Maw's towards Reinhart of years since.

"Wouldn't you like to know?" Maw replied instantly.

"I have to, you see, or I won't know what to bring you."

"Oh you're keen," said Maw. "I wouldn't take that away from you. Bring me the usual and double it because this lard is my son and he eats like a hippo."

Being young and pretty, the girl naturally would not look at Reinhart. She went away.

"Actually, it's the same menu every day," Maw explained. "Weak tea and greasy toast, waxy jam in a teeny paper cup. But I banter with that one. She's fresh."

"Why," Reinhart asked, "does she call you Molly?" Which was not her name.

Maw said smugly: "I told her to. It makes them feel intimate. Else they would spit in your face."

The girl was back immediately with the order. Reinhart found himself in a fantasy of her bronze breasts, uncovered beneath sparkling white nylon, but a vision of terror squads of black huskies, wearing jackboots and berets, trampled down his wonder. She had not yet looked at him.

Maw smeared her toast with the gorelike jam. "How's your wife?" She and Gen had always loathed each other on terms of the utmost formality.

"She threw me out today."

"That makes sense," Maw said, munching. Reinhart assumed this speech was but another manifestation of her senility—which was interesting in itself, Maw not being all that old; under seventy, he believed—but as she was wont to do without warning, she had turned coldly rational. "Now you can make something of yourself, Carlo, with that bitch off your back. I never said a word against her though until this juncture, and you know it. I have been the soul of diplomacy, but it sure cut my heart to see what she did to you."

Reinhart found this embarrassing but also oddly comforting, so much so that he could afford to throw a fish Gen's way.

"Well, I'm far from perfect."

"Don't I know that!" Maw said fervently. "I put up with you for twenty-some years less your Army time, and it often took the patience of a saint, but I succeeded in raising you to be a decent man. You are a stupid goof, you're disgusting overweight, I expect you've told your lies and done many a thing that won't pass muster, you may be a lazy atheist or what have you, but you're not nasty."

She pretty well hit the nail on the head. He had never been Maw's favorite, though an only child, but perhaps because of that she understood him, at least better than anyone else. Ardent affection never led her into mistakes of assessment, as happens so often with the spoiled son who thus in later life has no option but to go into crime or homosexuality simply to confound the hostile or indifferent world outside the nursery.

Maybe Maw characterized him nicely only for purposes of contrast to someone she liked even less, but hell, it was something, and Reinhart did not get much nowadays from anybody.

But to make a point of pride—Gen had been his choice, willy-nilly, for twenty-two years—Reinhart said: "Well, I'd just as soon not discuss negative matters. To look towards the horizon has always been my motto."

"While somebody has been kicking your feet out from under you," Maw observed. As long as he was down, she being a practical soul would rest her heel on his neck. "I figure you have come to pick my pocket, as usual," she went on, talking through toast.

Reinhart winced, though he knew any show of hurt would likely encourage Maw to continue working the pain-vein. On the other hand it would also put her finally in a benevolent mood. He wondered why he did not use this understanding of human justice when dealing with others. After reducing Germany and Japan to rubble, America had loaned them billions. God knows he lost often enough to make everyone love him. Trouble was, pride usually kept him from admitting failure to strangers.

"There's no getting away from the fact that you pulled me out of a bad jam with the gas station, Maw. I freely admit that. As Dad did, years back, with the TV store." He swallowed some tea, in which there seemed to be more than a little alum: his tongue grew thin.

"Your basic trouble is due to one thing, Carlo," said Maw. "I'd like to know where you got the idea you were a businessman. You used to talk about becoming a head-shrinker, years ago, when the government was footing the bill for your education merely because you laid about in uniform for a number of years. It strikes me that would have been the right vocation for you, for it's all nutsy talk of the kind you always specialized in. They got a couple of them here and I understand they pull down fifteen grand or more per annum, which no doubt is why it costs so much to stay here. It sure couldn't be the food."

Nevertheless Maw bit a great crescent from the next piece of toast.

"I got sidetracked," Reinhart said. "Marriage and all. Then my training under Claude Humbold gave me the idea that the real challenges lay in business."

"But Claude is the creative type. He has one of the biggest car dealerships in Southern Cal now, comes on the TV commercials all night long, I understand, selling autos to those Mexicans who come up to L.A. to make their chili-money. *You* got to get your sleep."

Reinhart smiled. "That's on video tape," he said cynically.

Maw sniffed. "I get a nice card from him every Christmas, along with a box of stuffed dates. But the point is, Claude's a born salesman. You always been too much of a materialist for that. You're like your late dad, except he never had big windy ideas. He worked for Ecumenical his life long, and when he retired he had his choice of several gifts, among them the movie camera which he took. He knew his limits, and he left me well fixed as a result. What do you have to show for going to college?"

Reinhart did not have the stomach to defend cultivation. In his day there had been a lot of talk, generally if not invariably by people who, because they had no gift for it, abused moneymaking—on the same principle by which the weak and awkward reviled athletics, the unarmed denounced violence, and to be fair, much as the illiterate hated and feared books—quite a blast of hot air to the effect that the sonnets of Milton would provide an expansion of interior horizons, an irradiation of soul, and intimations of immortality far in excess of those you could get from a pint of gin. This was to put it vulgarly, but if life was not vulgar it was not life.

Somewhere along the line, not long after pedagogues began to make decent salaries, one grew conscious he never heard that argument again. Presumably you now read *Samson Agonistes* so you could subsequently teach it and thereby pull down twelve thousand a year and live as high on the hog as a union carpenter. But meanwhile impatient Reinhart had gone into business. In a confusion of pre- and post-war credits he had had about a year more to go for his B.A. That was another thing he still intended to do when he found time. Meanwhile the college in reference was the same one in which Blaine was enrolled and which he had threatened, certainly not personally but rather as the voice of the mob, to destroy next semester unless the president submitted to various demands: the dropping of all academic requirements, the end of sexual distinctions in the toilets, and others.

"I could have taken a job," Reinhart said, "calling for a college education."

"But not if they wanted to see the sheepskin," Maw said. "It don't mean a thing unless you have got those letters. You could go ten years, and read every book, and you would still be an ignoramus when it comes to getting a good position. 'Let's see your B.A., my boy.' Nobody will listen to a complicated explanation as to why you happened to hang around college for years without getting one. Which information would in fact make you seem more of a loser than if you never went beyond high school. Records, Carlo, you got to have official records that come to some kind of conclusion."

She took some tea and flushed it through her dentures. "Let's face it, Carlo. You'll never see forty again. You are over the hill in that respect, as well as most others. What employer would take you as a present when he can have any bright youngster?" She winked at him. "You should have gone into police work years ago, rather than run around with that colored fellow. In those days he was only too happy to get your help, but now he'd cut your throat, I expect, merely for being born with a white skin." Maw made pious eyes, "I saw it all coming years ago and rooted for Max Schmeling, which didn't make me many friends, I tell you, and most of the people who would remember that are dead." One of the ex-post-facto delusions Maw was given to. Reinhart remembered quite clearly that she favored, with savage ardor, the American's cause in both fights, sitting beside the radio with clenched fists, crying, "Kill that dirty Nazi, Joe." Though she was of German descent. She did not like the buffoonizing of her breed by a dictator who looked like Charlie Chaplin. Neither did she like Chaplin, and when his later scrapes were publicized she would say, "He looks just like Hitler," though that was true only in reel life.

But just as Reinhart became surly when he read the ravings of Negro militants, he was still capable of a nostalgic defense of the race—or perhaps merely of his own old sentiments.

"They are under pressure, Maw. What they generally

destroy in those riots are their own neighborhoods. It may even be a form of self-hatred caused by—"

"Fooey," Maw said. "Show me an African country where they all drive lilac-colored Cadillacs."

"That's all changed now," said Reinhart. "Other times, other manners, Maw. They— Shh," he was relieved to be able to say, "here comes that waitress."

Maw instantly turned up a grinning face. "I was just telling my son here about your husband, Pauline, and his fine job at the U.S. Post Office. Bet he had to take a civil-service exam to get the appointment, did he not?"

"No, in fact it was political, Molly."

"Well, isn't that nice," Maw said, with a moue at Reinhart.

The waitress asked whether there would be seconds on tea. She was herself tea-colored, with a translucent effect. You not only saw Negroes everywhere nowadays, but they were often beautiful, and never black. Why they propagandized in favor of the latter adjective was but one of their many current peculiarities. But Reinhart was momentarily bored by the whole problem. What he would have liked to do was kiss this girl on her ripe orange mouth and bite her tan ear. Let's call time out and be utter savages, wallowing in sensuality.

Maw declined and the girl did not ask him, and went away.

The time had come. "Maw," he said. "How would you like to live forever?"

Shocking him, she answered jovially. He had expected a derisive snicker. She said: "I'm not about to turn up my toes, brother. So don't think my will will save you." When Maw had been in the years which now enmired him, she was a notorious hypochondriac, taking frequently to bed with imaginary attacks of leukemia, muscular fibrosis, and other then à la mode maladies, impersonating poor-devil neighbors and relatives who expired painfully enough to evoke her jealousy. But after Dad's demise, which, a modest man, he performed quietly in his sleep, without warning—his heart stopped, his face smiled at the ease with which he had got away, his right hand was, as usual, inserted between pillow and case, his feet pigeon-toed— when Dad was gone, taking with him her prime audience, Maw soon became a monster of good health, ate any-thing, walked robustly through the rain, and sought out drafts to sit in. It might well be her megalomaniac intent to live forever on her own steam.

"I'm not joking, Maw," Reinhart said. "What I am about to tell you is fantastic, incredible—"

"You mean that stuff about freezing, huh?"

Apparently he was never going to have a chance to spring it on anybody. "Oh, you saw the show," he said. "Well, do you know who that man was?"

"I didn't catch the name, but he looked just like that kid you went to school with years ago, that little one with the pimples."

"Aw, Maw," Reinhart groaned. "You spoiled it." She always managed to make him childish.

Maw cackled. "And that's what you'll be if you let them pop you into a deep-freeze: *spoiled.* Why, you can't even keep a pork chop frozen for long. Those doctors are all crooks, Carlo, and work hand in hand with the undertakers. They're like the people who make cars. Years ago a fellow invented a machine that would run on a aspirin tablet and water, and the auto people had him secretly murdered and sunk in concrete in the Detroit River."

"That would be the gasoline people, wouldn't it?" humoringly asked Reinhart. Not that he would put anything past the dirty sons of bitches who had made his last car, which happened to be a lemon.

"They're all in it together," Maw said, opening her purse. She withdrew a pack of cigarettes, plucked one out, lighted it, and inhaled so vigorously you might have seen smoke issue from her shoes. This was a recently acquired habit, perhaps more bravado against fate. Reinhart had long since given up the vice and now found the fetor of it nauseating, like that of singed hair or incinerating garbage. Maw kept blowing aureolas around his moonface.

"But, for the sake of argument, what if it worked?"

"The way I understand it," Maw said, "you wouldn't know for a thousand years whether you would be brought back to life or just stay like a snowman into eternity. That's a long time, Carlo, for an experiment. You might as well be dead forever as for ten centuries. And who's going to pay for a pig in a poke?"

"I don't suppose there has ever been a scientific advance or invention that has not been thought unfeasible when first announced," Reinhart said sententiously. "And yet here we are today with jet aircraft and rocket ships to outer space."

"I wouldn't whine about that. They got here, didn't they? What difference did it make when? I thought time was everlasting." Maw blew some more smoke into his face. "What's the hurry?"

"But here we are talking of the preservation of the individual self, Maw. That's what fascinates me. Can you conceive what it must be like as an insect? Nature has provided you with very little in the way of individual defense, and everything to the tribe. Or, coming up the ladder to warmblooded mammals—rodents, rabbits. I have always been struck by the failure of nature to give the bunny any weapon except a high birthrate. A particular rabbit will soon perish but the breed survives. But what does that mean to me? To lose all this personal consciousness! It takes many years to make a man, and then, as I believe George Bernard Shaw said, when that is finally accomplished, you die."

Maw peered at him. "You won't pass away for a while yet, Carlo, if that's what's bothering you. And if you keep on as you have been going, when the time comes to lay down, you will be mighty relieved. I'll tell you this: at your age a person broods more about death than at mine, because you have to stay in the game with impaired faculties. You're too old to retain your youthful vigor, yet too young to quit."

"Well, leaving me out of it," said Reinhart, "freezing seems to be the coming thing. Imagine if you had had a chance to put a few dollars on the Wright Brothers."

"I was waiting for the pitch," Maw said. "As I see it, you want some of my money to put into a business concerned with the freezing of bodies."

Reinhart swallowed the remaining puddle of tea. There were no leaves to read; they had probably brewed it from powder. "I had lunch with Bob Sweet recently. He's that guy I went to school with, you know. I have an opportunity to go in with him. He would give me a job, of course, but you know my personality is more of the entrepreneurial sort. I am not cut out for straight salaried work."

"So much the worse for you," said Maw, "for nowadays the big thing is not the wage but the side benefits, life insurance and medical."

"I could stand up on my own two hindlegs if I had something to put into the business, you see. And Sweet is a tycoon, Maw. Everything he does is gilt-edged." Reinhart had no assurance whatever that Sweet would let him invest in the Cryon Foundation, which furthermore had been described on the *Alp Show* as nonprofitmaking.

Reinhart was ignoring these considerations in favor of very serious estimate of his own constitution. He was no natural wage-slave. Perhaps no one was by birth, yet nature drafted the many as worker ants, as rodent gunfodder, for the greater good of the breed. By now Reinhart did not even like people. To preserve them in vast hosts, while at the same time reproduction was increasing madly in all quarters of the globe, was actually a scheme which, had he believed in its feasibility, would have been as repugnant as the reek of Maw's cigarette.

Which was as much as to say that not for a moment did he believe a frozen cadaver would ever be reanimated. If death was not a dependable fact, then life, as it had been lived since the dawn of man, had no form and, indeed, no process. The only thing you could rely on was the established truth that ripening and rot were the same, and the only, gauge of time. And where are you, Reinhart asked God, who might or might not Himself have expired, without time? I ask you. Even Einstein, who dabbled in other measurements as well, was dead.

Therefore if Reinhart made a business of what he saw as an impossible science, he would be by his own definition a swindler. To promise everlasting life: the grandest con game of them all, and the most mean. Terminal syphilis of the morality. He was not the nice boy of Maw's characterization. He had just not had the chance until now to be a dirty rat.

Maw sizzled out her cigarette in the teacup. "If you think you'll freeze me, buddy, you got a hole in the head. I'm not going to lay there in frost for centuries like a Sara Lee cheesecake. But you are probably right that many suckers will go for it. If they shell out for junk to make their hair grow back and for monkey-gland injections in Switzerland and believe in flying saucers and other evasions of reality, why, I guess you can expect them to pay even more to be immortal. And if I ever saw a successful crook, it's that Sweet. But how do you know his prey is not the people who would pay to be frozen, but rather the suckers who want to put money into the scheme to defraud the first?"

Occasionally Maw arranged in her own syntax certain terms from crossword puzzles, such as "evasions," "defraud," and, surely, "prey." Alone with what she supposed the vocabulary of a sibyl, she also assumed the mask:

slitted eyes, prominent groove of upper lip, high, rippled forehead.

"Of course," said Reinhart, "nothing is a sure thing. Not even death, now." What he meant as a chuckle sounded like a gasp of anguish. "Bob has nothing to gain from me. He could see I'm on my uppers."

"But you're the very type who is victimized," Maw asserted. "Man is not a wolf to other wolves."

"I was reading this review of a book about the aggressive instinct," said Reinhart. "It seems that wolves are not, either."

"Don't be pseudo-intellectual, Carlo. I don't want to cast my pearls before swine."

"Do I gather from that that the idea has some merit?"

"Listen," Maw said, slapping the table, "if I give you any money, it will be for the same reason as I have done so in the past."

Reinhart nodded. "Blood is thicker than water."

"Precisely." She smiled though hiding her teeth. "I might also be afraid you would knock me off and claim the whole bundle beforetime."

"Aw, Maw, don't joke about that sort of thing."

"Don't be such a fool, Carlo. You are my sole heir. I guess you didn't notice how I switched teacups with you. If you dropped that cyanide pellet you was palming, it's now in your own stomach, pal, and good luck to you."

Maw used her paranoia not only for fun. Undoubtedly she was on the point of loosening her purse strings now, but would try a few last-ditch maneuvers.

"I just wish I had your cunning," he said. "You outfoxed me again."

"Soon your face will turn blue and you'll be gasping for air," Maw happily predicted. "It's like fire in your gastric linings."

It is true that Reinhart proceeded sympathetically to feel a few symptoms, probably because of the acidulous tea which was running like sewage through his conduits, but nowadays he often found it difficult even to digest milk. With money in his pocket, however, he would eat nails with impunity. So he persisted, and Maw finally seized her black purse.

"How would five suit you, Carlo?"

"Hundreds, Maw?"

She giggled. "Dollars. Five simoleons." She waved a

wrinkled engraving of Lincoln at him. "You didn't tell me what that hag will demand in the divorce settlement. Whatever I give you, she'll shake you down for, don't you know that? You had best declare yourself a pauper."

"Gen knows I don't have anything now, and when I make good she'll be glad to see me again. I understand that much about women."

A doddering old lady was taking forever to pass their table.

Maw called to her: "Hey, Sal. Come and meet my son."

Reinhart rose and took her claw, which was weightless but suddenly closed like pincers on his hand, as his image drowned in her watery eyes.

"Sal is ninety-two, Carlo. I expect she'll be a candidate for your freezer any day now."

Sal continued to detain Reinhart with a steel wrist. He did not know what to do with her.

Maw watched this for a while, and then said: "Well, Sal, you got to be going. Say so long."

Sal mumbled something from a fixed mouth and released Reinhart's hand as though it were a load of gravel and hers an earthmover.

Reinhart sat down, saying: "Gee, Maw, you can embarrass a person."

"Not at all, Carlo. Out of sheer vanity Sal won't wear her hearing aid. She ain't as pitiful as she would like to make you think. Talk of being loaded, that old babe has got a hundred grand if a dollar. If you could talk her into freezing you'd have something. The only trouble is, she hates life. But that's the kind who lives longest." Maw popped out of her chair. "Come on, Carlo, I'll take you on at Ping-Pong. No, leave that five-spot for Pauline. I give her one once a week. Otherwise she gets uppity."

A veteran of Army dayrooms, noncoms' clubs, and nut-ward recreational facilities, Reinhart was proficient at table tennis, and he won several no-quarter-given-none-asked games with his mother, returning her smashing serves with a cunning Englished ball impossible to strike squarely. She threatened to splinter her paddle on his pate. But in the sequel she was also cowed, as everyone is by any kind of winner.

Reinhart left Senior City, in the rented car which he could now afford to return, with her check for five thousand dollars. Whether death would subsequently be altered, it was certain that he expected life to change for himself. He had fooled with aspects of residence, entertainment, and transportation—real estate, television sets, gasoline—but had never before dealt in fundamentals.

– 5 –

Here in the strangely barren office, behind the switched-on reception room starring the big with-it girl, Bob Sweet was another man than the one who had bought Reinhart lunch two days before.

"I've left my wife and moved out of that house," Reinhart told him, asking approval of the man who traced his own success to an escape from marriage. But Reinhart saw no interest behind the lenses.

"By accident," Reinhart went on, "I saw your *Alp Show*. So that is what you do. Pretty fabulous." Sweet continued to go through the papers on his desk. Anybody else's correspondence, especially when seen upside down, looks capricious.

Reinhart suddenly decided to be reckless.

"Hey, Bob," he called, as Sweet's pen, followed halfway by Sweet's head, fell onto the stack of papers and began here to initial, there to autograph. "You did make me a promise—"

Sweet's pen came up and pointed at Reinhart's nose, though his eyes stayed on the papers sorted by his left hand. "Revise that," he said.

"All right then, you mentioned you might—"

"Better," said Sweet. "I owe you nothing. If I chose to be sentimental at lunch, I may since have reviewed my feelings and found them indifferent to you. If you were not one of my tormentors years ago, as you claim, why should I help you now?"

"Excuse me, Bob, but does that make sense?" Reinhart's chair was of red, waxed leather, with brass studs suitable for the childish pretense that they were pushbuttons of a musical instrument or a spacecraft; press the right one and *zoom*, something would sound or ignite.

Sweet looked up from the papers, and in compensation his pen went back down. "Retribution," he said, "is all the more satisfying when benevolent. Imagine how devastat-

ing it would have been if the Israelis had sentenced
Eichmann to life among them, giving him a position of
trust in the government." He laughed, then stared bully-
ingly at Reinhart through the heavy-rimmed spectacles.
There was a day when glasses gave one a vulnerable look.
Now they seemed to be worn by most powerful people.
Weak eyes were an advertisement for the strong will, if
indeed the eyes so "corrected" had been at all wrong—
without his rims Sweet might be the most undistinguished
of men. Reinhart tried to recall how he had looked in
Gino's men's room while rinsing the lenses, when reen-
countered after an absence of a quarter-century, but
could not, which might have proved the point.

"My situation has changed dramatically since we last
spoke," Reinhart said. "I've come into some money."

"You would be wise not to let your wife know about
it," Sweet said, going back to his papers.

"I was wondering whether you might suggest an invest-
ment."

"U.S. savings bonds," Sweet answered instantly. "Or a
mutual fund that specializes in growth."

"Look here," said Reinhart. "Will you level with me for
old times' sake?"

"That's the way to get yourself lied to."

A rude note came from the intercom. Sweet threw a
switch, and the big girl's voice came croaking: "The calls
are building up, Bob," the use of which diminutive
confirmed Reinhart's suspicion that Sweet was laying her—
still, it was most unbusinesslike.

"All right," Sweet said to the box, "I'll be finished in
three minutes more."

You cocky bastard, Reinhart thought, if you think you
can dismiss me out of hand— But Sweet had been televised on a nationwide program, and he was rich. Reinhart
only had Maw's five grand, little enough these days. That
big insolent bitch in the reception room surely pulled
down a hundred a week or more.

Sweet said: "I had not forgotten. I had a credit check
run on you, Carl. It reads like the bill of indictment at a
war-crimes trial."

Reinhart blanched, though not at the quite fair characterization of his business history. "Turn that damn thing
off, will you? I don't want that girl to hear."

"Of course it's off," Sweet said quietly.

"She can first-name you all she wants, but I don't want
her to hear my misfortunes."

"Carl . . ."

"No, you hear me out, dammit. I'm getting the run-around. I don't mind kissing your ass up to a certain point, because that seems to me the role that fate has cast me in—"

"Carl."

"You've got it all, haven't you? So I have to sit here attending your pleasure."

"Bitterness is useless unless controlled," Sweet said kindly. "But I suppose if that were possible one would not be bitter in the first place. . . . So, anyway, runs the argument of the eventual suicide. Have you ever thought of doing away with yourself?"

"Every day," Reinhart said. "But then I think of the satisfaction it would give to all the shits, and I don't do it."

Sweet's pale eyebrows rose above the formidable black frames. "So it is bitterness that keeps you alive."

"You take that service station," Reinhart ranted. "My so-called friends could have kept me in business if they had taken the trouble to drive a quarter-mile. You could see me from the thruway, or the rooftop sign, anyway. They wouldn't do it. But they'll drive three miles out of town to patronize that shopping center where we had lunch the other day. They'll go four to the drive-in movie. I guess you also know that not long after the war I had a piece of the old theater in town, the Majestic where we used to spend Sunday afternoons as kids."

"Double-feature Westerns and six cartoons," Sweet said in a far-off voice.

"We ran on popcorn sales for a year or so before petering out. That's why I went into television sets, joining the competition that beat us, but was too late as usual."

"Timing is your trouble, Carl. You think the medium of business is money, but you are wrong. It is time. Trading stamps, for example, have peaked, and no longer will pull in a customer. The current thing is those lottery schemes, Double Dollars, Match-a-Bill, and so on, in which the patron gets half of some ticket or chit and must look for the matching part in future purchases."

"Criterion Gas, which was my franchise," said Reinhart, "gave matching sets of aluminum pots. They were quite nice. With each purchase and three ninety-eight the customer could get one set of four: pint, pint-and-a-half, quart and—"

"Don't torment yourself with bygone features," said
Sweet. "Time never returns but is always in fresh supply."

"I took a number of philosophy courses in college,"
Reinhart muttered, "but I should have majored in Business Admin. This is no civilization in which to live the life
of the mind."

"But can you," asked Sweet, ignoring Reinhart's self-
serving maunderings, "think of time as never-ending? Of
course you can, because we do habitually see it that way.
Which makes death so frightening: it cannot be imagined.
It cannot be imagined because it is nothing. You can
imagine being in excruciating pain—at least you think you
can until you are in it, and then you say, 'Incredible!' and
tell your friends it could not be described. But pain is a
quantitative value. From a toothache you can project the
grand agonies, having your appendix scooped out by a
pharmacist's aide with a rusty spoon while on submarine
duty in the remote Pacific without anesthesia or steriliza-
tion of instruments. A bullet to bite on and a slug of
bourbon from the captain's bottle."

He leaned his head against the high chairback of moss-
green leather. Reinhart imagined that he and Sweet sat in
a void of the sort represented in movie dream-scenes in
which the characters were supported on a cloud and their
horizontal locus not established by walls.

"Carl!" Sweet cried sharply.

"I closed my eyes to listen better," Reinhart explained.
"I'm not sleeping." Raising his lids he looked at the
window on his right, giving on a cityscape being smothered by smog but not without resistance: here and there
the pall, a kind of vast, science-fiction amoeba come from
outer space to devour our world, was punched through by
the fist of some commercial scructure, or pierced by a
churchly stiletto. Sweet's office did not suffer from deco-
rative excesses: one desk, two chairs, no rugs or things to
look at on the walls.

Again a signal from the intercom, which Sweet levered
over. The girl's voice was a mere electronic vibration, for
she happened to be one of those talking robots, Reinhart
realized, and would open the door soon and roll in on
casters, gesturing jerkily with mechanical arms. Something
eerie about this whole setup.

However, he listened to the message: "Bob, now hear
this! I'm on a hot line—"

"Get hold of yourself," said Sweet. "Breathe in deeply
through your nose for complete oxygenation, then release

it through your mouth." Static was evidence of her compliance.

Then she said: "He's on hold. Take it on Two."

"One moment, sir," Sweet told the mouthpiece, and resting the instrument in a rectangular container, pulled before him what appeared to be a small microphone and was subsequently proved to be by his talking into it. "Now please go ahead. You are speaking to Robert Sweet, president of the Cryon Foundation."

An amplified human sound emerged from one of the devices.

"My father is near death," said this voice. "Personally, I don't for a moment hold with this scheme of freezing. He is a crazy old man and—" A hard flat voice, but now it tore like paper. It was sobbing. Grief always seemed quite real to Reinhart; he might be gullible, but he was built that way. Cry at him and you could pick his pocket any old day—unless you were a callow Blaine blubbering over shorn locks. But this sorrow was the right kind, of a son for a father. After all, who usually died first?

"First, may I express my sympathy," said Bob Sweet into the microphone. "In the past that has often been a hollow sentiment. It used to be cruelly absurd to say anything about death. If I use a platitude now, what I have to suggest is far from routine."

"It might be weak-minded or fraudulent, though," the voice replied, recovering its obduracy. "I don't want any pitch. I promised the old man, you see. He has heard of your process. If it gives him hope . . ."

"I understand," Sweet said. Already he looked more accessible to Reinhart. He obviously had not yet got around to settling in the office. Soon it would be curtained, carpeted, and traversed by an energetic staff. He might traffic in alleged immortality, but he was a businessman. "I understand your doubts, and I believe I can answer them."

"I—" the voice began, then collapsed into a snort, shockingly near a giggle in fact. "I never thought I'd say this to any man, but are you in a position to freeze my dad when the moment comes? That's what he wants. Now, I am not a wealthy—"

"Sir," Bob said, "I am and I will, and furthermore I will not accept your money." He groped for the pen he had so recently wielded at Reinhart in remonstrance, keeping his eyes on the microphone as if something might escape from it.

Reinhart helpfully located and supplied the pen to Bob's twitching fingers.

"Just don't try to con me," the voice warned, quavering on the last words. It was interesting to Reinhart that in some people suspicion will contest with sorrow. "I can pay a fair price. What's your setup? Like a crematory?"

"I don't think you have quite the right idea of us," Bob told the soon-to-be-bereaved. "Can we talk soberly?"

"Sure, shoot," said the voice.

"I mean face to face, a personal interview."

"Look, my dad is likely to go at any time. How would it look for me to be off someplace gassing with you when he breathed his last? Can't you quote me a price here and now? What are you hiding, fellow?"

Bob removed his glasses. Now Reinhart remembered why he could not earlier remember how Bob had looked while rinsing his spectacles in Gino's washroom. The face tended to be indistinct, as though looking straight-on you were seeing it from the corner of your eye. Reinhart found it difficult to say why this was so. Only Bob's hair now had authority, the fuzzy gray sideburns, the rich, virile crest. His features were all very regular, like those shown in learn-cartooning-by-mail manuals, but the composite, which then should have been a Steve Canyon or Smilin' Jack, was, inexplicably, not.

Bob said patiently, colorlessly: "I am trying to explain that there will be no charge. This is a nonprofit enterprise." His fist clenched quickly, then slowly opened like an octopus testing its environment. "I can promise you nothing, but if you permit this experiment to take place, you might have a part in history. . . ." He lost his voice and raised his eyes hopelessly to Reinhart.

It was the most extraordinary thing. Reinhart wanted to cry: I'm sorry I thought you were a swindler but there are so many extant and, after all, to talk of abolishing Death—but I see you mean it.

Did he have a viable process? Reinhart did not know, or at the moment care, because *Bob was sincere*. Reinhart reached across the desk and seized the mike, a little ball of wire mesh.

He spoke fervently into it: "You just give us your name and address, and where the patient can be found. We'll arrange the rest. Let's set up an appointment. Better have the doctor there. This is a historical occasion. No, that's putting it too lamely. The Wright Brothers were small-time in this light. Your dad may live again! In a hundred, a thousand years, what do petty details matter? Napoleon, Caesar, Alexander the Great, they are all dust to stop a bunghole or however the quote goes, for Shakespeare too was a transitory incident. Can you understand, sir? Truth may change and Time itself, Life as we know it. Words, words. I beg of you, don't put any obstacles in the path. Don't question, don't doubt. You cannot lose. It finally comes down to that, does it not?"

The voice laughed.

Reinhart joined it, the wind of divine amusement in his sails. "It is crazy and frightening and brave and majestic. Think what man can do without the fear of death. The mind as yet cannot cope with so glorious a concept. But to put it simply: no mistake will be final. The whole idea of termination, of any sort, will be obsolete. Now, where can we find your father? If he is willing, how can you hesitate?"

The voice, which had continued to laugh in the regular rhythm of a machine whose function was to tumble that which it treated, wet wash or concrete, now stopped with a shudder.

"Greenwood Cemetery," it said. "He died in 1956."

Reinhart looked questioningly at Bob Sweet. "Well, sir," he said seriously. "I don't think ... Let me check with my associate." What a horrible disappointment. Surely the process would not ... The man was a crank. Reinhart was shrinking.

"Don't bother," said the voice. "You are as full of shit as a Christmas goose." And hung up.

Sweet wore his glasses again. "Not the first hoaxer, and not the last. Don't give it another thought."

Reinhart said: "I can understand an eccentric better than a joker, a demented or deluded person. But how do you explain a guy like this? All that trouble for a laugh?"

"Well, that's America, isn't it?" Sweet noted lightly as he pushed away the gadgets that had made the call public to the room at large, though actually privy only to himself and Reinhart. Why, in fact, had Sweet done that? When just previously he had been showing a definite disinclination to give Reinhart a role?

Jealously Reinhart said: "I believe he took you in for a while."

"He certainly did," Sweet admitted, seeming not to mind. "You learn to accept these things. One day someone will call who seems bogus, but will be serious. When the police get a bomb threat they have to check it out.

The 'public' is a collection of individuals though politicians pretend otherwise."

Reinhart shrugged knowingly though he still did not quite get it. "Bob," he said, "is there really a sound scientific basis for this freezing process?"

Sweet stared at him. "You seemed to have no doubts when exhorting our friend just now."

"A lot of that was the excitement of the moment, I guess. It is a wonderful vision when you're caught up in it. And the really formidable argument is that one cannot lose: he'll die anyway. Unless his heirs have to put out a lot of money. But you answered that objection, didn't you?"

"Not a penny for the first volunteer," Sweet said. "Now, if that is not an expression of good faith, I don't know what is."

"Especially from a man who understands money," Reinhart said. "That makes it all the more impressive. Just how did you get into this in the first place?"

A clout sounded against the door, and the big girl lumbered into the room. Reinhart had been prepared on arrival that morning for a row with her, but impassively she had sent him right in to Sweet. She wore an orange jersey dress, thin as a Navy skivvy shirt and hardly longer than the tail thereof.

"Excuse me, Bob," she said. "But I'm dying of suspense."

Sweet explained, and she dropped her massive mane in despair.

"Why are they so square?" she asked the floor. "People are dying every minute. Why can't we have one, just one?"

Sweet smiled gently at her, and then said to Reinhart: "Why don't you make up to Eunice? She's quite a nice girl."

Embarrassing Reinhart, of course. The bad blood between them was scarcely his fault. But, gallant as he instinctively was, he got out of the chair, nodded, murmured, and was prepared to shake hands if she extended hers.

"An old, old friend of mine," Sweet told her, leaning back with his hands on his nape, and, for Reinhart, "The best secretary I have ever had."

She kept her hands to herself, but peeped sideways through the edge of her hair. Reinhart wished she would wear a brassiere. Her protuberant nipples were large as percolator caps.

"Hi," she said, then glanced at her boss.

Sweet said easily: "Why don't you guys get to know each other?"

Why, thought Reinhart, an awful lot of *why's* are cropping up, amid a famine of *because*.

Sweet said: "People sometimes say cruel things through ignorance. Carl, for example, was being malicious about you earlier, but I'm sure he can revise his opinion."

Reinhart froze though not a corpse. Through gelid lips he mumbled: "Not true, miss. A sick joke, believe me."

"God," said she without apparent offense, "I was a little kid when those were in. I had a hula hoop. 'Can I interest you in a pair of Bermuda shorts, Mr. Toulouse-Lautrec?' That was one, wasn't it? I happened to understand it because I had seen the movie played by the man walking on his knees."

Sweet was smirking. What a swine he was, in some complicated way.

"I dote on movies," Eunice said humorlessly. "They seem to me to present the characteristic atmosphere of our kinetic time, along with rock. Words are out."

Reinhart was still humiliated. He sidled away to the window and looked on the characteristic atmosphere of our time, the smog-boa around the city's neck.

"Why don't you guys see a film together?" Sweet persisted. He was some kind of pervert. An air-conditioning outlet below the window was chilling Reinhart's genitals. He moved away.

"Look, Bob," he said. "Can we talk business?"

"What do you think?" Sweet asked Eunice. "Can we use this big hunk of man?" He smiled at Reinhart. "He is at liberty. He has no other current ties."

Eunice deliberately sized Reinhart up.

Sweet said: "This healthy brute."

She frowned and gathered in her gums, as in that device of mimicking the toothless, then released the lip-compression with a pop! "Umm." A glorious, carnivorous show of teeth. "I happen," said she, grinning, "to be free this evening."

Reinhart's eyebrows virtually met his cheekbones. He squinted out between.

"That will be all," Sweet said to Eunice, who replied: "OK, Bob." She turned, dropped a pencil on the floor, bent to fetch it with straight legs, and Reinhart saw the cheeks of her behind again. She breezed out.

Sweet threw his head back and pantomimed a howl of mirth. When the door was shut he leaned forward and said: "Hell, why not."

"I just want a piece of the business, Bob. I can put in five grand. That may not be much by your lights, but it does serve to show you I am not a beggar. Now I would be obliged to you if you would take me seriously. If you aren't interested, then throw me out."

"Come on, Carl, loosen up."

"You've changed since the other day, you know. Do you realize that? Is it a result of the credit check? I thought I had confessed to you already. Did you think I would kid you about my record? It's hopeless, I admit that freely."

"Even boastfully," said Sweet, shaking his head.

"I never have been a liar. I *am* proud of that. And I haven't been cruel. I don't think anybody could make that charge." Except Blaine, but father-son relations were private and, whatever, normal. "Nor am I dishonest."

"What strange things to brag about," said Sweet. "Do you really think that list contains anything to attract me? Even if it were true. Aren't you lying by implication right now? If precedents have any meaning—and you apparently believe they do—you will make a mess of any enterprise. Is it not dishonest then to offer yourself to me? Is it, in fact, not cruel? Because that is what you are doing." Bob smiled. " 'Take me though I'm worthless.' That is supposed to seem like candor, and I am supposed to conclude from it that you might be valuable for your honesty."

"No," said Reinhart. "I see how it looks, but what I meant was that I was straight in my business dealings, to the best of my ability. I never knowingly cheated anyone."

"But your creditors were forced to take a forty percent loss. Why would they care whether it was *knowingly!* These words are meaningless, Carl. And I wouldn't mind exploding another fixed idea of yours: that you are a *good guy.*"

Reinhart shook his head violently. "I never made that claim."

"It is implicit, once again, in your whole style. Even when you concede your judgment was bad, you mean instead your luck. Perhaps in some grand way, you put the blame on fate—it is bad luck your judgment is bad. How does that sound?"

"No," said Reinhart. "I'm not so childish as to believe in luck. I know a man makes his own. One can trace back to certain turnings in his life, which if not taken—or others which if taken, etcetera. For example, my marriage. I knew Genevieve was a snob when I married her. She got that from her father. I hated his guts on sight, and vice versa. And, farther back, my mother was never proud of me. I guess she loved me in her own way, but even when I got home from the Army she wouldn't listen to my stories but told me about the service experiences of the neighbor guys. She always acted—well, I know it sounds crazy, but, *jealous* of me. However, since my dad died she has changed. For one thing, she has become, sporadically, a paranoiac. Well, she's an old lady—"

"You're running off at the mouth, Carl, and confirming what I said."

Reinhart had sat down again in the leather chair, where he did not feel so big and exposed. Sweet now rose and wandered slowly about in his handsome suit of gray nailhead worsted and supple black oxfords.

"Let me tell you this, Carl. As long as material success escapes you, you regard it as an end. Women go along with this: getting the ones you want, controlling those you have, and so on. I'm not sneering at materialism, by any means. There are values in it. Art, for example, is certainly materialistic in itself and as to what it depicts. Had I lived a century ago I might have had a great house, full of rich, dusky oils and luxurious bronzes, stained glass illuminating the stairwells, and so on. This is not the time for that sort of thing. You see magazine photos of the apartments of public relations men: whitewashed walls, floor-to-ceiling paper posters, extruded-plastic trash to sit on. Like our reception room here, which incidentally was decorated by Eunice."

"Your clothes are certainly fine," said Reinhart.

Sweet nipped an inch of lapel between thumb and forefinger. "Forty dollars in Kowloon."

"What," asked wide-referenced Reinhart, "were you doing in Hong Kong?"

"Business or pleasure?" Sweet rhetorically demanded. "Neither, really. You know the old joke, Do you want to go around the world? No, I want to go someplace else. In Europe one year I took a tour of the world's tiniest countries, of which the largest was Luxembourg. San

Marino is the smallest. It has, if I am not mistaken, a Communist majority in its government, yet women have had the franchise there only since 1964."

Reinhart's right leg had got bored at his crossed-ankle position and gone to sleep. The day was when hearing a progression of apparent nonsequiturs he would immediately label the speaker a halfwit or rascal, but he had trudged into an age of nonlinear expression. He once had seen on the *Alp Show* a man pull a concertina to pieces while a girl in a bikini and space helmet bullwhipped a dummy and a greasy, squatting youth plucked at a one-stringed instrument imported from Asia. These persons professed academic connections with the fine-arts department of a major Eastern university.

"In short," said Sweet, perching his butt on the edge of the desk nearest Reinhart, "nothing makes any sense to me any more but the preservation of life. And if you think this is because I am unusually charitable, you are wrong, though I have placed my fortune at the disposal of this project. I was serious when I said I would freeze the first man at no cost to him. Yet I suspect that underneath it all you still think this is something of a racket." He thrust his arm at Reinhart. "No, I know you do. And why not? Nobody believes in God any more, but neither is there an ultimate faith in science. I'll tell you about myself. I used to fear Death. Now my feeling is a vicious hatred. I resent the hold it has over people as a fixed idea. But if you look at history you will find no idea has survived: the divine right of kings, the feudal code, slavery. And the earth was flat as a pancake until Columbus proved it otherwise."

Reinhart grinned. "You have to admit that Death is a hard nut to crack."

"I wonder," Sweet said in the tone of a man who does not.

"What I don't know," Reinhart admitted, "is just how you got into this, Bob. But as I look back on my intellectual history, I find that I relate to theories and ideas on the basis of the man who exemplifies them. Perhaps this is not the best way, but personality, in its widest sense, not charm or fluency alone, is what convinces me in the beginning."

"It is amazing, then, that you were so eloquent on the phone. Undoubtedly you feel the rightness about this endeavor, and that is important."

"What I sense, I think," said Reinhart, "is your basic selfishness. You do not want to die."

Sweet cocked his head. The definite margins between the grayness of his sideburns and the dark hair of the temples made Reinhart wonder whether he dyed one or the other, whether the brown or the gray was false. With this speculation he compensated for his admission of faith, which had been honest enough, but all men are competitive. Reinhart admired Sweet because the latter had done what he would have liked to do in life. He also hated him for it, in a healthy way.

Sweet said: "I want you to meet our scientific director. Have you got a minute?" He buzzed Eunice and told her to call his car. Then to Reinhart: "Are you serious about breaking up with your wife?"

"Why would I lie about that? It hardly puts me in a favorable light." Reinhart realized, when he saw Sweet depress the intercom key, that Eunice might have heard. "You seem to be throwing me at her, or vice versa, for some reason."

Sweet said levelly: "She's a nymphomaniac, Carl."

Reinhart's scalp crawled from nape to eyebrows. "Jesus, I'm embarrassed by my embarrassment. Mind you, I'm no prude, but I really haven't cheated on Gen all these years."

He didn't count of course his occasional visits to Gloria since Genevieve had preferred to sleep alone, because that was a business arrangement. Then there had been some friend of Gen's in the little-theater group, once back in '55 or '56, a neurasthenic, serpentine divorcee. A few kisses and fondling of neighbors' wives when drunk at parties and waiting in upstairs halls for the bathroom to empty.

A few other bits and pieces, and some forgotten totally no doubt, the point being that Reinhart had not fallen in love with anybody, something he had done frequently when unmarried, usually, in early youth, with girls of whom he had never gained carnal knowledge. Unlike many persons he never waxed nostalgic about bachelorhood. His lust for teen-agers nowadays was a romantic illusion, mixed with spite.

"You talk like some women's magazine article," Sweet said derisively. " 'Cheating.' A man has needs."

"This really embarrasses me, Bob." Why, in the Army Reinhart had been wont to talk of pussy for hours. But he had been young then, and it did not matter.

Sweet shrugged and went out into the reception room, where Eunice was plucking away at a typewriter, by no means competently. As far as Reinhart could see, she was the only employee at Cryon.

"We're going out to see Streckfuss," Sweet told her.

"Sure, Bob." She did not look up, being in the act of striking, with a long pale nail, an elusive key. She got the wrong one, tried again, saying, "Shhhh-ugar." Reinhart had not heard that in years. He wondered whether girls still said "funny-haha or funny-peculiar?" Her robust thighs were bare under the spindly typing table.

Reinhart was hoping she would not look at him, yet he could not forbear from watching her closely to see if she would. Sweet had probably just been baiting him.

"Come along, Carl," Sweet said, holding the door open.

Eunice glanced up indifferently at him. "You can pick me up here when you come back."

Reinhart followed Sweet into the corridor.

While they waited for the elevator, Sweet gave Reinhart an elbow to the ribs. "You're well padded, old fellow."

"I want to put one thing straight," Reinhart said in heat and fear. "I intend to return to Genevieve. I'm not going to let any woman throw me out of my own home. But I have to go back as a winner. Am I in, Bob?"

"We'll shake on it," Sweet said negligently, stepping into the cab, which was still quivering from its abrupt stop. It self-adjusted to Reinhart's excess weight.

"As soon as we're in the car, I'll write out a check," Reinhart said. He felt good. Yes, he would take Eunice out to dinner and bang her afterwards if that is what she wanted. "Thanks, Bob. I really mean it, and I swear to you that you won't regret your decision."

Sweet shook hands very quickly. "I can't offer you a piece of the business because we are a nonprofit organization, as you well know. Which would you prefer, a grant of money, which is to say, a lump sum such as we give to scientists for research projects, or a regular salary? Actually, the latter would still be a grant but one paid in installments like regular wages. This is, so far as has been determined, nontaxable. It has not been challenged yet. I think we might manage a grant, say, of fifteen thousand. That would seem reasonable at this time. After all, we are just getting under way. But perhaps before agreeing to any terms you would want to talk to Streckfuss."

Reinhart was giddy from the altitude of high numbers.

Of course, it was little enough to a man like Sweet, so he
tried to simulate professionality. "Perhaps I should," he
was saying as the elevator touched bottom. "Who is he?"

"A genius," Sweet said.

The Bentley waited at the curb directly in front of the
Bloor Building, in a no-parking, no-waiting, taxi-stand,
bus-stop, fire-zone crosswalk adorned with prohibitory
stripes and signs and a traffic policeman who sycophanti-
cally saluted Sweet. Allison, the old chauffeur, woke up as
the car settled under Reinhart's weight.

"Streckfuss, I take it," said Reinhart, "is at the scientific end of things."

"I brought him over a year or so ago, and have given
him the facilities he needs."

"That's a German name, isn't it?"

"Swiss," Sweet said. "French-speaking, but he can get
along in English."

Reinhart bent his neck in admiration. "You speak
French, too. I used to get along in German, but have
forgotten it all."

"I clowned around with Linguaphone records before I
went over there, but you pick up a lot when living in a
country. There's really no other way to learn a language."

"You lived in Europe?"

"It was a special type of living, I supposed. I spent
some time at Streckfuss' sanatorium."

"Is that right? Not tuberculosis, as in *The Magic
Mountain* by Thomas Mann?"

Sweet snapped his jaw, disposing of the question. No
man who worked his way up from pimples to a Bentley
did it on books.

"No, not TB," he said. "Time was my malady. Streckfuss is an authority on rejuvenation."

So that was Bob's secret. Monkey-gland injections,
Ponce de Sweet. Though it had worked—Sweet was certainly dynamic and his visible skin was taut, his trunk was
slender, his eyes clear—still there was something degrading in a reluctance to accept ordinary chronology. Sweet
managed it no doubt as well as could be, displaying not a
hint of second-childishness. Shopworn Reinhart himself
was more callow. Perhaps his very disappointment was
sophomoric. But he had been at least abstractly invigorat-
ed by what he had taken as Sweet's natural maintenance
of power. The self-made man now turned out to be partly
synthetic.

But was it not, on the other hand, futile to question the

origin of power? The Church had gone to seed when petty monks began to discuss how many angels might perch on a pinpoint.

"Do you think," he asked Sweet, "that he might rejuvenate me?"

Sweet's chuckle was elastic and liquid—as if in fact he were chewing those gumdrops of Reinhart's chronological youth called Chuckles.

"Hans will be glad to freeze you," he answered.

— 6 —

Streckfuss pronounced his name in the German fashion. "Shtreckfooss," said he, clicked his heels, and raised and lowered Reinhart's hand once only before dropping it. He wore an ankle-length white laboratory coat and stood in the foreground of a room full of rectangular devices along with vessels of glass. But nothing revolved or whirred; there were no jacob's ladders of electrical sparks, no scurrying troglodytes or other props of horror movies. However, the lab was rather cold, and Streckfuss had on a sweater beneath the gown, a currently fashionable one, in fact, with a turtleneck of wool around his skinny column of tendons.

"*Enchanté*," said he to Reinhart. To Sweet he said: "*Alors?*"

Reinhart peered down at Streckfuss' carrot nose, pitted cheeks, swarthy coloring, hectic, thick black hair, obsidian eyes which darted lizardlike up the fat bluff of Reinhart's front, froze briefly on his Adam's apple, and scampered down.

"Were you ever in Berlin?" Reinhart asked.

"*Jamais.*"

Sweet explained: "Hans is fluent in English except when he's very tired."

"*Jamais* means 'no,' doesn't it?" Reinhart asked them both, but it was Streckfuss who answered.

"Neffer," said he, showing a line of chipped yellow teeth. He grimaced at Reinhart, still denying him his eyes.

"Hans has an understandable bias against Germans," Sweet said.

"I certainly meant no insult," Reinhart told the little scientist. "I expect the world is full of lookalikes."

Streckfuss shrugged in a typical French gesture, at least in Hollywood movies, and made the typical French grunt. It sounded authentic enough. The fact remained however that Streckfuss looked and moved exactly like a strange little German Reinhart had known almost a quarter-

century before while serving in the Occupation of the
Teutonic capital; a person named Schatzi.

Streckfuss said to Sweet: *"Il est très gras, hein?"*

Sweet smiled or winced. "Well," he said in a bluff
voice, "here we are, Carl. What do you think of our
facilities?"

Outside, the building was an oblong of tile-faced cinderblock, ironically resembling a local crematorium which
it had been Reinhart's duty to accompany his father's
casket to. "I don't want to corrupt six feet of good
earth," always considerate Dad had said once long ago,
hence his disposal by fire. "He would have wanted this,"
said Maw as they sat side by side in a little chapel above
the furnace.

"Very impressive," Reinhart said now, in the layman's
ritual awe. He nodded at the nearest panel of dials set in
white enamel, then to a stainless-steel table full of
glassware, and made an inept joke, but he was nervous
for some reason. "Looks like a dairy."

Streckfuss' violent laugh suggested a lung condition,
then ceased abruptly, and he scuttled away as if on casters.

Sweet spoke confidentially to Reinhart: "He's a bit
eccentric."

Reinhart shivered slightly in the coolness. In the brief
intervals between air-conditioned buildings and cars he
had as usual exuded copious perspiration, which felt as if
it were now icily coagulating. There were also inhuman
odors abroad in this lab. In high-school general science he
and fun-loving pals had doctored both milk-specimens
with formaldehyde, corrupting an experiment supposed to
demonstrate the preservative function of that fluid, the
effectiveness of which could be measured only by the
presence of an untreated example which soured. Neither
half pint went bad for weeks. The dopey teacher kept
tasting them, yet stayed unpoisoned. But Reinhart could
well remember the first time he saw him doing it.

He thought of this now, perhaps because of the dairy
reference, but what he said to Sweet, also sotto voce,
was: "The damnedest thing. He's a dead ringer for this
German I knew."

Sweet said: "If it was so long ago, your German would
have changed in appearance by now."

"Of course," Reinhart said. "That did not occur to
me."

Streckfuss was perched on a high stool at an enamel
counter emanating from the wall. Before him was a sort

of rectangular glass fishtank from which sprouted many wires and tubes. From Reinhart's perspective these squirmy lengths seemed to grow from Streckfuss' own head, transforming him into a Gorgon. Away down at the far end of the windowless room a large metal cylinder, shaped like a space capsule, lay on its side in a wooden cradle. It claimed Reinhart's gaze because it was the thickest horizontal in his perspective. Everything else was tenuous, fragile, or polished blandly dumb like the tile walls. A man of his bulk felt uneasy in an enclosure full of wires and glassware, and Sweet stood there smiling at him inscrutably.

Suddenly he understood the function of the capsule.

"That's to hold the first frozen person, right?"

Sweet walked smartly down the corridor between the gimcracks of science, and Reinhart trailed him. It seemed to take forever to get there, and he sensed that on the way he passed bits of organic matter under glass.

Sweet thumped the tank with the heel of his hand. "A rocket ship into Time." The tank ominously replied with a boilerlike *clang*, rather less than hollow.

Reinhart blanched. "Good God," he said. "Is something or someone in there?"

"Not yet, worse luck." Sweet struck it again. "It is of necessity very thick, and the welds must be perfect. You wouldn't think, would you, that the program might hinge on the craft of a welder? Rather like the battle lost because the blacksmith forgot to put the nail in the shoe of the general's horse, etcetera. Young men aren't going into that trade any more, and the old welders tend to be pretty slipshod. Precision has been on the wane in all areas. But we are talking about a tank that must hold up for centuries. That means a perfect seal. The tiniest leak would be disastrous."

"Something I wanted to ask you, Bob. A pretty obvious consideration, really." Reinhart was about to lean on the tank but thought better of it on grounds of taste. "What if the power goes off, as it might at some point in that period of time? Remember the great New York blackout of some years ago? There go your frozen bodies out the window." Or into a cocked hat. He regretted his choice of jargon and sought to make up for it with passion. He struck the tank with a heavy fist. Very obdurate walls. Hit a Detroit fender that hard and you'd be through to the tire.

Sweet leaned comfortably against the capsule, crucifying his arms. His french cuffs were monogrammed. His initials were the beginning letters of RSVP, Reinhart realized pointlessly. Sweet's attitude was boyish. He seemed to have a personal feeling for the tank. He turned his hands over and stroked its curving sides as one might caress the globed surface of a woman.

"But no power is used, Carl. I forget you know almost nothing about the process. This is not a home-style deep-freeze full of Birdseye products which spoil when a storm brings down the high-tension lines. The body will be immersed in either liquid nitrogen or liquid helium." He frowned. "Did I not mention that on the *Alp Show?* We are talking of temperatures so low—well, let me say this by way of negative example. It has been suggested that when the program achieves public acceptance we might run out of space in which to store bodies. Also demand may at first exceed the supply of tanks and refrigerants. Therefore, could we not store some frozen people in Siberia or, better, the Antarctic, which is empty and otherwise useless?"

Reinhart raised his eyebrows while sucking his sore knuckles.

"The answer," Sweet said harshly, "happens to be no. *Not even Antarctica is cold enough.* Can you grasp that? Yet even in the comparative warmth of the South Pole, certain foods left there by Scott were maintained in an edible condition for decades. Spoiling, which is rot, which is death, is caused by bacteria, to put it simply. Bacteria cannot live at extremely low temperatures."

"Then how can people?" asked Reinhart. "That's another thing I wanted to inquire about. How do you explain freezing-to-death?"

Sweet tenderly patted his metallic baby. "A misnomer." He flexed his forehead and peered expectantly at Reinhart's elbow, attached to the arm whose fingers had gone to test the dampness in one under-shoulder cavity.

Reinhart himself curiously looked there too. Had he dipped his sleeve in some chemical? No, it was Streckfuss. He had stolen up silently. The floor was concrete, and he wore rubber-soled shoes, no, actually, rubbers, perhaps because of all the electricity hereabouts. At any rate, there he was at Reinhart's elbow. Reinhart, or so his fingertips would have it, was still gushing sweat though feeling generally cold: queer.

Streckfuss was of the same indeterminate age as his

Berlin double, but how long could anyone have kept that up?

"The popular impression of zese tings," Streckfuss said, glaring up at Reinhart, "is really what I should call literary. *Boom!* A man is *shot to death*. But he iss not, you see, except in cinema. Nor is poisoned, froze, electrocuted, and so on, *to death*. What happens is his vital organs are damaged so that they cannot continue to function properly and, *alors!* he dies zooner or later. It is not like to turn off a machine."

He was fluent enough in English, it seemed, with an accent that as yet could have been from anywhere: French or German uvular *r*'s, the occasional special treatment of sibilants, a difficulty with *th*, but a firm way with *h* alone that could not be called Gallic.

"Even," Streckfuss went on, "should a liffing body be disintegrated by explosion, literally blown into many fragments, bits of matter remain vital for a time."

Reinhart said: "You know what has always fascinated me? The running of a motion-picture film backwards, bringing the diver back up out of the water, sucking the splash-down into a mirrorlike surface of the pool, reassembling the cliffside blown off with dynamite."

Streckfuss ran a hand through his disorderly scalp, stretching the forehead ravines smooth, an instant and startling facelift. *"Quelle bêtise!"* said he to Sweet.

Sweet smiled at Reinhart. "I think it shows the right spirit. Carl is reluctant to accept the popular idea of reality with its narrowminded emphasis on finality."

"Of course," said Reinhart, "I know that is merely a trick of light and not existence."

"Still," said Sweet, "it is a beginning. Can you imagine what a man of some earlier century would say if exposed to that? He believed in unicorns and dragons without ever seeing one, yet accepted death as inevitable despite the material evidence of life which hummed through his veins."

"Well," Reinhart said, trying to contribute, "the belief in dragons has been traced to, I have read, the discovery of dinosaur remains—"

Streckfuss suddenly howled in rage. "Zis is no discussion!" he cried. "Vot are your credentials?" He slapped a small foot, clad in a shiny black rubber, on the concrete.

"I meant no—" Reinhart began.

"Silence!" cried Streckfuss, clearly making it a French word. *"Pas de mot encore!"* He clapped both hands to his

face and dry-washed it. Then stared at Sweet. "Ray-olly, Bopp." He marched back to his counter at the other end of the lab.

"What's wrong now?" asked Reinhart. "I don't understand much French."

"He's highly strung, Carl, as I told you. He'll be all right in a moment. . . . You see, it is not freezing as such that damages tissue. No one has ever 'frozen to death,' in the common sense of the phrase. Cold does not destroy, but rather preserves."

"But persons lost in the Arctic—"

"Exactly," said Sweet. "I know, I know. The damage may be caused by ice crystals which form in the body fluids, expanding and bursting the cells or puncturing vessels. What Hans was getting at, I think, is that the common supposition about causes of death is too general. There are poisons, for example, which cause death by suffocation; they arrest the muscles which work the lungs, or perhaps more subtly, derange the nerves which tell the muscles to move the lungs to take in and expel air. The body is a terribly complicated apparatus, Carl."

Streckfuss appeared to rest: his shaggy head was buried in his folded arms. He was rather a prima donna.

"But," Sweet went on, "there is much reason to believe that the damage is not done by freezing but in the existing procedures of thawing." He stared at Reinhart. "That is pretty revolutionary, don't you think? Can you remember as a boy being told to treat frostbite by rubbing the affected area with snow?"

"I have done it," said Reinhart. "Many times when out sledding—"

"No, you have not," Sweet said decisively. "Unless the area was not actually frostbitten. If it were you would have by that means ensured the loss of the limb. We know today that the effective therapy is boiling water or at any rate as hot as can be borne, and no abrasion of the tissue. Victims have not lost their toes to frostbite, but to its cure. Can you appreciate that?"

"If you say so."

"Hans could demonstrate it, if you like. As it happens this is now accepted medical practice. Your family doctor would concur."

"I doubt it," said Reinhart. "Doc Perse still prescribes mustard plasters for chest colds. He still has not caught up with the sulfa tablets, let alone penicillin. Of course, he is an oddity. I go to him merely for sentimental reasons.

Actually, I have never yet had a serious ailment, touch wood." But there wasn't any within reach. Reinhart loved wood, leather, ivory, and copper, but had spent his life amid galvanized metals and plastics. Perhaps he consulted Doc Perse merely because the old physician's waiting room offered a genuine horsehide sofa, if cracked. At least the stuffing it leaked was kapok and not that loathsome foam which looked like something a robot might ejaculate.

"That's just the point, Carl. Medicine has always lagged behind the other sciences. We are already at home in space, but a man can still die of a defective heart or even of an imperfectly executed transplant." Sweet sighed, but resumed energetically: "But not for much longer, in a historical sense. However, that wouldn't do you much good if you had a cardiac seizure today. One's own life is uniquely precious. Few people want to throw theirs away any more for a cause which will only benefit others."

"There are more fanatics around than ever," said Reinhart.

"Fanaticism fades away before the prospect of eternal life. True democracy is at last possible if everybody can live forever. A man who considers himself deprived has an eternity in which to redress the balance. Most of the old troubles are the result of envy. A Cadillac is attractive only if most people are driving Fords. To put it another way, he who has a morsel of moldy bread when others have nothing is rich. Life has always until now been comparative."

"I can't see that changing," said Reinhart.

"Then eliminate the dimension of Time, by which most social situations are measured. The Negroes are bitter, for example, that after a century they are still not first-class citizens. To put it personally, after forty-four years you are discouraged on reflection that half your life is gone with little to show for it."

"I wouldn't mind freezing my son," said Reinhart, "and awakening him just a few years hence to show him what an ass he had been."

Sweet finally left the support of the capsule. He poked Reinhart in the arm. "No, Carl, no one can make the decision for another, at least not while the other lives. However, there are interesting possibilities in matters of law. Surely prosecution for first-degree murder will be a thing of the past. A frozen victim is not dead. A so-called killer in this state of affairs is rather a thief. He has merely stolen a few years from the other. In time perhaps this will be considered merely as petty larceny. Nothing much has been taken from a man who has forever. The 'killer' will be charged for the expenses of freezing and the subsequent replacement of the vital organ that he damaged."

"I'll be damned," said Reinhart.

"Moreover, all current theories and practices concerning crime and punishment will be rendered obsolete. A persistently antisocial person will be frozen until the day when the surgeons can successfully replace his brain."

"If indeed that is the source of his difficulties," Reinhart observed. He believed that Sweet wanted him to play devil's advocate.

"Goes without saying. But we have already disposed of his economic, political, and racial motives, have we not? Under conditions of eternal life all 'problems' are by definition minor. Nothing can be *done to death*, you see. You could still be hungry but you won't starve. Swimming beyond your depth or incapacitated by cramps, you will not drown. Firemen overcome by smoke will not suffocate. The victims of poison would have spasms but not die—but why would anyone poison another in the first place if he could not eliminate him?"

Reinhart narrowed his eyes. He had thought of something. "Explosion," he said. "Referred to earlier by Doctor Streckfuss. Disintegration by blast, everything in fragments. I should say you are never going to abolish the human appetite for destruction. You are going to force it to be more subtle—or more gross, in the case of dynamite or whatever. And aren't you selling hatred short? I gather a body has to be frozen very quickly after death. The murderer polishes off his victim and hides the body for a week. Haha!"

"Aren't you the grisly one," said Sweet. "You're being perverse now simply for the sake of argument, I see. Let me tell you something more. There is a very real likelihood that science will one day be able to reproduce an entire organism from one living cell of that organism. That means, simply, that if one microscopic portion is recovered from blast or acid-bath or incineration or you-name-it, a new version of the same being can be re-grown."

Sweet said this almost wearily. His eyes were stark behind the black-rimmed lenses. For the first time Reinhart noticed that Sweet's nose was poreless, giving off a dull gloss, very unusual in a man of his age.

"In fact," Sweet went on, "this has already been done, in Europe, with frogs. One cell has been grown into a complete animal."

Reinhart had a strange feeling about Sweet. "Really?" he murmured, looking for visible seams in the neck, below the mastoid process.

"Well," Sweet said, taking Reinhart's arm again, "I know this is a lot to digest at once, old fellow, even for the sympathetic. You are faced with a complete reversal of everything you have known as fact all your life. It shakes a man up. I have gone through it myself. Along about our age, a fellow begins to sense his days are numbered. Then, when one grows old, he often swindles himself into welcoming an end to it all. This is of course fake. Nobody who is actually near death wants to die, but there is a natural need for human beings to want to feel in control. They *must* die, so they say they are ready. It's the old con job."

Sweet hooked his forearm through Reinhart's elbow. It felt like a metal tube. "C'mon," he said, "let's relax over a bite to eat."

They walked together down the aisle between the stainless-steel tables, electrical equipment, and the glass containers of fleshy nastiness, glimpsed by Reinhart on the way up.

Streckfuss was peering intensely at a dial above his counter. He made a brisk entry in a ledger and spun around at their approach. He was seemingly in a splendid mood now.

"Ah, gentlemen!" he cried. "Shall we feed? *Moi, j'ai faim, bien sûr! Et vous aussi, mon vieux?*"

He made a jolly, vulpine show of teeth at Reinhart, who smiled in return.

"*Jawohl,*" Reinhart answered. "*Ich bin sehr hungrig.*" He knew a few French phrases, like everybody else. He had gone through France years ago, armed with a U.S. Army phrasebook, on the way to Berlin, where he had known the little German called Schatzi.

Streckfuss twitched the very end of his long nose. He said to Sweet: "Sometimess Americans sink one foreign language is as good as anozzer."

Reinhart said: "It's your name, I suppose. 'Streckfuss' sounds German."

Sweet dropped his arm. "Come on, Carl. You're being

pretty offensive, you know, though I'm sure you regard it as a joke. But if you've had experience with Europeans it should be no secret that they do not understand this American penchant for kidding around."

Streckfuss, however, stayed in good humor. "Ah, have you forgotten about Dreyfus, sir?" he asked playfully, extending his jaw. There was something provocative in his imposture, if such it was, and it definitely was some sort of a, or one, or whatever—Reinhart found his own mental syntax performing awkward gymnastics. How in the world could a man look precisely the same for twenty-three years? On the other hand, was his own memory unchanged? Or at all reliable? He had once argued with Maw as to the location of an elm tree on the edge of Mrs. Bangor's property across the street from the Reinhart residence. Just after the war, pushing Dad's stalled auto down the driveway, the then-powerful ex-corporal had put too much beef behind it and the car escaped him, crossed the road, climbed the curb, and smote the elm. Mrs. B., a crotchety widow, had made a stink about it. Now she and Dad were dead, the tree was long since sawed down, and Maw produced a Brownie snapshot, taken during the same years, which clearly showed the trunk erecting itself a good ten feet to the left of where it would have had to stand to catch the car.

"I could hardly mean it as an insult," Reinhart said now. "I am myself of German descent. Though we never made much of it. I mean, we didn't go to *weinfests* or anything, let alone join the Bund."

"Frankly," said Streckfuss, grinning, "I do not care about your origins. It is your future which concairns me. *Vous êtes dans la merde de l'âge mûr.*"

Reinhart said to Sweet: "Look here, I don't understand French. I mean, that's not good manners either."

"You can address Hans directly," Sweet said in remonstration.

"He seems to be cursing at me," Reinhart said. "I thought I heard the only dirty word I know in French."

Sweet asked: "How would you describe your recent situation in life, Carl?"

Reinhart got it. "Is that how you say 'up shit creek' in French?" So Streckfuss had a sense of humor after all.

But the little doctor glared at him and asked: "Vy are you lahffing? What is the joke here? American astronowts wisecrack in orbit. What are the origins of this state of mind? *Merde alors!*"

Sweet winked at Reinhart. To Streckfuss he said: "What's on the menu today, Hans?" To Reinhart: "Hans is a skilled chef." To Streckfuss: "Carl has difficulties with his digestion, so none of your hot spices, please."

"No," Reinhart agreed, adding: "I also have some dental trouble. I have to take my meat well done."

Streckfuss went to a metal cabinet mounted above a stainless-steel sink featuring those high-looped faucets found in labs.

"You have a kitchen here?" Reinhart asked.

"Oh," said Sweet, "we have everything necessary to a well-balanced life—if you live like Hans. Frankly I find it a bit austere. It just occurred to me, Carl. If you have left home where are you staying now?"

Reinhart did not want to mention the Y, where though he had Maw's five grand he was yet registered. He had hoped to put the money in Sweet's business, but meanwhile he had to exist. All this was changed now by the new arrangement in which he was to pull down three hundred a week and retain the five thousand as well. He was in a position to take a luxury apartment with a wall of windows showing a night sky with a million stars. He could get his own car and have his teeth brought up to standard. He could buy Blaine a natural-shoulder Ivy League suit, a button-down oxford-cloth shirt, and a plain knitted tie, which, with heavy pebble-grain brogues and Argyle socks, was the really soigné costume of college men of his own era. And hire a bully to make Blaine put it on. He could buy Gen a decent mink jacket or an inferior full-length coat though still mink.

"I'm not settled yet, actually. I'm staying at a hotel for the moment. I'll probably end up back home when my wife gets over her mad. I'm really a family sort of guy, Bob. The swinging bachelor life never appealed to me even when I was in my twenties. A different girl every night, that sort of thing. Women are a hell of a lot of trouble. You have fewer problems if you stick to one, as big a pain in the ass as she might be. Anyway, generally speaking, I have found any woman is all the rest of them."

"I have heard that theory," Sweet replied sardonically. "The words that losers live by, if you can call it living. 'What good is money?' 'Power corrupts.' 'Who wants to live forever?' 'The bitch-goddess Success.' 'The bubble reputation.' 'It's not whether you win or lose but how you play the game.' No matter what the established good, it will be disparaged by those who cannot get some of it for themselves. The Christian religion is based on that principle, and some practitioners have become so highly skilled at its manipulation that they seemingly win with it for a time until somebody takes them seriously about turning the other cheek. He sees they really are helpless and blows their brains out."

"Have you ever considered this, Bob? That maybe they won, after all. In their own way, I mean. I doubt there would have been a Christian religion if Jesus had not been crucified."

"Balls, Carl. All you have is your own life and if you lose it you have lost. The reverse is that as long as you have your life you are winning. That's the sole truth behind all the complicated lies, all ethical systems, all that has been written or said or dreamed. When the vital spark leaves your body you turn into a lump of decaying matter. There is no serious distinction between a corpse and a turd."

Reinhart recoiled. He would not be able to eat lunch if the conversation continued in this vein, or intestine. He altered the direction slightly without seeking to steer away from Sweet's preoccupation. In the new job he supposed it would have to be his own as well.

"Speaking of marriage," he said. "I see all sorts of intricacies arising from the freezer program. Suppose a man dies and is frozen. Is he legally dead? Is his wife a widow? What becomes of his property? He may be revived later, but he is certainly as helpless as if he were dead."

"Be assured," Sweet answered, "that we are aware of these ramifications, and I shall be glad to discourse on them over lunch. Which I see is ready."

Reinhart saw with amazement that Streckfuss had done nothing but pull bottles out of the cabinet and shake from them pellets and powders into glass beakers. The little scientist now assembled the vessels on a white-enamel laboratory tray and lifted it, in cafeteria busboy style, fingertips back hand-heel forward, to his ear.

"La soupe!" he cried. *"Messieurs sont servis."*

Sweet pushed back the apparatus on a steel tabletop. One metal lab stool was nearby. He asked Reinhart to fetch two others. In so doing the stout man saw several smaller versions of the man-sized freezer capsule, demonstration models as it were, ranked upon a wall shelf.

"I have heard of this sort of instant concentrated nourishment," he said when seated, at his host's insistence, at the arbitrary head of the table. "But I haven't ever tried it."

Streckfuss took a handful of pills from one beaker and paid them out, two each, onto three round glass saucers.

"Fish course," he said, "accompanied by an unassuming little Sancerre with its typical flavor of unripe apples. There are keen palates which can identify from vich slope of zuh vineyard came the grapes." He poured an inch of colorless fluid from an Erlenmeyer flask into a beaker containing a pinch of powder and presented it to Reinhart.

"I'm supposed to drink this?" asked the latter, with a hearty chuckle, looking at Sweet for a confirmation of the absurdity. Reinhart supposed this could be fun. He had seen it in a movie once; the eater, a well-known comic, had been provided with cutlery, carved the little pills, etc.

"After inhaling the bouquet, of course," Streckfuss said, reaching to mix liquid and powder with a wooden tongue-depressor from which he first peeled the crackling paper, that funny translucent stuff you saw nowhere else any more. Reinhart always gagged when the doctor shoved one down his throat so as to peer at where it felt scratchy.

Reinhart twirled the contents under his nose. He scented nothing whatever. He took a bit on the end of his tongue. Nothing. It was certainly not the local water, though, which had the pronounced taste of chlorine.

Streckfuss hurled his skinny chin towards the ceiling. "Failed again!" said he. But his chagrin was obviously mock. "Try the *coquilles Saint-Jacques*, or are they *fruits de mer?*"

"Swallow whole or bite through?" asked Reinhart.

"Down zuh hatchway!"

"Aren't you guys going to eat?"

Sweet said. "Of course. I'm famished." He took the tablets in his palm and threw them into his open mouth, followed by a draft from his own beaker.

So Reinhart followed suit. If he were poisoned or drugged he would have company. It was precisely like taking two aspirins. Perhaps foolishly he was disappointed. He had more or less expected a flavor, though maybe not fish and wine exactly. Of course it was great in view of his dental problems, and not much less than real fish, which never filled him. Whenever Maw had fed him halibut as a boy he always slipped out and had a hamburger later on. In the early years of their marriage Gen had

occasionally prepared tunafish à la king, immersed in a
sauce of which catsup was a constituent. It was the
memory of such dishes that kept him from being bitter
about doing most of the family cooking.

Streckfuss thereupon poured himself a heaping handful
of the same tablets. "Gawd," said he. "I could eat siz stuff
till zuh cows come home." He threw them down his
gullet, which was pale as the throat of a water moccasin.

Sweet leaned significantly towards Reinhart. "Hans
never eats anything else."

"Really. You actually live on pills?"

You could see them going down through his Adam's
apple, in effect, one by one. He had closed his eyes in
pleasure. He took a swig from his own beaker of liquid
and made a gargling sound. Ah, there went the last
tablet.

"To put it vulgarly," he answered at length. "Nutrition-
ally speaking, zese tablets contain the same nourishment—
vitt-amins, protein, minerals, and so on—as an actual
serving of fish. Only the garbage is eliminated, and who
misses zat?"

Sweet spoke up. "I admit I can't as yet go along with
Hans in that respect. I still love my steak and would hate
to have to do without good red meat—"

Streckfuss interrupted. His long upper lip was keen
with pride. "I almost never have to defecate," he cried.
"Is that not a satisfactory situation? Not to have a long
snake of *matières fécales* coiled in your guts? It is not
enough that eating is useless. It is also filthy. Sink of
carrying about all that rubbish. Behind zuh average navel
lies a cesspool. Good heavens. Have you ever dissected a
cadaver?"

Reinhart took another drink at this point. He was not
nauseated, because this was nothing like eating. Another
advantage of Streckfuss' diet was that you could talk of
anything while ingesting it. Very utilitarian for a scientist.

"All right," Reinhart said. "But what happens to the
system if it is not used? Would the intestines not wither
up like deflated balloons?"

Streckfuss displayed some spiky teeth. "So comes the
role of the Streckfuss cocktail vich you seem to be enjoying merrily. Combining in the stomach with digestive
juices, it is transformed like a type of sludge—actually a
semisolid polyester foam—which moves through the bowels, not only supporting zem against collapse but scouring
them clean, thus making almost nil the likelihood of

noxious and uncomfortable gasses and guaranteeing immunity against hemorrhoids, among ozzer annoying embarrassments. I should suppose you are no stranger to piles?"

It was an odd but not unpleasant sensation, and thus far only moral. Reinhart could not as yet actually feel the detergent action. Perhaps he never would. If so, something would be lost, maybe not something infinitely precious, but definitely one of life's rhythms. Some people measured out their days by a schedule of eliminations. His parents used to be like that, Dad especially. And not just old fogies. Guys in the Army, shamelessly perched at stool, wincing in satisfaction—a whole line of them, in the morning, almost touching knees, for the latrines were stall-less—then exchanging jollity with the parallel line of shavers at the washbasins. Dogs however always looked anxious when hunched up: ancient racial memory, no doubt, from when the breed roamed wild and you could get jumped while helpless evacuating. Food was the preoccupation of all creatures in Nature. Only man had systematized its collection and all phases of its tour.

Reinhart answered Streckfuss' question. "Not one of my major complaints. A cocoa-butter suppository or two and I'm shipshape."

"Meat course," said the Swiss, dropping three green-colored capsules on Reinhart's dish. "I could continue the amusing conceit and ahsk whether your choice iss rare or well done but I sink I shawn't. My own manner of eating is while at vork to take which nutrients I need. I do not perform zis charade of sitting at table, mind you. I regard the mealtime customs as folly. Europeans still waste hours in zis preposterous ritual. I admire about your country the quick lunch, the instant foods. But they could be made more quicker still. These all-in-one breakfasts now available are a step in the right direction, though still rather vulgar. They are flavored with chocolate, no less."

The nay-saying John Calvin, Reinhart remembered, had been a Swiss. Yet Swiss chocolate was also famous, and, finally, watches.

"I'll join Bob," said Reinhart. "I don't relish the thought of giving up all pleasant sensory experiences. Though I don't live to eat, by any means."

Streckfuss looked at Reinhart's bulging jacket front and said: "You could have fooled us."

"The funny thing is that I don't eat all that much,"

Reinhart said. "Honestly. Is it not true, Doctor, that some people because of peculiar glandular—"

"No," Streckfuss said. "People get fat for one reason alone: gluttony."

Reinhart looked at Sweet. "I suppose I should take up jogging. That's the big thing now, isn't it, Bob?"

Sweet made a fist around his ration of green capsules and carried it to his mouth, swallowing elaborately. He said: "I come here to sit at Hans's feet, Carl. If he told me to climb into that vat of liquid nitrogen, I would do so without question. I may even come in time to enjoy this sort of meal."

"No," said Streckfuss, "not to enchoy it, old chap, but to disregard it."

"By the way," Sweet said to Reinhart, "Hans's title is 'professor.' Everybody in Central Europe is a doctor."

Somebody, or something, was smoking. Blue-gray whorls obscured Streckfuss' head. Reinhart smelled the transformer of the electric train he had owned as a boy, the scent of electricity, equivalent somehow to the music of the spheres, a comparison that made sense only in the reason of the morning half-dreams in which one anticipates, dreaming, the telephone bell which rings on cue in reality. Did I wake you up? the caller asks invariably, and you always lie. The odor of volts was called ozone. Reinhart was not totally helpless in the age of science. He had served in the Medical Department of the Army of the United States, and still remembered the main pressure points. If you get a head wound do you put a tourniquet around the neck? asked some joker, and the sergeant said all right you shitbum wiseguy. Streckfuss, reassembled his face and pressed it against Reinhart's, making owl eyes. Why if he did not eat food was his breath foul? No, that was ozone. Sweet was operated electrically. He had died and was revived as Streckfuss' creature. He was ageless and immortal. Open his shirt and you would see the wheels and wires. Imagine committing suicide by enclosing your head in a plastic shirt bag. Some did. Therefore the laundry printed a caution on each.

Reinhart knew he had passed out, but he did not know that he knew, and he was really not interested in why. He had never been good at quantitative judgments, barely squeaked through high-school math.

What was notable about his present state was the absolute absence of pain. In ordinary life this would have led only to suspicion or rather suspense, a related word.

In the beginning was the Word, the end is silence. This was, impossibly, neither. He certainly must tell his colleagues, when the experiment was concluded, that though in a sleep of ice, the brain made waves. Remembering that, he forgot all else and was resolved into a swirl of smoke or semen or snot and streamed towards a pinhole of light, entered it, and vanished.

Reinhart had a feeling that he had not closed his eyes. Nonetheless he opened them now and discovered himself still at table. The flasks and beakers had been removed, and his luncheon companions were conferring near the large freezer capsule. He checked himself for dizziness: flexed his neck, breathed deeply, seemed to pursue the ghost of a headache, detected nothing more, rose from the stool—had he kept his perch all the while?—took one step, and fell in a jointed, sequential fashion onto the concrete floor: knees, chest, chin.

Oddly enough, he hurt nowhere. However, he did not possess the coordination, or perhaps the will, to get up. From the tops of his eyes he saw a floorscape of metal legs and braces, and finally an oncoming pair of rubber overshoes. A hook or claw seized the neck of his jacket and raised him inexorably.

Having attained his feet, Reinhart said to the little Streckfuss: "Do you know you have just raised a dead weight of two hundred sixty-five pounds?" He felt OK. "With one hand," he added. Sweet slowly approached. Reinhart said to him: "I don't know what happened."

Streckfuss said: "Not by brute strength, I assure you, nor by magic." But he did not explain.

"Did I, or did I not, pass out at the table?" Reinhart asked Sweet.

"You dozed a bit," answered his friend. "We decided not to bother you."

"I might have had a reaction to those pills, might I not?"

"Very unlikely," said Streckfuss, "if you mean in any organic senssse. I cannot speak for your emotional constituseeyon. Exposure to new knowledge is zometimes exhowsting. But I suspect it is your habit to take a nap after a hearty meal."

"You know, that's right," Reinhart confessed. "But why did I just fall on my face?"

"I should suppose your leg was still asleep. It was twisted about the stool for zum time."

"Of course, of course. . . ." He stamped his foot, but the pins and needles, if such there had been, were now gone. Suddenly he felt hale. He leaped into the air and clicked his heels.

Streckfuss chortled.

Reinhart asked: "What did you do, give me a pep pill?" He felt both embarrassed and pleased. He would not have been surprised to find himself turning a cartwheel, something he could never manage as a slender child. "I don't know what it was I ate, but it worked."

"Still," Streckfuss said, "not everysing is possible through nutrition at this point. One as yet does not understand the precise role of adenosine triphosphate in the synthesis of cell protein, though it seems crucial. Ah, zuh fools!"

Reinhart raised his eyebrows at Sweet.

Who explained: "Hans refers to the people who oppose science by simple inertia. If you look at any past era you will see certain active enemies of truth but the mass of any population is merely negative. I have had some experience with the public. I know that if we could start a trend, Hans could have more bodies than he needs. If somehow we can make it attractive, people will so to speak line up to be frozen. Do you know that Pan Am has a waiting list for the first commercial flight to the moon?"

"If I might put in my two cents' worth," said Reinhart. He raised his hand in a routine movement and found to his surprise that it flew up over his head quick as a barnswallow. He pretended to yawn, as if he were stretching. "Ahhh. Excuse me. . . . But you can't quickly get anyone past the idea of death, even with the promise that it will be nullified—which, as you admit, you cannot even yet promise. If you could freeze and revive an animal, say—"

"Has been done," said Streckfuss. "Smith, of London, has frozen hamsters. Half the water in the little rodent brains was ice, the tiny bodies hard and rigid. And zese are mammals, mind you, warm-blooded creatures. Frozen hard as boards. When tawed, the little ahneemals were back on their wheels, revolving merrily, with bright beady little eyes."

Reinhart was victim to an access of sentimentality. His daughter had owned a hamster once. The nimble little bastard had run on his wheel all night. Daytimes he sacked in under a pile of rubbish. If Reinhart got up for a nocturnal pee he could hear that wheel squeaking. Winona eventually loved him to death. Silently she came to Reinhart and opened her fat hand.

"Aw," Reinhart said now. "The cute little devils."

Streckfuss sniffed. *"Chacun à son goût.* Kenyon has frozen dogss to the point of arresting all circulation, stopping zuh hearts for some time, bringing about clinical death. Then he revived the animals successfully."

"Why has this not been publicized?" Reinhart demanded of Sweet.

"A considerable literature is available. Experimentation in cryobiology is by no means new. Hans has been working in the field since the end of World War II."

"Where did you spend the war?" Reinhart stubbornly asked the professor.

"In Europe, of course. Vere else, for goodness sake?"

Reinhart made a gesture of acceptance, and again he was inadequately extravagant: his hands took wing. He must watch that on pain of looking swishy. "Just asking." If Streckfuss' specialty was rejuvenation, then he could be Schatzi from a quarter-century ago and he would not necessarily look older. Some such thought tramped across Reinhart's brain in muddy boots.

Streckfuss was leering at him through pupils of faceted jet beads with highlights in the shape of accents grave and acute. He had abnormally long earlobes, as if they had once begun to melt. Reinhart could not remember this detail about Schatzi.

"I would say," said Reinhart, "that publicity was the answer. I myself knew nothing about this whole subject until I saw you on TV, Bob." He had turned to look at Sweet, too swiftly, spinning on balls of feet like greased bearings, and almost revolved past the target. Whereas he should merely have turned his neck. His body had a will of its own.

Sweet said: "I think this is enough for today, Carl. Suffice it to say that wonders are within reach as of this moment. The situation is in a far more sophisticated state than was the case with aeronautics just prior to the Wright Brothers' lift-off at Kitty Hawk."

"Suda," said Reinhart. He had started to pronounce some other word or phrase. Instead this nonsense sound emerged. It was his own voice all right, and he had felt the breath hiss across his tongue. He proceeded to do it again, with an elaboration: "Suda, Kobe." He had lost control. Admitting which, in a rush of panic heat, he

regained it. "I don't know why I said that." He leered
redly at the others. "Strains of an old song, maybe.
Boopy-doopy-doo." He pretended to be dizzy and seized
Streckfuss' shoulder. Childish-feeling rubbery bones
writhed under his fingers. There was a sensitive nerve-
point beneath the shoulder-cap, if he could find it: would
make him wince and howl.

But the professor threw him off with only a twitch.
"Do not play the fool. Professor Isamu Suda, of the
medical college at Kobe in Japan. We are aware of his
successful experiment."

Again Reinhart's automatic pilot took over. He listened
to himself with amazement. "Professor Suda," said his
own voice, "froze a cat's brain to minus twenty degrees
Centigrade."

Sweet nodded to Streckfuss, and said to Reinhart:
"Yes? Go on."

"That's all I know," said Reinhart, less embarrassed by
now. He had begun to attain the freedom of the man in a
really extreme predicament, so sick, for example, that he
will puke in public. Shame is really anticipatory, whereas
fact is fact. He could not understand how he had gained
the stated information, and thus he felt no responsibility
for it.

Streckfuss spoke in a commanding voice. "Proceed."

"I'm sorry, that's it," Reinhart confessed. "You can't
get blood out of a turnip."

"Oh, you little rogue," Streckfuss said preposterously,
his wildest hair reaching no farther than Reinhart's breast
pocket. "You have been performing your investigations.
You have been pooling our legs, you fonny guy you."

"Wait a minute!" Reinhart cried. "Does the figure 203
mean anything?" He had seen this as if skywritten in the
azure of his mind.

Sweet said: "After two hundred and three days Suda
thawed the cat brain. The electroencephalograms recorded the resumption of normal brain waves."

Reinhart felt his scalp. "Gentlemen, I am nonplussed."

"Well," said Streckfuss, shaking himself within the laboratory coat. "It could be vorse." He padded to what
looked like a closet door, opened it only far enough to
admit his small body, and sidled through.

"What's in there?" Reinhart asked.

Sweet said: "His austere living quarters. An iron cot,
bookshelves, high-intensity reading lamp, a tiny washroom

containing a stall shower. I would give Hans anything he wants. That's it."

Reinhart saw rosy-fingered dawn. "He hypnotized me, didn't he? And planted certain suggestions, which I delivered on cue."

"What difference could it possibly make?" Sweet asked. *"Suda revived the cat brain and the electroencephalograms were virtually normal."*

"You mean it was still thinking? I wonder what about? Who knows what goes through a cat's brain when it is living naturally? I knew a guy once who told me that all cats are by nature schizophrenics. His psychiatrist furnished him with the theory. No doubt it would explain much in the feline temperament, which people sometimes call inscrutable." Reinhart pointed at the shelves bearing the smaller freezing capsules. "Looks as if the professor has got a few animals of his own."

"Hans has never published the results of his own work."

"Are they filled?" Reinhart asked, without much genuine wonder, because he now assumed they were, a small rigid hairy body in each, stiff-whiskered, tight-eyed, perhaps the tip of a yellow canine showing from the sealed lips, only the tail eluding rigor. If you found a deceased rat on the town dump, and you were a boy, or a primitive of any age, you plucked it up by that tapered terminal shoelace and swung it towards a quailing chum. "White mice? Hamsters?"

"Monkeys," said Sweet. "The next step is man."

— 7 —

The characters on the screen were either emotionless or showed some feeling at odds with the circumstances. A bony-faced blonde smiled at a squat brunette who addressed her angrily in a Scandinavian language, a tongue resembling German spoken while orally circulating some soft food, the vowels thus being rendered oval, the consonants bent. A beach full of round flat stones like poker chips, a marbled sky; the subtitles, as always with queer misprints, were flowing in superimposition across the ribs of a derelict skiff at the bottom of the picture: "You see, it is this way with mee. I . . . well . . have never been able to laugh easly—no! That is far from presise—" A large narrow man tramped into view, wearing a thick fisherman's sweater and an eyepatch. The brunette fixed her square shoulders at his clabbered salutation, untranslated, and failed to reply. The blonde wept silently in tight closeup of a face white as a giant aspirin.

"The birds, have you seen them?" read the rubric, beyond which lay a shot of the sea with its multitude of foamy hiccups. Who spoke, eyepatch or deep-voiced girl? The blonde was out of the running: she had had no lines from the outset, yet was the putative star. Had even, without motive, displayed one pale teat earlier on, then both buttocks, which were suddenly bulbous below elongated necks. She had pulled on slacks over no underwear. The brunette had fastened the blonde's brassiere hooks while sucking a cigarette and exuding dialogue rumpled in smoke.

Eunice sat on Reinhart's left, having insisted he precede her into the row. She made a breathy sound at the appearance of the male character, a gasp or cough or hiss. Reinhart had not known her long enough to specify which, nor had he, after an hour's viewing, oriented himself in the picture. He had not done much moviegoing in recent years. He had heard that commercial films were

129

on the verge of showing the act of coition itself. Perhaps this was the night. He hoped he would not snort in shame.

Why had Eunice wanted him on the wrong side of her? While pondering this he missed something that caused the audience to stir as one. A black dog was racing up a bluff above the ocean. The sound track was empty or the equipment had failed, the latter having been a frequent occurrence with the outmoded machinery of the Majestic during Reinhart's term of duty as part-owner. The audience would murmur, growl, and whistle, then stamp its mass foot, which of course led to dangerous structural reverberations. The usher nearest the warning button was supposed to push it and so alert the projectionist, an aged functionary who from time to time even confused the sequence of reels, accidentally defining the work of art as that which had a beginning, an end, and finally a middle. "I preferred it that way," he would assert arrogantly, armed with his sense that they could not afford a better man. He was also a cough-syrup junkie, a codeine-and-terpin-hydrate-head. All you had to do to get a bottle was sign your name, and in fact the old coot sometimes signed Reinhart's, as Reinhart discovered once when trying to buy a ration for a legitimate chest cold. One of the ushers, a lad with coltish eyes and maidenly ways, claimed the projectionist would goose him when, delivering the heavy hexagonal film carriers to the booth, he could not defend himself. "And I don't *like* that," he shrilled, rolling his hips and quitting. Many effeminate persons are not queer: rather they are the prey of queers, so Reinhart had read in a book by Dr. Brill years ago when he had been interested in psychiatry. Reinhart had in fact made discreet inquiries when hiring this usher. "Oh, no," said another boy, already employed, "Ralphie likes his nook-ie." Reinhart encouraged his people to talk straight with him, in their own jargon whenever possible. He posed as just one of the guys. This might have led to disciplinary problems had not business fallen away to the point that there was little for anyone to do except brood on his loneliness amid the vast reaches of the theater and thus welcome the quite rare encounter with the boss who found him. In the last months there was no audience with sufficient sense of itself to protest at breaks in sound and discontinuity of narrative.

Reinhart was led to observe that it is lack of community which makes for peace. Most theorists have it ass-backwards.

At last the dog, in the current offering, barked. Reinhart suspected the silence had been intentional, to bring about a certain dramatic effect. The device worked on Eunice, who grasping presumably at his left hand, which was plastered like an amoeba on the straining Dacron of his thigh, missed and instead found his member, bunched amidst a crotch-tangle of slippery wash-and-wear trousers and stiff white undershorts newly purchased. Squeezed it painfully. This intrusion was so unwarranted that he could not immediately assign it to his credence, and believed he had neglected to pluck out that last steel pin, concealed deep in the excess groin-stitching by Packer #2547, whose printed chit butterflied to the floor when, hopping on one leg, he donned the boxer-style garment with its continuous elastic waist.

The stocky dark woman was pouring wine for someone off camera, and who damnably might remain so for a half an hour without an identity-establishment. The dog was back, now being kicked by the man with the eyepatch, and the subtitles were suddenly slanted in italics: *Hell, of course, is not when you hungre, but—do you remember the Latvian song—*

A grim customer in balaclava helmet and goggles bulleted past on a one-man toboggan.

Reinhart involuntarily laughed aloud, so heartily as soon to infect a few souls widely dispersed and then the mass of the audience, in full diapason from fluty nickering to sousaphone bellow. As it happened what touched Reinhart off was not the picture, which to him was not absurd but irrelevant, but a sudden reflection on this moment, which when joined to a quadrillion others would eventually add up to a destiny. Here he sat, at the end of a day which began with his being thrown out of his home; passed through a laboratory featuring a mad scientist, played by a reputed Swiss, whose ambition was to find a corpse to freeze; to a motion-picture theater in which a large, lush girl whom he scarcely knew interminably clutched his organ of generation.

It was at this sequence that he had laughed, and when the audience joined him for the wrong reasons—if he set a precedent it was invariably unintentional—Eunice let him go.

She proceeded to contribute to the jollity, in a baritone buffola from her deep chest, though her speaking voice was considerably higher. Then the blonde's face appeared, but soon was partially obscured by the back of her head: the old mirror trick. Now raindrops bespattered close-up leaves, but a dry-faced, full-bearded ancient parted them with the rubber tip of his crutch. His nose-hairs were a rich growth. Why had that fad not caught on? Probably because you were nasally sparse-haired until too old to start a trend. Speaking of noses, the blonde at last spoke through hers. "One cannot possible have a motive for wanting to understand unless one is mad." Or at least so went the subtitle.

The blonde bun lay stolidly against her nape. Her pale eyes, out the other side, were fixed forever in the mirror, the camera ceased to crank, the picture was over.

"What devastating experience," groaned Eunice, leaving out the indefinite article, as if in mockery of the subtitles' frailties. The lights came on, and Reinhart winced at her. You got only a coming attraction, consisting tonight, meanly, of illuminated stills, and then the feature, at two fucking seventy-five a head. These art-movie houses did not maintain the incessantly bright screen of the Yahoo pleasure palaces and admitted no patrons during the feature. Until Reinhart was old enough to vote he had never seen a motion picture from the beginning but arrived always in medias res, part of the amusement being in orienting yourself. It could be done in a quarter-hour; known actors played predictable roles, and only a half-dozen plots were then extant.

"Do you think," he asked, modernizing his perspective, "that the dog was an erotic symbol vis-à-vis the girl?"

"I hope not," answered Eunice, hipping her way out the row though with her face at him, "unless as a put-on, Freud being so thoroughly out." She too was squinting with little grape-seed eyes.

In the aisle they intermingled with the throng. The population had got much huskier than that of old, or Reinhart had shrunk. Films outside the common run used to be attended mainly by pale, attenuated men and neurasthenic women with tight-pulled back hair and anteater noses, everybody wearing functional eyeglasses. Within twenty square feet he now saw three men as large as himself, all better-tailored, and one of them was a Negro steering a sepia Venus into him from the left: she was some four feet of leg in white satin pants, the waistband of which gave way only to her tiny, perfect breasts webbed in fishnet, and he was a burnished god in paisley

tunic adorned with bronze medallion and chain. Reinhart
did not mind the new garb when hung on admirable
frames. He had a romantic impulse to seize this pair and
tell them they were beautiful, but supposed it would be
taken for rank patronization. Instead he must take care
that his groin did not brush those shiny high buttocks now
just before him in the press.

Eunice was against his right shoulder, imprisoning his
arm throughout its length, the knuckles against an unresistant mass. The thought that it was her thigh did not
ignite his senses. In truth, he did not know what he was
doing in her company, but since he was here he would
discharge his responsibility.

He turned his head, taking a faceful of hair. Somehow
she got a hand up from below and cleared it, then
managed to slip the fingers between his thick chest and
fat arm, in which he immediately erected some muscle—
good triceps may get silted over in adipose tissue but they
do not dissolve.

"Don't do that," Eunice said sharply, people tried to
look, the colored girl stopped and stiffened, and Reinhart
slid right into her slippery groove. How adamant and
polished. He sucked himself back.

"Do what?" indignantly he demanded.

"Make it hard," said Eunice, grinning into his mouth.
She was either indifferent to publicity or craved it.

However, now that the reference sounded far worse,
their neighbors lost interest and returned, perhaps jealously, to the sort of public privacy once cultivated only by
heedless lovers. Everybody today had his own act; you
used to see more voyeurism, for example, when women
dressed modestly.

"I detest strong men," Eunice elucidated at last. "Violence appalls me, in any form, even the capability of it."

Against his better judgment Reinhart let his arm soften
into a column of fat. "All right," he said, "I don't want to
threaten you. But if we are mugged outside, don't expect
any help."

"You're a groove," Eunice said suddenly. "You had the
courage to laugh. Many would have forgotten this is
Casavini's first comedy."

An Italian name though the dialogue had been in
Swedish. It was news to Reinhart, but he held his tongue.
Suddenly the solid block of crowd disintegrated nonsensi-
cally, like a traffic jam, leaving no reasonable speculation
as to why the late clog, and they passed swiftly, almost at

a run, through the evacuating cloaca of the lobby onto an asphalt plain of snarling engines. By the time they had reached their vehicle, three-quarters of the other cars were already a stream of white and red lights along the highway. Eunice drove, because it was her automobile. "Nice car," Reinhart had said routinely when it was delivered by automation—weirdly came rolling off an elevator precisely opposite the painted line at which they had been directed to wait—in a reinforced-concrete garage around the corner from the Bloor Building. "What make is it?" "I don't know," Eunice had said. "It's some Plymouth or Ford or Buick or something. Look on the glove-compartment door. He gave it to me for graduation."

"Who?"

"My father."

Reinhart now said, hand on driver's door: "Let's have the key."

"It's open." She hurled her pelvis against him. "That's part of my thing. I don't want to keep anybody out of anywhere." When he held the door open she prodded him. "You first." Same thing as in the theater. He didn't get it. She explained: "That's one of the old hangups, and I find it patronizing."

Reinhart said: "Well, *I* find it difficult to slide under the steering wheel, if you want to know." He patted his midsection, forsaking vanity to make a point.

Eunice insinuated her hand under his, squealing: "You turn me on!" She palpitated his belt buckle, then plunged into the car. He plodded around the trunk. The other door was locked. He banged on the window as, obliviously, she started the engine. The handle was torn from his grasp when she backed out. Some sort of joke. She seemed infantile for a college graduate. She accelerated off and turned right, disappearing behind the theater, which was apparently an island surrounded by the parking lot. He turned to await her return. He was now alone on the blacktop, and the theater was already dark.

Now he could no longer hear the engine. Had she stopped somewhere behind? The funny thing was, when he and Sweet got back from the laboratory, she had taken it as pre-established that he and she would spend the evening together. And Bob had given him fifty dollars: "Think of it as the inaugural festivities for your new job." The nature of the job remained unspecified, but Reinhart assumed it would be in the area of promotion, really all the firm could do until the bodies began to come in. Then of course they would sell the freezing process and equipment. He could not believe the nonprofit angle would be permanent, Foundation or no. It was essential to the civilization to deal in money.

Suddenly he saw what had been wrong so far: the offer of a free freeze for the first volunteer. Nobody would believe in a deal in which eternity was handed over gratis. They should not only charge, but name a staggering price utterly beyond the resources of the average man, else they would not be taken seriously. Sweet might have made his bundle in some ruthless fashion—was there any other?—but he had become an impractical visionary.

An art theater in the country was only a recent phenomenon, owing to the rise in the suburban culture-level. Beyond the asphalt lay fields and woods, but there was a tract of medium-priced homes within a quarter mile and no doubt in the daylight one could see the beginning scars of what would soon be a new one encroaching on these meadows. Tonight's moon was the size of a toenail-paring. The pole-top fluorescents had gone off with the marquee lights. Maybe she had been waylaid back there by a pack of young toughs and was being gang-shagged at this moment.

Reinhart began to walk, feeling very chilly. He was over the hill when it came to violence. A man has a right to live in peace after forty. That's what young cops are for. Why wasn't this place patrolled? He continued to walk towards mutilation or death, or, if he failed to turn, straight towards the highway, where he might hitch a ride.

In time of danger fantasies resolved by cynicism are only debilitating. Reinhart was breathless when he got to the other side and his feet were great barges transporting stone down a muddy river. The car was parked, nose out, against the theater wall. His eyes were now habituated to the darkness and he saw Eunice sitting casually at the wheel.

She tooted the horn when he got close and cried out: "Going my way, stud?"

Under his breath he groaned. It was needed, when an older man kept company with a young girl, that he set the style, else you got the humiliating farce portrayed in corny movies, the panting bald-head trying to jitterbug or get kid-jargon through his false teeth, straining his varicose veins on the tennis court opposite the twinkle-toes in the swinging pleated skirt with a glimpse of panty that makes his leathery old hound-dog tongue water.

The fact was that Reinhart had always deplored horseplay in relationships with the other sex.

"I thought you might have got in some trouble back there," said he intelligibly though winded.

"You have a thing about danger outdoors. You have a terrible image of society."

"No," he lied, "I meant a flat tire or other breakdown." He went to the passenger's door again and, ending an annoying, even boring suspense, found it now unlocked.

In he climbed and, ignoring her bare thighs in the dashboard lights, said: "Tell me what you know about Professor Streckfuss."

"I haven't ever seen him. He never leaves the lab, and I never go there."

"Just as well," said Reinhart. Her answering look was searching and sober. Then she started the engine and drove out at a conservative speed.

Reinhart wondered whether he had offended her. He had perhaps forgotten how to talk to unattached girls. Flattery was surely always welcomed, but he would be hampered in its use in the absence of the standard motivation. He really had no wish to get to know her better. He had arrived at that time of life in which he could contemplate certain phenomena without brooding on their possible utility. This was one positive merit of middle age. He had not eaten since that queer chemical lunch at the lab, but he was not hungry now. For the moment he had no wants whatever. When he was younger he had called this state depression, because it had then been a sort of time-out between bouts of aspiration versus capacity. Now one sensed it was a state of morality which must resemble death. Even more valuable to the freezer program than a body which had clinically died of disease or accident, would be a well one.

It had been an overlong day already, and life was more exhausting than ever if it could not even be defined. Eunice drove quietly. Reinhart stole an objective look at her ripe, naked haunches and remembered how much it had meant to him at one time to seduce a girl. To get her to the point. The entry had often been anticlimactic. It was the surrender that mattered, the acquiescence to a superior will. Actually, he had never had such a victory in the supreme sense. He had never conquered a virgin. Someone else had always preceded him, even with Genevieve though she had made an elaborate pretense in the opposite direction, and anyway he married her.

No doubt he would die in that deprivation, but he did not care. Neither had he ever seen the Taj Mahal.

"You want to talk about your marriage?" Eunice suddenly asked him, in, at least by contrast, a loud voice. She kept her eyes on the road and her legs were tense, as usual with woman drivers. If a rabbit started up on the shoulder, she would brake them through the windshield. Reinhart groped for the ends of his seat belt.

She added: "Don't mind me. I'm the bold type." If not as a driver. She had fallen behind the bumper of a very slow car in the far-right lane and apparently settled in there.

Strangely enough, Reinhart found he was not embarrassed by her inquiry. "All right," he said. "I don't see any harm in it, especially in view of the fact that I've been married for almost as many years as you have been alive. That is an experience you are supposed to get used to when you get older. I never have. I mean, knowing someone as an adult with the same consciousness you had at a time when they were still a baby."

Eunice told him sternly: "I don't understand that at all, if you want to know."

"Let me explain if I can. The reason parents don't like to admit their children have grown up is that they knew them as infants."

"That's basic."

"Of course," said Reinhart. "But it is usually thought that people love the idea of dependents. What I am getting at is something else. I have more or less the same consciousness I had at, say, twenty-one, or whenever it was I became an adult. Now I have a son that age."

"How does he dress?" asked Eunice.

"There you are. I find that an odd question. I don't understand the point of view back of it. If you mentioned your father or brother, I would ask, 'What does he do?' "

"I might be putting you on," Eunice said seriously. "You always have to consider that."

"I always do, in fact," lied Reinhart. He saw with satisfaction that the slow car ahead was blinking at an upcoming exit.

"I don't believe I think consciously of being conscious," Eunice stated. "That's one of my hangups."

"I'll tell you this," said Reinhart. "You and Blaine use somewhat the same jargon, and my criticism of it is that it makes everything absolutely orderly. It's all hooks and grooves and bags. In my day we didn't sort things that much. A certain romance has been lost, which Blaine tries to make up for with gaudy costume and social theories designed to shock. I sometimes suspect it is all theater. What worries me is when the play is over."

He found himself relying on her sympathy, perhaps as the result of as arrogant an assumption as that of the stranger on the next bar stool, who assumes for no reason at all that you too are a vegetarian, atheist, or whatever his own persuasion. However, Reinhart was never really offended by the expression of any point of view, so long as its speaker expected no action from him. Perhaps keen observers of humanity could read that message on his face.

"What's your wife like?" Eunice asked.

"God Almighty," said Reinhart. "I got married in 1946." He was still searching with his hands for the seat belts. Now he discovered them wound up to the buckles on little reels. When extended they would not join; his girth was too large. "I wasn't this fat when I got married, though I was never skinny. Before the war I used to work out with weights. Young fellows in those days tried to build themselves up. Most people admired athletes. But I was quite a reader too. I had this idea of being well-rounded. I suppose the Athens of the fifth century B.C. wouldn't mean much to you, but it was a time when, allegedly, kings were philosophers and it was not rare to find a rather poetic sensibility in the body of a gymnast." He stretched his legs out comfortably underneath the dashboard, felt his shoes paw padded wires. "No doubt greatly exaggerated, as these things always are, but the idea has nobility."

"You know my idea of what is obscene?" Eunice asked. "Not sex, but war."

"I am certainly familiar with that theory," Reinhart answered, "and it sounds attractive. But I don't think it could have been sold to some poor devil about to be cremated alive in Auschwitz. I don't believe that growing old makes one wise, but you have survived quite a bit of history by the time you get there, and you remember so many things of which rigid opinions seem the most absurd."

Eunice said: "What I dig about the now music is it *says* something. It speaks to the whole person, in the name of compassion and fraternity and yet is fun at the same time. You know there are lots of people in this world who suffer all alone and are buried in a remote grave like Eleanor Rigby who kept her face in a jar."

Reinhart checked her countenance and saw solemn eyes focused here on the road and there on the lyrical plight of an imaginary personage. As it happened he was familiar with the song referred to, which was a favorite not of Blaine's but of Winona's. His daughter for obvious reasons was attracted to accounts of desolation. Blaine felt the Beatles had sold out when they took up with an Asiatic serenity-peddler who subsequently came to the United States and told a California college audience to respect their parents. Blaine's favorite rock group had next been a very American contingent of what appeared to be, on their album photo, faggot plug-uglies of the type once known as rough trade, led by a dervish whose leather trousers were cut so as to display, or simulate, the brutal swelling of a permanent erection, and whose songs were spasms of rage at those who refused to degenerate themselves in public. However, before long this aggregation turned up on the squarest of TV variety shows, where the MC defanged them by quoting their year's gross, an all-time high, and received the dutiful applause of the stout, eyeglassed audience when he asked for a "hand for these fine youngsters."

Reinhart repeated now what he had said then: "What matters most to a man, you will find, is his profession. I say encourage Negroes to become doctors and lawyers and the race problem will vanish overnight."

Blaine had replied with some standard abuse, but Eunice, who was after all somewhat older and, more importantly, worked at a job, pointed out that it might not be that easy. "I mean, the blacks have had it with the whole Western-civilization bag. I mean, I don't altogether grasp the concept with my honky hangup—it's completely phony to believe you can think black if you are white and evil to try—but that's as close as you can come in words because the English language is hopelessly corrupted."

Reinhart thought about that, and also about the possibility that she might be hopelessly insane. "But isn't it the only one we have here?" he asked, and turned the other way and stared out the window.

A built-up area had begun to accumulate on either side of the road, country branches of urban department stores, the covered arenas of discount houses, dispensing stations of soft ice cream, actually made with milk and expanded with compressed air. Another favorite of Winona's. Reinhart missed his daughter, which for him meant a feeling of unbearable tenderness and not an actual craving to be in her presence.

"I used to make it with this spade," Eunice said ruminatively, "and he dressed African." Quite tendentiously she went on: "It is often forgotten or never known that Africa is an immense continent, and the people of one area may be separated from those of another by thousands of miles and be as different as Finns are from the Portuguese."

"As it happens," Reinhart noted, "I *was* aware of that. I probably saw the same TV special that you did."

This pricked her. "I have never been uptight about the blacks," she said reprovingly.

"Why?" he asked as a wiseguy. "Because they are really brown?"

Eunice ignored this. "I used to have to meet him secretly," said she, "so as not to humiliate him. The whole situation is reversed from what I gather it used to be. Now it is we honkies who are considered inferior and must keep our place."

"The whole question of color is hard to figure out," Reinhart said without satirical intent. "I have never understood why Orientals are called yellow. I have never laid eyes on a Chinese or Japanese who came anywhere near that description. It doesn't make any sense at all." He cleared his throat resentfully. "Like so many other things you have heard for years and for which you can never find the source. My parents were always terrified of drafts. My dad would invariably develop a cold if one blew on him for three minutes, if he were in some sort of enclosure. On the other hand, he could cut grass or rake leaves all day in a stiff wind, which he found invigorating. What did this mean?"

He glanced at Eunice and added: "You may think I'm a running dog of the Establishment, but I have always questioned things." He had never seen such a dedicated driver as she, with fixed eyes and rigid limbs. When he drove with a passenger he was always flicking his head back and forth; he was even capable of swiveling his neck to converse with the back seat. Gen hated that practice, though Reinhart had a flawless insurance record. Also he was even more deft at manipulating a motor vehicle when half drunk, putting the lie to yet another cherished piece of general opinion.

"Now," he said, "scientists have definitely proved that colds come only from association with other people, that is, from germs so contracted. In the absence of such germs—"

"Viruses," said Eunice. The interruption astonished him. He had been certain she was not listening. Actually she was the normal sporadic auditor. Most people were incapable of listening to anything continuously, Reinhart had been made aware, even praise, hence the utility of filler, which perhaps was her misidentification of his current topic. Solid columns on race riots, mass murders, peace talks, then at the bottom of the page a dispatch from Nowheresville, Ark., to the effect that a gasoline tanker collided with a farmer's truckful of eggs; result: an omelette a hundred yards in diameter.

"Go on," she said, "make your point."

"Well," Reinhart admitted, "it's hardly mine. Just let me say that volunteers have sat with their bare feet in ice water all day, others have been exposed, naked, to chilling temperatures and cold drafts. None of these people contracted colds. Whereas individuals maintained in complete comfort, but in close proximity to others with stuffed noses, etcetera, came down with it. Yet the remarkable thing is that my dad really would catch a cold from a draft. I have observed that personally many times. Why? Ideas are weapons, as they used to say during World War II. One of these ideas, for example, was that the Japanese were little yellow-skinned monkeyfaces."

"My spade was a third-degree black belt in karate."

"Bob Sweet does karate too. For all I know he studied it in Japan."

"I never heard that about Bob," Eunice said sullenly. "But it doesn't sound anything like him. He's not well at all."

"You're kidding."

"Streckfuss keeps him alive," Eunice stated with stress. "But you can't turn back the clock, even with cellular therapy. Or at least *I* don't think so. Of course it's easy for me to say because I'm young, young, young!" She sang the last clause.

Then why don't you drive faster? Reinhart wanted to say. She was simply being spiteful, for the usual motives. Sweet was both her boss and elder.

He said instead: "Bob is a remarkable guy."

"Oh, I'm not putting him down really. But he's forty-*five*. Isn't it about time he grew up?"

"Look here, young lady," Reinhart spoke in real indignation, which however he wanted her to assume was mock—even though he had no designs on her person—"I'll have you know I am almost that age myself."

"But do you hang out in discothèques and do you half kill yourself at tennis and give demonstrations in water-skiing and otherwise compete with the kids?"

"I thought you said he wasn't well."

"Because of stuff like that."

"Eunice, has it ever been pointed out to you that you don't speak with logic? You just said that it did not sound like Bob to do karate, whereas it is all the more likely in view of what you tell me."

Eunice speeded up slightly, reminding Reinhart that he was still in the car. "When it comes to Bob," she said, "I am very sensitive. He has embarrassed me more than once. If he has taken up karate, I know why. It's because of that black I told you about. Oh, I could stand it if he merely wanted to ball me. That's a hangup of his generation." Reinhart appreciated the nicety; she could have said "your."

In return he said: "That should not offend you, true or not. You are an attractive girl."

She shrugged with her head. "So. O.K. But I meant that old Freudian bag. Bob was in analysis for years, with various shrinks."

"There is nothing abnormal or perverted about the desire of an older man," Reinhart asserted firmly, "for a younger girl. It is recognized as quite commonplace in many cultures. There is a good practical reason for it. If the desire is for flesh, then it is reasonable to want the flesh to be as lively as possible. In compensation, older women have generally a more generous spirit and a greater breadth of understanding." But he did not wish to be rude to present company. "I find it easy to talk to you, but that is not always the case." And Genevieve, the "older" woman he knew best, was hardly generous but was in perfect physical shape.

"Don't get me wrong," Eunice said. "I think you can swing all your life. I just don't dig this desperate scene."

"I doubt whether we should go on talking like this," Reinhart said. "Bob is my friend and our employer." Nevertheless he was enjoying it to the hilt. Having firmly accepted Sweet as a hero, he was now in a position to hear some dirt about him. So far her implications had been merely frivolous. Sweet had described her as a nymphomaniac, Reinhart reminded himself. It was her turn. Reinhart kept the advantage of having only lately joined the organization and thus was being contested for by both sides. He could of course give no encouragement to the lower echelons. Yet a physically attractive girl, whatever her rank in the power structure, had a certain force, even if you did not literally care to enjoy her favors. That was a curious thing. Reinhart certainly wanted Eunice to think well of him.

No, to be honest, he wanted her to desire him sexually. In the old days Reinhart's wish had been that a girl understand that he wanted her. One might have been somewhat wary of the female as aggressor—though taking her, of course, if she appealed. But only in recent years had he known an inclination to be—well, baldly, raped was probably the word. With this recognition he also understood that for him one's forties were not a romantic but rather a surrealistic era. Hopeless enough for a man of his years to get any feasible piece without paying for it. There was a certain womanish element in a man's middle age.

"Oh," said Eunice, "I've told him all this to his face. Hypocrisy has never been my thing. What I don't dig is this idea of his that he should want to make out with me, like it's some kind of law."

"I don't understand that at all," Reinhart confessed.

"Isn't that the Freudian cop-out? You are supposed to want to, so you can admit it and then free yourself from it and blow your mind?"

Trying to understand, Reinhart peered at her and saw a glossy longitudinal streak of what was evidently a tear which had lately passed that way, so diminishing itself as to be dropless when it reached the round, soft chin. At first he thought she must be allergic to some pollen currently on tour with the wind, but naturally the car was air-conditioned.

"Can you believe it?" he said. "Once, years ago, I thought of going into psychiatry as a career." He saw she was now definitely weeping. "I'm sorry. Did I say something wrong? I'm sure Bob has not intended to be obnoxious to you. These big operators sometimes forget that those of us in more modest positions in life are often oversensitive. We have less to think about outside ourselves. Rushing to drive through another big deal, they don't always notice they have bowled someone over."

She continued to sob and drive on. Since he had last

noticed the terrain they had left the highway and were now on a city street, in fact amidst an instant slum. Even a slow car makes quick transitions.

"Hey," he said, "we haven't eaten yet. God, that was a long movie. You can call me a Philistine but frankly I think it could have used some editing." Eunice had had some reason for wanting to see the film before dinner. What she had against Sweet might be merely that he had not made a pass at her. If she were nymphomaniacal that sort of neglect would hurt. But other than a few random gestures, the major one of which was her clutching his fly, obviously by accident and in oblivion, Reinhart had seen no evidence of the alleged disposition. Or had she heard, through the open intercom, Sweet apply the term to her? That was indeed cruel. Reinhart had sensed from the first that Sweet was a sadist, like many other powerful personages. By which he did not mean a figure in a pair of spurred boots and flicking a blacksnake whip, but rather a man who would use his inferiors by whim. The attractive thing about power was precisely that it tended to corrupt, else you had a thoroughly synthetic situation controlled by automata with their unsmirchable mechanical consciences.

At last Eunice shook her head and its twenty pounds of hair. Her large breasts nudged the steering wheel as she took the kind of breath that traditionally straightens one out.

"I guess you think I'm a drag too," said she.

Reinhart groaned compassionately. "Aw, don't say things like that. I don't know when I've had such a thoroughly pleasant evening. You know, I felt quite proud to be seen at the theater in your company, a lovely girl like you. I'll bet I was envied by many." It had just dawned on him that not only middle-aged flops like himself felt inadequate. A sense of losing was not exclusive to actual losers. One assumes the other guy is firmly in the saddle, but he may be a millionaire dying of cancer.

"What's that mean?" Eunice asked flatly. "Please don't put me on. If you don't want to fuck, just say so. I'll survive."

"But will I?" Reinhart managed to say lightly though his ears were revolving. He wondered why he had misheard. But what else could it be? Words were everywhere devalued now. Blaine habitually referred to anyone who held public office in terms which until only recently were rather technical labels for particular perversions.

"I can't get turned on by subtlety," she said. "You know, that creepy sort of stuff you see in old movies on TV, weird little looks, touches of the hand, candlelight and wine with some pimpy waiter grinning at the loving couple. Then a long, disgusting display of mouths pressed together. I actually think that is far more indecent than if they showed them going down on each other."

"You do?" Reinhart said politely. He was the sort who felt an obligation to respond fairly frequently when being addressed, with affirmative murmurs and rhetorical questions, but admired the man who could listen in serene silence and yet convey the impression of sympathetic interest.

Had she really said *going down?* Perhaps it had a different meaning nowadays. No, the context had been appropriate. But it was hard to be startled for long by nonchalance. He was always nervous on the way to Gloria's, but settled down when she shucked her clothes in that routine style of a whore. Once when her air-conditioner was on the fritz she had met him at the door barebreasted and it seemed the most natural thing in the world. He was not even impelled to stare at them.

"It'll have to be your place," Eunice said. "I don't want to go home. He's the kind who likes to watch, in case you didn't know. Maybe that shouldn't bug me, but I am basically quite conservative."

"Are you married?" Reinhart asked, already shaking his head. "I didn't know that. I don't like it. Really, Eunice, I just thought of this little excursion as a friendly thing between colleagues. I didn't pay any attention to what Bob said, believe me. I intend to go back to my wife when permitted. I'm too tired to begin anything new, especially dodging a husband."

Eunice laughed shrilly, almost whinnying, and turned a corner with flailing arms. "I live at home."

"Doesn't everybody?" In fact, he himself did not at the moment.

"I'm not married. Did he tell you I was? What a hangup he has."

"No," said Reinhart. Sweet was using him in some way, then. He had urged Reinhart to take her out. Perhaps it was not perverse, though. Maybe he was tired of her and trying to arrange her disposal in a manner that could be seen as humane. Mistresses, Reinhart had heard, were often tougher to change than wives, because legality did not enter the picture.

"Now I get it," Eunice said. "He thought you would be harmless."

True enough, but of course it hurt. Reinhart said, without conviction: "I'm old enough not to have to prove I am a man. That is a great relief, though it may indicate a lack of ambition. Whenever I begin to think otherwise, I feel my stomach rolling over my belt and my feet ache from carrying all this weight around. Have you heard that thing about inside every fat man is a skinny fellow trying to get out? Not correct in my case. My skeleton is glad to hide." Yet for the first time he had begun to feel a twinge of real desire for her. It was, for a change, born out of pity rather than envy.

"Tell me," she said, "about my father when he was young. You said you went to school with him."

Kooky as she was, she could have been joking in a cryptic way. Reinhart had a lifelong horror of being caught flatfooted by some unusual piece of information and then being jeered at when he gave it credence. The thing to do, as in most inchoate situations, was to rely on the Oriental mask of inscrutability.

So he explained in a style so literal as almost to be pussyfooting. "I just ran into him by accident last week, hadn't seen him in years. We weren't close in school, but I certainly never beat him up as he claims. He is thinking of some of the other guys."

"Oh, that's great!" cried Eunice. "That's fabulous. Tell me all about it. Was he hurt? Did he cry?"

– 8 –

When Reinhart had definitely established the fact that
Eunice was Sweet's daughter he refused, on principle, to
engage in further conversation pertaining to or reflecting
on that relationship. She grew sullen and at last began to
drive on the verge of recklessness, though not with what
could be called youthful zest and still not rapidly. Her
style was more like that of an oldster at the wheel, whose
distance gauges had seen better days. She almost
sideswiped a parked car or two, and taking one corner
scraped both left inside and right outside curbs, using all
of the available roadway, and it was not a one-way street.

They were now in one of those secondary business
districts, halfway into downtown, of closed shops which
yet kept their signs alight.

"Take the next right," Reinhart said. "I'm staying at
the YMCA."

He did not mind her knowing that now; not with what
he knew about her. He would dine alone in the Y cafeteria, if still open, or catch a hamburger special at a
nearby greasy spoon attended by a garrulous counterman.
Why Sweet and his daughter abused each other psycho-
pathically was none of his affair. He intended to stick to
business from now on.

He saw a drunken derelict, the emaciated, Christ-
bearded, skull-eyed sort whose stride was a rhythmic fall
inhibited at the last possible moment by the quick thrust
of a toe, from which he then proceeded to plunge again,
ad infinitum. Now there was a man they could freeze for
the price of a pint of muscatel. He wondered whether
Sweet had thought of him. Or maniacs, in institutions,
whose responsible kin would release them legally, in compassion or convenience. Persons on the point of suicide.
How could you reach them? Set up a phone number to
call, like the Alcoholics Anonymous hot line.

Eunice took a sharp left, into a narrow alleyway. Her underlip was still outthrust. Behind the thick façade of the buildings the passage entered a rectangular parking lot full of cars, some in motion, some at rest, and more of the former than the latter.

She stopped the automobile in an arbitrary situation and abandoned it briskly as if it were about to burst into flame. Reinhart followed suit, stamping his feet to restore lubrication to his joints, which stiffened up on long rides like those of a much older individual. The familiar stifling heat came up from the lot to strike his face, like the handle of a rake on whose tines you have stepped. Illumination was provided by many bare bulbs surrounding and also intermingling with the painted letters on a sign over a flight of concrete steps descending to a subterranean doorway. THE GASTROINTESTINAL SYSTEM said the sign and the doorway was modeled in an uncomfortably evocative form, the jamb rounded, the door itself consisting of two leaves meeting in a center cleft and radiating painted stress or pursing lines of a compressed sphincter. Unless one was physician, deviate, or contortionist he rarely saw a rectum, yet knew how it looked even in a giant representation constructed of alien materials.

Having entered, they were in a colonic passage lined with rippling pink plastic. Reinhart paid seven-fifty in entrance fees to a barbarously coiffed girl behind a grilled window let into this wall. There was nothing hokey or stylish about the way they collected money or the iron bars. A large noncommittal fellow, wearing a judo outfit, pressed a little rubber stamp onto the backs of their left hands. Reinhart saw a vague, fleeting impression fading into the fat on his, but no ink.

"You didn't get me," he said, but the man amiably ignored him.

Eunice said: "It's ultraviolet," and placed her hand beneath a bullet-lamp jutting from the wall. The date appeared magically on her flesh in greenish-yellow glow.

"What's he, the bouncer?" Reinhart whispered as they proceeded.

"Yes," she answered. "I just hate this place, but it happens to be where it's at."

"What?"

"I wish I knew," she said. Suddenly they were among many heads of hair, most of them below Reinhart's chin so that he seemed to be wading neck-deep in a streamful of swimming beaver. Luckily Eunice was tall enough to be seen. Reinhart was afraid to enjoy his frottage with small round bodies on pain of identifying them as boys'. The one currently under his nose smelled like pizza. He could not tell whether it particularly was coming or going, or the crowd in general, for that matter. But the pressure was soft and undemanding, and though some sounds were strident he could identify no malignancy.

He made way with his hands, feeling such surfaces as leather, real and fake, and sheepskin. He saw few faces and no eyes. And what he took as heads might have been sometimes beards and moustaches or even feathers, pelts.

At last he reached the end of the Large Intestine and the entrance to a large, amorphous room where Eunice stood gazing at the crowd which filled it in intermittent flashes of light alternating with a more startling blackout that wiped everyone from view.

He said to Eunice, who was there and gone by turns— it was queer to address a person under such conditions— "You have pulled a fast one. I'm no discothèque swinger."

"Neither am I," she said fervently. "I go around in a dream since the assassinations. This country's going to explode, and nobody's doing a damn thing about it. If you go peepee, buy me a joint, willya?"

"Huh?"

"There is always somebody selling sticks of pot in the men's toilet," she explained, her white face disappearing in mid-sentence.

"That would make a swell impression on Bob," said Reinhart. "Take his daughter out and feed her marijuana. Come on, Eunice." He laughed hopefully. "This is a big act of yours; isn't it? I've seen you at the desk. You're a sensible working girl. This is all clothes and talk. I could match it with now-forgotten stunts of my own era: drinking at college dances, driving the old man's car sixty miles an hour while standing outside on the running board— they had a hand throttle then that you could pull out and leave there, a pretty murderous practice, you'd reach in through the window and steer. There were guys who would get crazy drunk and play Russian roulette with three chambers filled."

"We can't even get a decent gun-control law," Eunice wailed.

"I suppose a registered gun can't kill anybody," Reinhart asked ironically. What a pointless discussion. He should leave her there and return to his monastic bed at the Y.

"I'm hungry suddenly," she said.

"Can you eat here?"

"Not here, in the Cecum. The restaurant part is called the Stomach."

"Cute," said Reinhart because he thought he should.

"I hate it," said Eunice. "I detest cleverness in words, I would love a restaurant called Restaurant. I used to have a puppy and called him Dog."

Yet you don't say Daddy, Reinhart was about to point out, but she was in motion again. He called out: "Don't go too fast or I'll lose you in the periods of darkness, which seem to be getting longer."

Still no music. What were these people doing? She took his hand. Then colored lights began to stream from the ceiling and flow down the walls, accompanied by an electric drone. The floor, where Reinhart could see it, looked metallic. The human-tissuelike walls began to undulate. A dais made itself slowly known with back-lighting. On it were four lumpy silhouettes, one of which developed four limbs in a spotlight and screamed, in a spray of spittle: "Suck my nose! Eat my snot! Lick my armpits, and I will tell you, I will tell you, of babeh will I tell you, love ain't what, love ain't what you thought, it ain't what you thought when you puked your scum and burned our hearts, it ain't what—"

Reinhart poked his nose into Eunice's ear—neither was her hair precisely fragrant: what became of the dab of perfume at the temples which had been traditional among womankind?—and said: "I can see why they don't serve meals in here."

"Don't mind that," she shouted back. "Those lyrics refer to pot and LSD and napalm, and not what they actually say."

"Why?" he cried. "Why don't they just say it then?"

"Because they're cop-outs, that's why," screamed Eunice. "The Chancres have a big recording contract. They are Establishment now. Fuck them. Let's go and feed."

Reinhart's assumption proved incorrect: the Chancres' ranting was piped into the Stomach, regardless of its references, which continued to be nauseating, but after a time only by formal definition. The rhythm, the persistent drum-thud and electrical moan soon anesthetized the lyrics and they sleepwalked through the infinite repetitions. The Stomach was a more standard roomful of booths and tables and lighted now and again with bare bulbs mounted on a wall of fake brick. There were also candles placed

on reversed coffee cups, a cunning idea, though it would
have made better sense, Reinhart believed, to put them in
the bowl of the cups to catch more wax.

Eunice had led him through a queue of passive persons
to an empty booth. She had inherited Bob's authoritative
manner in public. Another fellow wearing a Japanese
fighting suit appeared and said pleasantly to Reinhart:
"You can't have this. People have waited in line."

Eunice said to him, with calm ferocity: "Eat me,
man."

He walked away, rubbing his chin with the exaggerated
knobbed knuckles of his right fist. He was only about five
feet six or seven and slightly built. They must rely on the
psychological effect of their gear, thought Reinhart.
Bouncers used to be his own size or larger and with
fearsome countenances. But karate got publicity everywhere these days because of its exotic cries and spectacles. Reinhart had watched a midget break a brick with
his fingers on TV, emitting a hiss of low density. "But
isn't it essentially *aggressive?*" asked the MC, with socially
concerned eyebrows. "Certainly not," said the dwarf. "If I
can do it, a woman can do it."

There was everywhere a tendency to ask irrelevant
questions, matched by a determination to answer different
ones equally ungermane. Reinhart studied the menu.
Things were getting back to normal. There were catsup
blobs and a shred of meat stuck to the card, and printed
on it were the designations of seven kinds of solid steak as
well as chopped, sliced, cubed, shredded, and pounded
versions of the same, in addition to the specialty of the
house: Stomach Steak.

A fifteen-year-old girl stood at Reinhart's elbow, naked
from waist down. He was scared to look directly at her.

Eunice ordered: "Stomach Steak sandwich on white,
French fries, large Coke."

Now Reinhart looked at the waitress and saw she was
at least thirty-five years old but small and with long black
hair. She wore a black turtleneck sweater, armless, and a
bikini bottom. She had flat breasts, slender hips, and
pouches under her eyes.

She said: "And you, baby?"

"Join me in a drink?" Reinhart asked Eunice.

"We don't sell hard stuff," said the waitress. "Don't put
me on."

Eunice added that her steak must be *very* well done,
and Reinhart played a game of asking for rare gastro-

nomic creations like Swiss on rye, scrambled eggs, vegetable soup, and so on, until the waitress was fed up and took her leave. "OK," he shouted at her twitching little bottom, "chopped steak."

"You do a pretty fair put-on yourself," Eunice noted with a certain admiration.

"Necessity," he admitted candidly. One thing could be said for Eunice: she elicited from him no falsity in the service of pride. "Between my teeth and my stomach there's not much I can eat with impunity. . . . So you're Bob's daughter," he found himself saying in defiance. "I can't get over that."

"I wish I could." Eunice squeezed the plastic container of mustard, shaped like a tube of house-caulking, stercoraceously encrusted at the nozzle. The one for catsup was a big red replica of a tomato, smeared with maroon. Reinhart flicked away some spilled sugar and put his forearms down. He hadn't got rid of it all and felt a sandy grating.

"I guess your complaint is that he doesn't understand you," he said. "Same old story. Nothing new today except that everybody's more vocal. I wonder if that's a gain? I'm pretty tired of propaganda from any side. I wonder if life really should not be hopeless as a condition of normalcy." He wondered if that was really what he meant.

"Bob got custody of me. My mother lives in Hungary. She ran away with a defector during the Cold War—actually, by the old definition, a traitor. He was a rocket engineer." Eunice looked bored. "Bob is a fascist. He is connected with the military-industrial complex. The CIA subsidizes the Cryon Foundation."

"I thought they pulled out of that sort of thing."

"Well, they *would* subsidize it if they were still doing it. Hey, I forgot to order potato chips."

"No, you didn't," Reinhart said. "Oh no, that was French fries."

"I want them both."

How infantile she was.

She screamed and pounded on the table, and in fear he said: "OK, OK."

She asked: "Do you think I'm putting you on?"

Reinhart had a burst of inspiration. "Only when you cry," he said.

She was staring into his eyes. "I dig you," she said.

This embarrassed him, of course. What he actually wanted was not to be here at all, to twist a magic ring

and wake up somewhere else. Reinhart took no position
on the question of Shakespeare's identity, but he did hold
with the theory that fatso Hamlet spoke literally in wishing his too solid flesh would resolve itself into a dew.

Eunice still stared admiringly or perhaps merely near-
sightedly at him. She apparently expected something. He
turned his head away and pawed the ground in a shit-
kicking maneuver. And then it was he saw his son.

Blaine was moving amid a unisex group settling into a
booth across the room. The light was poor but Reinhart
would know him anywhere now with that plucked head.
With the naked neck he resembled a baby vulture. Reinhart blew out his and Eunice's candle. "Fire upsets me,"
he said. "With its mindless consumption. Out, I say, out,
brief candle."

"You're out of sight," Eunice said with unwitting sense.
The young-bodied waitress with the old face swooped in
and slid their dishes to them: two Stomach Steak sandwiches on dead-white, gummy-textured bread. French
fries. Two large Cokes. Eunice squeezed a flood of catsup
over every available surface. Reinhart salted down his
meat and, taking a bite, identified it as more or less
uniform cartilage. Eunice was chomping away, her eyes
crossing with every bite.

Reinhart stole a look at Blaine from behind the decora-
tive flange that made the booth round-shouldered. As bad
luck would have it, his son sat on the outside of the party
and persons had suddenly ceased to walk between them.
Fate had arranged a clear field of vision. Blaine might
glance across at any moment. The nearest wall bulbs were
close enough to illuminate Reinhart but too far away to
extinguish unobtrusively. Reinhart was within his rights to
be here and with a female friend. Blaine's mother after
all had thrown him out of the house. Yet no father likes a
son to catch him with a strange woman. Something deeper in this than loyalty to wife and mother, bearing emotional similarity perhaps to one's distaste to be seen in the
nude by his offspring. When Blaine was ten or twelve
years younger he used to burst in on Reinhart in the
bathtub and grin inscrutably.

The other reason Reinhart had for now wishing to
avoid him was more generous: this was Blaine's kind of
place and his father did not wish to infringe upon his
privacy in it. In truth he did not want to know Blaine out
of the house. They were not the kind of people who, had
they not been related, would have been friends. This had

been true in all of Reinhart's familial arrangements since birth.

When Reinhart next saw Eunice's plate only a smear of red marked where her food had been.

She followed his eyes and said: "That's the way I am. I might not eat again for twenty-four hours." Swallowed the rest of her Coke in a rush of chipped ice.

Reinhart pushed his plate away. "Turns out I am off my feed," he said. "Let's get the check and blow."

Growing more self-congratulatory than ever, she shook all of her hair and stared arrogantly around the room. At least the type of woman who was overfond of her own vivacity had not vanished.

If Reinhart had correctly sized up that little waitress he would never see her again without a heroic search. By nature he was suited for the kind of restaurant depicted in the old drawing-room comedies he admired, the obsequiously attendant maître d'hôtel in the dinner jacket, et al., but had lived his life in hashhouses with indifferent if not insolent help. Even now with Sweet's fifty clams in the kitty and backed up by Maw's five grand on deposit. He could have dined at L'Etable de Cochons, where local debutantes were always being feted. Well, next time.

Thinking which he realized that all in all, and in a weird way, he was enjoying the company of Eunice. Bob had no doubt trusted him to keep her out of trouble, while the nympho talk was designed to maintain his interest. Sooner or later Reinhart found that sense still reigned, back of puzzling façades. People were basically the same as ever. They just said more today.

Eunice cried: "Hey, I see somebody I know." She slid from the booth and started across towards Blaine, of course, and Reinhart's fat was in the fire.

So came he to hide in the toilet, having got there in a wounded-animal progress which however seemed to attract no attention from the crowd of young persons oblivious to all but their own costumes. But two of those karate-clad attendants were inside the men's room, and he abruptly straightened up.

"It was the roundhouse kick," one was saying. "Perfect focus. Then a *shuto* to the neck, quick turn and—"

"Did they allow contact?" asked the other.

"Not to the face, but none of the lower belts had any control and were slaughtering one another."

"How'd the trophies look?"

"Cheap. It was a crappy tournament. But the demonstrations were good. You know Hojiwara?"

"The *sensei* at the Midtown Y?"

"He blocked arrows shot at him. Then broke five boards with a *nukite*. That shook up Kim, you know, the Korean who has his own *dojo?* He was sitting there sneering. He can break eight boards with a *shuto* or *empi* or five with his head, but when Hojiwara went through them with his fingertips Kim like to shit."

Reinhart, standing at a stall, loosened his belt with the other hand. He had either got fatter, while eating virtually nothing all day, or was bloated with emptiness. It had been years since he was able to see his member in that stance. He still thought of the Japs as enemies in the late war. Funny how their hand-to-hand techniques were now popular. The old movies always showed a little treacherous slant-eyed judo man being eventually defeated by the honest one-two of the brawny American boxer with the Irish face.

As he rinsed his hands the karate men left and an old-fashioned-looking young fellow entered, wearing an Ivy League sack suit, regimental tie, black wingtip shoes, short sideburns. Reinhart was delighted to see an example of a type he had supposed to be deplorably dead. Clean-cut chap, neat to a fault. Washed a pair of already impeccable hands, scornfully eschewed the stained roller towel, and dried them on a very white breast-pocket handkerchief.

Reinhart cautiously opened the toilet door and, peeping out, saw an oncoming Blaine within ten feet. He backtracked rapidly into a booth and, locking it, crouched there. He heard the rush of air as his son entered.

"Hi, man," said Blaine's voice.

Nobody else was available but the Ivy League type, and therefore it had to be he who replied: "Five."

"Shit, man, that's high."

"Gimme the bread or fuck off."

"I'm not saying I won't," said Blaine. A rustle. Reinhart essayed a look over the door of the booth. He saw the back of Blaine's head and half the Ivy League face with a white parting of hair and one hazel eye. Which, flickering, saw him. The suited youth pushed Blaine violently. "You fink bastard," he said. "I thought that slob looked like a bull." Blaine's back struck the door in front of Reinhart, who now had hooked his chin over it and got a vibration in his Adam's apple.

Ivy League dashed for the exit, but the returning ka-rate men appeared when he had a yard still to go. They wore those Nipponese rubber sandals.

"Wait a minute, you guys!"

"I thought we warned you a couple times," said one bouncer. He extended his right foot behind him and bent his left knee. The well-dressed fellow shuffled backwards.

"Come on, you guys, I got the message."

The bouncer pursued him in a strange dragging walk, in which his erect trunk and horizontal shoulder line did not alter. His fists were closed and held against the body, one high and one low.

"You won't do it to me again," said the Ivy Leaguer. He brought a knife from the flapped pocket of his pin-striped jacket, switching open the blade en route.

His inexorable pursuer took another gliding step, re-maining noncommittal, but the other bouncer smiled radi-antly. He took from his belt two slender sticks joined top to top by eight inches of cord. Holding one, whirling the other through the air in a lateral figure-of-eight, he envel-oped the thrusting knife in an abstract design of motion terminating in a soft report as the rod struck the wrist. The knife fell skittering on the concrete.

Blaine's back was heaving against the booth. Behind it his father took the emergency measure that had always served him at moments of violence: absolute paralysis. Only the eyeballs moved. If you are good enough at it you will be taken for a boulder and go unnoticed.

"You don't learn," said the bouncer in the stylized stance. "You just don't learn."

"Then call the bulls. There's one in the toilet. Help me, man!" cried the fellow in the natural-shouldered suit, staring at Reinhart's face. "I got my rights to protection." His eyes definitely showed anguish. He was rather pathet-ic as any creature at bay.

"You peddle shit in here and you pull a concealed weapon. Man, I don't know what you could be thinking of," said the praying-mantis bouncer with a kind of gleeful regret. Then he kicked him once high in the vest and when the head bowed over he caught the chin on an upthrust elbow and the groin on a lifting knee. As the victim descended from this assault he was struck at least thrice by blurred fists on snapping wrists. When he lay upon the floor the security-man leaped onto his face.

The other bouncer turned to look at Blaine, who quickly threw him two wispy cigarettes and, crossing his arms and compressing his chin, sank to the concrete and made himself into an unresistant ball.

"Don't you want to see my flying kick?" asked the disappointed enforcer. He waded over Blaine and handed Reinhart the reefers, as they were once termed.

Reinhart shook his head. "I'm not a cop. I'm just a patron."

So the other bouncer went through the pockets of the recumbent pusher, found a lighter, and the two lit up. Reinhart thought it amazing that athletes would smoke marijuana. He sat down on the closed toilet, from which situation he could see part of Blaine's body under the door.

Before long the bouncers' trade-talk conversation went out of the men's room. Blaine stirred and became a pair of feet in the familiar boots of reversed cowhide. Reinhart rose and peeped out. Blaine was searching the unconscious pusher. But he seemed to find nothing and left without a glance towards the booth. He was wearing a blue military tunic with black frogs. How easily the young passed through experiences nowadays.

Two other costumed youths came in, had a piss, and left, oblivious to the fallen. At last Reinhart stepped out, ran some water into cupped hands, and threw it into the gory face of the man on the floor. After an instant of tentative awakening, the victim groaned, flung his arms out dramatically, and after a single convulsive jerk seemed to die. Reinhart kneeled and was on the point of some test of vitality, rolling back an eyelid or the like, when the pusher struck him violently, leaped half-erect, and dashed out the door.

End of episode. When Reinhart emerged from the men's room his presence was still unknown to Blaine, but he no longer cared. His son buying marijuana. But actually that bothered him less than Blaine's demonstrated ability to handle himself under stress. He had never learned that from his old man. It made Reinhart feel very rotten indeed, totally useless. He might otherwise have come to Blaine's aid, and both of them would have been beaten savagely and thus reunited in blood. Such sentimental speculations had gone through Reinhart's head in that instant in which the bouncer had advanced on Blaine, as well as the normal disinclination to get hurt.

Blaine certainly lived in a different world, which Reinhart contrasted not to his own current one but that of his own teens and early twenties. There had been then quite as much violence, but it seemed to have more effect.

The pusher apparently was an old hand at being punished by these karate men, and, for their side, they did not have him arrested. The performance would no doubt be repeated soon again. Why were none of the principals bored?

Over the P.A. system continued the same tune that had begun when Reinhart and Eunice had entered the Gastrointestinal System. The lead Chancre was still screaming: "Oh babeh I will tell you. . ." How long could they keep that up? Not only the Chancres, who no doubt by design did not seem true persons, but the other people, these organisms in human form. When Reinhart was younger he had sought control over experience, basic to which was an escape from imposed rituals, like church, rigid political credos, and social biases. The object was not to repeat anything compulsively.

Reinhart looked around for the pusher. He would have liked to ask him a few things. He had, however, no questions for Blaine, who in many earlier colloquies had explained that marijuana and the stronger hallucinogens were needed because his, Reinhart's, generation had mortified human consciousness. How could you talk to a boy whose vocabulary contained only collective nouns? There was more hope for the pusher, who was an outright criminal and so, presumably, his own man, out to make a buck and not change the quality of life. Yet he too was a repeater.

When Reinhart's eyes were adjusted to the darkness —the latrine had been bright—he saw Eunice's silhouette. She was not at Blaine's booth but at a nearby table. His panic had been practically for nought. He found his check and, catching the little old waitress, paid her off. He moved his bulk towards the Small Intestine. This exit however was blocked by those karate men, who were at the moment hammering down a longhaired youth with an exceedingly bad complexion.

Reinhart backed away from this and collided with Eunice.

She draped herself on his shoulder and said: "Let's split. Unless you wanna see an underground movie in the Pancreas. It's a gay gang-bang, I think, the same old crap. This place used to be a groove when it first opened but it's turned into the same old cop-out full of fake freaks. I wouldn't come here ever except for the food.

That's good because the Mafia runs the kitchen and wops love to eat."

"You don't mean gangsters are out there frying steaks?"

"That's neat!" She nickered. "What a scene, chalk-stripe suits, floppy white felt hats, tommy guns! You know who I dig? George Raft!"

But Reinhart had seen these pictures first time around, which was another thing entirely. It made him despondent to hear youngsters with a taste for the Thirties. They were out to take all and earn nothing. Past eras were recalled for their amusement, minus the pain and depriva-tion of those who survived them. You never ran into nostalgia for breadlines and apple-selling veterans. Rein-hart could wax quite indignant on this subject, though he himself had always eaten his three square per diem. His father had somehow got along. He had always meant to ask him how, but had never done so while the man lived. Yet when Blaine ranted about the dreadful state of America now, Reinhart was wont to bring up the Depres-sion.

They made a buffeting and buffeted exit at the opposite side of the room from the commotion, going out a door under a naked red fire bulb. In an alleyway of trashcans, Reinhart felt he had left something undone. That had been his son back there, buying marijuana in a manner that suggested extensive practice. He wondered at his own reluctance to come out of hiding and decided his motive had been simple shame. It was comforting to make admis-sions. He had rather been father to the pusher, who at least was working for a living.

This of course was a reflection of anguish, but, as women invariably will, Eunice chose that moment to say, squeezing his arm, which he still always forgot was fat until someone did that: "You know what I dig about rapping with you? You are always in an up mood."

At the debouchment of the alley into the parking lot stood another karate man, eating a hero sandwich leaking oil and tomatoes. It suddenly occurred to Reinhart to check something Bob Sweet had told him on their first meeting at Gino's.

"Excuse me," he said. "Do you know about something called kung fu?"

A paper-thin slice of salami disappeared between the bouncer's lips. "Chinese martial art," said he, sucking next a black olive from the sandwich, whirling it in his mouth, and ejecting the seed, all of this with no hands. Reinhart had not been able to eat much of his steak sandwich and this show made him ravenous.

"See," he said, turning reluctantly away to Eunice. "I told you Bob did karate. He certainly had the name straight." Eunice shrugged. This however was the sort of thing that Reinhart found important: small details but fitting into a mosaic, etc. "He said he got his black belt in kung fu."

"Bullshit, man," said the bouncer, who had heard. "There isn't no belt system in kung fu. Everybody wears a black *gi*. And what I don't like about it is you wear shoes too."

On the way to the car Reinhart asked: "What's a *gi?*"

Eunice said: "Uniform. Bob's a pathological liar."

She was probably just overwrought. It was interesting to Reinhart how this father and child abused each other to third persons. He himself, in contrast, would never calumniate Blaine to anyone outside the family. Of course Blaine probably besmirched his dad's name to anybody who would listen.

The idea of this depressed Reinhart all over again, and also made him aggressive when they reached the car. He opened the door and forced Eunice to get in in the normal, mannerly fashion. He closed the door on her and talked through the window.

She said, in affectionate threat, "I'll get you for that."

"Look," said he, "I'll just walk to the Y. It's just a couple blocks from here. Really."

"I might as well drop you," Eunice said. "It makes more sense."

"I could use the fresh air and exercise."

"You just don't like being with me, is that it?" She turned her big soft head away.

"I thought we went through something of this sort earlier," said Reinhart. "Look, I'm an old guy, and after a day with a specialist in rejuvenation and an evening of youthful pleasures, I feel twice the age I was to begin with. And I don't even have a real home to go and recuperate in."

And surely enough, Eunice said tragically: "I wish I didn't have a home." She reached out and clutched his wrist. "I'm scared to go there. You don't know what Bob is like."

Reinhart's scalp prickled. He put together her earlier cryptic comments with this current evidence of apprehen-

sion and got something ugly. When she had suggested that
Sweet had a sexual interest in her, Reinhart had not yet
known she was his daughter. But fashion had also
changed as to interference in the internal affairs of others. When Reinhart was young all decent persons had
wanted the U.S. to go to the aid of Western Europe; now
it was precisely the same sort of people who demanded
that America let Southeast Asia alone.

He grimaced. "I can't be policeman to all the world."
There was no getting away from the fact that the clichés
of journalism were often useful for disposing of an
uncomfortable subject.

Her voice broke as she said: "I don't have anybody to
talk to."

Try your clergyman or family doctor, Reinhart wanted
to say, à la the popular psychologists. He had read that
in, of course, Los Angeles there was a telephone number
which could be dialed by distressed young victims of
parental fascism. The sage at the other end of the wire
gave them love, no doubt literally if they got within
clutching distance. A good way to get young stuff.

But an unhappy girl is an altogether different entity
when you confront her in reality, just as an actual starving beggar is something other than he appears when a
mere digit on a list of miseries in far-off India.

Reinhart said: "I used to be the kind of guy who would
get involved in the troubles of other people. But my help
invariably succeeded only in getting them deeper. I don't
even speak of my own burned fingers, which presumably
shouldn't matter to the Good Samaritan. I really mean
quite seriously that emotional problems are better left
alone by my type of person. I no longer have faith in my
own judgment. Time will do what it wants to anyway."

She was plucking at his sleeve. A car started up nearby
and roared past, as it were scorching his behind. It was
possible that her movement had had no reference to
saving his life. Still the idea occurred to him that she was
perhaps not the typical young solipsist.

"I'll see you in the office tomorrow," he said. "You
know, the freezer program puts a whole new complexion
on human troubles. If it works nothing is permanent any
more. If we are trapped in a situation, it is but for a
limited term. Think of that." He would himself try to keep
it in mind, which was not easy what with the habits of a
lifetime.

"I never figured you for a cop-out," Eunice said, deep

within the darkness of the car. "I thought I could count on you."

"The thing I can't swallow," Reinhart said indignantly, "is being given all this responsibility. You feed and clothe a child and expose him to your principles. What the hell else are you supposed to do? I never expected my parents to be perfect. My dad, for example, never gave me any useful advice his life long, and my mother criticized me incessantly. They might not have been the kind of people I would have chosen as friends, and I always felt superior to them, yet I managed to love and respect them as parents. Why then must my own son be a Blaine? Because I have failed in business? But he hates business. And my wife. I tell you she stopped giving me any moral support whatever as soon as we were married."

He stopped abruptly. "I'm sorry, Eunice. This is unforgivable of me. It's what happens in middle age. Another person's troubles only remind you of your own. When you get to really old age they please you by contrast. The old-timers at Senior City get a charge from the death of a colleague—another one gone and I am still here, that sort of thing." He poked his face in the window. "Human beings are vile. That's the best advice I can give you. Like any other general rule it has as many exceptions as applications, but it is a useful position from which to start. Then you won't be disillusioned by swinishness on the one hand, while on the other you will be pleasantly surprised occasionally when decency appears unexpectedly."

After a moment of quiet she ordered, in a low but intense voice: "Get in the car."

He complied, with a hot face, cold limbs, and an absence of will. She drove through the downtown shopping district, now dark, to an even darker area, near the river, of depressed commercial buildings, seedy warehouses, and the like, the sort of neighborhood which is seemingly dangerous because deserted but actually quite safe for the same reason, criminals being the most gregarious of men.

What's this? Reinhart asked himself when they stopped adjacent to a steel-shuttered loading platform and several enormous trucks of the breed that look stupid when not in use and brutal when they are. But he followed her as she left the car and, opening a door in a tall, skinny building next to the warehouse, entered a feebly lighted hallway and stepped around the unconscious derelict

sprawling there covered with whiskers and slime and an
Army overcoat showing two stripes on the arm—in fact,
Reinhart's own late rank.

At the base of the stair Eunice halted and said: "Some
friends have a loft here."

"OK," said Reinhart, who felt liberated from something
or other. They proceeded to climb many flights, a murky
journey between sporadically illuminated landings. The
bare backs of her thighs were just ahead of him under the
appreviated hem, massive columns so firm they gleamed
in the twilight. Going up such a steep staircase as a boy
he would have goosed a male predecessor and stooped to
see a girl's pants or, better, the tops of a woman's silk
stockings. He could remember as far back as when most
were rolled. However, it was no joke to carry his weight
ever upward.

At last through a haze of exhaustion he discerned that
they were no longer mounting but moved along a level
surface. Eunice opened a sagging door. He followed her
into a room too dark to have identifiable dimensions.
Nearby were bodies prone, supine, or hip-propped, and
many were intertwined with others. A couple of candles,
erected in saucers, flickered over the scene. Everybody
seemed to be smoking. Reinhart of course recognized the
odor as that of marijuana smoke, which he had lately
smelled, for the first time in his life, in the men's room at
the Stomach, when the bouncers lighted up—though it
was far from a new indulgence, and had been used by
certain schoolmates of his years ago, or so it was alleged
then, for there are always legendary wild men mixed
among the hordes of routine clods, creative types who are
drinking, fucking, dope-taking while the jerks are drearily
grinding their noses.

A pleasant fragrance rather like that of a brushfield
being burned. Reinhart had smoked various weeds as a
kid exploring local meadows and woodlands: there had
been one sort of tall reed which, intact, you could hurl as
a spear or, cut into lengths, smoke. Inhaling marijuana, so
said many leading authorities, you did far less damage to
your system than came from boozing. Other spokesmen
were opposed. But Reinhart felt the essential argument
was as to ethics rather than health. Did not this effluvium
wither the will to succeed as well as asphyxiate the moral
values?

An answer was immediately forthcoming. Eunice
leaned over and plucked the joint from one of the beards

on the floor, who gave her no opposition, and then found
an area where she herself could sprawl and did so. Reinhart joined her there with considerable difficulty. He
would rather climb stairs than sit upon a floor. An erect
body distributed its weight more effectively than one
folded or heaped upon itself like a pillowcase full of wet
laundry.

Her first drag was rather shallow, for all the atmosphere of the place: which is to say he had been prepared
to see her ingest what was left of the butt in one great
suck, the glow swooping towards her lips.

Chewing dramatically on the smoke, she handed the
little twisted, wretched thing to Reinhart. He had given
up cigarettes years before and in the years since puffed
only on the occasional cigar presented by business acquaintances. The thought of inhaling had become repugnant to him. To fill the lungs with the fumes of burning
vegetable matter, to inflame the delicate linings, to con-
strict the fine blood vessels, to condense black tar in his
interior passages—but marijuana was not tobacco, and
might indeed be less harmful. If so, what a joke.

So he took a moderate draft, inhaled cautiously, felt
temporarily dizzy, and returned the butt to Eunice.

She leaned into him and said: "You can freak out
here, do your own thing, with nobody on your back. I
wish it was the whole world."

Reinhart hoped it was not, his thing being wearing a
shirt and tie and a wash-and-wear suit, shaving every
morning, and trying to make a go at business. He was
neither well dressed nor prosperous, it went without saying, but still could see no future for himself in universal
fecklessness. How could you freak out in the absence of
will? Yet had not the Moros, inflamed by hashish, run
amok, causing the U.S. Army to adopt the .45-caliber
automatic pistol, the heavy slug from which would knock
a man ass over elbow if it struck so little as the tip of his
smallest finger? Some old Army sergeant told him that
twenty-five years before, beer-belly rolling over web belt,
stained campaign hat. "I was loaded on soured pineapple
juice mixed with medical alcohol give me by a nurse I put
the blocks to, when out of the jungle runs this brown
monkey gook and I fired the whole fuckin' magazine at
him and never hit him once but into the earlobe, but it
turned the little dicklicker upside down and dropped him
like a stone and his crooked sword went flying." The
Philippine Insurrection happened to have occurred circa

1900. Sarge told the story during basic training in
1942–43, at which time he had been no older than thirty-
five, younger by a decade than Reinhart was right now.

Those were the days when older guys had a license to
tell outrageous lies to their juniors and were not really
believed by the latter but were definitely respected and
admired for so doing. It was a kind of convention, half-
comic without being absurd. His back to the wall, Reinhart would have relied on Sarge for responsible leader-
ship; one could reasonably expect him to live up to his
bullcrap.

At his next turn Reinhart took another drag, and
leaned back to relieve the pressure that the top of his
belly was putting on his lungs. Eunice also extended
herself and then rolled onto him. Big as she was, her
weight did not oppress, as he feared it might when he felt
her coming over. She was mass without volume.

He tried to hand the butt to her, but that proved
impossible in the new arrangement. He had gradually
begun to inhale, and supposed he was coming under the
influence when he sensed no discomfort of lung. Eunice
was wriggling gently against him, but in a practical rather
than an erotic way, as if they lay in bed together and she
adjusted the tangle of sheets.

Suddenly his tie was inhibiting, and he had the illusion
that his head had inflated with smoke and would detach
and float away. He took another drag to speed this
pleasant process, but his hand, working at cross purposes,
rose to open his collar. He decided to open his eyes
without determining whether they were closed. He had
never before been in a position to play such jokes on his
body. Eunice's hair was in his face.

What a time to play the fool. He tried to get the butt
to his mouth but her head was in the way. He found
himself smoking her tongue instead. In the fourth or fifth
grade you would hold your tongue and say either: "The
teacher has a big red apple" or "I saw the cowboy's
lasso," and you heard a dirty word. In earlier years the
game played at recess was called Catch the Girls: chase a
plump little blonde in green tam and mittens on a string,
capture and bear-hug her, that was the game, which was
fun and sometimes made you want to peepee. Junior
Dodge once went to the toilet in his pants, back in the
cloakroom. Carlo Reinhart played a bumblebee in the
spring pageant, in muslin wings and a yellow-striped knit
cap, cardboard stinger in his tail. He squashed a banana

in his schoolbag and you could smell it there all year.
High-top boots, with a pocket to carry a scout knife,
included with some brands. Cut a wedge from his left
index finger when sharpening a pencil, a little hunk of
flesh which tumbled to the desk, pale, too startled to
bleed; he instantly popped it back in the finger and
wrapped around his handkerchief, crackling with dried
snot. In a few days it had healed up, stayed a welt for years,
after decades showed a whitish trace.

Having traveled up to the present on the dangling digit
of destiny, Reinhart identified the surging movement at
his groin as Eunice's spasmodic pelvis. How strange it had
been to get the first hard-on while dancing and subsequently duck-walk, thrilling in shame, Could she feel it? Sure,
and loved it, so said Roy Moody, class filthmonger. Nobody yet had "hairs," as they were called to distinguish
them from the kind in the scalp. Roy once pulled a lock
from a janitor's brush and stuck them on his crotch with
mucilage. Roy once found in his father's sock-drawer,
beneath the balled lisle, a little eight-paged cartoon book
showing Toots & Casper having at each other with, re-
spectively, a great bushy orifice and an enormous war-
club. Roy claimed some impossible record in meat-
beating. Many people were shamelessly candid about their
experiences. Wendley, that tall guy from Alabama in
Army basic training, always came back from pass with
some unlikely story: claimed to have screwed a chicken
once. Lies, lies, yet stranger phenomena were on record.
Wendley acted everything out but was never disgusting.
Even the chaplain's assistant would laugh. This type of
humor could not be explained to anyone who had not
been there. The Army was the first and last place Reinhart felt a sense of community.

He was getting maudlin now and had even lost his
cigarette. Searching for it, his hands swept over Eunice's
bare behind. Of course, that made sense: earlier, when
she writhed, she had been pulling off her pants, a commonplace event hardly worth noting. He must find that
other butt, puff on it, fill his lungs and the lacunae in his
memory, flee his humdrum present. But everywhere he
searched he felt irrelevant bare flesh. She was a nice girl
but obstructive. Either his hands were larger than normal
or her naked breasts were smaller than they had looked
under fabric. Old Blaine had certainly been right about
the liberation afforded by pot. Reinhart didn't give a fig
for career, home, or flag. He had no plans for what he

would do when he grew up. All existing categories were
exposed as fraudulent, including diet. He loved the feel,
from within, of his rippling fat, the soft adipose tissue
clothed in thin skin of fishbelly white, marbled with blue
blood vessels and dappled with hair. The great kidney
pads that hung like hams over his belt behind, the lateral
folds in front, the loose meat under his arms, the massive
vault of gut.

He grew quite lascivious towards himself and, forgetting about Eunice, assumed her body was an increment of
his own, bigger and better than ever, a veritable Moby
among the routine dicks of the world. But womanlike she
made jealous assaults against his self-possession. The difference from every other time this had happened in his life
was that he now remained impervious to capture. Oh, he
might be denuded, chafed into erection, and inserted well
within her, but it was a fantasy over which he could at
any time exert control, held off so doing only because her
hollow assurance she was being loved amused him. Go
right ahead, my dear lady, plunge and withdraw, for all
the good it will do you. Little do you suspect I am not
involved in your desperation. . . .

He was quite comfortable on the hard floor and not at
all embarrassed to note that the nearest of his fellows had
risen from a recumbent figure to a sitting shadow and
could be seen applauding though without sound, unless
Reinhart's vision and hearing were out of synchroniza-
tion, in which case the handclaps would no doubt come
along later.

"Go, man, go," said his neighbor thickly, then toppled
over again to the supine.

Reinhart thought: we are being watched, like a hog
and a sow rolling in the muck of the pigpen, oink, oink.
The longer he went without a puff, the more inebriated he
became. He thought he might chance a nap, Eunice being
no longer near his face but far, far away, murmuring,
breathing, bobbing, ardent though mechanical at some
new project. She really seemed to find him useful.

His spirit playfully left his flesh and from an attitude of
levitation reveled in new, penetrating perspectives, studying at once the kelpish hair, blanched skin, and blanket of
fat and the underlying organs which they armored:
liquor-sponge of liver, oysterish stomach growing a pearl
of ulcer, entwined-caterpillar bowels, grapelike gonads.
He was one huge mixture of metaphors, but he was alone

now. Eunice was now seen in a coupling with another
figure beyond his feet.

That he was nude and recumbent also proved an anachronistic illusion. Surely he had been so earlier, but now
he stood in the hallway outside, watching the police
mount the narrow staircase.

"Up here, officers."

The saturnine men in the lead, in plainclothes, impatiently signaled for silence. Reinhart stepped aside and the
enforcers kicked down the door without trying the nonex-
istent lock, ran in, and made noises.

Reinhart sat on the first step, head in hands, no longer
hallucinating but still sufficiently narcotized to feel no
vicarious hurt from the beating his recent companions
were sustaining inside—if one could judge by the sounds.

In a moment the detective emerged and asked: "A kid
of yours in there?"

"I doubt it," Reinhart said lightly, then, rising, corrected himself: "I mean, certainly not! I looked. I was relieved he wasn't when I smelt the marijuana."

The officer snorted. "That's not weed, at least not what
I found. It's dried lettuce leaves, made up to look like
joints of grass. Some pusher probably got a few bucks out
of them for it, stupid punks. And not the first time. But
what do they care? They can pretend they're high and
fuck one another." He gave Reinhart a look of primitive
compassion. "Go home, mister. Your kid is shaming you
someplace else tonight, on your money and in your car,
shitting on everything you believe in and have worked like
a dog for." He commiseratingly patted Reinhart's shoulder with his left hand. Reinhart noticed he dangled a
short sap in his right, rather cunningly worked in leather
braiding.

"My kid?" Reinhart said with a jerky elbow motion
intended to convey indignant pride. "My kid put in two
years at the front in Vietnam, came back decorated and
shellshocked. He's earned his right to be a bit confused.
Look what this country's turned into behind his back
while he's been putting his life on the line: orgies and
draft dodgers and race riots and punks taking over colleges, buying and selling narcotics in the toilets of discothèques. And what are you guys doing about it? Why
the hell do I pay taxes? Why don't you go down and clean
up the Gastrointestinal System?"

The detective took a step in moral retreat. "You don't
know what we have to put up with, sir. When I entered

the Force a cop had a certain respect. Oh, sure, we were supposed to be lower class and stupid and our idea of living was a pregnant wife and a little house in the suburbs and we took orders from the Church, a policeman wasn't ever anybody's idea of prestige, you know that, but I'll tell you this." His voice broke. "No beautiful, rich, and educated young girl with a new car and a wardrobe I couldn't buy with a month's salary ever called you a motherfucker. I've been wounded twice in line of duty. If some hood was holed up here with a machine gun and a stack of grenades it would be me who had to go in and get him." He was practically crying. "Me, the motherfucker, I would go in and get my belly shot out and they'd give me an inspector's funeral and my wife the insurance plus what the boys collected in the hat. You know what I get paid for wading in chin-high shit for twenty-two years?"

"Not enough, I'm certain," said Reinhart, returning the pat. "I didn't mean any personal criticism, Captain."

"Lieutenant. You don't get promoted fast unless your tongue's up a politician's asshole." But Reinhart's message seemed to mollify him. He took some air and said: "I'll look out for your boy in the future. I'll give him a break if I can. They might call me a sadistic pig, but I am anything but. I could tell you many an occasion when— but you wouldn't believe me. Trouble is the public's on the side of the lawbreaker nowadays." He struck the boss of the newel post with his sap, making a curiously soft yet heavy report causing the rail to tremble around the corner of the next landing. "I'm a veteran too," he added. "What's his name?"

"Sweet," said Reinhart. "Bob Sweet, Jr." This was off the top of his head, and out before he remembered Eunice. He must flee before they collected her name.

"He's probably got good stuff in him, Mr. Sweet. You can't last long if you're a fag in the Green Berets." Thuds and cries of pain from the room caused a grimacing reaction in the lieutenant. He said: "It's the girls who break my back, dirty little whores, fouler-mouthed than the boys. We got a dilly in there. A nympho: she called me motherfucker."

Fearfully, already descending the stairs, Reinhart asked: "Did you get her name?"

The lieutenant scowled down, slapping his palm with the blackjack. "Reinhart, it was. Eunice Reinhart. You tell your boy to stay away from her."

9

Reinhart stopped at the bank next morning to pick up at least enough cash to reimburse Bob—considering the way the evening had turned out, he felt obliged to make that gesture—and discovered that Maw had stopped payment on the check for five grand.

As expected, Eunice was not at her desk in the Cryon office. She was probably in irons in a dungeon full of jeering prostitutes. He was in an ugly position, though the initiative had been all hers.

He went into the inner office. The desk chair was empty, the washroom door ajar. He had no stomach this morning for announcing himself blatantly. He raised his fist to knock, but had arrived at an angle through which he could see a lighted strip of half a Bob Sweet, standing before a washbowl in T-shirt and trousers. Bob's head was crystal bald except for the sideburns. At the moment he was installing in his mouth a complete set of dentures. Having seated them with a thumb at either extremity, Sweet squeezed a dot of cream from a tube here and there on the inside of a toupee and placed it upon his crown, pressing it to establish adherence.

The upper margin of a stiff garment, apparently a kind of corset, rose above the waistband of his pants. He was seen tugging at it before donning a shirt. This was interesting to Reinhart, who was much too obese for any agent of compression to have signally altered the profile of his trunk. Sweet was demonstrably not fat, but he must have a sagging belly—more degrading, in a way, than over-all adiposity. Reinhart was stout everywhere, consistent from elephant-leg neck to big feet-flappers. His scalp was thick—and rather linty, he saw as he unconsciously ruffled it. Hardly a tooth was not stuffed with silver, and three were synthetic and removable on a wire but the shells of the others were real and of his own origination.

He found himself gliding backwards, away from the

bathroom door, as silently as he had arrived. Sweet had not noticed him. A man putting himself together from scratch did not look for distractions.

The sight was fundamentally more shocking than anything that had happened the night before. Reinhart really found it easier than he might admit to accept any evidence that today's youth were depraved: a historical phenomenon. He was far from astounded that Maw had stopped payment on his check—that of course was merely personal. Back in the outer office he sat down on a chair and realized that he habitually assumed the worst of others, and had furthermore done so for so many years that the process had by use become agreeable. He was comfortable in a world full of malice and corruption.

But Bob Sweet was a man of his own generation who had seemed to escape the accumulated penalties of four decades. Oh, there were other examples, fifty-year-old movie stars who married schoolgirls, sexagenarian statesmen with unflagging energy, but Reinhart did not know them except as newspaper and TV myths. Sweet was his age-old acquaintance and newfound friend, and he now proved to be a collection of detachable parts.

Reinhart's head was in his hands when Eunice came in. His shoes, 11-D, as usual needed a shine. When he reached puberty his dad, instead of a sex-talk, had given him a characteristic rule of life: "Always keep your shoes polished and your clothes brushed and you'll find that the doors will open for you." Reinhart had always found it impossible to imagine what Dad had been like as a youth.

"Hi," said Eunice cheerily. He answered but did not look up. Her own square-tipped, purple-patent-leather shoes marched by. The cushion of her chair sighed and the swivel squeaked.

He had not a clue to what she expected of him today, question, apology, carnal nostalgia, or indignation. And brutally he did not care. She had no right make demands on a man of forty-four. Still, he was in better or at least more authentic shape than her father.

"I'm sorry," he said therefore. "I went out in the hall and tried to ward them off, but you can't do much with cops intent on a raid. Frankly I couldn't see it would do any good for me to get beaten up too."

"I thought you split before the bust," she said. "I was so freaked out I couldn't remember."

He looked up at last. She had a new hairdo: ringlets alternating with dangly droopy locks rather like truncated pigtails, the whole slanting generally upward from low forehead to high crown with many intervening elaborations, false starts, and cul-de-sacs characteristic of dream-architecture as well as certain schools of pastry decoration.

Reinhart was momentarily diverted from the mainstream. "When did you get that?" He looked at his simulated Omega. "I didn't know the beauty shops were open this early."

"There's a cat named Reynard Fox who's open all night. The hookers all go there. I might have gone there. I don't remember. How does it look? I haven't really seen it." She squinted. "This light is killing me. I can't find my glasses."

She searched the desk drawers with more desperation than necessary. Everything was a performance. She found the rose-tinted, window-glass, googoo-eyed spectacles and put them on. She stood up. The waistband of her blue satin bellbottom slacks ended only at the protrusion of her breasts.

"Oh come on," Reinhart said. He had tried several times to tell Blaine that in any dramatic offering there should be an occasional intermission so the audience could empty its bladders or buy popcorn. He tried it on her. "I happen to know that wasn't marijuana you were smoking but lettuce leaves." Too late he saw that the possession of such information compromised him.

But Eunice failed to make the inference. She said: "I don't know about that. I was really freaking out on my own thing."

Sex? Reinhart would not ask. Both Sweets were enigmas but had rapidly revealed themselves as the kind which any attempt to solve would only further becloud as well as peculiarly humiliate the investigator.

He said lamely: "Well, I'm relieved to see you don't have any broken bones. Are you out on bail?"

She laughed. "Not bloody likely. They took it out in trade." She wore a blouse of the window-curtain material called dotted swiss and as usual her paps were on display. Reinhart had had her, but he saw her now with no sense of ownership, perhaps because she looked so new. Degeneration seemed to refresh her. "All charges dropped, if you forgive the pun." She stuck a finger into her forehead. "Hey, you know something? Cops are all premature ejaculators."

Was he being baited? But it never took if done by anybody but his wife or son. He nodded amiably.

"Is Bob in yet?" she asked and strode, bouncing, to the door of the inner office. And Reinhart wanted to scream: *Don't go in there for God's sake,* as if, being Sweet's daughter, she would not know her father's façade could be pulled to pieces; but the main reason he did not was that Sweet then appeared, the whole man and so well arranged that Reinhart had once again to suspend his disbelief. Sweet might wear a toupee and dentures, but they were the best money could buy and represented a strong man's dominion over nature.

"Good, you're here," he said to Reinhart. "Let's go. We have a candidate."

Eunice squealed in some sort of emotion, and Reinhart leaped to his feet, discarding all other issues.

Sweet thrust a memo at Eunice: "Tell Hans to meet us at this address." He passed rapidly into the corridor. Reinhart gave Eunice a little salute of no particular significance and fell in at heel.

"I gather you have reason to believe this is not a hoax," he said.

The elevator gaped. Stepping in, Sweet responded: "It's better than that." Which was not an answer. But then Sweet said: "He's a Negro." Which certainly was.

"I have been here before," said Reinhart, staring out the window of the Bentley at the ramshackle house. This was no example of the famed, inexplicable déjà vu, but a true memory of twenty years before, at which time the porch had been in the same state of disrepair, collapse apparently imminent but now proved not so as to that era, since it still stood. Sometimes certain edifices were interminably arrested at an arbitrary point of their decline.

Shortly after returning from the war, Reinhart had enjoyed an association, in several projects, with a person of color named Splendor Mainwaring, an impractical fellow, something of a visionary, a man in whom grace and style so took precedence over common sense that his enterprises often failed but were never in bad taste.

Splendor often lost particularly but, unlike Reinhart, could not be termed a general loser. That crucial distinction, perhaps, gave each a motive to drift away from the other. For years they had seldom seen each other even accidentally while both continued to reside in a suburb of

fewer than ten thousand souls, though not in the same
neighborhoods. This was the same period in which the
status of Negroes had improved conspicuously. Not since
the fall of Japan had their access to local movies been
denied and the emergency provision printed on the tickets
—"We reserve the right to change prices wtihout notice"—passed into disuse except as applied to drunk and/
or disorderly types of any breed. As if to supply a fine
moral problem for a gross gauge, an inebriated and ob-
streperous Splendor had once applied for admission and
been turned away. He had also once done time for possessing heroin. He had worked as an automobile mechanic
and once hired a store-front church in which to give an
inspirational address, then vanished in one of his moods,
leaving Reinhart, blind drunk, with the task. Finally,
when Reinhart, then working for Humbold Realty, had
been suckered into heading up a construction company
actually controlled by Humbold, the mayor, and the police chief, and awarded a contract, engineered by the
same cabal, to dig an extension to the town sewer, he had
taken on Splendor as his aide. This project was not
successful.

Splendor and Reinhart since had gone their separate
ways, and the latter could not have said what his old
friend did for a living. Through the years Reinhart was
occasionally hailed by a brown face in a passing car, or
vice versa. He had always intended to renew the friendship when he got a minute or a pretext, but time was in
ever shorter supply after he reached thirty.

After confessing that he recognized the house, Reinhart
sighed and said: "Then it must be his father. I met him
once, a damn nice guy."

"You know these people?" Sweet asked suspiciously.

"Mainwaring?"

"That's the name." Reinhart started to get out, but Bob
seized his arm. "Do you mind explaining?"

"Don't you remember Splendor?" Reinhart asked. "He
went to school with us, a year or two ahead. He was a
star athlete, for one. Don't you recall the basketball team
that went to the state finals? It was his touchdown that
won the Thanksgiving game in '39 or '40. He won more
letters than anybody, a record that probably still stands.
He got good grades too. I belive Splendor was salutatori-
an of his graduating class." Sweet's toupee was a beautifully authentic-looking article, except where the gray
sideburns began abruptly: an observation Reinhart had

made the day before, when he had not known of the
counterfeit.

Sweet made a disdainful mouth. "All I can recall are
the guys who picked on me. Not an era I look back on
with much sentiment, Carl."

Reinhart was suddenly victim to an imminent loss of
nerve, teetered as it were on the threshold. He looked up
and down the street for a mob. "Say, Bob," he said. "I
suppose it's safe enough here? This car is quite a target."

"Don't be an ass," Sweet said, pushingly indicating he
should get out.

En route up the cracked walk, Reinhart said: "It's a
weird feeling." Memory had calmed him. "It has changed
so little I almost expect to see his sister open the door as
she did the first time I ever came here. She was one of
the most beautiful girls I have ever seen in my life." He
dropped his voice. "But she seemed to be mute. At least I
never heard her say a word." The images of years past
were much more vivid than those of last night. Yes, he
had reached that age.

He fell back a few steps before they mounted the
porch, so that the worn stairs, precarious two decades
ago, would not receive their combined imposition.

The porch floor sounded thin as a drumskin. There was
less mesh on the screen door than of old, and Sweet
reached through it and rapped on the wooden portal.
While they waited Reinhart peeped around at the neighborhood. Like most palefaces he had always been more
or less scared of Negroes. There were many explanations
for this, sociological, sexual, statistical, and historical,
and at any given time Reinhart honored that of whichever
persuasion met his current needs, which were largely
formulated by what he saw in the media of information.

The person who opened the door to Sweet's summons
wore military garb, though not of our side. In fact it
looked rather German, specifically SS, being black with
white piping, and the pants were those wide-winged
breeches, flaring out of high boots, which had done so
little, pictorially speaking, for the late Heinrich Himmler,
perhaps because of his petit-bourgeois figure. However,
this chap, whose skin was quite light, not so swarthy,
actually, as many of your average Nordic-descended
Midwesterners toasted by the summer sun, stood as tall as
Reinhart and much trimmer. He had a boy's hips, a girl's
waist, and a bull chest. He would also have been very
handsome of countenance had he shaved off the continu-

ous beard which joined the sideburns. Reinhart had quite enough of hair, having served too long as Blaine's father.

This lad seemed to be in his early twenties. Reinhart thought his expression could be called menacing, but Bob Sweet, having wrested a fortune out of the world's most competitive economy, did not know fear of ought but death.

"Mr. Mainwaring?" he inquired. "I am Robert Sweet of the Cryon Foundation, and this is my associate, Mr. Reinhart. I believe you called us about a certain sad matter."

The young man said levelly: "I did. In a minute I will join you in your car." He closed the door.

Reinhart felt terrible. "God," he said to Sweet, "that might be Splendor's son, and if so, it's probably Splendor who is dying."

Sweet nodded briskly, but waited until they were back in the Bentley before making a response.

"I don't know about the patient," he said. "But that fellow happens to be a militant leader who publicly goes under the name of Captain Bruno Storm: a nom de guerre, I gather, since he answered to 'Mainwaring.' Didn't you recognize him from the newspaper and television? He is an officer of a group called the Black Assassins."

Reinhart said: "I'll be damned. Sure I have. My son told me Storm was invited to address the local bar association and began by addressing them as 'Scum' and said he looked forward to shooting them all and raping their wives, daughters, and mothers. He received a standing ovation when he finished." Reinhart struck his own fat thigh. "There is talk he may be hired to head up the black studies department at the University. How does a guy like that get away with it, Bob? Do you understand it? I had a run-in with a neighbor once some years ago in which I said, you know how you will, something about punching him in the nose. I didn't touch him but he threatened me with legal action for assault. Luckily there were no witnesses and his lawyer talked him out of it. That's me. This guy threatens a whole roomful of lawyers, uses obscene language in public, boasts of his criminal intent, and they applaud him and pay a fat fee."

Sweet characteristically shrugged while studying some papers he had taken from his attaché case. "Don't worry about it, Carl."

"Let me tell you," Reinhart went on, in part fleeing from thoughts of the dying Splendor, "if I were black, I would probably be a fire-eater too. But I am not. Why should I go through life listening to the troubles of other people when nobody listens to mine? I have never been a white-supremacist reactionary. In fact I have always been a liberal. I abhore the extreme. But I tell you I will defend myself if anybody approaches me with violence."

Sweet looked up from his documents. "We are of course prepared to do the freezing gratis, but there is no point in reminding them of that. If he offers to pay, it might be considered patronizing if we turn him down. He does get these substantial lecture fees." Sweet showed his impeccable (false!) teeth.

Reinhart dropped his case. The death of a friend was something else. Reinhart said: "This becomes unbearable when I hear the practical details. I tell you, I knew Splendor. He was a mixture of extreme vulnerability with, at times, inattentiveness to reality. I have had friends die, as well as enemies and slight acquaintances. This strikes me especially hard because I never decided which he was. Over the years I have always had in the back of my mind an intent to get to know him again, and better. But you know how it goes, things we leave undone."

Sweet said, at his papers again: "Now you're getting mawkish, Carl. Sentimentalizing always has been useless, but now it is outmoded as well. Have you forgotten that through cryonics we are going to *preserve* his life? Instead you are talking like an undertaker."

If it works, Reinhart thought for the first time in quite a while, but seeing Sweet's toupee, false teeth, and corset and recognizing the mess he had made of Eunice, Reinhart's faith had been strained. Sweet pointed past him and he looked and saw Captain Storm coming towards the car with an assured, martial stride. The young man now wore a black-leather belt from which a pistol swung in a closed holster, and a high-peaked, shiny-billed cap approriate to his uniform.

Reinhart opened the door and Storm entered. His broad shoulders made the back seat crowded at the upper level but a good four inches of leather upholstery separated his narrow ass from Reinhart's spill of flesh.

Reinhart breathed deeply and said: "Is it your father who is ill? Splendor Mainwaring? I knew him years ago before you were born."

"Yes," the tan young man answered emotionlessly. "He is dying of cancer."

The dreaded word. The popular designation of Reinhart's astrological sign had been changed to "Moon People" to avoid it. Even "dying" had a preferable sound, because there were options in what it signified, in its means, that is: Reinhart's dad had died in his sleep; others in a trice, by their own hand, for example, in an instant of glare. But "cancer" submitted to no interpretation: the body slowly began to devour itself until it had consumed a vital organ, a process measured in pain-time, by which moments were eternities of agony.

There was no feasible response to this information, and Reinhart accepted it in silence. But Sweet spoke up in an efficient voice from his other side, not even bending across Reinhart to look at Storm.

"Regrettable. I hope he has not been in too much physical agony. That's no joke, of course, but it will end with his clinical death, which for the first time in the history of the human race will be truly a beginning rather than an end. I'm not attacking religion here. There are many concepts regarding an afterlife and I have no quarrel with any of them including reincarnation. That is one of the beauties of the freezer program. It violates nobody's faith, because it preserves life. It does not bring people back from the past. It keeps them living. Clinical death, you see, is not absolute. Compare the body to an automobile. The fuel pump goes bad, the car stops but is not a total ruin. Replace the failing part, she runs like new. You would be a fool to sell an otherwise perfectly good automobile to the junkman."

Reinhart was conscious that the Negro had begun to stiffen while Sweet spoke.

Captain Storm said: "Don't feel you have to put it into simple-minded terms for my benefit, please. I have read your literature. I am familiar with your argument and your projected technique, draining of the blood and perfusing the circulatory system with dimethyl sulfoxide and glycerine, then freezing the body with liquid nitrogen." He cleared his throat. "This has been done successfully with simple organisms and simpler human tissues, but with nothing of even moderate size in human terms or any complexity of function. Therefore don't give me any of your jive. This is not my idea, but my father's. He has always been a Tom when it comes to white so-called science."

Which happened to be true, Reinhart remembered. Splendor had been addicted to obviously fraudulent theories. Still, Reinhart did not like the implication of these remarks and wanted to tell him: This is the sort of attitude that turns us sympathetic whites away, and you need us. Or did he? After all, he was armed. And as Blaine explained it, the New Blacks wanted to go it alone. But when precisely that had been suggested by the Old Whites they had been called fascists.

To live by the definitions of other people was to be always a swine.

But Sweet naturally took no offense. "Our literature," he said, "lags behind the research. Necessarily so. New things come in with breathtaking frequency. To keep abreast of continuing developments we would have to publish a daily newspaper. Carl can tell you about Suda's experiments in Japan."

The Negro grunted. He said: "I could have predicted you would work in a person of color."

Reinhart looked out the window, past Storm's goatee, and saw three more Black Assassins standing on the porch of the house. They were all armed with long guns and adorned with crossed cartridge belts of the Pancho Villa design.

Storm said: "Shall we get rolling?"

"Which hospital?" asked Sweet.

"I took him out. White medicine was killing him."

Reinhart could smell the leather of the holster. He asked: "Doesn't your dad live here any more?"

A snort. "No, he has a lovely little house in Whitetown. He is singlehandedly bringing down the real-estate values. I bought it for him, and I'll tell you why. A man ought to achieve his aim before he dies, even if it is to be a lickspittle to white values. I don't blame him. He is a product, not a maker. If you are treated like a thing all your life, you become one. You'll find that in the works of Immanuel Kant."

Reinhart was stung, less by the anti-white stuff, which was fairly routine these days, than by the characterization of his old friend. If anybody had been an individual to a point well past eccentricity, it was Splendor Mainwaring. Reinhart began to suspect that Splendor's son was a blackfaced version of Blaine. So Negro offspring also turned against their progenitors, demonstrating again the foolishness of drawing fundamental distinctions between races.

It took some courage for Reinhart to speak to this armed young man against a background of storm troopers.

He stared at the haughty brown face. "Look," he said, "the Splendor I knew kissed the ass of no man. He stood by and for himself, and he suffered for it before you were born, young fellow. He had a personal vision and pursued it alone. He wasn't backed up by an army. I don't mean to intrude into your family life, but often someone from outside can see things that are missed, especially by sons."

Captain Storm was sneering at him. "Naturally you would say that. You are white."

"I'm getting tired of that word," said Reinhart.

"You're getting tired of it!" This was said with what seemed to Reinhart more hurt than anger, however—or perhaps that was merely the interpretation of Reinhart's always ready tendency to sympathize with his vis-à-vis in a social situation.

"I'm sorry," the fat man said. "This is no time to argue." He put out his hand. "I'm Carl, by the way."

The Negro drew away in horror. *"I* don't want to be on intimate terms with you. Christ Almighty." He made a dramatic grimace towards his comrades on the porch.

Sweet asked for the address, and Captain Storm gave a number and street that were most familiar. Reinhart had grown up there. It was his parents' old house.

In his mind's eye Reinhart still saw the place as it had not been for years, with the willow tree in the front yard, long since a vanished loser to some arboreal malady; the old porch fence of his childhood, between the palings of which he had once got his head stuck and Dad had to saw one off and never replaced it.

The façade had been painted since his parents' residence. He supposed Storm would see something vulgarly significant in the bone or dead- or lily-white, but in fact it had always been dressed in that color or lack of same, which anyway would turn soot-gray before the painter sent in his bill.

So many emotions were available as the Bentley came to rest at the curb that Reinhart was hard put to make a choice. His childhood home, his old friend, a Negro, moribund, yet getting a crack at eternal life, their hostile sons, the synthetic Sweet and his disturbed daughter—O for a portmanteau response in which he could dump the lot, along with his years, resurrect the willow tree and climb into its topmost branches as he had been wont to do of yore, peeping down at the passing parade, hidden and superior.

Children were swooping and hooting through adjacent yards. In the Negro district Reinhart had been too preoccupied to notice persons other than the Black Assassins, but some must have been abroad because the season was summer. The yards at hand were all of the same size and unseparated by hedge or pickets, and three lawns distant stood a hairy-bellied man, stripped to the waist, gawking shamelessly. At that range Captain Storm might look like a black cop, Reinhart thought. He himself waved at the man, who might turn out to be another old schoolmate, more routine than Bob Sweet. The man did not return the salute. Instead he scratched his navel with one hand and raised to his mouth the beer can in the other. He was the sort who might at any moment say, "Now hear this," and release some gas. In the other direction stood a spiky-figured woman wearing a droopy playsuit and a science-fiction hairdo of pink plastic curlers, and bitching a little snot.

The arrival of another car diverted Reinhart from the stocktaking of the neighborhood. It was a black Cadillac of ancient vintage and held the contingent of uniformed and armed Negroes last seen on the porch across town. They parked ten yeards beyond the Bentley and stayed inside.

Sweet's old chauffeur went to sleep again as the odd threesome of which Reinhart was a member left the car.

Reinhart asked the back of Storm's tunic, which must have been unbelievably hot under the sky's open forge: "Those guys with you?"

"My bodyguards," the young man said, glancing back and giving Reinhart an angled view of his face that was suddenly reminiscent of Splendor's sister, this boy's aunt, the exquisite Loretta. Where would we all be now if Reinhart had made an interracial marriage? For one, had certain chromosomes dominated, Blaine would undoubtedly have been a Black Assassin.

But a stout walnut-colored woman in nurse's whites opened the door before anyone knocked, and Storm, Bob Sweet, and Reinhart entered the house in that order.

Captain Storm greeted the nurse with a lavish geniality that contrasted interestingly with his gelid manner towards the whites, and he made no introductions. But being plump and in her forties, the woman nonetheless smiled at Reinhart. Whatever anybody said, fat people really were generally good-natured, especially to other adipose types, he supposed because they had their number, like fellow soldiers and ethnic siblings.

Reinhart crossed the threshold, passing his old home door with its familiar bronze knocker, a lion's face frozen in a belch or yawn, but then he saw the hospital bed in the far corner of the room where the superheterodyne had once stood and later the television.

And upon it a wasted old brown man whom it seemed peculiarly indecent to advance upon with one's own pink bulk. Splendor in his prime was tall as Reinhart and more gracefully assembled, strong yet lithe, with sensitive musculature that seemed to have its own consciousness. This wizened creature clawed feebly at the sheet which covered but did not disguise its corporeal ruin of twigs and wire. The face on the pillow was a caricature, a tourist's souvenir, carved into a coconut. No platitude is outmoded when it comes to dying, which is itself a cliché endlessly repeated. Yet Reinhart found himself incapable of utterance. To see his old friend in this situation was another thing than to entertain its possibility while riding hither. "All men die" is easy enough for you to say, but that each actually does, without benefit of quotation marks, cannot be abstracted, represented, or demonstrated by the living.

There was a glitter in the eyeholes of the skull. Reinhart did not expect to be recognized, indeed would have preferred not to be embarrassed by proof of his now irrelevant identity, but a ghastly rictal movement was already under way.

"Carlo," said the dying man. The pronunciation was astonishingly normal in timbre and volume. "How terribly nice. I am touched by your grief, old fellow. But it is misplaced. I may die, but in the words of the late great militarist, I shall return."

"You certainly shall, Splendor," Reinhart was quick to say, wiping his eye—which, judging from Splendor's speech, must have been wet. However, it wasn't; yet he *had* been grieving and perhaps would go on to do even more of it, switching focus from Splendor's terminal illness to his naïve faith in the freezer program. How typical of his old friend to be dying painfully on the one hand and on the other to be so jolly of soul.

It was also rather too grisly an incongruity for Reinhart to bear if he had to look at his friend's visage while juggling the factors, so he stared at a white-enameled table full of glassware filled with liquids and solids which were of course inefficacious, else the patient would not have been where he was: the offensive rubbish of medical science, a good thing on which to take out one's spite against illness.

Reinhart said: "Meet Bob Sweet."

Splendor put out a terrible appendage, a wiry structure of the sort found in the ruin of burned-out houses, whose late function it took a while to identify: ah, a lampshade frame. Ah, a hand. Sweet shook it forthrightly.

He said: "We all know what has been said on certain historic occasions, Mr. Mainwaring. The 'What hath God wrought' sort of thing. Now we can begin to write *our* script. The responsibility is staggering. It will be quoted forever. How do you feel as the first man to have a crack at eternal life?"

In spite of himself Reinhart looked again at Splendor, from under whose sheets a rubber tube traveled to an upended bottle hanging on a chromium pole. For a moment Reinhart thought of it that way: that Splendor was being drained, against gravity, into the bottle—certainly not; he was being fed intravenously. But when you were being devoured by cancer, where did your carnal mass go? Matter can neither be destroyed nor created. Splendor had been physically a splendid man. There could be scarcely seventy pounds of him left. Dying was, among other things, a materialistic mystery.

Reinhart asked: "Should you be talking this much? We don't want to tire you."

Splendor laughed distantly, his sheet trembling. "I'm useless for anything else. . . . Who can say what the world will be when I awake from that long sleep? Man by then, physically speaking, may be largely synthetic. And what kind of morality he will embrace may be an utterly different thing from what we have seen. All religions have been responses to the fact of death. Those promising an afterlife have generally demanded adherence to a code comprising many prohibitions referring to the weaknesses of the flesh. What does the worship of God have to do with eating pork or not? A great deal, if you were an old desert Jew or Moslem. You might die from tainted meat. . . ."

Dying had not changed Splendor. He had always loved this sort of concept-spinning. And now, of course, nobody could say it was not appropriate to his condition, but Sweet had a job to do, one which would certainly benefit Splendor if it worked and would not hurt him if it failed.

There was a noise at the front door. The nurse opened it to reveal the party of Black Assassins surrounding the small figure of Streckfuss, who was grinning obsequiously.

"Madame," he said to the nurse. "I am expected, *s'il vous plaît.* Could you explain to zese gentlemen—" He looked and saw Sweet. "Ah, Bopp!" Streckfuss coyly clawed the air in salutation and started in, but left the threshold, walking in air, as the two guards lifted him at the elbows.

Sweet turned to Captain Storm, who subsequently made a signal to his stalwarts. The little scientist scampered inside as soon as he was released.

"You are the afflicted?" he asked the recumbent Splendor.

"No doubt about it," Splendor said amiably.

"*Alors!*" Streckfuss cried, peering at the ghastly face on the pillow. "Intestinal malignancy?"

Reinhart's own bowels squirmed. "Must we talk of these things now?" he asked. "You can go over the whole situation with his doctor."

Splendor's eyes were quick. He said: "You are a principal in this project, Carlo?"

"Splendor, I have come as a friend, you know that, but I was not aware until the call came in. May I say this is not a profitmaking venture."

But Splendor was answering Streckfuss. "You can tell that by looking at my face? Great God, you must be gifted. Yes, it is my colon."

"I expect zey wanted to remove it surgically," Streckfuss said, nodding obsessively. "Surgery has no blace in medicine. I call it carpentry! It is but a hobby, did you know? But practiced on living tissue." He was developing a fury and glared at Splendor.

"They were at a loss," said the patient.

The little Swiss shouted: "Of course zey were. So anozzer living person is taken to pieces. The large intestine is of course virtually useless. We could do quite well to be born wissout a colon. But having one, we make it of necessity part of our integrity. You do not excize a piece of zuh body without affecting the unity of the whole, threatening the very fine equilibrium of blood, nerves, muscles, the distribution of weight, zuh ahnatomical zymmetry."

"Listen to that, Raymond," said Splendor, putting an eye towards his son, who remained at the rear.

Captain Storm shrugged. "I am forced to," he said with evident disgust.

"Raymond is a mechanistic rationalist," Splendor explained.

In the presence of his father he seemed much more of a boy. Reinhart had known Splendor's own dad slightly, and it was interesting to compare the three generations. Splendor had always been rather loftily superior to his father, a small, lively man who, the first time Reinhart had come upon him, had been burning a car for the insurance. A more practical type than his son. There was a theory that a grandfather's traits jumped a generation and landed in the grandson. Reinhart was inclined to take Storm's militarism seriously, not the uniform so much as the gun. Something new in the Mainwaring family was the hostility towards white men. But Storm had displayed less of it since entering the sickroom. Instead he was now sulky. That is why he seemed more boyish than earlier. Reinhart saw that relations with Blaine would probably be less abrasive if he, Reinhart, were dying: a radical solution.

"Splendor," said Reinhart, "I think before we proceed, we should get hold of your doctor. He may take some convincing if he is the conservative sort. But if you insist he must finally give way. It certainly helps to find you in such a positive frame of mind."

"Carlo," Splendor said, "we live in a remarkable time. The phony is constantly turning into the real, and vice versa. God knows what the world will be when I am revived."

Reinhart felt suddenly impelled to make a sanctimonious utterance. Here he was, a stranger in his boyhood home. If he searched the baseboards he would surely find certain dents he had put there with a toy tractor almost forty years before—the kind of damage too slight to repair, too inconsequential to be noticed by anybody but the maker thereof; the world was full of that sort of evidence, which lasted long after great buildings and massive bridges were pulled down for the erection of other transitory phenomena. Enormous mountains had been leveled for the railroads, for example, and now the latter were on their way out. The trick to survival was to accomplish something of no utility, and so small as to be inconspicuous.

However, what he said was designed to conceal his actual feelings, which seemed overly personal and perhaps downright racist. He kept telling himself that if his old home had to be occupied by someone else, how nice it was a Negro, to whom it represented progress. And the truth was that Reinhart never missed this place once Dad had died. All the same he found himself hating Splendor for choosing this house to die in.

Therefore he said: "I hope when you return to the world the people of all races will be living like brothers."

From behind him Captain Storm howled. "I knew he'd get around to saying that sooner or later. A black man lies there eaten up by white disease, cheated and lied to by white doctors, in a white house for which we had to pay the white owner three times what it was worth, listening to white quacks promise him eternal life, and sure as shit one of them will talk about brotherhood."

All this while Streckfuss had been nosing around the table, peering into bottles and vials, and now he lifted the sheet which covered Splendor and inspected him. Thank God the angle was not one from which Reinhart could see much. Reinhart backed away into the opposite corner, the former site of a drumtop table which for years had borne a picture of himself at twelve. The same was now displayed on Maw's dresser at Senior City. She was partial to the image, the last on which he would ever be represented with a grin.

"Raymond," said Splendor over Streckfuss' bent head, "if you must use foul language it will not be in my presence."

"I'm leaving," his son said. At the door he blurted boyishly: "I'm sorry, sir." And went out onto the porch.

Reinhart was careful to look at the floor, but he was most favorably impressed. Also he was astounded. Had he remonstrated with Blaine in this fashion the upshot would have been much worse than the original infraction.

"He's a good boy," said Splendor, "but he is inclined to talk too much." He shifted slightly under Streckfuss' examination.

Reinhart said: "He's a fine-looking fellow. I didn't even know you were married, Splendor. We've got a lot of personal history to fill in for each other."

Splendor seemed detached from Streckfuss' rummaging about on him. There must not be much left to freeze. The restorers of the future would have their work cut out for them; Reinhart had always assumed the first man they froze would be a stranger to him. He felt now as if he were in the position of a doctor who treated a member of his own family. He himself would be part of Splendor's memory, arrested in ice: an eerie thought.

Streckfuss replaced the sheet at Splendor's chin and straightened up. "I must have a specimen of your your-reen," he said. "I can make you comfortable meanwhile. Do not please take any more of zeze poisons." He pointed to the medication on the table. "And zis nourishment is useless." The hanging bottle. "I shall replace it with something else. But if your physician knows about zis he will undoubtedly object. Therefore discharge him."

Splendor said calmly: "In view of my condition that won't be simple."

"It is your damned life, is it not?" Streckfuss asked indignantly. But then he made an abrupt gesture. "Yes, it would look zuspicious. Above all, my presence must not be made known." He peered violently around the room. So did Reinhart. The nurse was not there at the moment. "Mr. Mainwaring," the Swiss went on, "I must tell you that I am not licensed to practice medicine in this country. Are you troubled by zis disclosure?"

"Not much," said Splendor. "You see, I'm dying."

Streckfuss narrowed his eyes and looked towards Reinhart. "Perhaps," he said.

"Freezing is not illegal," said Reinhart. "Bob has that all checked out. As far as law is concerned, the body is dead—forgive me, Splendor, talking this way, but—"

"I want all the details," said Splendor. "Squeamishness is for those who plan to stay deceased."

Reinhart went to the bedside. "Old friend," he said, "everything's going to come out all right. By the way, I don't know whether you know it, but this happens to be the house in which I was raised."

Splendor smiled wearily. "Yes, I know that. It gives me a feeling I suppose you could call serenity." He closed his eyes, and the nurse returned to show out the trio from Cryon.

10

"Why," said Maw, "you big sentimental slob. When you were little you wouldn't let me cuddle you. I'd come near you as a baby and you would ball your tiny fists. So don't get sloppy at this late date."

Reinhart had asked her if she remembered holding him as an infant, and what lullabies he had seemed to like especially. They sat in her room at Senior City. The bed did up to form a sofa of modern design. The other furniture was all-purpose as it stood, no converting necessary, and made of an impervious synthetic wood that looked like plastic and could not be touched by the results of routine forgetfulness: a cigarette dropped onto the coffee-occasional-bedside-card table would dwindle away harmlessly into gray powder and could be whisked off with a Kleenex.

"OK, then," said Reinhart, coming clean. "What I really came about was that check you gave me the other day. You see, it bounced."

Maw grinned into his face, though not with amusement. "Far from accidental, buddy-boy," she said.

Reinhart's smile signified polite incomprehension. "I'm a little confused, Maw. So much has happened to me in the last couple of days, I'm a little slow on the draw."

"That's rich. When were you speedy?"

"Look," said her son, "all you had to do was refuse if you didn't want to give me any money. Why go through such an elaborate performance?" He was sitting in an icy draft as usual: another air-conditioning duct was spraying him with chill. And because the outlet was concealed he could not divine whether the cold wind was above, or to the side.

"Carlo," Maw said, "you misrepresented your situation the other day. I have often known you for a fool but never a liar. You have degenerated, boy. I expect you are on your way to the gutter. People homeward bound from

188

a hard day's work will see your body slumped against a wall, an empty wine bottle nearby and the flies buzzing around your stinking mouth."

Maw always had been capable of creating vivid word-pictures on unpleasant themes. "A shuffling bum in an old Army overcoat, eating in soup kitchens and sleeping in a fifty-cent flop," she went on. "That's how sex maniacs invariably end."

She had confused two types of going-bad, perhaps owing to her old prejudice against strong drink. Maw always saw alcoholism behind any villainy. Hitler, a famous teetotaler, was to her but another boozer. It was useless to attack this lifelong mania, but the juxtaposition of sex was quite new.

"Maw, do you intend to explain this assault on my integrity?" The persistent draft was causing his neck to stiffen. It seemed to issue from the blank wall, painted in dusty rose, behind his head, but there was no visible grille.

"I'll talk turkey with you, Carlo. Hardly had you left here the other day when your son made his appearance and showed me how you went at him with a shears. I consider that a vicious stunt—"

In traditional fashion Reinhart was always a child in Maw's presence, but mention of Blaine made him a father, a competitor as parent, and furious.

"He's lucky I didn't cut his throat. My conscience is clean towards that boy, I have given him everything, and he has turned out completely rotten. He had bad blood in him from his mother's side. That's the only explanation. I never used to believe in heredity, but I see it working in him." Reinhart slammed a hand on the vinyl armrest. It felt like cold liver. He stared wildly around the room. "And where is that goddam air-conditioning coming from? Can't you turn the lousy thing off? I'm catching cold, for God's sake."

Now, like many another free-swinging temperament, Maw pulled in her horns when the other guy grew aggressive. She shrank into the bed-couch and pulled her cardigan together. "Try to get hold of yourself, Carlo. You are a huge man and you are shouting. And if you go about threatening old ladies and young children you should maybe get professional treatment." She looked into her lap. "You are real lucky, you know, that Genevieve never chose to make more of it and put the cops on you."

"Oh, come on," Reinhart roared. "The police would

give me a medal for cutting off those golden locks. They hate hippies and punks."

Maw said modestly: "I don't refer to that incident and I think you know it. Let me go back in time, Carlo, for a few years. You were five, Carlo, a little towhaired tyke, playing down cellar with that little Wisely girl who lived next door then and the same age as you, and your dad happened to look into the basement window from outside in search of whether he had forgotten a rake indoors, and he marched around to me on the front porch and says: 'Carlo is piddling in front of the little Wisely.' That cellar toilet we had, remember? With the door open. Now you know your dad, he was not a buttinsky. He considered it impolite to even correct a tiny snotnosed kid like yourself. I says: 'George, you must go down there, and get that boy out of the basement with his pants closed. If he begins that young to show a filthy inclination, God knows where he will turn up later.' Well sir, your dad went back and takes another glimpse in case he made an error, so careful he was, then he comes back and I says: 'Did you do it?' 'No,' he says, 'for the little Wisely has her own underwear down at her ankles and hands on her tiny hips and is demonstrating herself.' "

Maw made a strange triumphant face at Reinhart, who proceeded to guffaw. Had he forgotten this experience he might have been embarrassed, but as it happened he remembered it fairly well, from that long ago, except that in his memory Emma Wisely was absolutely smooth between the legs. Not seeing the organ he had expected, he saw nothing else. It was an early example, in his experience, of the limitations of the eyewitness.

"Kid stuff, Maw!" Reinhart howled. Then he had a sobering thought. Emma Wisely was today forty-four years old, wherever she was, you could count on that, whether rich or poor, loved or damned. He wondered jealously whether she was also overweight.

Maw threw back her head and magnified her eyeballs behind the lower half of her bifocals. "You might jeer, Carlo, being as huge a monstrosity as you are today, and get away with it, but I never tolerated impudence and insolence when you was a child."

Reinhart decided to humor her. "True enough, Maw. I can well recall your favorite admonitions, which tended towards violence." He smiled. "You always had a way with words."

For some reason this had the opposite effect from that

intended. Maw flared up, shook her fist at him, and said: "You won't think it's so funny when you're picking your teeth up off the floor."

"Gee," said Reinhart, "how that takes me back over the years."

Maw made one of her quick changes. "Not that I blame you exclusively by any means. You were a clean boy up to then, and I expect that little devil lured you into it, being no better than a common prostitute. Still, the seed took root. I never told you this, but your third-grade teacher, a couple of years later, sent me a note to the effect you were inclined to drop your pencil and shoot your beady eyes up her skirts. For this reason she moved you to the very back of the classroom."

Reinhart sagged in the chair. Of this crime he had no recollection, nor little of the teacher. He had a succession of reedy spinsters in those days, of whom he had a horror when they stood close. All females were repugnant to him until he was almost out of grade school, and then suddenly he had started to play with himself over the mental image of any at all, including comic-strip characters, but he still did not enjoy the company of actual girls. Next he began frequently to fall in love but never with any object of his self-abuse. And so on into young manhood. A routine and sometimes a rather sordid story. He was not obsessed, as many were, with his own sexual history. His adult lust had been for money.

"All right, Maw, I was a regular Marquis de Sade as a boy. Let's leave it at that."

"I wish you had, Carlo. But then you got hooked up with this Genevieve. I know that was for sex pure and simple, but I never opened my mouth at the time."

"For Christ's sake, Maw! I married her."

"For sex, Carlo, and no mistake. It don't change a thing that you made it legal." Maw shook her head and cackled. Her senility was really getting out of hand. Reinhart had an ugly thought: perhaps she should be put out of his misery, then hastily assured his conscience that the possibility occurred to him only because he feared and abhorred the event of her death. There was a name for that technique: you hypocritically hoped for what you feared, so as to disarm the devil.

He asked abruptly: "What bearing does this have on your bad check, Maw?"

"Don't give me that D.A. look, Carlo. You had your chance to study law and you never did it, with all the free education of the GI Bill, which you wasted on Liberal Arts. And you never have been artistic in one iota. As for the Liberal, as you know your dad and me were always Republicans, straight through from Warren G. Harding. And let me tell you: your son agrees with me."

Reinhart caught his lower lip and pinched it painfully. "Blaine?"

"Oh sure!" Maw crowed. "He told me liberals like yourself are what's wrong with the country, and the young kids would like to see you all shot. Your generation has botched everything from the word Go. We seniors and the youngsters see eye to eye on that. You have sold out the world to Communism and whipped the colored people into a frenzy, built up a national debt, and you are losing the war. Look at the labor unions, run by gangsters, and the schoolteachers are all atheists and traitors, and the niggers think the world owes them a living."

"So you and Blaine are making common cause," Reinhart said rigidly. "That figures. You always were a big free-lover, anarchist, nihilist, and junkie, just like him."

Maw grinned. "Don't think you can sweet-talk me out of this, Carlo. Good sense usually skips a generation. Blainey has made the dean's list every semester he has gone to college. He's smart as a whip and no chip off your blockhead."

"He also had a plan to kidnap the dean and burn his office," Reinhart said. "I suppose he told you about that. But a police spy informed the dean, who prudently went to an out-of-town conference that day. Imagine an important official being run out of his own college by some longhaired little rotters."

"That's another thing, Carlo. You are neurotic about hair. I could understand if you was bald which you are not. I call it cute for those young fellows to let their locks sprout. It's surely better than those crew cuts of your day and I wish you would let yours grow a little. You look mighty old-fashioned, Carlo. If you watched TV you would appreciate that all the New York personalities have taken up the hairy style. You're not In, Carlo. In fact, you are downright square: that skinny tie, for example, and you're one of the last left with a white button-down shirt."

"I'll be damned," said Reinhart.

"I say thank God that Blaine never inherited your foul mouth, either," said Maw. "Even as a tiny child you were always saying poopoo and doodoo. I have many a time

believed the babies got mixed up in the hospital and I
brought home the illegitimate offspring of some thug and
a cootch dancer."

Reinhart started to say—

But Maw held him off. "Yeah, the check," said she.
"You are quite the monomaniac on some subjects. Which
brings me back to sex. See, I know about the little
teenybopper next door." She pridefully explained: "That's
what they call them, teenyboppers, if you are With It."
Then her face, amazingly smooth for her age, took on the
hue of bad blood. "She's a child, Carlo. Even I never
thought you'd come to that. You could be locked away in
the penitentiary for fifty years, and the other inmates,
even murderers, all despise the sex criminal and will knife
him with shivs they fashion from metal fragments from
the license-plate shop."

Somehow Blaine, or Gen, or perhaps the girl herself,
had discovered his voyeurism. This was indeed a crisis.
You could never clear yourself of charges of sexual unorthodoxy. Reinhart had once read a magazine article
about some poor devil accused and convicted at law of
indecent exposure. Another man's subsequent confession
had eventually cleared him—the familiar case of
lookalikes. All the same, injustice's victim had to change
his name and move to another town. Though flung in
error, shame's stain persisted.

And Reinhart was caught dead to rights. That in European cultures the dirty old scopophiliac was a tradition
figure of farce; that Reinhart though venially guilty had
caught Blaine in mortal miscreance; that the girl's habitual failure to lower her blind suggested conscious exhibitionism—the fine moral complexities would be overlooked.

On the other hand Reinhart was democracy's child and
did not bear the burden of proof.

"Maw," he said, "that bathroom screen never has fit
properly, and you know how sloppy workmen are today
and how insolent when you call them to rights. I prefer
the old-fashioned type to these combination screen and
storm windows, anyway. Remember when Dad and I used
to change them every spring and fall? It was a ritual. Ah,
those were the days."

He said this knowing full well that his mother was
utterly devoid of nostalgia, whereas it was his own major
emotion, so much so that ten years hence, if he lived that
long, he might even look back on this currently dreadful

indictment with perhaps no actual pleasure but at least relief that he had survived it: if he did. Obsolete horrors got more and more quaint as they receded in time. So he watched a teen-ager undress. She would smile at that when seventy-five and he long since pushing up the daisies.

He had all but eased himself out of panic when Maw bared her dentures at him.

"You are warped worse than I thought, Carlo. I have a mind to go to that telephone across the room and call the cops down on you. Yapping about window screens at a time like this, when that little girl is carrying your child."

For a moment Reinhart actually interpreted this curious statement to mean the girl next door was bearing Blaine, his child, on her body, between spread legs. Yes, he had suspected that was the case, and it was deplorable. He was also willing to accept that general, journalistic guilt that all parents are saddled with by public spokesmen for the crimes of their children, but in particularities his conscience was impeccable. Time and again he had spoken to Blaine about honor, pride, responsibility, courage, and manhood; the need for hard work and meeting your bills: the moral gauge of human actions, nothing pompous, mind you, about God and flag, but as to whether a projected action would injure another.

And not only that. He had also omitted mention of the tiresome truth that every action by one person inevitably hurt someone else, so that incessant decency required incessant analysis of the sort of the practice of which had made him both unpopular and poor. Why discourage the boy?

But he supposed he had known all the while that what Maw meant was he, forty-four years old, two hundred and sixty-five pounds of middle-aged blubber, had climbed wheezing, sweating, between the tender thighs of this young girl and drenched her intimate channels with seed.

He checked up on this assumption: "The teen-ager next door to the house where I used to live?"

Maw nodded smugly.

"Where I lived until a couple of days ago?"

Maw scratched her chin.

"From which Gen threw me out?"

Maw pulled the lobe of her right ear. She was wearing silver, iridescent nail polish.

"This girl claims I—" What was the idiom when talking

to a mother? In four decades this subject had never come
up in a personal, illicit way. "She is—" *Shit*, Reinhart said
to himself, *that dirty little lying cunt, says I fucked her,
does she?* But it was bravado.

"Carlo," Maw said, though without a trace of worry,
"you are turning purple all over your head. I'd have my
blood pressure taken if I was you. You are not too young
to die of a heart attack, given your excess weight."

He was also suffocating. Injustice alone would not
cause these symptoms. Captain Dreyfus survived many
years on Devil's Island. Innocent men often spent their
best days, in terms of health both psychic and physical,
while awaiting execution.

As Reinhart continued to fight for air, Maw said: "I
think I would be capable of murdering you with my bare
hands would it not make the scandal known. Also, did I
not think that person you married was responsible in
part." Maw glared at him. "Which doesn't lessen your
guilt one whit, you filthy, disgusting hog. But it was her
who got you into sex in the first place. I can't forget that.
You never knew what it was until she got hold of you. It's
like drinking. You take a sip and you are hooked for
life."

Reinhart suddenly remembered that under the new
scheme of things it was no longer really malignant to
hope for someone's clinical death. You could merely wish
them into the freezer. He began to breathe with less
effort.

"This girl has made certain accusations," he said. Now
he felt a pricking in his chest as if the point of a knife
were seeking entry. Reinhart had already cried Wolf
several times to his doctor on the occasion of mere gas
pains. The real strike would no doubt catch him by
surprise, far from the haunts of medical men, hardly here
in Senior City with its resident practitioners. Anyway, he
was born to be hanged.

"I wouldn't waste your breath, short as it is," said
Maw. "I have always lived by common decency, but am
also a realist to whom what is done is done. Little Blainey
somehow in that house of evil grew up to be a saint, don't
ask me how and kindly don't make a dirty grin if I say
that whatever example I set might have been useful to
him. You don't know this because you haven't set foot
back there since She threw you out and you better not try
either, but Blaine is marrying this child to give *her* child a

name and that is why I cut off your five thousand and gave it to him."

"I see," Reinhart said, feeling the pain fizz away as he moved his shoulders—but how could gas get way up there? "He told you the whole story himself. That figures. The whole thing makes beautiful sense. I predict that you and Gen will even make your peace one of these days." Reinhart lifted himself up. "But what I will never understand is why you all hate me so much. I am really a likable guy. In every other case on record, people have been fond of the man who never gets anywhere, especially if he's fat."

Maw said: "The world is changing, Carlo, and you haven't kept up. The young kids are taking over from your kind. They don't know you don't have anything to take over. They just see you are big and in your forties."

"Aw, not you too, Maw!" Reinhart sighed cavernously and sank his hands into the droopy pockets of the wash-and-wear jacket. "You won't believe a word of this, but I'm going to say the truth if it kills me. Not me, but my saintly son Blaine got that girl pregnant, and he will use your five grand not to get married on but to buy marijuana and gasoline for Molotov cocktails with which to burn down Western civilization. And in the name of what? I can understand what makes Communists in Latin America and Asia and Black Assassins here—and it's not poverty, incidentally, but pride—even when I don't agree with it and would shoot back if shot at. I get the point, that is. Violence and lawlessness, even downright anarchy, have their attractions sometimes. Who doesn't get enraged at the way things are? I always loved the Marx Brothers for that reason. But to live life like the cast of *Horse-feathers*, to accomplish nothing but to harass everybody who has—"

"Which certainly isn't you," said Maw. "I shouldn't wonder if it was pride with Blainey, also. He don't have any in you."

Reinhart struck a dramatic stance. "Maw," he said, looking down at her, "you are hardly one to get morally sanctimonious, when you skinned the Mainwarings on the sale of the house."

Maw laughed till her eyes were wet behind her spectacles. "I sure did, Carlo. The best way to make anybody equal is to rub their nose in the facts of life. I set a certain price and would have sold it to anyone who coughed up the loot, including a little green Martian with aerials on his head. It so happened those colored people were the only ones who would meet it. I bet the neighbors could kill me."

That had the ring of truth, which of course has many clappers to its bell. Maw was right, Captain Storm was right, and so were the neighbors whose property was devalued: hardworking stiffs who had no other assets. Would it help, Reinhart wondered, if I nail myself to a cross and absorb everybody's interpretation?

He said quietly to his mother: "We have reached a crisis. I am afraid, Maw, that unless you reject this vile accusation against me, I shall not be able to see you again."

"It's real twisted when you think of it, Carlo. To this coming child you will be both father and grandad." Maw yawned. "Time for my nap now. Kindly close the door gently when you leave." Her eyes closed and her head fell slowly towards her lap.

A goat, of all things, was tethered outside the laboratory. The goat was a favorite animal of the comic strips, and frequently shown devouring tin cans, then butting fat people in the ass, which impact projected them high in the air, and they might be seen in the last frame hanging helplessly aloft, the spike of a church steeple through their pants seat. Reinhart had lived most of his life no farther than ten miles from genuine farmland, yet this was all he had heard about goats: lies, lies.

This goat had not been provided with anything to eat, and no natural foodstuffs grew on the hard unsodded earth, alternating with the asphalt driveway, that constituted the approach or yard of the lab. The animal gave Reinhart a brief, seemingly indifferent glance as he unloaded himself from the car, then swung around its lean buttocks in exchange for its wispy beard.

Reinhart sniffed and opened the door. Inside it was cold and dark after the sun, and Streckfuss, emerging from a chilly shadow, advanced on him with an enormous hunting knife.

"En garde!" cried the diminutive scientist, crisscrossing the air with vigorous slices.

Reinhart shrank aside, as well as a fat man could manage, and Streckfuss passed into the outdoors with a derisive laugh that suggested a cloved-hoofed, medium-size animal with horns or perhaps a certain satanic quality of his own.

Sweet, standing near a laboratory table, wore a long white coat to match Streckfuss'. He looked professional to the point of bogusness, rather like one of those pseudo-doctors of the early days of TV, who showed graphs and quoted statistics in support of some cosmetic, since forbidden by federal ruling to appear in costume.

"Bob," Reinhart said by way of greeting, "you certainly make a convincing doc."

Sweet pointed. "Get yourself a coat and mask from the autoclave." His own surgical mask was slung loosely from his neck.

"Me?" asked Reinhart. "Is this a joke? I'm at a loss when it comes to science, and think I might get sick to the stomach if I have to watch you prepare to freeze that goat." He understood suddenly the significance of the captive outside.

"Nonsense. You're talking like a schoolgirl, Carl." Sweet also wore rubber gloves. He was lining up a rank of steel instruments on an enamel stand.

"Are you always Hans's assistant in these things?" Reinhart asked. Certainly not with AMA approval, he thought, and then remembered animals, not persons, had been specimens thus far. Yet it might be an indication of quackery to come. They were preparing, after all, for the freezing of Splendor Mainwaring. "Isn't that unorthodox?"

Sweet nodded. "Naturally. Unorthodoxy is Hans's great strength. Orthodox medicine abandons the patient at time of clinical death."

"But surely we have to clear the way legally, with a death certificate from a licensed physician, and don't you have to get something from or through an undertaker? I mean, I don't think we can spirit away a body—"

"For a goat?" asked Bob. "Not even the ASPCA would go that far. Don't worry, my lawyers are all set for the moment we get a human body."

Overhead was a battery of lights, real surgery equipment. Bob's hands cast no shadows. Reinhart noted that, just as Sweet added: "If we ever do."

"What do you mean?" asked Reinhart. He hated this lab: no place to sit, and he hesitated to lean on anything. Then he lost his need for support, receiving an access of energy from a sudden suspicion that he had, at long last, caught Sweet out. "Is Splendor Mainwaring not human? Must we wait for a lily-white corpse?"

Now that he thought about it, all the local undertaking

establishments were Jim Crow. Another old schoolmate, a mortician, had once assured Reinhart that if an attempt were made by a Negro cabal to impose a colored corpse upon him, he intended to evade it by professing his inability to work with exotic cosmetics. For all Reinhart knew that was authentic; you can't argue with a professional in his own field. But it was morally unpleasant. However, Reinhart was in no position to make waves. Also, though cremation was his wish for his own disposal, officious survivors might well have his remains trundled into the rear door of Schmutzig & Sons Mortuary, where, remembering the argument, the undertaker might vengefully make him up like a piece of waxed fruit—which he would in fact do anyway, Dad's reason for choosing fire for himself.

At that point Streckfuss came in, dragging the goat on its neck rope, its hard heels sliding on the concrete floor. Even without traction it was a strong and stubborn beast and all the small scientist could manage.

He shouted to Reinhart for help. The goat had braced its behind against a metal tableleg now, the line went slack, and the animal lowered its head almost to the floor. Reinhart never took his eyes off it. True, it looked half-grown with but stub-horns, but the nastiest bite he had ever sustained was from the tiny fangs of a Pekinese with its rotten little pushed-in face. He mistrusted everything small and young, hit it off well with aged St. Bernards of the sorrowful countenance.

Streckfuss thrust the rope-end at him, not the friendly frayed hemp of yore but hardly more than a thread of smooth, cold, slimy white nylon. A wonder that the loop at the other end had not cut the animal's throat. In sympathy for the creature, Reinhart took the line gingerly.

The goat's charge ripped it from his hands, and missed Streckfuss, if indeed he had been its aim. In panic it opted for the impasse of the corner with the sinks rather than the long westward run of the lab, relatively open, except for the freezer capsule, in the final quarter.

Then, as Reinhart approached reluctantly, slowed and yet made inexorable by his usual moral decision—that whether or not he caught the goat, someone would, and put it to death, and freeze it, and he, Reinhart, might at least be gentler—the animal feint-nodded to the left, then ran into Streckfuss' quarters, the door of which was ajar.

Reinhart pushed in after, and saw a bedroom as remarkable for its asceticism, for which Sweet had prepared him, as for its filth: twisted yellow sheets on the unmade bed, a greasy sock underfoot, sheets of paper widely disseminated, some whole, some in fragments, and others balled. Reinhart's nose-hairs erected at the sour odor—though that might have been the goat.

The animal had galloped beyond into the open bath-room, a claustral place indeed, windowless, and with one of those ceiling exhaust fans activated by the switch which worked the lights, as in a Holiday Inn. Nature at bay: a goat in a bathroom. Streaked gray shaggy crea-ture, snuffling over a Fu Manchu chin. Its natural set of mouth was a thin, mocking smile.

The washbowl was slimy. Soap scum had dried to powder on the chromium taps, and flecks of toothpaste bespattered the mirror. Streckfuss was unsanitary for a scientist. Toilet lid and seat were in the up position. So he would not have to look within even by accident, Reinhart kicked them down. The crash was registered by the goat's flaring ears, but its body did not move.

"I'm sorry," said Reinhart. "What it comes down to is that we are superior to you in force. There's no answer to that, believe me."

A young animal, with half-grown horns. He himself was an old goat to young girls. The experience with Eunice was too recent to be digested into any kind of self-esteem. Where had goats acquired a reputation for lust?

He bent and reached for the trailing rope, the end of which terminated a casual S-loop under the basin. An in-souciant movement of the goat's head flicked it away from his grasping fingers. Another effort similarly thwart-ed suggested that the animal not only was efficacious, albeit crudely, in the basic physical laws governing mo-tion and stasis, but demonstrated them with deliberate malice. That it also seemed amused was probably the sentimental anthropomorphism of a poetaster: nature, raining, did not weep at funerals or, shining, smile on young love, and its fauna, unless corrupted by domestic-ity like obsequious dogs, had no sense of humor.

Reinhart however, a long way from his ancestor simi-ans, felt at this juncture a certain sense of comedy—even with the classic significance, that in which Dante called his poem comic because it had a happy ending though few laughs on the way there: this goat, alone among his breed, was to have eternal life imposed upon it. His tormentors were his saviors—ever the claim of the tyrant in the past, but now, by the miracle of modern science, salvation was no longer a false promise.

Reinhart pursued the goat with greater ardor. Amazing how nimble it was within such a strait enclosure. With scarecrowing arms Reinhart could almost touch both walls of the bathroom, yet could not lay a hand on the animal, which by almost casual movements involving only its hairy neck eluded him.

The stink was formidable, but again Reinhart hesitated to lay it altogether at the goat's door. Streckfuss' little temple of sanitation was quite a sty, the bathtub filled with dirty laundry, a yellow looped brush, loathsomely stained, standing in the corner behind the toilet. The overhead fan, set above the tub, made more noise than ventilation, roaring like a rocket engine while the room stank, and to put it off one must needs extinguish the light.

The goat was getting Reinhart's. The latter took a breather, hands akimboed on the spare truck tire circumventing his waist in reaction to the belt.

"Well," he said, "you're certainly getting my," etc., and the goat pantomimed butting him in the testicles but actually moved only an inch in that direction, then threw up its narrow snout and, beard dangling, uttered a horse- or goat-laugh.

Sweet said from the doorway: "What the hell are you doing in there, Carl?"

Always a sexual tinge to this question when asked of someone in a bathroom. Reinhart felt a ghost of his old childhood apprehension dating from even before he had begun to dabble in self-abuse.

Bob said: "Just grab the rope and bring the goat out. That should be simple enough."

And was. The animal docilely watched Reinhart pick up the nylon line, and followed its tension as he trudged back into the lab. In observance of a code of honor, Reinhart did not turn once to determine whether he might be butted at this eleventh hour, but marched on, following Bob to the prepared table, where Streckfuss waited impatiently. Upon delivery Reinhart intended to make himself scarce.

There was a time in his life when bubbling blood, by reason of surgery or accident, did not provide horror. But without prior notice this strong stomach had weakened through the years, and he did not now, interesting as it might be, wish to watch the goat's blood exchanged for gelatine, preceded, one trusted, by some type of anesthetization. Streckfuss would never try to hold down a goat while pouring ether onto a muslin cone covering its nose and mouth—which had been done to Reinhart prior to his tonsillectomy in 1931 and it took three persons to restrain him.

The Swiss however was holding a bladed instrument. Under his direction Bob lifted the animal's hindquarters, and Reinhart took the shoulders. In this intimate relationship, the hairy head against his chest, Reinhart could affirm that the goat indeed stank in its own right, but in a ripe animal way like the cowpie into which your shoe has trod while wandering spring meadows.

The beast was no longer reluctant to struggle, and its flailing hoofs were superb weapons of which Reinhart had been unaware until he sustained several savage blows, sure to be remembered by blue-green blotches on the morrow.

As might have been expected, Sweet had less trouble with the back end, owing to the nature of the man and the nature of the part. In psychoanalysis the patient traditionally faces away from the doctor, and Reinhart remembered why: Freud could not bear to see those eyes. He shut his own and encircled and subdued the thrashing forelegs with his thick arms. This of necessity brought his face near the goat's, his chest against its shoulder. The animal was on the table, and half of Reinhart with it. They paused together, Reinhart to breathe heavily of the stench, the goat, after a tentative shudder, to accept, with the stoical realism of the beast, the superior power further resistance to which would be quixotic. Simple creatures eat, fuck, fight according to their needs and opportunities, peddle no ideologies and bear no grudges.

Reinhart opened his eye to seek the goat's. They might at this point exchange understanding of a basic kind, two mammals, haired, air-breathing, their females viviparous and milk-secreting. Reinhart did not expect to be loved immediately. He found the goat's eye to be shut, squeezed, pursed like a nonfunctional button-hole at the cuff of a jacket sleeve.

Streckfuss cried: "Still hold it!"

He had cut its throat with a scalpel and was catching its blood in a pail.

"There is no other way," Bob Sweet was saying. "Any kind of injection might permeate and corrupt the cells.

The living body is an entity, Carl, the internal affairs of which are complicated and subtle. Hans is not a cruel man. He does not torture his laboratory animals. As a trained physician his knife is swift and sure. The goat did not suffer needlessly, and gave up his life to save your friend's. I should say that is sufficient moral justification."

Reinhart had not fainted like a Victorian heroine. No, he had stayed afoot through the dissection, first maintaining the goat in close restraint until the last quiver—gory from wrists to neck, for Streckfuss was none too precise with either scalpel or bucket and also in the early stages the goat's head was capable of movement; then watching as the Swiss dehaired the belly with a power clipper.

Next Streckfuss made one vertical and one horizontal slash, spread the flaps of skin, and plunged both hands into the squirmy viscera and rummaged around as if he were looking for the odd sock in a laundry bag. Reinhart still assumed this was preparatory to freezing. A massive job of reconstruction would be needed at thawing time—unless the supposition was that by then the work of this mess would be done by noncorrosive gears and transistors, a single unit dropped in, hooked up.

Reinhart continued not to faint—the goat was after all not human—as Streckfuss serially emerged with several organs and dropped them into basins which Bob carried away.

At last he had pretty well exhausted the stock of the first-rate parts, the big publicity hounds like heart and liver, most of which Reinhart, a hypochondriac as well as a former medical soldier, recognized. The actual guts, that gooey stew through which coiled a Loch Lomond serpent simulated in vacuum-cleaner hose, Streckfuss passed over, to swoop below and snip off the testicles. Above the gauze mask Bob's eyes were more than businesslike when these slid like oiled olives across the basin.

"There is a test called Aberhalden," Sweet explained, "performed on the urine of the patient. Hans is one of the few men in the world, and the only one in America at present, who have mastered its analytic intricacies. In brief, this test indicates whether the organs are functioning properly, and if not, which are at fault. Hans has determined that Mainwaring suffers from a malfunction of the liver, specifically in the production of bile, which plays an essential role in the digestion of fats in the intestines."

Reinhart was feeling better. He was always receptive to reason. "I see," he said. "This will be recorded on the records that accompany the freezer capsule, so that when the liver-transplant technique has been perfected, Splendor can be thawed, given a new one, and revived." God, but this still sounded like science fiction—as did space travel only ten years before, and no doubt the telephone in its day. "And also a new large intestine, I suppose."

"No, no," Bob said. "We are not going to freeze Mainwaring, at least not yet. Hans thinks he might be able to save him."

Reinhart shook his fist. "You would never try that on a white man."

Streckfuss was furiously busy at another table, chopping some organic-looking substance in a glass dish. Making lunch again, no doubt. This was a place in which Hieronymous Bosch would have felt quite at home.

"I tell you, Bob," Reinhart stated gravely, "if you persist, I will personally call the police."

Sweet flexed his arms as one does to suggest a hale condition. "God knows I am myself Exhibit A." He bounced on his toes. He was still wearing the androgynous gown, and there was something obscene about the demonstration of vigor.

"Did you hear me, Bob?"

Sweet went so far as lustily to gnash his artificial teeth in a grin of braggadocio virility. Then he said more soberly: "Of course Mainwaring's degeneration is well advanced. Too bad Hans couldn't have got to him earlier. But once this biliary malfunction is straightened up, he should be back on his feet, a better man than before—in fact, rejuvenated."

Reinhart gave up on the warnings: one, because Bob paid no attention to them, and for another, he had heard the magic word, and furthermore pronounced without the smirk which had been its natural accompaniment since Ponce de León explored Florida, finding only alligators and sawgrass. To go back and start all over again, with the faculties of twenty and the memories of forty-four. Of course he was thinking of himself and not Splendor. Could it be serious?

"Do you have to be dying to get this treatment?" he asked.

And now Bob heard him, and answered: "I have tried to tell you a number of times, Carl, that I myself have received Hans's cell therapy, and here I stand as proof: Old age is a disease, and can be arrested right now, cured altogether perhaps still in our lifetimes. In this light *noth-*

ing else is serious—can't you see that? The treasuries of all nations should be put at the disposal of the researchers in this field. Men like Hans, who is alone here and practicing illegally, in fact. But there are several in Europe, some accepted and even honored by their countries, if the countries are small enough. In America especially, which should be foremost in this sacred mission, medical theory and practice persist, ignorantly, cowardly, in the same old negative approach."

Sweet laughed savagely, his ordinarily dispassionate mask extruding at appropriate points to produce, with the white cassock, the look of a celebrant of a proscribed religion, all the more righteous as well as merciless therefor. "The President," he cried, "will probably die at no more than eighty years of age. The most powerful man on earth. He can put people on the moon, while his own cells waste away."

"Chemicals," said Reinhart, "I know, are the big things now. The emphasis has shifted from the emotional, psychosomatic approach to drugs—"

"No," Sweet interrupted firmly. "Not chemicals but the basic unit of life, the cell, capable of infinite regeneration. We are not solid, Carl. We are assemblages of cells adhering together."

"True," Reinhart agreed. "You take any solid, even inanimate. It is no more than a cluster of molecules. They say that if you were deft enough you could slip your hand through a wall, between the atoms. Anyway, I saw once during the war, in England, Exeter Cathedral, I believe it was, a piece of wood that had been driven into a stone pillar by a bomb blast."

"Bopp," Streckfuss called. He held aloft an enormous syringe, of the kind used by veterinarians on people in movie comedies.

Sweet strode to the table. He opened his surgical gown at the back-parting and got his hands inside.

Reinhart saw that the tube of the hypodermic was filled with a suspension of pink globules, a slippery, gooey mess that reminded him in texture and form of that cocktail-party horror, orange caviar.

Bob's pants collapsed around his ankles, followed by his undershorts. He lifted one side of the gown, revealing a hairy haunch, and Streckfuss drove the needle into the ham so presented and began slowly to depress the plunger.

Reinhart believed it was more polite to go around to

the other side of the table, facing Bob, whose neck, however, was twisted and head inclined so that he could watch his buttock ingesting the weird nourishment.

"Which organ," asked Reinhart, "are you getting?"

"Testicles." Sweet was very matter-of-fact. He did not bother to look around and check out this statement on Reinhart's countenance, for obviously there was no irony in it. He was having minced goat balls injected into his rump—doesn't everybody? was the implication.

After that was done, over to Splendor's house Streck-fuss would go and shoot the poor devil full of chopped goat's liver. Reinhart was not the one to stand in his way. Splendor was dying anyhow.

– 11 –

There were various possibilities: that Blaine had lied to
Maw, in whole or part; that the girl had lied to Blaine;
that each was lying to the other; that Maw was lying
deliberately or suffering from senile delusions or merely
making a malicious joke in stopping the check.

Blaine of course was quite capable of the bad feeling
behind this bit of character-assassination, and he certainly
would be in the market for revenge. He was a pretty ugly
kid without his long golden locks. To Reinhart's taste he
had not been much with them. Up to puberty he had
resembled his father. Then for no good reason he had
begun to get this ratty look along with the change of
voice and a skin condition. At fourteen or fifteen, when
acne was still in vogue, he had a faceful of purple welts.
Sympathetically Reinhart supplied him with a new type of
lotion—advertised on late-afternoon teen dance shows
which, during idle periods, Reinhart tuned in on to watch
the jouncing thoraxes and sturdy thighs of adolescent
girls—the kind that masked the lesions with a beige cosmetic while "hidden medication did its work." But Blaine
was by then already well embarked on his career of
defiance—though not as yet openly vile.

Reinhart knew his own trouble as a father resulted
from a preoccupation with the ideal which actuality delighted in continually proving impractical. Hence he was
ever insecure. To Blaine he could not speak straight
without considering the ironies. He had not been able to
order him to do his homework, say, without reflecting on
a number of considerations which, evident in his voice,
vitiated the command to a mere wheedle devoid of
sufficient reason. For one, Blaine had always got good
grades without apparent study. For another, Reinhart
abhorred the idea of enforced learning as illiberal, un-
American, antidemocratic, and contrary to the best psy-
chosocial theory. The life of the mind must be pursued by

207

love alone. He had heard often enough that Shakespeare
will be hated if read under compulsion. At the same time
he was secretly pleased to have had *As You Like It*
rammed down his own throat as a high-school freshman,
else he would have preserved nothing from those days but
memories of *Reader's Digest* accounts of now-outmoded
scientific breakthroughs.

Reinhart had always lacked the essential of the com-
mander: the conviction not that his orders were sensible
or just, but that they would be carried out.

A brassard labeled DAD and a steel helmet, that was
what Reinhart needed, nightstick, handcuffs. As one
grows older he becomes more of a policeman. Yet his
own father had been anything but a cop, and Reinhart
could not remember having defied him. They had this
instinctive, tacit agreement by which each observed the
decencies towards the other. When their needs conflicted,
something was always worked out. If Reinhart was supposed to cut the grass, on the one hand, and play ball
with his pals, on the other, his custom was to put the
situation to Dad, who would always find a civilized exit
from the dilemma.

"Why don't you mow the front lawn, Carlo, which
shows? That shouldn't take so long, whereas the back,
which is larger, you can leave for when it is convenient,
on account of nobody sees it as much."

For his part, Reinhart then would accept only pro rata
payment, twenty cents out of the fifty which he got for the
whole job, taking the remainder when he completed the
back yard, which indeed he would do promptly after the
ball game.

It had been so simple, sensible, and just, and both
parties habitually acted with honor. Common decency,
Reinhart was wont glibly to think as a very young man, is
all that's necessary for a world without conflict. He saw a
ghost of this theory in the contemporary vogue among
youth for "love," though, typically, exaggerated by the
passing of the years. Just as you could not get a lawn
mowed any more for fifty cents, so inflation had affected
ethics. Decency was not enough, and the English, who
seemed to have invented it, no longer had their empire,
were in fact virtually bankrupt. Why should you have to
love a man to give him justice? Though Reinhart did, of
course, love Dad, but he might have done as much for a
stranger.

Blaine however, in his day, neither played ball nor cut

the grass, though the fee for the latter was now three dollars and the tool, provided by the employer, a gasoline-powered device for which no effort was needed beyond a gentle guidance. A young girl could have run it, and in fact, Winona sometimes did, or came outside, anyway, while Reinhart was making it roar, and "helped." What had she been then, eight or nine? Always large for her years.

What had Blaine done, if not sports and not work? He had a puppet show of his own making, quite cunning, cardboard theater, finger-puppets suggested by that glove-style hot-dish handler Gen had, the palm of which was decorated as a comic rabbit face in fragments of colored felt. Blaine himself stitched up a cast of characters on his mother's Singer, then manipulated them and spoke in several voices to a script of his own composition. Genevieve naturally believed this a confirmation of the boy's genius, predicted by her father when Blaine had been christened with his own name. Never having been herself a boy, she was not equipped, as was Reinhart, with the experience from which to assess the accomplishment as rather routine. At ten or eleven Reinhart had made his own comic strip, using a set of rubber stamps which, inked on resilient pad and carefully positioned on the paper and pressed, left the representation of circus animals, clowns, bareback riders, and aerialists. It was far from easy to make neat impressions, properly aligned, but the real creativity came in on the writing of the accompanying narration, painstakingly lettered in a box at the bottom of each frame.

Genevieve said: "Aren't you ashamed of yourself? Jealous of a young boy? Who is furthermore your own son? You make me sick."

But the moral question was: Why should Blaine get everything? He already had early youth, perfect health, and an allowance of five dollars a week for which he performed no chores. For the weekly four bits Reinhart had also, when the grass was out of season, raked leaves, shoveled snow, and organized the basement. Having begun these jobs as a son, he continued them as a father, getting help from his father when a son, but when a father himself he worked alone, except of course for sporadic aid from Winona, whose will was good but whose effectuality was impaired by daydreaming, the practical use of only her left hand, her right ever occupied with wedge of cake or jelly doughnut, and a flow of tears whenever she flushed an insect from "his little house."

While Blainey was indoors running up puppet dresses on the sewing machine. At that time he reminded Reinhart of Genevieve's brother Kenworthy, who after a career of harassing them in their courtship, had gone off to the Navy and thence to New York, where he allegedly had enjoyed success as an interior decorator, though he never visited back or wrote. Gen once displayed a page from one of those snotty fashion magazines, showing a serpentine model lounging amidst a total environment of jaguarskin, to carpet, wall, and ceiling which an entire jungle must have been emptied. Among the credits one read: *"Mise en scène*—Kenworthy Raven."

"What I wonder," Reinhart had noted, "is who shot those wild animals. You can't drop a jaguar with a slap from a limp wrist."

"I think you are a dirty shit," said Gen, who had developed quite a foul mouth over the years though she was careful to use it only when they were home alone.

At parties she was most demure of speech, even when, as the punchbowl got down to the discolored orange rounds, the rest of the crowd waxed raunchy. From the sort of smut related by a Harry Healy, whose conceit it was to use physician's jargon ("He palpated her clitoris with his glans . . ."), Genevieve would indeed retreat to the lavatory or, finding it occupied, to the bedchamber-checkroom and sit sulkily upon the piled coats. Reinhart became privy to this practice once when, leading Harriet Birdsall, who loosened up to the point of harlotry after two drinks, to a private place so they could join tongues and he cup her rather juvenile buttock-globes in his large paws, they staggered into a bedroom and saw Gen; fortunately her head was turned away and he could pretend he came to fetch her for leaving.

But what did Gen want? Reinhart had had less of a clue each succeeding twelvemonth of an era lasting twenty-two years. Pregnant with what turned out to be Blaine, which was to say for a period of ten months immediately following their marriage—the nine bearing Blaine added to the one for the pretense of pregnancy, by means of which she had induced Reinhart to marry her—Gen lay about in a wrapper and read mystery novels, the sort set in country estates and peopled with tea-pouring dowagers who disposed of parvenus with devastating adjectives,

trust-fund lawyers, lapdogs, and rose gardens, the lot
pussyfooting around in New or Old England.

Yet Genevieve had never shown a penetrating interest
in Reinhart's schemes to make money—if the grand life
was what she wanted, with upstairs maids and porte
cocheres and snowy napery. It was not. That happened to
be Reinhart's own dream. He understood that people did
not necessarily lust for that which they read about. Reinhart liked private-eye yarns, but he neither wished to be a
shamus nor live in California. On the other hand, though
he could not endure ten pages of the sissy type of thriller
he would have liked to be an intimate of the houses
depicted therein or, better, own one of sufficient magnitude to require a "staff."

Money. So simple was his need. The strange thing was
that in the early days, when Gen and he both worked for
Humbold the realtor, she had been quite ambitious for
him. On the strength of her urging and her expertise in
office matters, he had even squeezed a raise out of
Claude. Pregnancy had changed her, and Reinhart as
well. He insisted she quit her job: he would not have a
child of his carried to employment for another man. (So
early did he begin to give Blaine special treatment!)
Neither would he let her turn a hand at home. He did the
meals and cleaning himself, and of course when the baby
came, with all its requirements, it would have been
shameful to dump all the old duties on Gen in addition.
In fact Reinhart also took on several of the feedings and
most of the diaper-changings—it was not unpleasant to
deal with the intake and outgo of one's own flesh, and in
the cradle Blaine was a dead ringer for Reinhart, in
miniature and surely much finer-made, but with ears set
at the same angle and the characteristic depression of the
cranium just below the summit in back.

Genevieve's descent was allegedly *echt* English, at least
on her father's side. Her mother was a dim figure, apparently some kind of spiritualist crank, though in twenty
years Reinhart had not talked with her more than an
aggregate of twenty minutes, and that mainly on the
phone if he called the Raven house and she answered. In
nonelectronic encounters he had seldom seen her except
in the company of his father-in-law, to characterize whom
as an arrogant, tyrannical, narcissistic, and thoroughly
nasty king of pricks was to circumlocute to the point of
mealy-mouthed inarticulation.

And yet Reinhart had had to name his own son after

this individual, had been forced to watch another Blaine grow to majority. The two Blaines of course got on famously, demonstrating what's in a name after all, for Reinhart's father-in-law was a blatant fascist in marvelous physical trim though a drunkard.

He claimed to be a former Marine officer and had the uniform and Jap combat souvenirs to back him up, though no doubt these could have been acquired by purchase or theft from the genuine article, and such an item as the gold incisor tooth—reputedly knocked by him personally, with the horizontal butt-stroke of an M-1 carbine, from a Nipponese monkey-mouth on the Canal or Iwo—could have been swiped from a local dentist. (He had been trained at "Tico" and shipped out of "Dago." His jargon had an authentic sound.) Stolen from the dentist, because the elder Blaine was never known to pay for services rendered or goods received, and being a lawyer by training and an indeterminate period of practice before he was disbarred, he could not effectively be bluffed by his creditors.

Reinhart for example usually owed certain debts, like the one at Gino's restaurant, but he would pay them when he could and at no time did he challenge the basic principle of obligation. But his father-in-law, who frequented the haute cuisine establishments downtown— L'Etable à Cochon and the Epicure's Nook in the Shade-Milton Hotel—might eat three-quarters of a dish before returning it to the kitchen as ill-prepared, spray a mouthful of wine through his perfect teeth and send back the bottle, abuse the waiters and the maître d', then sign the check including tip, and not only never pay it but if he were subjected to the proprietor's importunities, threaten to boycott the place forever. He was of course only dunned by mail. On personal appearances he received a red carpet the nap of which grew deeper and the obsequiousness with which it was unrolled more slavish in the degree of his indebtedness.

Reinhart finally worked out an explanation: for one, his father-in-law persistently put on their mettle those persons whose business it was to cater to what began as a basic human need for nourishment and became a highly stylized self-indulgence. Obviously you did not require *caneton aux cerises* for life. Existentially speaking, such a menu was most arbitrary, even irrelevant. Therefore it would be difficult to establish that payment for it was necessary in the absolute moral sense in which a hungry man was

obliged to return money for the hamburger filling his but
lately hollow maw.

The other thing was that the elder Blaine actually
cowed these persons with his connoisseurship, which was
authentic at least in passion. Though the servitors were a
mixed bag of nationalities, some from no farther than
Kentucky, the chefs were approximate Frenchmen, and
more than once a baggy white toque drooped in contri-
tion as the haricots flageolets were identified as rather
American Great Northern or the eggs Benedict were
smothered in hollandaise and not sauce Mornay or if the
latter, the constituent cheese was domestic and not imported Swiss. Perhaps his father-in-law was a genuine
gastronome, or merely a shrewd psychologist. It was not
likely that Reinhart, who bought California wine by the
gallon, could fault him on technical matters.

What interested Reinhart in all this was Raven's assurance. The man was a monster of certainty. He could
survey a room in a single glance and identify its inhabi-
tants as base swine or sum up a historical situation, for
others fraught with agonizing complexity, with the stark
statement, "The coons are taking over everywhere." But
organized right-wing groups were beyond his pale, with
their flabby faces and loutish clothes, and anybody Southern because of the accent, and Hitler and his associates
had all been grotesquely deformed in body. Raven could
not endure people who deviated from the physical norm
in any direction, fat or bone, wore facial hair, walked
with an irregular stride, or whose nostrils, ears, eyebrows,
etc., were either exceptionally tiny or gross.

He was particularly a nut on posture, and might strike
Reinhart painfully in the small of the back if he passed
behind him—probably a holdover from his officer-days,
but after the breaking-in period of the marriage, Reinhart
felt within his rights to protest. Raven however was a
master in rising above what he considered meanness. He
would not argue. For that matter he would not fight
though he kept himself in beautiful trim in the gymnasium
of his club (on the upstairs bulletin board of which his
name was permanently posted as being in arrears on
dues), hefting barbells and making the cable weights
scream.

Raven's style was not everywhere triumphant. The lower on the social scale his involvements, the more likely the
resistance, and the attendant of a parking lot, say, being
virtually immune to any kind of approach, in fact sharing

with Raven a sense of disjunction from the rest of humankind, would fetch his car with no more grace than a sane man would expect, abusing the transmission and brakes, ripping the ticket from the hand, spitting on the ground, the usual series of natural uglinesses. Raven's practice was to get back of the wheel, close and lock the door, and, lowering the window two inches, call out in a penetrating but not loud voice: "You are a filthy hyena." Oftentimes the attendant was too far sunk in the mire of his spirit to hear the statement or at any rate to apprehend and/or apply it to himself. But on at least one occasion, Reinhart being present, a short, underweight fellow, with a ripe boil on his cheek, correctly divined he was the target of an insult and ran to the window uttering obscene imprecations. At which Raven smiled victoriously through the glass, turning once to show Reinhart, and accelerated into the street.

The truth was, Reinhart envied his father-in-law. He too loathed persons who were paid to render service and did it badly, but found himself paralyzed when it came to entering a complaint: his conscience would invariably begin to snivel about how little the flunky must earn in wages, how dreary the job, how limited the opportunity. In the old days Reinhard would swallow his bile and congratulate himself on his compassion. He now had the courage anyway to admit his failure to protest was due exclusively to cowardice.

Raven's solution was perfect, but you had to be a scoundrel to execute it. What Reinhart envied in his father-in-law was not finally the arrogance in itself, but rather the solipsism of which it was a product, and he hated him the more, without sympathizing with any of Raven's victims. On his side Raven had always been more or less oblivious to Reinhart. Yet, in the early days Reinhart had often found himself, willy-nilly, in his father-in-law's company. More than once he had come upon a drunken Raven and helped him home. Reinhart himself was wont to soak his depression in strong drink, which made his spirit despair even more strenuously and his body swell with fat, but though twenty-odd years older, Raven seemed immune to the deleterious effects of liquor. His belly was flat and his wind inexhaustible, at least by Reinhart, who had many occasions on which to gauge it, for Raven in his cups could become quite bestial when pursued, leaping onto bartops and car roofs and

swinging on overhead projections with a simian's insouciance.

As a lawyer he had seemed rarely to have a client. The
only one Reinhart could remember was the streetwalker
who had hired Raven to beat a bum rap brought by a
vice-squad dick who had been getting freebies from her
for six months in exchange for immunity and then treach-
erously, to fill an arrest-quota in response to a mayoral
cleanup push, put the collar on her. While planning her
defense, Raven went into one of his crazy drunks and
gave his client a savage pummeling. The hooker took *him*
to court and won. Another issue of this incident was his
disbarment.

But Raven not only survived the experience but
through it became favorably known to the fellowship of
local pimpery, who recognized a kindred soul when it
came to handling women and retained his services for a
decent annual stipend. He could not practice, but dispensed advice equipping the clients to represent themselves quite effectively.

Gen did not know the whole story, and overrode with
screams and howls Reinhart's attempts to put her in the
picture. To her Raven was still "the greatest Daddy who
ever lived," her literal inscription on the cards accompanying Xmas and birthday gifts. Reviewing this state of
affairs in a mirror, Reinhart could watch himself turn
blue.

But as his own daughter grew into a usable consciousness, Reinhart recognized that he might well be the Raven
to Winona's Genevieve. The girl worshiped him. It had
not been little Blaine who smeared aerosol-canned
whipped-cream substitute on his cheeks and scraped it off
with a pencil, in imitation of his shaving Dad, but
Winona, who subsequently licked off the froth and swallowed it. When hardly out of the staggering stage she had
already begun to pick up Reinhart's peculiar stride. It was
amusing to see that little blob loping along a block away,
and of course touching as well.

Or when, still too young to read—which was in fact
somewhat later than normal, for though not in any sense
"retarded," Winona was very patient about acquiring new
skills—she would sit next him on the sofa and pore over a
book chosen to resemble his in size and color, with her
eyes cornered so as to see his expression and simulate it
upon her own visage. As Reinhart did not usually reflect
on his face the emotions derived from the written word,

Winona grew ever more strenuous in her surveillance until, leaning over, she lost her balance and fell across his lap. It was of course impossible to read under this well-motivated harassment, and if Reinhart was eager for the book he took it into the toilet, where he seldom got settled before Gen or Blaine wanted to flush him from cover.

But if, as was more likely with every year of life, he found the narrative or explosion indifferent to his needs—the quenching of a thirst for fantasy-adventure and the confirmation of favorite prejudices—he would help Winona back onto her seat and pretend to resume reading but actually daydream while making grimaces, smirks, scowls, and even the occasional belly-laugh for her benefit. Each of which she would simulate in turn.

Sometimes they both held their volumes upside down. She was not *that* stupid or young. She knew that he knew. A charming little game of affection. There was no getting away from the fact that he was loved and in the only right way: uncritically. But it was also unfortunately true that one, or to be candid, he, tended to undervalue that which came so naturally without condition. That was to say, he got less joy from Winona's total approval than despair from Blaine's rejection.

Part of this was sheer snobbery, Blaine being older and considerably more clever than his sister. This might be a rotten consideration, but Reinhart had come to manhood in a day when psychoanalysis and other forms of secular rationalism demanded that the truth be told, to oneself at least, however hideous.

Then there was the sexual distinction. Growing up to womanhood equipped with the expressions of a male face would be impractical for Winona. Whereas, those were precisely what Blaine could use as an adult, as well as a virile moral code comprising such basics as an initial respect for everybody, its reluctant withdrawal individually from the unworthy and, if necessary, replacement by the just use of strength—the obvious points, simple enough to make theoretically though in practice complex. Seldom had Reinhart been satisfied with his own performance on these principles, but that they were manly he had no doubt.

But from the first Blaine had taken his own cue from Genevieve as to ethics. What he wanted was always right. Why? Because it was what he wanted. A continuous circle, self-perpetuating, and above all neat, whereas Rein-

hart's soul-searching, weighing of alternatives, and identification of motives were a disordered procedure, and
after all of that the issue might well be self-destructive.

Reinhart was never pompous, to be which you must
have power, and he aways wore the familiar soft button-
down collar of oxford cloth. Receptivity to all points of
view was his natural habit. Reinhart should have been
Blaine's best friend, that was the pity. As a drab bour-
geois father Reinhart was actually in disguise, wearing the
same makeup, which aged like skin, that had served him
as middle-class son. Underneath it throbbed the questing
mind of a philosopher-king, vitalized by the blood of a
poet's expansive heart. His own parents had never had a
clue to his true character. Why cannot they see me as a
prince? he had asked in vain for the last time, and joined
the Army at eighteen. He was careful not to have the
same failing with Blaine. Had read him King Arthur
when the boy was six or seven. Reinhart was wont to
exaggerate when estimating the boy had been friendly
enough as a tot. He would often apply to his father to be
read to on retiring—Reinhart of course never forced
this.

Blainey's favorite was Sir Galahad, the pure, the dedicated, whose strength was that of ten because his heart
was squeaky clean—a sexless, priggish, obsessive compul-
sive by Reinhart's own measurement even as a child.
Reinhart naturally preferred Launcelot, who carried
about him an aura of stain even in the bowdlerized
versions for children. Both were water over the dam now,
of course, except that Blaine wore his hair like the
Perfect Knight, which may have been one of the leavings,
and there was also the possibility, now that Reinhart
thought about it, that Blaine believed his own morality to
be Galahadic.

He had already begun in high school to find the existing
social structure as a matrix of fraud, sheathed in lies.
Reinhart had made something of the same discovery in
his own day; it was scarcely an original apprehension.
Later Reinhart decided that whether or not it would stand
up as a universal truth, it was immediately attractive in
the degree to which one had no responsibility, which was
to say, did no work.

In his first job, the selling of real estate, it had soon
become apparent that one could not at the same time
survive in commerce and adhere to the letter of certain
moral maxims. As a result tradition had worked out a

kind of gentleman's agreement, never vocally articulated but more or less understood by all parties, to the effect that each side would screw as good a deal as he could from the other, and the state of the market, an objective gauge and no respecter of personalities, would determine who came out the better. In a seller's market the vendor had the upper hand, but a recession would eventually come along. And anyway, once the buyer made a purchase, he was himself a potential seller: think of that, ad infinitum.

But Blaine was only a high-school sophomore, wise fool, when he arrived at an opinion adverse to the whole idea of private property. "The land should belong to the people." Generous and noble sentiment, but redundant: every single property-owner in the world was a human being or an institution comprising many. Blaine of course meant commonality, pure communism in fact, and who had not dabbled in that vision as a beardless stripling? And then grew up, at least in America, to see the mess made by the Post Office, the Army, and other public agencies. Reinhart would rather buy a house from a crooked finagler like his old boss Claude Humbold than be issued one by some prick of a bureaucrat.

"But if there were no private enterprise all the good men would have to work for the government," said Blaine, with his already well-developed air of Q.E.D., already offensive in its implication that at fifteen he could recognize a truth that idiot Dad had missed for thirty-eight years.

"But that's just it, Blainey," Reinhart cried vehemently. "There are no good men in that sense!"

He had him there, and Blaine winced, his blue eyes pale as skim milk. He seemed ready to weep. Disillusionment hit him hard.

"You see," Reinhart pressed on while he had the advantage, "in certain situations all men act the same, or most—there are always eccentrics—which does not refer to good or evil, really. They will try to make a profit. If the monetary type of gain is outlawed, as in Russia, then in power. People are a competitive race as well as gregarious—there may be some connection. Other herd-type beasts have instinctive hierarchies of power. They follow a leader who has whipped the other aspirants. So do we, but in human life the leaders are usually not big, strapping physical warriors but rather men with cunning, often quite small in body, as was Adolf Hitler, who was actually a flop at every other form of endeavor than handling people."

Blaine's tears turned out to be not a whimpering reaction to the force of Reinhart's analysis but the symptom of a suppressed rage which he now proceeded to liberate.

"You," he said, making a highly particular form of recognition, "you"—he actually pointed at Reinhart—"you are a defender of the status quo of substandard housing, underdeveloped countries, the poor and the wretched all over the face of the earth."

Reinhart moved quickly to say: "I think I get your point of argument, but there's no call to get personal, Blaine. Of course I am not offended, but—"

"That's what's wrong with you. That's why you tolerate social evils like racism—it's not personal. But it should be. It should be the personal agony of every human being. You should not be able to sleep at night."

In fact Reinhart was suffering from insomnia at this very period, which was that of his gas-station venture, in which all his resources and then some were tied up, and They had already begun to construct the superhighway which would bypass him. They, the people with power and money. Blaine should see Them as the common enemy.

"Look, son," he said. "I can hardly keep ahead of the bill collectors. We might lose our home unless I use every bit of my mind and spirit in my own business. I wish the poor well and deplore the way Negroes are treated in some areas of this country. Look, I always vote for liberals. What else can I do and at the same time look after my own interests, which are also yours and your mother's and sister's? A man's first obligation is to his own family."

"Human beings are dying of neglect," said Blaine. "And all you think of is your bankbook."

With its balance of $27.24. If Reinhart thought of that, he thought of trash indeed. A far-right fringe group had lately circulated an open letter to all taxpayers, branding several local social-science teachers as Commies. Reinhart had grinned and discarded the missive, but it now occurred to him that Blaine might be under such tutelage.

"Do you get this stuff in school?"

Blaine loftily replied: "I get it from the President of the United States."

"Oh, a millionaire by inheritance," was Reinhart's riposte. "They always grieve for the poor." It was mean, but he was somewhat cynical about Blaine's adoration of the Kennedys, as he would not have been were they penniless, homely, and dull—but then Blaine would not have worshiped them. "Anyway," he went on, "I voted for him. You can't fault me on that."

"Then why aren't you thinking of what you can do for your country instead of what it can do for you?" Blainey asked indignantly. A few years later he would savagely reject such political rhetoric—except that spewed forth by the white bums and colored criminals who called themselves revolutionary—but at this time his hair was still short and he wore much the same kind of buttondown collar as Reinhart, and a V-necked sweater in maroon.

All at once Reinhart understood he was being admonished by an adolescent boy for utterly arbitrary, imaginary failures. Were he to tolerate this he might next be accused of allowing cancer to spread unchecked and hurricanes to devastate the Caribbean.

"How dare you speak to me in that tone! I won't answer to a fifteen-year-old boy for whatever I do or don't. And I don't admire Communists. I saw plenty of Russian soldiers in Berlin and they were nobody to emulate, dirty apelike bums who went around raping German girls." Actually Reinhart had never seen this in practice, and the Russkies he encountered seemed like pretty nice guys, smiling at and saluting everybody, but he wanted to end the colloquy on an aggressive note of his own.

Blaine gave him a long stare. Reinhart was never good at eye-to-eye combat. He looked instead at his son's chin, already elongating from the roundness of boyhood. The thin mouth could be an implication of cruelty, the lower lip almost flat and thus not so much a lip as the inferior margin of a gash. He was still too young and fair to shave. He smoked on the sly, but not much. Probably grabbed a beer now and again, but in general he was not a rebel in his personal habits. Dad had never spied on Reinhart, and Reinhart returned the favor to his own son. There had never been a curfew on Blaine, but he rarely stayed out late and whether he had shiftless cronies was not apparent. Occasionally when Reinhart rose from bed to take a post-midnight pee, he could hear the dim murmur of Blaine's radio, never music, probably one of those all-night talk shows out of New York. The boy always got good grades, yet one seldom caught him with an open schoolbook. But he read much, and not in clothbound

volumes borrowed from the public library, as had been
Reinhart's adolescent practice, but rather from paperbacks
purchased on his own and usually those of quality both
in matter and format, costing a dollar ninety-five and up.
This impressed Reinhart, who would casually buy the
dearest whiskey, but thought much wine and most books
snobbishly overpriced, and if you got a lemon you were
stuck with an item whose resale value was nil.

The sidesplitting yet sophisticated novels of Thorne
Smith were among the fare on which Reinhart had
feasted at age fifteen and beyond, and also the texts of
drawing-room comedies of the New York stage: cocktails, dinner jackets, Manhattan penthouses, weekends in
Bucks County, and elegant women. Above all, elegant
women.

Two of Blaine's books were about whores: *Maggie, A
Girl of the Streets* and *Moll Flanders,* and he also seemed
to have taken an interest in the scandalous situation in the
turn-of-the-century slaughterhouses of Chicago, as represented by Upton Sinclair in *The Jungle.* Real fun reading. *Crime and Punishment* was at first more understandable: not too many years earlier Blaine had doted on the
sadistic comic books which slipped by the committee of
clergymen and other public meddlers who withheld their
imprimatur from depictions of pain and gore.

"Do you know," Reinhart had tried to tell him, "that
Dostoevski was once condemned to death as a member of
a student revolutionary group, a pretty harmless bunch,
actually put in front of a firing squad, which cocked its
rifles, aimed, and—the sentence was commuted at the last
moment. That sort of thing will affect a man."

Blaine showed no fascination with the personal side of
this. He blithely assumed it was normal to submerge the
self in a cause, even extinguish it utterly, and the peculiar
experiences of the author intrigued him not at all, nor for
that matter the personality of Raskolnikov, whom he humorlessly interpreted as a premature Marxist, striking
down capitalism in the figure of the old woman money
lender.

In other words he was not only a tedious lad but also a
ruthless one, at least insofar as his imagination went.
Reinhart found himself yearning for the bygone days of
the puppet show, then, following the gunfire in Dallas, he
would have settled for the first phase of Blaine's social
consciousness. Blaine had already acquired the belief that
the CIA was the Mr. Big behind the "military-industrial

complex" which held Presidents captive and manipulated governments so as to murder decency and imprison virtue. Blaine admired Kennedy, then, because he thought him vulnerable. And Reinhart had to admit he had a point when the man was shot down. But look at the killer: a runt, a eunuch, a failure, acting utterly on his own. You might even say Oswald proved the power of individualism in a world supposedly controlled by the blocs to which he had no access.

But it could have been predicted that Blaine would embrace the more outlandish of the conspiracy theories, and from initial grief he turned soon, perhaps in over-compensation, to thoroughgoing savagery. In a society in which a Kennedy could be murdered, this adolescent grew to legal manhood with a conviction to the effect that all existing institutions were at the same time moribund and insanely malignant, rotten at the foundation but in the superstructure terribly efficacious for evil purposes. And everybody knows a dying tyrant is the most wanton.

Thus all acts of America as a state were perforce wicked: if apparently kind, as in the provision of grain to starving Asiatic populations, then worse because hypocritical, exploitation in disguise. One preferred a candid war as more honest: like Vietnam, where "we" devastated the country and incinerated children for sport, Texas-style. And with reference to civil rights, a redneck illiterate coonbaiter was preferred over the slimy degenerate who worked for integration of the races and a social détente in which goodwill and right reason were applied.

Yet fundamentally the situation was purely personal. That's what galled Reinhart. He might have found it entertaining had he never become a father or had he sired another kind of son. Or had his own son maintained the current point of view without reference to his father, Reinhart might well have applauded first his self-sufficiency, and then his energy and courage in attacking the heroes and superstitions of the herd. Reinhart had never his life long held a brief for prating politicians, demagogic chauvinists, or nay-saying bigots. He was also ready to admit that many liberals, persons of goodwill, were, being human, vulnerable to the charge of hypocrisy and suffered from poor vision, distraction, boredom. Excruciating injustices remained, even in America, and there were no doubt lands abroad where the initial form of totalitarianism might arguably be preferable to general starvation. There were many types of killers, and as far as Reinhart was concerned Ché might not be the worst.

Blaine had a perfect right to his opinions on public issues. When the chips were down Reinhart could defend few shibboleths.

Though the businessman quailed at televised pictures of burning stores in Detroit and Cleveland, and the Caucasian in him rankled, the failed shopkeeper, the near-bankrupt knew a certain vengeful delight. The thing was that in a time when Negroes themselves were rejecting the role, Reinhart felt more and more like an old-style nigger.

But, surveying the field, and distinguishing essence from the accidents of bad breaks, ill winds, and, yes, poor judgment, he could identify only one human enemy as responsible for his personal ruin: a rotten little punk against whom he had never seriously offended, whom he had once cherished and indeed yet loved.

No, two. He telephoned the other at her place of work—just after watching Sweet get the shot of goat testicles, though there was no apparent connection; Reinhart had to get the straight dope on this libel about his congress with the girl next door; all right, it did then concern his virility—and invited her to lunch.

Genevieve accepted too quickly. It was ominous.

– 12 –

For several years Gen had been employed in a dress shop
or, properly, a "boutique" and there was more than jargon
to distinguish it from the emporia of yore: for one, an
incessant din of canned hard-rock issued from concealed
speakers; for another, the salesgirls were high-schoolers
and dressed in the wares of the house, skinny sleeveless
sweaters thin as the membrane of an egg and over no
underwear, and either flared-leg pants rising nowhere near
the navel in front and in the rear swooping in and out of
the apple-cleft, exaggerating the behinds of even the boyish, or a skirt so short as to be no more than a vulva-
valance. The skirt was in cooler seasons undershot by
colored tights, but they summered now with naked tan
legs. They were all longhaired, perverse-babyfaced,
flawlessly complexioned, loose-limbed, blatantly incarnate,
and spoke habitually to Reinhart in fluty little yips.

Not that he loitered therein unduly, enjoying freeby
ogles, scenes for which were in abundance: the shameless
little customer-wenches seldom drew the curtain if indeed
they used a booth at all and did not strip, indifferent as
Polynesians, before some rack which took their fancy and
tried on a succession of its burdens. No, Reinhart generally
avoided the place, at the cost of his eye but to the
protection of his heart. If he had to meet Gen at the shop
he would from the threshold shout the nature of his
mission to the nearest salesgirl and then wait at the curb,
somberly inspecting the dog feces, yellow sputum, and rain-
stained cigarette ends in the gutter.

Gen was manager of the establishment, one of a chain
of six throughout the metropolitan area, and pulled down
two hundred dollars a week, better than Reinhart had
ever cleared from any of his business stunts, and was
probably underpaid at that. For the place raked in massive amounts of hard cash from its spoiled clientele, or
rather their adoring daddies, all natural and not the sugar

brand of a wiser era. The comic-strip wife, walking blind behind her embrace of high-piled dress boxes, had been replaced by the adolescent superconsumer.

Reinhart's tendency was to put other people's daughters and his own son in the same category. Winona was not so classifiable, and Gen kept her isolated from the boutique clothes, having her rotundity covered instead in the modest garments typical of earlier decades and still offered for sale, no doubt with rural areas in mind, in Sears and Monkey Ward catalogues, of which anyway Winona loved to study the colored pictures while dribbling them with piccalilli from an upended sandwich.

The point was that Genevieve did not yearn to see Reinhart inside the shop, not with reference to his voyeurism clandestine or candid—Gen was never jealous; she was incapable of that much respect for him—it was merely that she liked to suppress all knowledge of their relationship from those not already privy to it. She had never spelled this out for Reinhart, but he needed no house to fall on him. Emerging from the door while he stood expectantly on the sidewalk, she would march past without a word or glance or an iota of acknowledgment that he was physically there, let alone attendant and her relative by law. Falling in behind, he often felt as if he might be taken by a neutral observer as sex criminal or purse snatcher.

Once she had come out accompanied by a lithe man who was scarcely thirty, Reinhart judged, and dressed, shoed, moustached, and coiffed in killingly high fashion, jacket vented to his shoulderblades, shoes with buckles, silky handlebar on his upper lip, and sideburns pointing to the corners of his mouth. Past Reinhart they flowed and when the fat husband, correctly identifying the smart youth as one of the owners of the chain—there were three, and pooling their years they could not have come up with ninety and they were already rich though having begun on a shoestring—when Reinhart, who had a merchandising idea or two of his own of which he would have liked to make this young genius aware, pushed up, begged pardon, and sought to introduce himself, the debonair chap without looking handed him a quarter and continued his conversation with Gen, who never batted an eye.

Today Reinhart opened the purple door and stuck his crew cut into the interior clamorous with music and papered in swirls of orange and lavender, with now and again an outsized wall-mounted blowup of a hooligan motorcyclist on which had been superimposed the face of the current President. Or a mug shot of John Dillinger, who when Reinhart was a boy had been fingered by the Lady in Red and gunned down in Chicago by Melvin Purvis of the G-Men after emerging from a movie called *Manhattan Melodrama,* costarring Clark Gable and William Powell—a newspaper extra with full details had been hawked through the quiet avenues of Reinhart's suburb. And a depiction of Shirley Temple, looking weirdly old in this magnitude, with a well-preserved Stepin Fetchit, lately and anachronistically adopted as chief whipping boy by embittered Negroes, though in his days of glory he had owned three Rolls Royces at the same time.

You couldn't possibly understand that era unless you had lived through it.

Reinhart stuck his head in and spoke to a passing minisalesgirl, who had been born no earlier than the last years of the Korean War, which had furthermore been postclimactic to the real one in which he had served under arms.

"Would you tell Miss Raven I am waiting for her, please." Gen used her maiden name for business.

In one revolution of eye the girl assessed and dismissed him. "OK." She proceeded to take her time, stacking floppy-brimmed felt hats onto a china cranium which when bald displayed the phrenological scheme. He moved out to the curb, below which the gutter filth lay in eleventh-hour stasis in anticipation of the streetcleaning machine, bearing down on it, with whirling brushes, from the corner. Prudent Reinhart stepped back to the middle of a sidewalk suddenly thronged with pedestrians ejected frenetically from doorways on the toe of noon. All the tables would be gone everywhere if Gen made him wait.

"Hi, Carl. How they hangin'?" said a man who bumped him without apology, an individual he recognized as Gus Kruse, an auto-parts retailer who had once put Reinhart onto a job-lot of tires he himself could not use: a truckload of the old wide whitewalls, after the skinny ones had come in, at a wholesale price you could not reject. Reinhart, who then had his gas station, rubber-painted these in black and sold them to clients for peanuts as a come-on. But the paint peeled off within fifty miles, and even after the refunds he had lost friends.

"Gus," he said and listlessly accepted a smaller hand which yet managed to hurt his. "How's business?"

"I'll live," answered Kruse. "I regard the big boys in the shopping center as a challenge, though they hurt me the first year." He had a patch of peeled red on the brown of his nose: found time to sun, so wasn't killing himself. He made the same speech whenever encountered, followed by the same lie that a giant chain had tried to buy him out for a fortune.

"What are you doing these days?" Kruse asked, showing two stained teeth through the slot left behind by the pipe he sucked all day behind the counter.

"Oh, things," Reinhart guardedly stated. Freezing the dead was not something you revealed flatly on a public sidewalk.

"Listen, Carl," Kruse said, nastily confidential. He burned garbage in that pipe. He hung a finger in the crook of Reinhart's elbow. "If you need something to tide you over, I could take on another man in the stockroom."

Reinhart's grin was like the yawn of one of the great carnivores. "Gus," he said, "why don't you take a flying fuck at a rolling doughnut?"

Kruse peered so closely his eyes crossed. "You are quite the skunk, aren't you?" Off he went.

Up yours, thought Reinhart, though initially at a loss to explain why Kruse had evoked from him this vicious response. Then he remembered he was meeting Genevieve. He hoped he had not exhausted his armament in the phony skirmish.

At this moment Gen emerged from the shop. She wore a suit of lime-green linen. Her hair was pulled back so tight as to make her forehead smooth as metal and her eyes slanted. She also wore small earrings and long moss-colored gloves. He had forgotten when it was that Gen last smiled at him. You could not count such occasions as when, the previous winter, he had slipped on an icy walk and plunged into a snowdrift which concealed a spiky hedge. Then she had laughed aloud.

Reinhart was more than a little embarrassed to see this woman with whom he had lived twenty-two years and was now separated from.

She asked practically: "Where to?"

He had of course not chosen a place. He was unconsciously stubborn about that. Never in his life when meeting Gen for an outside meal had he come with a restau-

rant in mind. This habit had been the stimulus for many
quarrels on rainy streetcorners, in curbed cars and hotel
lobbies. He tried desperately now to cover up.

"I thought Al & Grace's. There's not much choice down
here."

Continuing in the same monotone, Gen said: "Al &
Grace's has been closed for six months since the fire. We
could take the car and go to Gino's." Did Reinhart see or
imagine a malicious star falling through her eye?

"That's a thought," said he.

"Not a happy one," Gen said. "Gino called the house
last night, and it wasn't to give you a medal."

"That guinea will get every cent I owe him."

"I will not listen to your ethnithets," said Gen, for once
eloquent in her garbling of language though utterly false
in feeling. Her father habitually used "jigaboo," "yid,"
and other offensive sobriquets.

"Don't get on your high horse with me," he warned her
icily, then immediately tried his once-fetching grin: freck-
le-faced Tom Sawyer caught with his hand in the sugar-
bowl, as played by a cloying child star realizing a homosexual director's fantasy of boyhood. "Of course you're
right. I didn't come to quarrel."

"Don't crawl on your belly, Carl." A group of pedestrians streamed between them, and by the time the field was
clear Gen had got ten yards up the street with her
imperious walk, which she must have been brushing up on
lately through old Lana Turner movies on TV, because it
was pretty outlandish. To pull that off she should be
wearing those padded shoulders of wartime.

When he reached her she was already in the car and
airing it. He folded himself up and got into the right-hand
portion of the bench seat, which was so far forward as
almost to touch the dashboard, Gen being short of leg.
What this arrangement did to Reinhart's knees was hideous; he felt like a double amputee.

"Going to call me, huh?" he asked. "Going to Gino's
anyhow. You think I haven't got the nerve. I'll show
you."

Gen was a woman driver, absolutely devoid of a sense
of communion between herself and the two hundred
horses pulling a ton of metal at her command. Sporadic
braking caused the skirt to climb and remind Reinhart of
her rather elegant, lean haunch. She did not know the
thigh-problem which bedeviled most women of her years
and even younger. In general she had the sort of timeless

look that might hold out indefinitely. Her calves were
somewhat sinewy. She wore a scent that irritated Reinhart's nose with imprecise memory. Somewhere in the
mists of the past was a girl who had had the same smell.
It was definitely associated with an archaic desire of his,
one that he had perhaps gratified but in an indeterminate
way.

Genevieve had a plate of lettuce leaves intermingled
with boiled shrimp. What with the pressure on him Reinhart opted for a simple egg dish and was served instead
with seemingly a folded sheet of kraft paper inundated in
a sauce the color and texture of what you found on
sidewalks frequented by sick derelicts: a so-called Spanish
omelette. The waitress was the same as on that day with
Sweet, but she showed no memory of him, good or ill. He
had been prepared for this by Gino's performance at the
front door: "Good afternoon, folks. I hope yuz enjoy
your meal."

"Let's get down to business," Gen said, taking a lady-
like bite of unbuttered Rye-Krisp while simultaneously
looking at Reinhart and plunging her fork into the salad
and bringing nothing back. It was some sort of trick. The
lettuce did not adhere to the tines. Only when she repeated it did he see his body symbolically spread-eagled
on the plate. "And after this," she went on, "all communication will be conducted through our respectful lawyers.
You can rest insured that while I don't want to do you
any favors, I am no more anxious for publicity than you
are in this area."

Reinhart straightened his shoulders. "Genevieve, the
language is not friendly to you. I haven't a clue to what
you are trying to say. The sole reason I am here right
now is to investigate a vile story, a vicious canard, allegedly circulated about me by none other than our own
son. It exceeds the imagination for utter evil. We seem to
have raised a Doctor Goebbels."

Genevieve was manifestly so unmoved by what Reinhart thought a telling statement as to suggest she was in
the dark. Well then, the situation could be worse, being
shared only by Blaine, Maw, and himself. In fact, it was
not then serious, but merely a device by which Blaine had
bilked Maw of some more money to spend on narcotics
and the disintegration of society.

He smiled. "I may be exaggerating. Hell, he's still just a
kid. At his age I was goofing around Berlin, drinking

medical alcohol and chasing fräuleins. Plenty of things from then wouldn't pass muster."

With amazement he accepted a brown-stained mustard pot handed him by Gen, who said, oblivious to his commentary: "The problem is of course what you could provide. You don't own anything. You don't earn anything. But if you have some money stashed away I mean to find it." She took a drink of iced tea and her teeth clicked against the glass. The lemon round was still hooked onto the rim. Reinhart was never guilty of that kind of oversight: yet he was supposed to be the slob. At home she was wont to yawn without covering her mouth, especially when listening to a theory on which he waxed passionate.

"Genevieve, do you really suppose me the kind of person who would hold out on you?"

"Don't get me started on the list," she said, emptying into the tea two more of the little packets in which Gino's sugar was dispensed. The table was littered with torn paper and cellophane from the Rye-Krisps. Reinhart hated to eat out of a wastebasket.

"I'll give you a hundred dollars to tell me one instance," he cried, carelessly.

Gen said: "I knew you had secret funds. I always knew it, you bastard, for all your poor-mouthing. Many a time I have worn threadbare clothes so you could sneak over to see that whore."

Reinhart's tongue grew large as a cucumber. He poured coffee on it, but there was no room, and the liquid ran out at both corners of his mouth. He napkinned thoroughly. She was faking, of course. When Reinhart went to see Gloria he took the precautions of an atom spy, circled the block twice to isolate shadowers, knelt in front of the apartment house as if to tie a shoelace, and still half-crabbed, darted inside. If he passed another tenant in her hallway, he kept going as though on official business for the gas and electric company and doubled back.

So much for that. The moral implications were much more outrageous. He had not begun to visit Gloria until after Gen had got her job, which date also marked the latter's exclusion of him from her bed. That he had spent on lust what she required for life's necessities was a vicious lie. He was impeccable on this score.

"Don't try to impress me with your filthy talk," he said. "I'm clean as Sir Galahad."

Gen masticated a shrimp. She looked at one of his eyes

and said, switching midway to the other: "Gloria, apartment Nine-C, the Stuart Arms, 386 Winddolph Avenue, phone HArwood 5-8305."

Reinhart experienced a strange revelation of his own character. He might have broken down had she got it all wrong, or in any essential part. He could not have withstood a false accusation. Genuine tourist Reinhart, arrested in an Iron Curtain land on a charge of espionage, would need little torture to confess, but Reinhart the secret agent would die mute. He was unmanned not by the triumph of justice but rather by its failure.

He was now as cool as had been his Spanish omelette on delivery. "You are protesting too much," he said, quoting a line he had never really understood, but if he didn't she would hardly, she was really a vulgar, mindless bitch and always had been, he could never share books or ideas with her, he had knocked her up and married her and let himself in for twenty-two years of boredom when it had not been agony.

"I know you're from a long line of aristocratic drunks and deadbeats," he said, "but I'll tell you this: I think you have bad taste." Gen regarded her own taste as authoritative, and aspersions on that of another person were her maximum in obloquy. At Nuremberg she would have charged Goering with bad taste, dropping all other counts, and hanged him. So Reinhart now awaited a ferocious counterattack.

It never came. Instead Gen recited a bill of particulars: "Visits on May twenty-seventh, June eighteenth, June twentieth, July third, usually during the middle of the afternoon, though once in early evening." She turned her fork around and with the end of the shaft pretended to compute the gross expenditure on the bare Masonite between Gino's paper lunch mats, which were imprinted with a map of the shopping center. "At twenty-five per bang, that's not a tidy sum." She was hopeless with colloquial usage. Indeed it was a very tidy sum, and Reinhart himself wondered where he had got the money.

Of course he always managed, by skillful shopping, taking advantage of today's specials at supermarkets, buying in bulk, etc., to save a few dollars from the food money Gen gave him each week. But even so, even so. Oh yes, that's right, he had pawned his grandfather's gold watch in May, skunk that he was, and spent the proceeds on purchased cooze. Also a silver-backed set of military brushes left him by Dad. Sometimes he was rotten to the

core. However, the net from these amounted to seven
dollars fifty cents. Maw had tipped him on several occasions and laid fifty dollars on him for his birthday, but the
latter postdated the specified events in Gen's charges, and
with Gloria it had been cash on the barrelhead.

Reinhart shook his finger at her. "You've been sold a
bill of goods, Genevieve, by some unscrupulous, private
detective. That's a racket, didn't you know? He takes
your money and makes up a report out of the whole
cloth. I'm surprised you would be so naïve. You're
scarcely a young girl any more."

At last he had stung her. She said: "I'll outlive you,
you bastard."

It was then he remembered from whence he had got
the bulk of the money spent on Gloria's professional
services: he had stolen it from a secret cache maintained
by Genevieve in an old pointy-toed shoe in the rear of the
closet floor.

Happy in that memory, he said: "Of course we could
sit here all day and be bitchy, but where would it get us?
Or we could act like mature persons who have shared
quite a bit of life together, good times and bad. I am
certainly willing to admit that I am not perfect." He was
grinning over the theft, from which he had got away
scot-free. Apparently she never counted the lode, which
represented a holdout of her own from the common
weal: a roll of twenties mainly, filling the shoe like a fat
set of toes.

"What gets me," said Gen, "is, for all your sneers about
my lack of formal education, look at where yours got
you. And then I think back a long, long way—you have
had half my life—and realize I never respected you,
never. Not once, not from the first. *Sorry* for you is what
I have felt from the beginning, and now disgust." She
waved a fork-held lettuce shard at him. "But nobody can
say I did not observe my side of the bargain. I'm a
lawyer's daughter. Show me a contract and I will live up
to it. That's my nature."

Reinhart loathed the way she ate lettuce and soft-boiled
eggs and dangled a shoe at the end of her big toe when
she talked on the phone and cleared her throat while
perusing the newspaper, nonchalantly ignoring the major
stories, and opened a magazine from the rear and riffled
through it forwards, stopping at ads, clearing her throat
again, and *pitching* it aside, never putting it merely down,
when finished. He especially hated the way she drove a

car or it drove her, and her Sunday housecoat, her trimming off with surgical precision the thinnest strip of fat from boiled ham, her application of mayonnaise rather than mustard to cheese, her gnawing of an apple in the style of a man.

There were many other cavils, and laid end to end the lot added up to a list it was niggardly to draw. Reinhart did not believe the old saw about the little things in marriage. That was the stuff for Maggie and Jiggs jokes. It was the big things that had ruined his—insofar as he would admit it had been ruined. Gen had never liked him at all. He preferred that theory to hers about not respecting him. What did respect have to do between husband and wife? He had heard of a college professor who married an ex-whore who turned out to be fabulous as cook, mother, mate. There were many criminals with loyal wives, so loyal indeed that, if the stories were true, they would screw prison guards to further escape schemes.

If you really liked somebody you would put up with a great deal, and if you loved them you would accept anything, even a situation in which you held nothing in common except home and children and life. Reinhart believed this implicitly though when spelled out it might seem nonsensical, but so did everything else: why for example live at all when you were sure to die?

"Half my goddam life!" Gen repeated, dropping fork and lettuce onto the plate. "Only my childhood was my own. You got everything else, mister, and you have soiled it all. But do you know what? For all the reasons I have to hate your guts, I still only feel *sorry* for you. Sorry, for Christ's sake! How do you like them apples?"

Reinhart toyed with his omelette and, on the wagon today, drank some water which managed, in a glass full of ice, to taste musty.

"I'm going to startle you, Gen," he said at last. "I'm going to admit you are right in many respects. But look here: I have never run off with another woman. And, two, I have never done anything with malice. Let me explain that point—"

For no reason whatever Genevieve chose that juncture at which to blow up. "Why, you pompous son of a bitch! Who do you think you're talking to? I'm not a prostitute."

"You're no lady, either," Reinhart retorted, but somewhat quizzically. Gen had never had a sense of discourse as an exchange, but to attack him on his magnanimous admission was either shameful or insane. "Will you listen?" he cried. "I'm not arguing. And why the prostitute reference? You've got whores on the brain today—"

"Actually," Gen said, calm again, "I shouldn't make too much of that if I were you. You'll never break me, don't you realize that? You never have in all these years of hell." She took some iced tea in her mouth, and the lemon disk slipped off and fell with a plop. Reinhart picked it up, nasty wet thing, and put it into the ashtray amidst Gen's three cigarette ends, which stuck to it. Gen swallowed audibly: another trick he had always hated; and her lips quivered in aftertaste. "You'd be surprised how cool I was."

"No, I wouldn't," said Reinhart, almost without thinking. "You see, I've been to bed with you."

Gen lighted a new cigarette and filled the air with a great blue exhalation. Then she laughed coarsely. "Naturally I knew about your spyglasses for months. But I never made the connection. I really instinctively think the best of my fellowman. I suppose I am still a child in that way. I actually thought you were using them for birdwatching. You always used to be yapping in your sickening, sentimental way about how the same wrens return every year to that birdhouse in the elm tree which you made in manual-training class in 1937." She extinguished her cigarette in a mayonnaise-laden lettuce leaf and lighted another.

Reinhart gathered from the evidence of the long butt that she was genuinely exercised now: usually she smoked them down to the filter, and had never coughed in her life. This flouting of currently fashionable medical lore never failed to impress him. Gen was quite brave or desperate or indifferent, perhaps all three at once, for that everyone is a combination goes without saying. Of course, the first was easy for her because she had no imagination. Genevieve was the starkest realist he had ever known, and surely at the bottom of her contempt for him was his easy recourse to fantasy. In the early days of their marriage he had been wont to say: "I'll take you to Europe, darling, when we get a buck ahead, and we will picnic on bread, cheese, and wine on the banks of the Seine." To which she would respond: "But meanwhile the sewer has backed up through the basement drain."

Reinhart took some more water onto his palate, warmed it, and identified the subtle ethers of chlorine. So

Gen was privy to his Peeping Tom act, but only on circumstantial evidence. Funny she herself had provided him with at least an arguable motive: the wren house could be seen from the bathroom—if you removed the screen, hung yourself halfway out the window, and had the jointed neck of a marionette. But it was not like his wife to be generous in any regard. If she opened the door of the cell, it was to shoot him as he attempted to escape. You learn these things in years of cohabitation.

"Go on," he said with tented fingers over his nose, a saturnine eye on either side. "Go on, I'm enjoying this."

"I am only too familiar with your fascination with the bodies of other people," Gen said, "which is why I for one cannot undress in your presence. Though married you always made me feel"—she giggled, though not with good feeling—"*filthy*. Frankly, when I go to the john I always bolt the door and stuff Kleenex in the keyhole. I can't get over this idea that you are watching, waiting, might bust in on some pretext."

It was true that Gen had always been weird about bathrooms: for example, invariably holding it all evening when they were out someplace, even at a private house. Often she insisted on leaving a party early only because she had to get home to take a leak. Winona had picked up a phase of this peculiarity, perhaps: *vide* her difficulties in movie restrooms. Too bad that inheritance has such an easy job with the uncomfortable traits.

"The girl," Gen went on, "is young enough to be your daughter, but then you were a dirty old man at twenty-two." She violently waved her cigarette. Of course for some time they had been attracting persons at nearby tables. In a moment Reinhart decided he would do something, rout these kibitzers with a direct stare, or laugh encouragement at Genevieve and say: "You've certainly got your lines down pat. The play will be a smash." In years past she had dabbled in the local Little Theater.

"I couldn't care less," she added. "Oh, there were times long ago when I was quite embarrassed to be in the company of a sex fiend, but then I decided to consider the source or else I would go crazy like the Southern lady that Marlon Brando raped in the picture, always seating me in a restaurant so you'd get a good view under the next table that was occupied by any female at all from Campfire Girl to somebody's grandma and finding excuses to take Blaine to the skating rink when he hated to skate so you could see behinds under those short skirts and I

guess even you are aware there was something fishy in me
refusing to go to any beach with you." She dropped her
cigarette and let it sizzle. "I knew I could drown while
you were watching crotches."

What an ugly rhyme. However, Bob Sweet had also
accused Reinhart of undue ogling, and he would have had
no ulterior motive. Or would he? Perhaps you could never
say that of anybody. Whatever, the girl on the other side
of the first table to their northeast was wearing panty
hose and not the gartered stockings he had first taken
them for.

"That must have been a thrilling sight for her," said
Gen. "But with your enormous belly hanging down, how
did you expect her to see it?"

"Pardon?"

"When I was twelve," Gen said, "a paperhanger working in our house showed me his business. You know what?
I laughed out loud, I really did. I guess you would think I
was scarred for life, huh? That's all you know."

He might have known that she, his original enemy,
would come up with something far worse than young
Blaine could ever manage. Experience tells in these matters, and sex. By a sleight of hand, voyeurism, of which
he was guilty, had been transformed into exhibitionism,
which he had not practiced since the incident with Emma
Wisely at age five. If naked in Genevieve's presence,
taken by surprise, he would at least cup a palm. He was
funny that way. But she was right as to effective tactics:
this was far worse than Maw's version. It was pride-
making to receive an accusation of potency. A man of his
years and girth topping a beautiful sixteen-year-old. Mil-
lionaires and movie producers did it as a routine, and
measured their force in the envy of lesser breeds. Whereas
he could still remember, from decades ago, the scandal in
his neighborhood when the director of the Methodist
choir allegedly stood stark in a window and flapped his
genitals at a passing schoolgirl. Of weaker stuff than the
young Genevieve, she screamed like a peacock all the way
to the police station and though the charges were later
dropped the man was ruined, leaving town with his family. Years hence classmates of Reinhart would still point
at the house and say: "That's where old Sinclair used to
show his whang to Bettysue English." Who, as chance
would have it, was for a time Reinhart's high-school girl
friend in a fleshless, jokey arrangement. She was still

around town, now older, like Reinhart, than old Sinclair in his moment of truth.

"Let me get this straight," Reinhart said. "You are accusing me of exposing myself to the girl next door?"

Gen made a surly gesture.

"It so happens, my dear Genevieve, that the bathroom window is four feet above the floor. To show myself there below the midpoint of my chest would require remarkable acrobatics or a stepladder."

"It doesn't surprise me you would cover your tracks," Gen replied. "But I should warn you that you have the right to remain silent and refuse to answer questions; anything you say may be used against you in a court of law; you have a right to consult an attorney—"

"You'd be laughed out of any court in the land," said Reinhart, giving her tit for tat in pretentious dramatization, though he had not had her histrionic experience. In the Little Theater Gen had distinguished herself in several roles: the Hildy Johnson part in *The Front Page*, originally written for a man but played by Rosalind Russell in the well-known old movie, now accessible on TV (perhaps the source of Gen's square-shouldered stride); and one of the major female characterizations in a shortened version of *Twelfth Night* prepared by the group's director, a vivacious smalltown swish, this reported by the local weekly as: "Genevieve Raven (Mrs. Carl O. Reinhart) plays the viola."

Thus both roles remembered now by Reinhart, though there had been others, were transvestite. You could see where Blaine got his implicit encouragement to cross sides in styles of dress—in addition, that is, to the current cultural trend.

He was suddenly amazed to see Gen snap her fingers, precisely as he had done the other day while drunk, at the same waitress, and order another glass of iced tea. Her tumbler was instantly replenished from a clinking pitcher. Far from taking offense, the waitress said: "Sure, honey." The cunts were in a conspiracy to take over the country. Reinhart sensed his paranoia might be better described as simple misogyny.

"Now," said Genevieve, pouring more sugar from more little envelopes and making more litter, "it is common knowledge that the kind of man who recourses to whores is basically a homosexual. Added to that, this exposing ... I've done some thinking lately, Carl, no doubt long overdue . . . I can remember certain things now. Does the subject of costume parties ring a bell?"

Ten or fifteen years before, they had belonged to a set that went in for that sort of amusement, a horror to Reinhart. When heavy, you are restricted to comic impostures, figures from opera buffo, the singing cowboy's grotesque sidekick, big fat pirate, obese chef, et al., and once Gen had insisted they go in together (assembling themselves in the bushes outside) as an elephant, of which she was the slender forequarters and mask with dangling trunk, and he the mammoth thorax and rump.

Nonetheless the reminiscence brought back the ghost of happier times, when Blaine was a child. Reinhart seized upon it, perhaps more to distract himself than Genevieve.

"Do you remember?" he asked, "that occasion on which I went as Hermann Goering? And Blainey asked in his piping voice: 'Who's Hermann Goering?' " Too late he recalled that neither had Gen known, though she had lived through the appropriate era. She had no general knowledge at all, though she was anything but stupid. He had never divined that cast of her character.

"Frankly, what sticks in my mind," said Gen, "is the time Randy Hines came dressed like Shirley Temple, and you were fascinated with him."

Hines, in real life a matter-of-fact sort of guy, something in sales, and a golf bore, had thoroughly depilated his calves for the role. His feet were positively tiny in the Mary Janes, and he showed exquisite legs, at least as far as the knee, where his razor-patience had run out. Hairy locker-room thighs traveled on to the short skirt and ruffled panties revealed when he pirouetted. "Fascinated" was imprecise for Reinhart's reaction. He marveled at Hines's bravado in essaying the little tap dance and the falsetto rendition of "The Good Ship Lollypop." He would not have guessed he had it in him.

"No, Gen, no. That won't work," he said now.

"You don't think I thought you would admit it?" she asked. "It's a pity, though, you wasted all that time on call girls and exposing yourself, etcetera, when I can see right through you. It also indicates the basic lack of trust on your part of our marriage. If I hate you for anything, it's that. If in the beginning you would have come to me and made a clean breast of it, we might have had a different story. 'Genevieve, I prefer men. That's the way I'm made, I'm afraid. I am willing to get therapy.' "

Gen broke off her imaginary dialogue to light still
another cigarette. The amount of rubbish she could create
in the course of a simple luncheon was remarkable, and
of course that waitress never emptied the ashtray. Reinhart could not stand it any more, and asked the people at
the table nearest his right hand if, since they were not
using their receptacle, he might borrow it. A business type
said OK, it was his funeral, giving Reinhart the bitter
thought that while he had given up smoking years ago, he
might well contract lung cancer from breathing the air
near Gen.

He must ask his doctor about it, as well as the uncon-
scionable length of time it took him to pee nowadays: the
old prostate could not last forever. A cholesterol count
might also be a good idea. He refused to let Gen's latest
knife penetrate the skin.

"Go on," he urged her. "Tell me more about my
passion for Randy Hines."

"Of course, as we all know," Gen went on, "psychothera-
py doesn't usually work with homosexuals, but in your
case it would at least help you to accept yourself, and not
to do ridiculous degrading things to demonstrate the viril-
ty you have not got."

She leaned against the back of her seat. With his mind's
eye Reinhart cut off her hair and saw her father's face.
He was willing to admit that over the years it was he, and
not Gen, who had changed. She had really never been
anything but his harshest critic, becoming tolerant, though
seldom tender, at times when he admitted the justice of
her position, which was at best negative and at worst in
no feasible relationship with actuality, as now. She had
never for example given him psychic support in his business ventures. She—

Gen broke into his thoughts, right on target. "Like your
crazy get-rich-quick schemes, your grand-ose dreams that
any fool could see were—uh, dreams."

"Then why didn't you?" asked Reinhart prosaically,
after this verse.

"Don't kid yourself, I wouldn't let you suck me in. I
would have rather cut out my tongue than cast aspersions
on your sacred delusions. You hate women bad enough to
begin with, and I never would fall into a position where
you could accuse me of castrating you. I always detected
your game. You couldn't blame any of your flops on me.
But what I hadn't counted on was that you would still
build up this hatred no matter what I did. Why? Simply

because I was the nearest female. How dumb I was. But then you got me when I was a virgin—"

"No matter how violently we have ever quarreled, Genevieve, I have never challenged that goddam lie of yours," Reinhart cried. Of course their neighbors had heard everything she said, and when Reinhart turned and glared they brazenly grinned into his chops. So he would now take equal time. But halfway through his first sentence, peripheral vision told him they had risen and were leaving the table. Come back here, you rotten bastards!

"I know you have some sort of need to maintain that fiction, and I respected it in the worst moments. But why should I suppress it any more, with the kind of crap you're trying to pull on me now? Blaine got the idea from you that I will take infinite punishment and never fight back. Well, I cut off his lousy hair. And to you I say: I remember very clearly the first time I had you, in the back seat of my dad's car, parked in Cherry Wood, to which you in fact had directed me, whereas I thought I was taking you home. And I want to tell you something, Miss Phony Virgin: it was like falling into a well."

He would not let her ruin his big line this time. He hastily withdrew from the table and repaired to the familiar men's room, where while he waited for a stall, a nearby booth opened and a whisper issued from it: "Psst, I'm Chuck." Reinhart nodded and turned away. *"Chuck,* you know! *Make love not war,"* persisted the importuner. A urinal was free, and Reinhart took it. He tried to finish as quickly as the man on his right but for various reasons failed. All at once he was quite alone in the room, except for the pervert in the booth, who was hissing again. The thing is, Reinhart reasoned in terror, if I beat him up it will only seem as if I am the kind of latent who mistreats overt ones.

God, this was taking forever. He must go to the doctor tomorrow and have the gland palpated, though it was a miserable experience. "Finger wave" was the Army word for it. There was also some sort of scope they ran up through your tool, in serious cases.

"Keep quiet in there!" he ordered the faggot. "I am armed and will kill you."

"Goody! How thrilling," said the fag. "Wouldn't you like to beat me savagely to begin?"

This was ridiculous. One should never get into a colloquy with a degenerate. But he was finished peeing at last, and then the door opened and in came Gino. Reinhart had never thought he would be glad to see him, but he was.

Looking into Gino's pockmarks, Reinhart said: "You ought to clean out your restroom, Gino, or the vice squad will be on your neck."

Upon that note the booth opened and a plain-faced individual emerged to shove a small leather folder at Reinhart. On one leaf was a badge and on the other, behind clear plastic, an identification card, depicting the bearer and characterizing him as a county detective.

"We're way ahead of you, pal," said the dick, and went back to his stakeout inside the booth.

Gino was shaking his head. "You take the cake, my friend, for sheer gall. I don't care the little lady settled your bill in full. I would still cream you if you wasn't escorting her tuhday."

Gen was gone when he returned to the table, and the waitress was smearing a wet gray rag across the Formica. He got out his wallet. The girl shook her head: "She picked it up."

"Thanks for another wonderful eating experience," Reinhart wasted his time in saying. For the girl heard it as straight, and said, with the outthrust lower lip of the woman speaking man-to-man: "Give people the best, and they'll come back."

In a way Reinhart never expected to see Genevieve again in his life, but of course when he emerged from the front door onto the asphalt, there she was, waiting for him in the car. He reminded himself again as he had so many times throughout the years, that aggression will get you everywhere. He should have begun to insult her the day they were married. But though he knew this was sound practice, Reinhart was a pacifist in the depths of his stomach. There had never been a close correspondence between what he knew and what he felt. It was all very well to say Stand Up for Your Rights! But if you were talking to someone for whom lying down was instinctive, say an oppossum, you had your work cut out for you.

But he squared his shoulders now and strode around to the driver's door, opened it, and said: "Move over. I'm taking the wheel."

Oddly enough she complied, and he breathed again. He moved the seat back as far as it would go. Gen looked smaller with all that space between her and the dashboard. He gunned across the blacktop, maneuvering easily among other vehicles, and at the entrance onto the highway played chicken with an oncoming panel truck, crept farther and farther into the lane until it slowed to allow him ingress, the driver waving in angry acquiescence.

"Genevieve," Reinhart said, "I want to make two points. First, whatever you think, I have always been sympathetic to your plight. I know it hasn't been enough for you to be just a wife and mother, and it's useless to bring up the time of one's grandmaw when people were content to be housewives. You remember that feminist group you belonged to a couple of years back. Well, it may surprise you to know I read your literature thoroughly, and it was far from being altogether idiotic, though perhaps, for polemic purposes, the message was put in an exaggerated form. To get attention today you have to be outlandish." The car was tooling along.

Reinhart gave her a quick glance. " 'Combination janitor, chauffeur, and whore,' as I remember, is how they characterized the American wife."

This organization had been named GIRLS, an acronym in the fashion of the times: Get Into Resistance against Lackeydom Soon, was its strained referent. Like so many movements since the dawn of man, hardly had it designed the letterhead when factionalism reduced it to impotence. That near-Lesbians had been attracted to its banner, along with a host of women extremely unattractive in either person or manner, was to be expected, but the defection of one of its spinster officers into a peculiarly authoritarian marriage, in which her husband often manacled her to the bedposts and, in spurred boots and black cape, whipped her raw, was ruinous. Neighbors called the police, and the newspaper had made great sport with the affair.

"I thought it was great when you took up the theater," Reinhart went on. "I would not have stood in your way had you wanted to turn professional."

Actually, at the time, Reinhart had been quite jealous. He had himself shown a dramatic gift when, in high-school speech class, he portrayed an Irish peasant in *Spreading the News,* by Lady Gregory. However, when he auditioned for the Little Theater's production of *The Man Who Came to Dinner* (the part of Banjo known to be modeled on Harpo Marx), director G. Lloyd Havermill disqualified him, and proceeded to cast Genevieve as the female lead. Reinhart was only human.

"Yet," he went on now, motoring along the bland high-way, "I was sympathetic when you quit the group entire-

ly. As you know, I have never been a joiner, I have
preferred to go it on my own. Of course, that's the tough
way because you haven't got anybody else to blame."

Gen was taking all this in. She had got something out
of her system in the restaurant, so perhaps it had been
worth doing. It was therapeutic to vent one's spleen: all
authorities were agreed on that.

"But to any kind of sensitive spirit, the power plays and
infighting that go on in groups are insupportable. One
begins to wonder whether he hasn't better things to do."

What had happened in the Little Theater was routine:
a cabal had formed and outmaneuvered the Old Guard,
of which Gen was a member. Perhaps because of this
experience Gen had joined the Young Turks in GIRLS,
only to have that organization collapse through bad publicity.

"If you remember," Reinhart continued, "you went into
a long depression after Blaine was born. I don't pretend
to know what it's like to give life to a new person, but I am
sure the strain is remarkable. I know I felt guilty about
filling you with it." A piece of inadvertent arrogance. "I
mean, contributing my part.

"But then, if you recall, once Blaine was ready to go to
kindergarten you believed you would miss having a baby
to look after, so we had Winona." Whom Gen had never
quite liked, from the first. For one thing Winona had been
much larger to deliver, after having been heavier to
carry, than Blaine. Then for quite a while Winona's eyes
failed to coagulate, as Reinhart thought of it: the irises
floating like raw eggs. And she could not tolerate Gen's
milk, and one of her feet was almost covered with a
maroon blotch. These proved minor matters in the sequel,
eyes OK and the stain had dwindled through the years,
but Gen had probably not recovered from the initial
shock. Talking of the poor devils who had two-headed
babies and Mongoloids, etc., was to no avail. Blaine had
been absolutely flawless and had slid out as smoothly as if
he had been tenth-born, whereas Gen had labored with
Winona for some ghastly length of time.

Some anxious maniac was overtaking them at high
speed, weaving in and out of traffic. Probably stinko as
well. That kind of prick was never arrested, yet Reinhart
was once given a ticket for a broken taillight.

"Now that I think about it," Reinhart said, "until you
got the boutique job you had as many false starts as I did.
It is not easy for one to find the proper role in modern

civilization. In the old days everyone was assigned a position in life. You were born a serf and stayed one. It is difficult to deal with freedom. You take me, I was interested in so many things when young I couldn't decide on any."

The madman's car had swung in behind Reinhart's bumper and stayed there. Reinhart didn't like it; you could never tell when a guy like that would let go again.

"My main purpose in asking you to lunch today got sidetracked by our interesting discussion of other matters. I've finally found it. The opportunity I've been looking for for years. I ran into an old high-school friend named Robert Sweet. He is a pretty fantastic individual, made a million in business and has now gone into scientific research. I don't know if you have ever heard of a thing called cryonics, the freezing of human beings immediately after death, but—there is a guy behind us who is blinking a red light." Reinhart adjusted the rear-vision mirror. "He is some kind of nut. You should have seen how he was driving before, and now this red light. The cops should take a person like that off the highway, but you never see one when you want him."

Gen now made her first statement since getting into the automobile. She looked out the back window. "That's an unmarked police car," she said. "Pull over onto the shoulder."

Reinhart braked slowly. Probably another broken taillight. Gen never took care of her car.

When the guy got out he was revealed in breeches and puttees, and put on the trooper's hat he had concealed for his imposture, stinking stunt.

He was a youngish fellow, with a face that could have passed anywhere. Through Reinhart's window he said: "Why didn't you stop as soon as I signaled?"

"I didn't know who you were," Reinhart answered indignantly.

"Are you aware of the speed limit here?"

"Fifty, isn't it?"

"You're certainly right about that," said the policeman. "I clocked you at fifty-two. That's two miles over the limit and therefore you were breaking the law."

"Two miles? Is that serious, officer?"

"My personal interpretation doesn't count, sir."

"Isn't that just the trouble?"

"Sir?" This man had no expression whatever. Reinhart

found himself longing for the old-time brute of a traffic cop, sneering and abusing his power.

"With modern times," Reinhart said. "We are people, not things."

"May I have your license and registration, sir?"

Reinhart handed his license over, saying: "You don't agree? You see me as a number on a document, don't you?"

"Oh, shut your goddam mouth." For a moment Reinhart was gratified to think he had pierced the officer's plastic hide, but the speech had been in soprano and came from behind his own back.

"Why," asked the cop, "won't you give me your registration?"

"This is not my car."

"Did you steal it?" the officer asked abstractedly, reading Reinhart's license.

"Yes!" Reinhart cried, before turning to ask Gen for the document.

"Keep your hands in sight and get out slowly," said the cop, unbuttoning the flap of his holster.

When Reinhart had performed the first part of the charade, he was directed to spread-eagle himself on the side of the hood.

"This is carrying the joke too far," he said. "My wife owns this vehicle and she has the registration."

The policeman forced him against the hood and felt him all over, including between the legs, thus devaluing a childhood fantasy of Reinhart's to the effect that one could pack a rod in a kind of jockstrap and get away with it when frisked. The cop did not linger there. He was no deviate. Still, if he had been, one would have been at his mercy. Reinhart determined to write a letter of protest to his state senator.

"Can I get back in now?" he asked, with his cheek flattened against the veneer of road film. No answer, so Reinhart straightened up. Gen was giving the registration to the cop. Reinhart wondered how many cars had passed while he underwent his humiliation.

Having returned the papers, the officer said: "Let me give you a piece of advice, sir. You should not clown around in these matters."

Reinhart nodded like a chastened schoolboy.

"You look like a respectable gentleman. You wouldn't want to get into a terrible accident and kill your wife. So you get where you're going a little bit later, so what?"

"No ticket," Reinhart said when they were underway again. "But I had to listen to a lot of Dutch-uncle crap. Fortunately I know how to deal with those characters. It's fashionable now to hate cops the way Blaine does, but most of it is empty rhetoric, as usual, on the part of people who have had no experience with them. A cop is not necessarily a fascist. If you seem respectable to him he will treat you decently enough."

"And if," Gen said, "when he looks inside your registration he finds a folded ten-dollar bill, he won't give you a ticket."

Reinhart's cheeks puckered. "Why couldn't you have got it out faster then? Letting me be put through that degradation."

"Was it me who told him the car was stolen?"

"Shit," said Reinhart.

"Up yours," said Gen.

Reinhart checked himself. "I am going to astound you out of your skull, Genevieve. I am genuinely going to rise above this incident, which would have crippled me only a week ago." He kept the speedometer needle at forty. "To resume, I have become associated with Bob Sweet's Cry-on Foundation at a handsome figure. But perhaps more important than the money is the feeling that one is doing something valuable—in this case, believe it or not, developing a process that may result in eternal life for humankind."

Other cars streamed past them, obviously at speeds in excess of fifty mph.

"Naturally, success is not guaranteed, but incredible results have already been achieved, enough so that one is not lunatic to hope, to dream—"

"What is your specific job?" asked Gen.

"I suppose you might describe it as public relations. Not all my duties have been spelled out. I have just been taken on."

"It sounds like a quack thing to me."

"I thought you were receptive to new ideas, Genevieve. You pick up all Blaine's callow theories, which are old as hell. When did you ever hear of the possibility of everlasting life, literally speaking? Can you grasp that?"

Gen sniffed at the windshield. "I'm not impressed."

"What the hell would impress you, then?" But Gen was hopeless at science and technology. She had once stripped the gears of an electric can-opener.

"Look," said he, "this age will be remembered not

because boys wore shoulder-length hair, but rather because man went to the moon, and, perhaps, also conquered death. Blaine is anything but avant-garde. The
real revolutionaries are those crew-cut guys alone up in
space, while their loyal families wait on the ground, going
to Sunday school and subscribing to the *Reader's Digest*."

Cars kept zooming by. The eternal flux, mankind in
motion, but from outer space you could see only geograph-
ical distinctions, blurred by clouds, but the world apparently looked just like a ball-of-the-world, South America
with its elongated tail, the boot of Italy: amazing. Matter
was so rich, and there were tears in things.

Gen said, with a hint of worry: "I'm not putting down
science. What I seriously question is your part in this,
Carl. Your only association with medical affairs is in
being a lifelong hypochondriac. Who are you going to
freeze, your mother? You had better, because you can't
get along without her."

"I haven't been able, ever, to get along *with* her,"
Reinhart said semifacetiously.

"You are given to cute sayings, but you really should
examine that relationship, Carl. That has been the trouble
all along. A mama's boy like you should never have got
married in the first place."

The turn-off for the old business district lay just ahead,
a hairpin for which you had to brake down to twenty. So
occupied, Reinhart was not in a situation in which to
formulate a rejoinder, and Genevieve, with her keen
knowledge of practical psychology, exploited the advantage.

"I suppose what you'll want to do now is set up
housekeeping with her again. I'd move into Senior City if
I were you. And we'll have to set up some sort of escala-
tor arrangement on the child support and alimony, should
she leave you all that money," and so on, spite, spite,
spite.

Oddly enough a parking spot offered itself quite near
the boutique. Reinhart entered into a competition for it
with an insane female who was backing at high speed the
length of the block. To save time he had to nose in at an
angle, but he won.

He returned the keys to Gen, who said: "OK, Carl. No
reason why we can't act like intelligent people and let our
lawyers handle the rest of it." She laughed quite prettily.
He was again conscious of her scent, as he had been on

the trip out, and he now remembered the other girl it reminded him of: also Genevieve, though looking back he could see how that one developed into this one, given his own contribution.

The woman he had beaten out for the parking spot, a slender young-mother type in sunglasses, with freckled arms tensed against the steering wheel, had stopped opposite his window and was cursing him.

"Blow it out your barracks bag," Reinhart told her, fetching up an old one from the days before she had even been born, fresh bitch.

Her response was in a series of Anglo-Saxon expletives, dating from much farther back.

Reinhart turned to Gen: "Forget about all that bravado talk. Look, I'm starting at fifteen thousand per annum, which is actually some sort of grant that according to Bob is tax-free. This is guaranteed." He put his hand on her hard knee and said wryly: "This is a sure thing, because I'm not running it."

Gen began to melt in an unprecedented style. She put her hand on top of Reinhart's, she showed him her softening eyes, she spoke in a voice which, relative to her usual, was benedictory.

"You know, Carl," she said, "I'm not the worst person in the world."

Reinhart was moved, while at the same time feeling the satisfaction of cynicism confirmed: he knew that quoting the figures would do the job. And why not? Money was properly enough a gauge of virility in a day when violence was widely condemned. Women had to have some means of measurement, and men a goal.

"You're the best wife I ever had," he told her, taking the uncomfortable edge off his sentimentality with a bit of irony.

"But," Gen said with her loving look he had not seen for so many years, "there is someone else."

Oh, that's perfectly OK, Reinhart almost said from the depths of his bliss, an emotion that always made him tolerant of others' foibles.

"Somehow I knew you'd understand," said Gen.

Something was clicking in Reinhart's mouth: his teeth seemed to be chattering in mid-July.

He said: "I suppose you wouldn't want to tell me who."

Gen smiled at the bridge of his nose. "All right, then. You'd know eventually anyway. Harlan Flan."

"The owner of these dress shops," said Reinhart, who had heard the name often enough. "He's under thirty still, isn't he?"

"Imagine," said Gen. "Falling in love again."

The title of Marlene Dietrich's biggest hit.

There were moods in which Reinhart could admit to himself that his peeping at the girl next door constituted prima facie evidence that he was a dirty old man, a term which was recognized everywhere in the culture—though not in that of many Oriental societies—as referring to a comic condition. The desire to commit a crime conjoined with the inability or lack of equipment so to do was for some reason humorous throughout Western civilization. Look at those movies in which a gang of inept thugs tried to rob a bank and botched it: their failure made them downright lovable.

The reverse did not lead to commensurate conclusions. For grown women who lusted for younger men there existed, so far as he knew, no handy term. Life was by no means to be described as an equilibrium.

That is an obvious, even platitudinous conclusion, is it not, Reinhart? His imaginary playmate, as a child, Jim Jackson, had always called him "Reinhart," whereas Reinhart had always used Jim's full name. Jim Jackson was an older boy and did everything better than Reinhart. He was useful because Reinhart had no real brother, and one often felt the need to discuss things with someone intimate. Not that Jim Jackson was at all benevolent. More often than not he was a ruthless critic of his creator, and a natural one-upman. Whereas Reinhart felt like a sodden sandbag when he tried to chin himself, Jim Jackson would seize the bar and rise and fall like the moving part of a machine. Then when Reinhart's turn came, Jim Jackson would hang on his knees.

Had he not been one's own invention one would have loathed him. From what Reinhart gathered from friends who had genuine older brothers, the latter acted like Jim Jackson within the family. The difference was that Jim Jackson, unlike a real brother, behaved traitorously when Reinhart was under attack from outside. When, for example, Reinhart was five years old, he was beaten up in a public park by a great big girl of ten or eleven, who stole his orange popsicle. He might have run away from her had not Jim Jackson said: "Don't be scared. You're a boy." So she slapped Reinhart in the face, and Jim Jackson said: "You can't hit her back because she's a girl and you're a boy." She took away Reinhart's popsicle. Jim Jackson said: "What a crybaby you are. You got beaten up by a girl."

Somewhere along the line Jim Jackson was replaced by Reinhart's conscience, which as in all exchanges was both better and worse. If Reinhart wanted to he could expunge Jim Jackson on the moment: he always had that over him as an ultimate. "You can do anything better than I can because I made you that way!" Reinhart might cry, in the sort of chagrin that is a form of satisfaction. But with conscience, he was himself Jim Jackson, and aware of a terrible loss of power.

It had been almost forty years since Jim Jackson's retirement from the scene, but it was still too soon for his reappearance. Reinhart computed that he should have another two decades before true senility settled in, bringing with it the incunabula of the first to the second childhood. Blaine would then be where Reinhart was now, hopefully with a son of his own, an arch-conservative of the kind who undoubtedly would be, in the then-current backlash fashion, a pursed-lip Puritan with cropped skull, militaristic, traditionally religious, and biased against any form of deviation from the white middle-class norns. Thought of this brought a wince of pleasure to Reinhart's rheumy old eyes.

Yet it seemed to be Jim Jackson who spoke now in Reinhart's thoughts. *You're still the same old horse's ass, boy,* he said next. *For forty years. That must be some kind of record.*

Reinhart shrugged in mock modesty. Even with Jim Jackson he had to keep up appearances. *Still the same old irony, too,* Jim Jackson said. *You should get a new style.*

I know, said Reinhart.

On the other hand, your strategy has always worked beautifully. The other guy always turns out to be the shit. So why change now? You are better than any of them. Isn't that the idea?

Your interpretation tends to corrupt, said Reinhart. They all have their reasons, which, under the aspect of

eternity, may be as good as mine. Take Gen. Think she'd
be running off with this young kid if it had been I instead
of him who owned the string of shops? And Blaine. He
could have been the typical pleasure-loving punk that I
was myself: Joe College porkpie hats and old cars with
corny slogans written on them in whitewash, Andy Hardy
and his infantile values. But no, not him. He might have
an abrasive manner, but he is probably right that the
system is rotten, the fucking IBM machines have taken
over, social injustice is still rife—

When was it not?

But every young man should have a right to learn that
for himself.

*In fact, it may be a dangerous error to look at life in
terms of justice. It leads to quantitative judgments, quo-
tas, rosters, the relative sizes of mobs, and fucking computers. You see, it is precisely those persons who take
justice most seriously who are most unjust. . . . Why are
you defending your family?*

Because they are my family.

You are, said Jim Jackson, *the most unjust man I have
ever known.*

Reinhart was standing at the parapet of the observation
tower of the Bloor Building, the forty-seventh tallest
building in the United States, its rating having fallen since
the thirties, when it was constructed, owing to more
recent erections elsewhere from coast to coast. He was
not armed with its current rank as suicide-site, always a
subsidiary function of skyscrapers, but that it had known
such use was not only established by his memory but also
confirmed by the rusty meshwork rising three feet above
his head to terminate in an in-curving section of stranded
barbed wire. A nimble individual could still get over it, no
doubt, but he would likely cut his hands—which might
well dissuade a certain fastidious type of neurotic.

You would get your clothes rusty, said Jim Jackson.
Why don't you try weed-killer?

Because it would be painful!

Sleeping pills.

I wouldn't like the feeling of going to sleep when it
would be fraudulent, Reinhart said. Funny. If I want to
die, I want to die. Beginning it as a nap seems wrong,
that's all. And to get my shotgun I'd have to go home.
Slashing the wrists in the YMCA showers, that's pretty
squalid. Anyway, the fags swarm all over you as soon as
you come in the door there. Then there's hanging, but a

body of my weight would pull any fixture from any
ceiling and crack the floor it fell onto, leading only to
more embarrassment. More irony, I'm afraid. A man
without a home has a pressing motive for suicide but
lacks the privacy in which to commit it. So I came up
here. Now I can test the various hypotheses as to death
resulting from a fall from a great height. Some say one is
unconscious before hitting the ground, owing to the rush
of wind or fright itself. I have watched movies taken in
the air of free-fall parachutists, an ever more popular
sport. They assume the attitude of swimmers.

*Enough bravado, said Jim Jackson. I'm familiar with
your lifelong taste for fantasy-executions: Ronald Colman
walking bravely to the guillotine, the guys who before the
firing squad spurn the blindfold and make sardonic quips.
In real life a man's bowels open on the way to the
gallows, and many victims of the electric chair must be
carried there. When the human body hits the ground from
a fall of sufficient height, fragments of it fly off to
considerable distances, including the head, which owing to
its spherical shape might bounce and roll for yards. The
progress of the head of the last jumper from this observation deck is a case in point, but was never traced in the
newspapers for reasons of delicacy. High over an old
Volkswagen on the first bounce, leaping on the second
over a brand-new Camaro with racing stripe and wide-
oval tires, then under a Number 10 bus—*

You think I don't have enough guts?

*I am simply reminding you that reality is ineluctable.
The price must be paid. Suicide is certainly one effective
means of dealing with your problem; indeed, the most
certain of immediate success, but it is not free and unen-
cumbered.*

But look at the alternative, said Reinhart. I can't show
my face again in town if Genevieve marries this Flan.

*You would kill yourself because of social humiliation?
Isn't that a superficial motive?*

You would talk me out of suicide because the means I
have chosen are unaesthetic. I don't call that serious. I
would be well out of it by the time my head went
bouncing down the street.

*But you think the other people in town are mainly
bastards anyway. So why do you care what they think of
you?*

It's funny how that happens. No matter how low your

opinion is of another guy, you want him to be favorably impressed by you. I've noticed that when dunned by panhandlers.

Better get started, then, said Jim Jackson. *A man with your figure won't have an easy time with this fence.*

Not yet. That guard has his eye on me. He is suspicious of a person who comes up here alone and talks to himself.

"Well sir," Reinhart said aloud, very loud, walking towards the functionary. "You can sure see for miles and the people look like ants and the view is really something."

He was a man of about Reinhart's age, and broken veins in the nose suggested he was no stranger to a drink. This was a job calling for little ambition and no intelligence whatever. Reinhart saw in close-up that the guard's look was very dull indeed. One could probably climb up the wire right in front of him without challenging his manifest disaffiliation. "It's a long way down," Reinhart added, reaching his quota of clichés from high places.

" 'Though every prospect pleases, and only man is vile,' " said the guard.

"Hey, I know that one," Reinhart said. "Only isn't the first word 'Where'?"

"No," the guard stated firmly, bringing up from the hip a paperbound volume into which his right index finger was embedded. He opened the book and read:

> "What though the spicy breezes
>   Blow soft o'er Ceylon's isle,
> Though every prospect pleases,
>   And only man is vile.

Bishop Heber, 1782-1826."

"Is that right. I would have said Dryden or possibly Pope, I don't know why."

The guard leafed through the book. "Here's the Pope," he said. " 'The vulgar boil, the learned roast an egg.' I don't get that. . . . Here's one:

> Men, some to business, some to pleasure take
> But every woman is at heart a rake.

I don't get that either.

See how the world its veterans rewards!
A youth of frolics, an old age of cards.

I'm a veteran," he added quizzically, "and that's a crock
of shit."

"Me too," said Reinhart. "But I don't think he means
'veteran' in the sense of the American armed forces. He
lived a couple of centuries ago and was English."

"I was in England for a year before the invasion," said
the guard, "and I didn't like one little bit of it. I picked
up a whore once in the blackout and when we got to her
place and she put on the light, she had two sore eyes.
How do you like that?"

He was one of those bitter individuals who are also
cryptic. "Who was the other guy you mentioned?" he
asked, thumbing roughly through the book. "Drysdale?"

"Dryden," said Reinhart. "Those names are always
linked, Pope and Dryden, like Shelley and Keats."

"Billy Jones and Ernie Haire, the Interwoven Pair,"
the guard said. "I never went to college."

"Didn't you take advantage of the GI Bill?" Reinhart
asked with a lack of sympathy.

"Fuck *that*," said the guard. He had one long hair
growing from his left ear, and several ancient blackheads
spotted here and there about his face. Reinhart could
never understand the sort of persistent inattention which
would permit that.

"I hardly ever get around to reading poetry any more,"
he however said. "I guess it is a great thing to kill time
with up here."

The guard flashed the cover of the book. "This isn't
poetry," said he. "It's quotations. Somebody left it here.
They leave all kinda things here, you wouldn't believe it,
though it ain't as bad as the bus. I used to drive a city
bus. I found a truss the other day; you know, for a
rupture. You find dirty jockstraps, false teeth, a dozen
new shirts still in cellophane, a dead parrot, a live turkey,
but the damnedest was once I found a fresh turd, it
looked human, could have been a dog's, but that part of
the deck was empty for hours." He suddenly guffawed.
"Maybe it was mine!" Stuck his head into the book again.
"Hey, here you go, Dryden:

My thoughtless youth was winged with vain desires,
My manhood, long misled by wandering fires,
Followed false lights; and when their glimpse was gone,

My pride struck out new sparkles of her own.
Such was I, such by nature still I am.
Be thine the glory, and be mine the shame."

Reinhart said: "I suppose this fence is to keep people from jumping over?"

"Naw," said the guard. "To keep jerks from throwing things down. You'd be surprised: drop a penny and it would go through some character's head like a bullet."

This shed new light on the problem of self-disposal. If Reinhart could get someone to drop a coin while he stood on the sidewalk below.

"Well we're all alone up here today."

"It's still early. Towards noon in summer you get the groups. Girl Scouts and such, and they toss their garbage down if you don't stop them. People are pigs. We used to have a mesh with bigger openings and them pigs would push garbage through them. When I drove the bus lots of people would piss in the back seat, especially on the last run at night, and more than once I caught young kids playing stink-finger back there."

Reinhart was looking northwards, verifying by the subtle curve of the horizon that the earth was truly round.

"Know something?" said the guard. "That isn't bad. When I was younger I used to think nookie made the world go around, but now I get more pleasure out of taking a good old-fashioned dump."

Why "old-fashioned," Reinhart wondered. Had youth also somehow corrupted that function? But he doubted that the guard was precise about language.

"You be surprised," the man went on, "I get a lot of propositions up here." He leered into space.

"Is that right?" Reinhart asked idly. He supposed he was playing for time. Had the fence not been there he might already be a squash of protoplasm on the sidewalk. What a thing that would be for passersby to see: apropos of nothing, the sudden hurtle, the horrendous smash, the flying parts.

"The young ones are the worst," the guard went on. He searched for something in Reinhart's eyes. "Know what I mean? They start real young nowadays." He moved closer, though the deck was windswept and empty.

"I guess prosperity does it," Reinhart said. "Kids are healthier than when we were children, during the Depression." He stepped back before the guard could breathe on him. There were certain people you knew had bad breath.

"Ooooah-ugh," the guard muttered obscenely. "Some of them little Girl Scouts and them fat behinds and bobbing titties already. Mmmmpf. Ohhh." He gave Reinhart a rolling display of ocular veins. "I had a beaut the other day, a little twelve-year-old fatty who was trying to put a banana skin through the wire. I says, 'I ought to take your panties down and tan your little keyster,' and she says, cocking that pretty fat butt, with them fresh, soft boobies poking out around her neckerchief—"

The man was a raving pervert.

Reinhart wrinkled his nose. "You better watch yourself, fella," he said. "They could lock you up and throw the key away."

"Shit," said the guard. "Little pussy like that don't tell their mamas what they do these days. She knows what it's all about. She says, 'I'll peel your banana for you.' Huh?"

Reinhart stated frostily: "I happen to be a father."

"Me too," the guard agreed with enthusiasm.

"I'm going around on the sunny side," Reinhart said. The filthy swine. He should turn him in, but in any kind of sex thing a person had to be caught in the act. That is, when Reinhart was plaintiff. When he was defendant, however, any fantastic insinuation or outright lie was accepted as evidence, as in the case of his alleged relations with the girl next door, who was far from being twelve and had the build of a brood mare.

The guard trailed him, however, saying: "Hey, should I get her to bring a friend? We could get a bottle of wine—"

Reinhart turned furiously. "Screw you and your rotten perversions, you degenerate. What gives you the right to address me in that fashion? Can't you understand: *I came up here to jump off.*"

The guard showed a mouthful of discolored fillings: was either smiling or preparing to bite. "OK, guy, we get Boy Scout groups too, if that's your game."

When you are absolutely in the right, you can stare any man down. This was one of the many useless assumptions on which Reinhart grew up, it being often exemplified in morally instructive novels like Ralph Henry Barbour's *Honor of the School* and movies about the United States Military Academy. However, as expected, the guard refused to quail. He molested underage girls without a hint of self-doubt. Where did everybody else get their assurance?

"You write poetry, do you?" slyly asked the guard, and cocked his arm on his hip as if carrying a large loaf of bread.

"Look," Reinhart said. "I came up here to kill myself. Why do you persistently ignore that?"

"Because you are a big fat twenty-four-carat pansy," the guard answered. "This place attracts creeps for some reason, but you take the cake, buster. Now get yourself down to the street pronto or I'll blow the whistle on you."

The elevator was around on the sunny side. Reinhart walked there at a grave and dignified pace appropriate to a man of his years. Crossing the clean, ruthless angle of shadow, he was smothered by the white blanket of sun. Under an Indian-scout hand across his eyebrows, he saw another patron of the observation deck, a slightly built youngish chap with carrot hair, freckles, and all-American smile,

"Hi there!" cried this fellow.

Reinhart returned the greeting. He noticed that the lad had before him on a high tripod a quite realistic-looking rifle equipped with a telescopic sight. Probably an advertising stunt of some sort. They had the damnedest gimmicks nowadays, often skirting the margins of bad taste.

Reinhart rode the elevator down to the twenty-seventh floor, and entered the offices of the Cryon Foundation.

"How are you making it, Carl?" Eunice asked negligently.

"I was just up on top of the building with an idea of jumping off but was sidetracked."

"Groovy!" she said, typing away.

Reinhart had no sense of having been physically intimate with her, amazingly enough. Perhaps it had never happened.

He said: "Would you mind telling me what it is you're always typing? We never seem to do any ordinary business."

"The scenario for a blue movie," she said soberly, then peeped at him over enormous hexagonal glasses with raspberry-colored lenses. "How does that grab you?"

He nodded silently.

"I'm no swinger, Carl. I'm just a scared little girl."

"Is Bob in yet?"

"Bob's in Berne."

"Switzerland?"

"If you say so. I never could read a map."

"Eunice, are you putting me on again?"

"It's not a film but a play," she said. "The cast is nude, but the girls wear dildoes and the boys artificial vulvas. You can buy them by mail from California—"

"All right, all right, but when do you expect Bob to come back?"

"Never. I put a bomb in his attaché case. Hey," she cried, "the silence in here is deafening." She did something to a little black cylinder, which turned out to be a transistor radio.

". . . has not yet been identified," said a synthetic voice from the tiny speaker.

"Which could be said of us all," Eunice contributed, and switched to blaring rock.

Reinhart escaped into Bob Sweet's office. He still had no duties, and would have found it strange were he not preoccupied with personal matters. He looked outside in the southwards direction and noted he was colateral with the floor of a neighboring building in which all the windows were broken but one, and saw that shatter before his eyes and a human figure behind it go over like a silhouette of cardboard.

He dashed back and seized Eunice's radio.

". . . known dead and sixteen wounded at the latest count. Police snipers have been sent to the top floors of surrounding buildings but none of these is as high as the Bloor Building, forty-seventh tallest edifice in the continental United States and constructed in 193—"

"There's a madman with a rifle on the observation deck," said Reinhart. "I just talked to him. I thought it was an advertising stunt. I took the elevator and—"

Eunice spilled the contents of a vial onto the bright orange desk blotter. "Take a Librium, Carl," she said. "You got withdrawal symptoms."

"No, Eunice, this is real. Listen—" Reinhart turned up the Vol, small as a pimple on this set.

"And now back to our normal broadcasting schedule," said the radio. "This is your station for news. Roundups on the hour, summaries on the half hour, headlines on the quarter hour, key words every five minutes. The current amount in the Treasure Chest is $164.47, the magic phrase for this five-minute segment is: Bloor Building Mass Murderer. If we choose your number from the

Fortune Barrel and you can give both Treasure Chest number and the magic phrase, I'll come to your house and punch you in the mouth, yessirree, this is your old D.J. and sex fiend Fats O'Hafey and we're right here for the next twelve hours giving you the best in the squarest sounds this side of heaven—"

"He's killing people from up there!" Reinhart cried. "Mass murderer. Jesus Christ." He ran around the dial, in a circulation of nonsense sounds, but no further information seemed available on the moment.

"A little, mild-mannered, red-headed young guy, said 'Hi' to me, looked like he wouldn't say 'Shit' if he had a mouthful."

"Look here, Carl," Eunice said, pointing at him with an enormous index finger. "I don't like that kind of talk. You keep a civil tongue in your head."

"Huh? People are being shot down in the next building! Which one is that? The Ecumenical Life Insurance? Home office of my dad's old outfit?"

She was staring at him balefully. "You might apologize."

"Brother, when I think how close I was to him—"

"You cunnilinguist!" Eunice screamed. "You can't swear at me. I don't know you that well."

"Oh. I'm sorry, Eunice. I beg your pardon. I'm not at my best today. You see, I went up to the roof—"

She laughed till her glasses were wet. "You're really uptight, aren't you? I never knew anybody I could put on so easy. I'm really wild about you." She rose without warning and engulfed him in an asphyxiating embrace, opening her mouth sufficiently wide to block all his air intakes.

"What brings this on?" he said, positively hurling her to arm's length, forgetting she was mainly mass without weight, a difference between big girls and large men.

"Violence," she cried, getting free and running into Bob's office, presumably to watch the carnage across the way, but when Reinhart got there she had most of her clothes off and was falling onto the couch.

"Do me," she said. "Do me and do me again."

Reinhart had one whale of a postcoital depression, a despair the profundity of which made further serious deliberation on suicide impossible—because the urge to destroy oneself is entertained practically only about halfway down the pit; any farther along and there is no will left with which to accomplish it.

Eunice said into his ear: "My generation never knew a time before the Bomb." She took her head off his shoulder and turned it into the loose bolster against the wall, talking into nubby tweed over foam rubber.

She said: "Most of Bob's money is in numbered accounts in Swiss banks."

Reinhart gratefully took a purchase on this reality. "You wouldn't know," he asked, "when I am supposed to get my first paycheck? And shouldn't we get dressed in case somebody walks in? . . . My wife is getting married to a guy who is fifteen years younger than she, her boss, in fact. The strange thing is that though I am forty-four I have a feeling I have not got started in life."

Eunice turned back and lightly bit the end of his nose. He noticed that he suddenly found her ingratiating. She was the only female he had ever known, except the daughter of his loins, who did not make him feel inadequate. He pinched her earlobe affectionately.

"Which reminds me," she said. "I'm going to get that pierced. Is it lunchtime yet? There are some Gypsies in an empty store down on Third Street." She hurled herself off the couch and walked naked to the window. "Hey, the bulls are shooting back from the roof of Ecumenical." She put her fingers on her hips and did a bump and grind at them. She turned around, blinding Reinhart with sheer nudity in sunshine.

She said: "Everybody married I know is a freak. You know, that scene, porno-Polaroid shots, 'strapping young couple, interested in discipline, would like to meet persons of like interests, of both sexes.' "

"I have always believed the incidence of that sort of thing was exaggerated," said Reinhart. "But then, I have lived a sheltered life for years." It was not an easy admission. Indeed, had they not recently been joined, Reinhart would not have possessed the courage with which to make it. Confessing to a twenty-two-year-old girl that her life was more exciting than his—he who when young had made a vow he would always live an adventure and never get trapped in the mire of the commonplace.

"I used to belong to a sex club," Eunice said. "There was a girl there who made it with a chimp." She sat down on the couch, giving Reinhart a profile of collapsed left breast. "Or tried to, I guess it was. He never got one up." Her elaborate coiffure was already gone, after twenty-four hours, and the abundant hair now was divided by a straight part and fell simply. She had, in that position, extremely slender arms, almost concave in the biceps, but big, round, polished shoulder-caps.

She said: "You know what? I don't feel anything at the time."

Reinhart's will wasn't getting any stronger. He knew he should get up and wash, but the moist, vulnerable feeling in his midsection happened to be babyishly in answer to his need of the moment.

Eunice said: "But I do later on. Like vodka. You take a drink of vodka and you don't taste anything. But later on your stomach glows."

At last Reinhart said: "I guess you're talking about sex. I always thought of it as private. I guess that's a hangup of my generation." She had him talking that way now. Well, why not if he was laying her? It was the least he could do.

He sat up from the waist, his legs still stretched behind her, and finger-walked along the trough of her spine.

"Why," she asked her navel, "are you so kind to me?"

"I like you," Reinhart said sincerely. "There is something awfully nice about you. You are friendly. That may not sound like great praise on the face of it, but the fact is that the world seems hostile to me nowadays. I don't meet many people I like."

"I know what you mean. Everybody has always hated me. I see people staring at me in the street and saying to themselves: 'I detest that bitch.'" Eunice wore a queer grin.

"Well, you don't want to get paranoid," Reinhart said. She had the smoothest back he had ever touched. He could not for example find her shoulder blades. "Probably if you were able to know what they were really thinking it would not be about you at all." Nevertheless he had also had this feeling many times.

"No, no," Eunice insisted. "Because they say things. They address me rudely. Some old woman in carpet slippers shuffled past me yesterday, muttering, 'You stupid cunt.'"

"A crank, undoubtedly. They're everywhere these days. People driven mad by the pressures of life, talking to themselves."

"Are you just saying that to make me feel good?"

"Certainly not!" he lied. He put his arms around her waist and leaned his old head against her young back. "You got everything going for you. If you think you've got problems now, wait till you're older."

"No, I won't," Eunice cried desperately. "I'm going to kill myself on the last day of my twenty-ninth year."

"What kind of talk is that? How dare you say that to me, when I am forty-four already, and especially in view of my just having come down from the roof, where as I told you I was thinking seriously of jumping off. Instead I was distracted. So will you be, in your day."

She struggled from his embrace, saying: "Why? Lots of people knock themselves off all the time. It's not so hard to do. You don't have to do anything violent. You can just swallow a handful of pills."

"That's the loser's way," Reinhart said scornfully.

"But I *am* a loser!" She pushed him down and began to punch his chest, and not altogether in fun, either: she was a strong girl. "And I don't want to win, and I don't want your sympathy, and I'm going to punish you for your arrogance." She proceeded to act on her statement and Reinhart was the victim of a savage pummeling, which up to a certain point was stimulating, but as her fists worked up towards his face he became apprehensive. He immobilized her with overlapping limbs.

There was a confused mass of hair and squashed features against his face. She said into his cheekbone: "What do you have to complain about?"

So that was it: jealousy. She saw him as a competitor in ill fortune. Perhaps it would help if he specified his.

"My wife is leaving me after twenty-two years of marriage," he said. "I have never been a raving success at business, and it has been years since we got along well. But is that any excuse? I am a guy with a strong sense of home and family, far stronger in fact than my instinct for a profession. Do you think that makes me effeminate? Maybe. But I don't have a home now. Do you know how that makes me feel? And the funny thing is that at last, in this association with Bob, I have a successful connection."

"You wanna bet?" Eunice asked, flushing him with her warm, wet breath. "I regard it as only a matter of time before Bob is indicted."

"No, Eunice," Reinhart said. "I am only too familiar with the fashion nowadays of children accusing their parents of weird and exotic crimes."

"It doesn't seem funny to you that you haven't been given any duties?"

"I've thought about it," Reinhart answered smugly. "But I can't be hurt. I don't have anything further to lose.

That's one big advantage. I gather that in part anyway this project is a sort of tax dodge, but what isn't? And Streckfuss really is doing things, freezing monkeys, dissecting goats. I saw him do the latter, and ruined a suit in the bargain."

"See, that's why I don't ever want to be old," Eunice said. "Cynicism terrifies me." She shuddered against him.

"That's a meaningless word," Reinhart said. "And one of my son's favorites, as you might expect. Look, life is various and complex. The state of Israel owes its existence to Hitler. Paradoxical, eh?"

"I think you oversimplify."

"Like all women you have a way of steering away from the subject. My point is, suppose what you imply about Bob is true, and by the way I assume that any successful businessman is something of a crook by a certain rigid definition if not often by a loose one."

"And you condone this."

"I? What the hell difference does it make what *my* position is?" Reinhart asked. "I'm not Secretary of Commerce. I've been through all this, Eunice, believe me. Once when I was young, and again with Blaine." But perhaps never with more unreality than while clasping a naked girl on top of him.

"Do you know something?" Eunice said. "I don't believe in love. I mean on the personal level. I mean I believe in it among groups and in international relations and that scene, you know, but not between individuals. In fact, I don't believe in the validity of individuals, which just means exploitation of the weaker by the stronger."

Reinhart could not resist asking sardonically: "You wouldn't expect it to be the other way around?"

"Why do you make fun of me?" She whimpered. "I'm doing the best I can."

Reinhart was both exasperated and gratified. He liked being thought cruel by a great big beautiful girl he had mistreated in no way, but he was puzzled as to his next move, which would undoubtedly be interpreted by her with no reference to his actual motives. Even a girl to whom you were making love was *somebody else,* and you were *other people* to her. Absolutely uncorrupted communication was never possible, especially with a woman. They are quite different from us, Reinhart thought. For twenty-two years Genevieve had no idea of what was going through his mind at a given moment. She would rise and switch off the TV in the middle of a program with which he was fascinated. "I saw your pained expression," she would say knowingly. Or invite for dinner people he despised. "Frankly I can't stand them, but they are your friends." He had always assumed this was sheer bitchiness, but now he entertained the suspicion that Gen, too, was doing the best she could.

And Maw, in her day, as well. "I bet you missed my pineapple upside-down cake," she said after he came home from the Army, and levered out an enormous wedge comprising two disks of quondam fruit now burned thin and black as miniature phonograph records. Whereas he had always uniquely detested that breed of pastry.

He had a terrible thought that all women were doing their best most of the time, and whatever the results could not be faulted as to motive—if you could talk of motives when it came to women; "pretexts" was probably a better term. They do not proceed according to the principles of plane geometry, as one becomes aware when he strolls behind one in the street. A woman cannot walk in a straight line, a peculiarity that becomes crucial when you try to get past her on a crowded sidewalk.

Women had always been Reinhart's nightmare, not in the homosexual sense of maternal castratress—Maw had certainly never suffocated him with excessive warmth—but despite strenuous efforts he could never understand what they wanted, and accepted the deficiency as his own.

"Well, I'll tell you," he said now. "That's certainly good enough for me."

"What is?" Eunice was peering suspiciously into his face at a range of a quarter-inch.

"Your best."

"Oh." Her head sank.

Hell, once again he had said the wrong thing. He might have been big with women had he been born mute.

"Don't you think we should get up?" he asked anyway.

"Why?"

"It's probably noon by now. What a strange morning I've put in. I have made the same reflection on many recent days. I suppose unusual experiences if frequent enough can come to seem routine. For example, we are being very cool about the mad sniper on the roof. People are being shot down, and what do we care?" Reinhart took one hand away from her sacroiliac and snapped his fingers.

It was a mistake. She broke free from his remaining arm and began to beat him up again. And, even though under a rain of blows, he managed to see that a man had entered the room. This person was armed with an Insta- matic camera, with a so-called flashcube that clicked around for every shot until all four sides were exhausted. Reinhart used to have such a Kodak, but forgot it for ten seconds in a superhighway men's room and it was gone forever.

The man departed with as little warning as he had come.

"Obviously a detective in the employ of my wife," Reinhart said.

The spasmodic flashes had subdued Eunice. She snug- gled up and asked: "What's she uptight about?"

"I guess there's no point in getting dressed now," Rein- hart said.

Then another man, small and very fair, came in and spoke in an odd accent. "Where could I find Doctor Streckfuss?"

Eunice raised her head off Reinhart's chest. "Sorry," said she, "but we are not permitted to give information about our personnel. Company policy."

The man shrugged and retired.

"Bob told me to say that," Eunice said. "He is manic about invasions of privacy, wiretaps, and all that shit." She arose and swiftly put on her pants.

"Why would anyone be looking for Streckfuss?" Rein- hart asked.

"That's suspicious, isn't it? You don't suppose he could be a war criminal?"

"I hate war," Eunice said automatically. Her little skirt was actually culottes.

"The Israelis are still looking for Martin Bormann, I understand."

"Oh yeah?"

"You don't have any idea who he is, do you?"

"No."

"I mean Bormann, not Streckfuss."

"I don't know a fucking thing," said Eunice. "I don't even know what I did last night. I was on speed, proba- bly."

Reinhart continued to ride for a few more stations on

his train of thought. "If you have seen pictures of Israel, you know that many Jews are blond."

"I don't know," Eunice said, performing the necessary contortions to hook up her blouse. "Jews are out, I think. Blacks may not last much longer, either. I am beginning to turn off from the ethnic bag. Do you dig soul food? It's all fried."

"Nazi doctors performed all kinds of experiments on the inmates of concentration camps."

"So did the doctor at the camp I went to as a kid," said Eunice. "He balled me. He wasn't a real medical doctor, but a shrink, a psychosexual existentialist with bulging eyes and a funny smell like mustard. I think he was queer for my T-shirt—you know, with Camp Fuckaduck written across the boobs."

"I can't get over the idea that Streckfuss looks familiar to me." Reinhart was tying his shoes.

"He wanted to marry me," Eunice said. "But an oppressive society would have persecuted us. I was fourteen and he was fifty-eight."

"Please, Eunice," said Reinhart. "This is serious."

She giggled. "You just don't dig, do you? I have always had this thing for old men. I can't make it with anybody else. And you're fat besides! You are too much! I want to marry you and live in a little house in the suburbs and go to church and PTA meetings and make the kids costumes for the Halloween parade." She was crying now.

Reinhart was still distracted. "All right, all right. But I should have stopped that guy and got his story. I have thought Streckfuss a sinister character ever since I laid eyes on him. The trouble with science is that it's amoral."

"That is positively brilliant, and I love you," said Eunice.

– 14 –

After having lain low under an ineffectual barrage by the police, the sniper had released the jammed elevator, descended to the lobby, bought a packet of cheese crackers at the newsstand, and surrendered himself. His name was Lloyd Alvis, and he gave his profession as Protestant ministerial student. The police allowed him to eat his crackers and pose for TV news shots.

The totals would not be in for several days, but 6 persons had positively been killed, with 2 others it was touch-and-go, and although the early report that 16 individuals had been wounded was an approximation owing to the difficulty of taking an accurate count while the firefight was in progress and hinging on whether those lightly flecked with cuts from broken glass should be included in the same tally with those struck by lead slugs in vital organs, not to go into the question of relative states of impairment, the media of public information nevertheless could aver that in terms of casualties this was the second highest toll-taking by a rifleman shooting from the observation tower of an edifice. It was of course the worst disaster in which the Bloor Building, the 47th tallest in the continental USA, had ever figured, the second worst having taken place in 1951 when a pair of middle-aged lovers leaped off hand-in-hand, after the man's old mother had once again refused him permission to wed.

A psychiatrist from the staff of the local med school assessed Alvis, on the basis of what he had read about him in the earliest dispatches, as a latent homosexual with whipping fantasies, probably impotent, and suffering from penis-inferiority and constipation. "To Alvis the Bloor Building represented a gigantic phallus, of which the observation deck was the glans and the discharge of his rifle an ejaculation."

Reinhart could remember the day, not long ago, when you could not have got away with using even such medi-

cal terminology in a newspaper. For example, twenty
years before, when a Marine on furlough had beaten to
death a traveling salesman in a downtown hotel room,
only knowledgeable ex-servicemen (and practicing deviates) could have grasped from the mealy-mouthed report-
age any clue to the motive.

Because he had known none of the victims nor the
perpetrator, and because the building in Alvis' sights had
not, after all, contained the home office of the Ecumenical Insurance Company, his dad's old firm, but rather the
Consolidated Electrical, Reinhart saw the importance of
the incident as consisting in his failure to recognize Alvis
as a sniper and take measures to inhibit the man. Thus he
coldbloodedly interpreted this public catastrophe in a personal way: he had passed up a chance to become a
hero.

He was watching the TV newscast on a color set in the
lounge at the Y. From time to time he peeped through an
eye-corner at a thin, attenuated person who sat next him
on the institutional sofa and gasped at things on the
screen. Oddly enough, they were the only two viewers.
The other residents apparently had better fish to fry.

At last Reinhart said: "You know, I was up on that
roof. I saw that guy. I spoke to him."

This person wore a thin mesh shirt of canary yellow.
He recrossed his legs the other way and looked towards
the tip of Reinhart's nose. "You must have been
benumbed with dread."

"Actually, I didn't even recognize what he was
doing."

"I can understand *that*," said the individual, who could
have been any age across a range of twenty years. "He
looks positively harmless." He whipped his legs around
again. "You never know, do you? We live in such a sick
society. I was in the movies the other night when a huge,
gross man sat down beside me and with no preliminary
demanded that I do a filthy thing to him. The film was
Dr. Dolittle."

"I haven't seen it yet," said Reinhart.

"What amazes me is the assumption other people have
that one exists for their pleasure. An utter stranger." He
put his chin against his chest. "Small wonder that poor
things like Alvis run amok. And now they'll try him for
murder and strap that frail, white little body in the
electric chair."

"Of course he's quite mad," said Reinhart. "I agree with you there."

"I *abhor* violence," the man moaned. "This incident will make me sick for days. Oh why, why do these things happen?" He had shy young eyes in an old face, and his dun-colored hair was combed down across his forehead at a slant. "I really must go before they show lovely little Oriental boys being barbecued with napalm."

But he made no move to leave. Instead he extended both soft calfskin loafers and shivered them. "He forcibly took my hand and pressed it between his heaving thighs," he said. "I threatened to scream for the usher, but you don't see ushers any more. A movie theater seems to be entirely automatic nowadays, like an elevator."

He was apparently a nonfaggot sissy. There were such, Reinhart knew, often sires to large families.

"What a rotten experience," said Reinhart, glad to get his mind off his own problems for a while, though he found it hard to put himself into these shoes.

"It was hideous, I assure you. And my grief served to make him more ardent. Perhaps poor Alvis had to undergo this sort of thing."

It was interesting to Reinhart that a good many people interpreted the world's phenomena in a fashion peculiar to themselves.

"Oh, I don't know," he said. "It might have been pure chance."

"Which experience?" asked the man. "Mine or Alvis's?"

"Everybody's."

The man looked around the room. No one else was near them. He said: "Let's go up to my room and have a pillow fight."

Reinhart shook his head judiciously.

"Strip and sting each other with towels."

Reinhart said, very calmly: "You're the second deviate, though of a different type, that I have met today. Would you mind telling me why?"

"I'm not queer!" the man replied. "I admit to being immature, but what can you expect in this sort of world? Who wants to grow up? I shall continue to look at life like a child, never losing my sense of wonder."

"Wait a minute," said Reinhart. "I'm not criticizing you. Please answer my question. Do I look like the sort of fellow who would play snap-the-towel with another man?

Or do I look like the type who would want to do whatever you can do with a preadolescent schoolgirl?"

"Does Alvis look like a killer?"

Reinhart paused for a moment, then asked: "You're not by any chance putting me on? You're not another disguised cop?"

"I know a state trooper," said the man, "who is as gay as they come."

"Why don't people like you get hold of yourselves?" asked Reinhart. "Aren't you just being self-indulgent?"

"You spoke to me first," the man said snippishly, rose, and left the room.

Two of the public telephones in the lobby did not function. On the third Reinhart dialed his former home. Winona answered, of all people. It was strange, suddenly to enter her special frame of reference, stepping out of fantastic reality into, so to speak, a realistic fantasy.

"Hi, Darry," said she through a mouthful of something. "Hold on. This pizza is dripping. . . . Hi!"

"I bet you put it down on some polished surface, dear," Reinhart said with more nostalgia than reproval. When she came to his attention, he missed her badly.

"There's an anchovy on the phone!" She giggled and a smashing noise ensued. "There, it's off. What can I do for you?"

"How are you, darling? Are you being treated well?"

"Oh, sure. Though something puzzles me. Why don't you eat here any more, Daddy?"

"I don't sleep there, either, Winona. I don't live there at all, in fact."

"Is there some reason for that? You're not mad at me, are you, Poppy? I thought you had all you wanted of that cake. A great big piece was missing, and I thought you had eaten it. Can you possibly forgive me?" She began to weep.

"Now don't do that," said Reinhart. "Winona, stop that this instant! Do you hear me? The cake undoubtedly arrived after my exit, and no issue. . . . Winona?"

"Well, you know when I get hungry I can't help myself." She made some snuffling sounds.

"Unfortunately, dear," said Reinhart, "I did not have a chance to explain to you earlier that your mother and I have decided to go our separate ways. We have different careers, you know. It is as simple as that. Time marches on. Before you know it, you'll be off on your own. Have you picked a profession yet?"

Winona answered gaily: "Still airline stewardess. You get to see the world for free!" She chortled.

"That's just fine," Reinhart said, deflecting his sigh. "But you've still a couple of years of high school left. Maybe something else will turn up. I wouldn't set my heart on any one thing, Winona. Maybe a millionaire will marry you."

She said soberly: "I don't want to get married. I hate fights."

This caught Reinhart in a sensitive place. "I'm sorry about that, dear. . . ." But he really didn't know what else to say that would neither confirm her desolate view nor hypocritically deny it. "You might think about Scandinavian Airlines," he said. "I think they serve smorgasbord. . . . Say, Winona, is your mother there?"

"I'll call her. But, Daddy, will I ever see you again in all my life?"

"You certainly will, dear. I'm going to get my own apartment any day now, and the first thing I'm going to do is make a big potful of chili con carne and—"

"With spaghetti?"

"Sure, if you want it, and grated cheese and chopped onions and a fried egg on top. Then strawberry shortcake to follow."

"Bread pudding! Please, Daddy."

"You name it, Winona."

"Golly, I love you, Daddy. I'll get Mother."

But a male voice came on next. Reinhart at first took it for Harlan Flan, Gen's boss and intended, and the swelling veins closed his throat.

Fighting this effect, he gave himself over to glottal adjustments while the voice said: "Sir, you are an unmitigated scoundrel."

It was Gen's father, the elder Blaine. He went on: "Only my girl's intercession saved you from a savage thrashing at my hands the day you brought her home, years ago, after molesting her repeatedly and then conducting a charade before a J.P. to escape prosecution. Years of pain and humiliation ensued, brightened only by her magnificent son. Else I would have stepped in earlier and crushed you like the sewer rat you are."

Reinhart actually felt a certain relief. "One good thing has come out of it," he said. "I don't have to be polite to you any more, you yellow skunk. The next time I see you, Raven, and I don't care how old you are, I am going to hit you in the mouth with all my might and watch what happens to your front teeth."

Raven cleared his throat. He said: "There's no reason why we can't conduct ourselves like gentlemen. In fact, it will be easier on all parties if your lawyer handles it. I say that for your own good, Carl. Personally I have never considered myself your enemy."

"I know it was you who told Genevieve about a certain Gloria," said Reinhart. "But sending that photographer today was lower than I thought even you could sink."

Raven regained some of his aplomb. "I reject that allegation," said he. "I sent no cameraman anywhere. I can state that without fear of contradiction."

"You knew about Gloria because you are a whores' lawyer," Reinhart said. He felt reckless though having taken in no liquids recently except the Y's watery coffee. "That in my opinion is worse than being a client, any old day."

Raven was almost back to normal. "I abhor hooliganism," he said. "It must be expunged without mercy. Excessive pigmentation is not an ameliorating circumstance. I carry a derringer now in my waistcoat pocket. If anyone toys with me I'll blow off his kinky head."

Reinhart stared at the dirty wall of the phone booth, with its smeared numbers. In all these years he had never recognized that Raven was insane. He felt deprived. You cannot hate a madman.

He said: "This has nothing to do with colored people."

"The lines of battle are clearly drawn at last," said Raven, "and that is a relief."

Reinhart said, with a sudden suspicion: "Are you talking to me?"

"I am discussing social matters with my splendid grandson," Raven replied. "I find, to my immense gratification, that we are very close in our thinking. He is in the mainstream of the Raven tradition. Our men are bold, our women compassionate."

"If Blaine is near the phone, I want to speak to him."

"He is shaking his head in negation," said Raven. "You have alienated the youth with your liberal mess of pottage, with your sheenylike quest for the quick buck, with your elastic nigger morality." Reinhart could hear a peal of Blaine II's offstage laughter.

"Raven," he said, "I never thought I'd feel any sympathy for you, but I do now. You are being had. Ordinarily that wouldn't bother me, because I have always considered your opinions loathsome, but I now find yours preferable to his, because you are quite alone. It would be different of course were we in Nazi Germany. But Blaine not only wants to destroy this country: he may be capable of bringing that destruction about. You are merely an isolated crank—"

Raven was apparently talking to Blaine again: "I'd like to see that entire community razed and the earth sown with salt. I have always believed Chicago an abomination."

The Windy City had been the site of several of the conventions at which Raven's form of revelry had verged on the pathological. He had bombed pedestrians with beer bottles from a window in the Palmer House, and on another occasion had started, by willfully igniting the drapes, the fire that gutted a suite in the Blackstone Hotel.

"Raven, Raven, you don't know what you're doing!"

Raven said to him: "You jest, surely. We are wading chest-high through a swamp of excrement. My club has been forced to accept as members a half-dozen gorillas who take their lunch with Coca-Cola and perfume the showers with swarthy sweat. I carry a cattle-prod in the locker room, I who have yet to adjust to the obscene sight of hairy Jewboys on the jogging track, I must await my turn on the trampoline back of a squat simian."

"Raven," Reinhart cried. "Blaine admires the black militants. They don't want to join your club. They want to burn it down."

"I'll supply the petrol," said Raven. "If we have to have coons, then I say let them be as savage as possible and not pretend to be gentlemen. I respect the warlike Watusi, who remain in Africa. We have been the recipient of the scum of all lands, drink-rotted Irishmen, Neapolitan thugs, pigfaced Heinie draft-dodgers, and the cretinous coolies from Asia who cannot iron a shirt without leaving scorchmarks. Standards of excellence have vanished out of memory. It takes a first-class letter four days to travel across town. I am seldom served a glass of wine that is not flecked with sediment. I raise an arm to hail a taxi and my wristwatch strap disintegrates, and the cabman, arrogant with the success of his last strike, the settlement of which assured him a handsome income for cruising empty all day, ignores me. In all this city I cannot find a man who can tune a Weber carburetor, or French-polish burl walnut, or repair a Purdy shotgun, or clean a Lock hat."

Someone began to bang on the glass of the booth.

Reinhart said: "All right, these are capricious matters, Raven, mainly errors of omission and so on. What I am trying to tell you is that Blaine has no program whatever. He merely wants to destroy what exists. He has no plan to rebuild. His aims are all vicious, wanton, and—"

"As are mine," said Raven. "I should like to detonate a nuclear weapon in the District of Columbia. I should warn only the Marine commandant, certainly not those potbellied, eyeglassed, baggy-uniformed buffoons of the Army who have permitted a ragtag band of rickshaw-pullers to humiliate them in the Orient."

Reinhart looked out to see who was waiting for the phone, and a willowy young man stuck out a purple tongue at him.

"What was that stuff about Chicago?" Reinhart asked with sudden urgency.

"The Democrat Convention," Raven answered. "My grandson intends to go there and disrupt it, and I am wishing him Godspeed and a steady trigger finger. I'd like to see the charlatan they nominate dropped, on television, with one well-placed round." Raven snickered. "But I have warned him off the Mannlicher-Carcano, with Japanese scope, which is not effective in less than three." He turned serious. "Oswald was trained in the Corps, so we must blame the weapon."

Reinhart let the handpiece dangle and pushed out of the booth. He was conscious that the waiting fairy made an aspirate remark but he did not register its details. He made his way to the directory rack, against the exterior wall of the third booth, and searched for the listing of the FBI. There was none. "Faze, Harry L." gave way to "Fealy, Mrs. Marjorie." All his life Reinhart had been impersonally adjured to "contact your local FBI office" if he sighted a wanted man or had reason to believe a federal law might be broken in the foreseeable future. Little did he suspect they would have an unlisted number.

The whole thing was a lie, J. Edgar Hoover a composite photograph of the platonic ideal of a watchdog. Reinhart knew he was panicking, and loosened his belt buckle. But a good many public figures had been gunned down in the 1960's, from Malcolm X across the spectrum to the American Nazi Rockwell. Anybody eminent, for good or ill, was a clay pigeon. Hey, there's a top guy: let's be egalitarian and cut him down! This had replaced the old cry: Let's get a beer, or play cool, or get a piece of ass!

Get hold of yourself, Reinhart. Reflect. Use the old cocoanut. Of course: he must look under "Federal." There it was. He kept repeating the number as he rushed in and out of the two dead-phone booths. The fag was vivaciously using the third. Reinhart pounded on the glass, and the swish opened the door a crack to say, furiously: "Go pee in your hat!"

Reinhart convinced himself he had transposed certain digits in the FBI number. He decided to look it up again when he found another working telephone. He stepped out of the Y into the night air, a mixture of heat and soot with the consistency of tear gas. The police could flush a killer from his stronghold by lobbing in canisters of ozone.

Reinhart saw three dark figures coming towards him when he reached the end of the block. They were between street lamps, and he could not ascertain their degree of pigmentation. On such a night everybody was Negro. Reinhart wondered whether *he* might be scaring *them*, but found this technique unconvincing, and crossed the street on a long slant. When he was opposite the trio he saw they were white priests. Well, you never knew. It was exactly a man of goodwill like himself who would be attacked by vengeful blacks, whereas a Blaine Raven would go scotfree. He saw a sidewalk phone booth, gained it, and heaved himself inside. He was now imprisoned in a lighted glass cube, visible at great range to night-stalkers, whereas for his part he could see only reflections of himself.

The black plastic directory-holder hung limp. A vandal had made away with the book and also the center-disk of the dial. The armored cable had also been chewed at, and when Reinhart lifted the handpiece it disintegrated into separate parts. Somehow he reunited them, put his dime in the slot, and wonderfully heard the electronic hum. He screwed in the cap of the mouthpiece. Someone had mutilated this device for no motive that was apparent to him, just as they chopped up park benches and destroyed public drinking fountains. Prosperous schoolboys had burned a bus last term. Jubilant fans had wrecked an entire stadium after their college had won the traditional Thanksgiving football contest. None of these incidents could be called valid social protests.

He did what he should have done earlier, got the FBI number from Information and used it. When it was answered, he hung up. Dialed half of it a second time and hung up. Neither experience nor fantasy prepared him to blow the whistle on his son. He had nothing on him but hearsay. A skinny young kid could not merely shoot a public figure. Though both Oswald and Sirhan had so done. But Blaine did not believe in violence—his abhorrence of it was so great he thought anyone advocating it should be shot. He believed that the president of a university in which there was an ROTC unit should be hanged and not in effigy. He was an absolute pacifist, but had cheered at the Communist gains in the Tet Offensive. He thought the President should be put to death as a war criminal, but he advocated Ché Guevara's theory that what the world needed was more Vietnams.

But he was personally pacific: witness his behavior in the men's room at the Gastrointestinal System. Of course, he had been alone and unarmed. But he had always hated guns as a boy. It had been Reinhart who played with the cardboard shooting gallery, plastic parakeets which when hit with a cork from a little spring-powered rifle revolved on a wire.

A veritable monster of a Negro was glowering at Reinhart through the phone-booth glass and would put an eight-inch switchblade in his belly when he emerged. With such a fiend it would not serve to hand over one's wallet. He would take that anyway when he ransacked your inert body. He would punish Reinhart for what the slaveholders had done before Reinhart's forebears had set foot in America.

Reinhart slid the door open. He said: "I am unarmed and nonviolent."

The Negro came around from the side. He said: "I am sorry to trouble you, but my wife is pregnant and about to deliver and my car has broken down." He was seething with worry.

Reinhart said: "That's OK. She will be just OK. Don't you worry. Everything will come out just fine."

He remembered how it had been when Gen's time had come. Speeding to the hospital, Reinhart had been ticketed by a traffic cop who was totally ignorant of the traditions of emergency. Reinhart had a history of encounters with literal policemen and letter-of-the-law. Gen hadn't helped, her coat arranged in such a fashion that she did not look pregnant, and nonchalantly smoked a cigarette though ten minutes earlier she had threatened to deliver on the garage floor.

He could not imagine Blaine with a gun. It was of course pure rhetoric. Reinhart could well recall youth's easy way with verbal extravagance.

He watched the Negro talk anxiously into the phone. He felt a proprietary interest in the man's baby, as yet unborn, cute little chocolate-colored rascal who might grow up into a hate-crazed militant. You never knew. What a lottery it was.

But nowadays people realized their threats. Negro gangs waged open warfare with municipal police departments. Students set out candidly to destroy hallowed old colleges. He had himself seen Blaine buying marijuana and standing naked in the bedroom of the girl next door. He had perused some statistics in a national magazine which revealed that a certain percentage of eleven-year-olds had already had sexual intercourse. There were now organized revolutionaries in high schools.

Public order would soon be a thing of the past. Already the streets were jungles. Had that colored guy been a ruffian, Reinhart would have had his back to the wall, alone. Passersby would have averted their heads, motorists speeding by. The old beat cop was now in a car, unavailable unless you broke a traffic law. The Supreme Court freed convicted murderers on technicalities. Peace-parade marchers carried the enemy flag. Heroin users were on the relief rolls. The President pleased everybody when he said he would quit at the end of the term. The war was apparently lost but would not end.

In a certain state of mind you could say that life in America was shitty, though the standard of living was at an all-time high. In the abstract the idea of dropping whatever impotent windbag the Democrats nominated was not without attraction. Line him up in the old cross-hairs, take a breath, let it half out, and squeeze. It was spoiled by his being a man, a skinful of protoplasm that would run like an egg when the shell was broken.

"Are you all right?" It was the Negro gentleman, who had left the booth. In his own extremity he could yet feel concern for a stranger. This gave Reinhart a lump in the throat.

"I'm a little heat-sick I think," he answered. "Did you get an ambulance?"

"My brother-in-law is coming right over. You can always count on him. I must get back. You take care of yourself, you hear?" He was walking backwards. "Go home and put a cold rag on your forehead."

Reinhart knew a great love for the race. Victims of persecution were invariably the nicest people. For example, never in his life had Reinhart met a nasty Jew. And even Captain Storm had not been impolite. . . . He must not panic. There were all sorts of decent folks around. America was still the only place on earth where you could quickly make a million, and one of the few where you could state your case and be heard.

Blaine was no Lee Harvey Oswald. Rest assured, the Democratic Convention would be the same old bore of endless "caucuses," ugly word, and "Man who" speeches. Reinhart had been worn out for organized politics as a boy in a Republican family: on the other side it had been Roosevelt every time.

Problems enough remained: the divorce, the false accusation of paternity, the possibility of Streckfuss being an old Nazi, and the disappearance of Bob Sweet. There was a bill for the room rent in Reinhart's box at the Y.

"Listen," he said to Eunice on entering the office next morning. "I am out of funds. Can't you cable Bob to authorize some money for me? Or can I sign a chit for petty cash?"

Eunice wore a chain-mail dickey, a breastplate of linked brass coins, over bare flesh. When she exhaled it hung loose, beyond her breasts.

"I can never remember town names or book titles or airplane schedules," she said indifferently. "If I want to fly somewhere I go to the airport and say, 'Where would you like to send me?' I might end up on Air Pakistan and land in Karachi. Which reminds me. Would you like some *chota hazri?*"

While Reinhart colored, assuming this was an obscene term similar to poongtang, Eunice threw a paper bag at him. When opened it revealed a glazed doughnut.

"That's 'breakfast' in Urdu," she said. "I used to know this Moslem hockey player. You know how they say 'groovy'? *Bahote khoob!*"

Reinhart had not eaten breakfast, having no money. He took a bite of the doughnut, which was rather clammy from being kept in a closed bag.

"Do you know that Sikhs must live by a number of rules?" She persisted. "For example they must always carry a comb. And they never undress completely their life long. So they bathe with one arm still in their underwear."

"Eunice," Reinhart said with a mouthful of glazed, very yeasty doughnut, "this is serious, about my money. I don't have any."

"Sorry I drank all the coffee," Eunice replied. "It's hard to get a dry doughnut down. Why don't you make a deal with your wife: you will agree not to contest the divorce if the price is right?"

"How do you know about that?" Reinhart cried forgetfully, in shame, but then remembered, among other things, the private detective who had taken their picture. For which Raven had disclaimed responsibility: something weird about that incident. "Listen, ten bucks from petty cash would help."

"Our petty cash is down to an airmail stamp and a Brazilian cruzeiro," Eunice said gaily. "But if you want to talk to Bob, why don't you?"

"I don't know where he is!" Reinhart shouted.

Eunice wore a tiny pair of Ben Franklin glasses, with intense green lenses. She looked over them at Reinhart and said gravely: "Are you aware, Carl, how easily you tend to freak out? To lose all control? Really, is it worth it?" She extended two index fingers and brought them simultaneously to the keyboard of her typewriter. "You see, I can't do it. I can't jam this machine. Isn't that fantastic? It simply won't allow two keys to be struck at the same time."

In annoyance Reinhart marched into the inner office, slamming the door behind him, and there sat Bob Sweet.

"Back from Switzerland?" Reinhart cried. "In one day?"

"It could be done," Sweet said. "But of course I didn't. What are you talking of, Carl?"

"Eunice told me yesterday that you were in Berne."

"Berne is a little town forty-five miles northwest of this city," said Sweet. "I have some interests there."

"Oh yeah. We used to play basketball against their team. I went up once to see a game: a bunch of guys in that old Ford, all painted up, of Billy Wright's. We had flat pints of drugstore wine and cheap cigars, and Specks Cunningham had to stop and get out to puke." What stupid amusements had been popular in Reinhart's high-school days.

Sweet's eyes narrowed behind the black frames. "Two of the guys who used to pick on me."

"No," said Reinhart, "not Specks and Billy. They were idiots, but pretty good guys. Specks got killed in the Army—on the maneuvers in the States, oddly enough. He had apparently camouflaged his sleeping bag so well that a Jeep ran over it with him inside—"

"Spare me the details," Sweet said. "I couldn't care less. I don't collect the disasters of mediocrities."

Reinhart was slightly stung. He said: "Look, Bob. I hope you won't think it bad taste if I ask you when I will get paid. I am hard up at the moment. I owe my room rent at the Y, for one thing."

"I thought you had five grand. Did not you offer to put five grand into the business?"

Reinhart sat on the edge of the desk. "It's a sordid tale. My son slandered me to my mother, who stopped the check."

"You stood still for this?"

"What could I do? She was always a harsh critic of me and now she verges on senility."

"Are you her principal heir?"

"Unless she changes her will, which she probably wants to do now."

Sweet arose and began to stride slowly about the room. "Carl, I'm going to talk turkey to you. I don't know if you are aware that nature is ruthless. Animals, for example, with the exception of a few domesticated creatures, are totally self-concerned. There are old pet dogs who allegedly sit by the grave when their masters die and howl endlessly. But even this may be only because they have lost their meal ticket. Horses learn cunning tricks because they are rewarded for doing so. Nothing of the human moral code obtains anywhere in the wild. Kindness, pity, honor, and so on, are purely intellectual constructions, and as we know, beasts are incapable of abstract reasoning. For example, the whole concept of incest is uniquely human. Members of animal families regularly mate with one another. Where did we get our idea of the horror in that?"

"Well," said Reinhart, "Freud says—"

"OK," Sweet said. "But then where are you? An ape will still have relations with its sister, and we won't. But we will deify the illegitimate son of a carpenter whose preaching consists simply of advising us to be losers in every transaction. Can you find an animal who would turn the other cheek? Do you see a lesson in that?"

"Yes," said Reinhart, "but one that I reject. That old

Army saying: 'If you can't eat it or fuck it, piss on it.' "
After snickering—Reinhart always found cynicism funny,
probably because it scared him—he went on: "We're not
animals, Bob."

"I quite agree," said Sweet. "There is no lesson in
animals, in fact. I brought up the subject so as to dispose
of it. It is a phony argument. There are those who whine
about why we have wars when animals don't. Well, neither do we screw our close blood-relatives. The truth is
that men have made themselves from scratch. We have
invented our ethical codes from the whole cloth. They
have nothing to do with instinct. They are, in the truest
sense of the term, unnatural. And have got more so
throughout the centuries, arriving at the present when we
have at last abolished death."

Reinhart winced. He asked: "Isn't that a premature
claim, Bob?"

Sweet was near at hand suddenly. He seized Reinhart's
lapels and said: "Yesterday Hans thawed a monkey that
had been frozen for six weeks. Last night it ate a banana.
This morning it was seen masturbating."

– 15 –

The monkey gave Reinhart a quick, peevish look and then avoided his eyes. In the animal world, Reinhart had read in one of those popular natural-history books, the fixed stare signifies hostility. Beasts peer at one another only when preparing to tangle. Reinhart had once stared at a king cobra, through the zoo glass, and the serpent erected three feet of its length, which when added to the height of the cage above the spectators' floor brought its flaring hood to Reinhart's eye-level. They peered at each other, slender snake and fat man: chilling exchange for the latter. Folk wisdom held that a serpent's gaze could hypnotize. "Looks like a piece of hose," said Genevieve, coming up alongside, and the cobra wilted and glided away like a stream of water seeking its lowest level.

Bob Sweet was pouring champagne into laboratory beakers.

"I know you don't drink, Hans, but surely this once." He handed a vessel to the little scientist and another to Reinhart, then hoisted his own. "To Professor Doctor Johann Streckfuss!" To Reinhart: "You are a man of words, Carl. Here is your opportunity to utter a few that will be historical."

"I am?" asked Reinhart, who felt irrelevant, displaced. Nevertheless he stared at Streckfuss, who looked away like an animal. Reinhart's memory whirred, as if a computer in a TV satire, and ejected a card. " 'If he has seen farther than most, it is because he is standing on the shoulders of a giant.' "

Streckfuss' flecked eyes were on him now. "Isaac Newton, no?" he asked.

"I believe so," said Reinhart. "No offense. I really don't know what to say. I really find it incredible."

"Bottoms up," said Sweet, and Reinhart was about to comply when he felt his wrist being detained by a weird little agency, a tiny animate manacle. He had lowered his

283

arm while thinking of the quotation, his back to the cage. He now saw a thin limb, all tendons and gray hair, thrusting through the bars. A parody of a human hand clutched his wrist.

"Isn't that cute," said Sweet, who had never before, in Reinhart's presence, displayed his sentimental side. Bob bent over the cage. "Does he have a name?"

"Otto," said Streckfuss.

Reinhart's wrist was still in restraint. "Shall I give him some champagne?" he asked. "He has, after all, come back from the dead. What a story he would have to tell, if he could speak."

"That I doubt," Streckfuss replied dryly. "Undoubtedly, like most of zuh human race, he would speak in platitudes." He put his own champagne down untasted and walked to a steel table full of vessels and wire.

"Drink up, Carl!" Sweet cried.

Reinhart plucked the monkey fingers off his forearm, one by one. The last two closed on some of his wrist hair and pulled it painfully. "Ouch!" Reinhart said. "You little bastard." He had never thought monkeys cute. They were more like dirty old men than charming children (as in fact were, nowadays, many children). He lifted the beaker and put it to his closed lips. He intended from now on to be careful about what he ate or drank in this lab. Seeing Sweet fill his own mouth, however, and having previously watched him uncork the bottle, Reinhart at last admitted the bubbles to his tongue.

Bob poured some more for both of them. "Come on, Carl, live a little." He put the bottle down and, picking up the mushroom-shaped cork, gave it to the monkey, who examined it gravely, hanging by the other paw from an exercise bar of wood.

Reinhart turned away from the cage. "You couldn't tell by looking at him, could you?"

"That's the amazing thing," Sweet said. "Hans is something else, isn't he? He is not the least excited by his triumph. Mark my words, he won't even bother to go to Stockholm for his Nobel Prize. He makes the rest of us seem pretty cheap."

Reinhart shrugged in secret, while Bob gazed worshipfully at Streckfuss' back. Reinhart did not feel cheap. For some reason he was jealous.

He heard himself say: "Well, of course, scientific discoveries come so frequently nowadays that they seem almost routine. Since I was a boy—" He was struck in the nape by a small projectile traveling at speed. The monkey had thrown the champagne cork at him.

Sweet did not see, or ignored, the incident. "A point of no return for the human race," he said quietly. "All the old reality must go."

Reinhart decided that throwing the cork back would be a degrading action for a superior animal. He kicked it skitteringly across the cement: it had been the little metal cap that hurt. Otto was sitting now, his knuckles on the cage floor, very fine fingers with the opposable thumb of the primate clan, by using which to build bridges and aqueducts man had established his earthly control. Otto used his hands to clutch bananas and play with himself.

Otto was sitting on his furry balls, pretending to reflect. He was medum-sized as his tribe went, about as large as a cocker spaniel, his gray fur tinged with yellow, over pink skin. If, that was to say, he had actually been frozen. Streckfuss had assertedly removed him from the capsule with no witnesses present.

Reinhart had an impulse. He went to the cage, turned his back on it, and lowered the beaker of champagne to the length of his arm, concealing it with his body from Bob.

Sweet swallowed the last of his own portion and gave himself more from the dripping bottle, risen from the disposable paper ice bucket imprinted with a picture of the Eiffel Tower. They had stopped en route at a liquor store to get so outfitted. Reinhart, glancing down, moved the vessel against the bars. He had known it was too wide to go through, but he was now apprised of the equivalent fact that so was the monkey's head too large to come out, and apes are not equipped with the extensive tongue of a dog.

"I understand Hans's reluctance to gloat prematurely," Bob said as if to himself. "He won't be satisfied until he has frozen a man and thawed him. It's as simple as that." He nodded abstractly, not at anyone, and drank.

Reinhart dropped his other hand after rubbing his forehead and sought the sliding bar that opened the door of the cage. Before he found it, Sweet turned to him.

"Let's have your glass, Carl. You are strangely calm. Some contrast with your usual gung-ho personality."

Reinhart was forced to bring up the champagne to mouth level, but he did not drink. He asked: "Me?"

"Yes, you. You always had a lot of life, even back in

school. Remember how you used to come up and bruise a guy and shout?"

"There you go again, Bob. I tell you you are confusing me with other people. Warren First was the one who did that."

"Show your shoulder-cap and say, 'Look where the horse bit me,' while ramming your knuckles into somebody's crotch." Sweet grimaced. He swallowed some champagne, which foamed against his teeth. Reinhart suddenly recalled they were false.

"I tell you that was Warnie First. He died just last year. He was a three-pack-a-day man."

"You don't smoke, do you, Carl?" Bob asked, pouring himself the last of the wine. "And you certainly don't drink much. You may be somewhat overweight, but I imagine that if you haven't had any indications to the contrary your internal organs are all functioning well."

Reinhart was rather flattered at this. "Well, seriously, I guess I haven't done too badly. Whenever I have a bit of heartburn I suspect it's an ulcer, but the X-rays don't lie. My teeth could use some work. Sporadically I do a bit of boozing, but switched from bourbon to vodka some years ago. Fewer esters, I read, or a different kind anyway: not as damaging to the system. My blood pressure is high, which is inevitable in a man of my weight, and I don't get enough exercise. Also should cut down on fats and carbohydrates—" He was jerked backwards. The monkey had seized his coattail. Amazingly his recovery did not cause the wine to spill.

Sweet had glanced away just prior to this contretemps. His glance did not return until Reinhart was again in a normal stance. Bob seemed to be playing the role of a parent who manages to miss his child's harassment of another individual. Gen used to be like that when Blaine was four and in his shin-kicking phase.

Reinhart lowered the beaker again and the monkey struck it from his hand.

Sweet could not fail to notice the smashing of Pyrex. Yet he did. Damn, there went Reinhart's plot to get the ape drunk. The champagne bottle was empty, upended in the slush.

"Sorry," Reinhart said.

"Why? To be in good health, with all your parts functioning?" cried Bob. He hurled his empty beaker at the opposite wall. Before the crash was heard he had plucked out his dentures. "My scalp is false, too," he said from a funny, rubbery mouth.

Reinhart was shocked into silence. The fact was not new to him but the motive behind the revelation was.

"That's not the measure of a man, Bob."

Sweet perversely chose to interpret this statement as mockery. "I don't need your sympathy," he said clenching his face as if it were a fist.

Reinhart said: "I didn't mean to be patronizing." He spat his own dental bridge into the palm of his hand, waved it, and put it back. "I've got this myself, and it doesn't even fit. At least you have the wherewithal to buy the best."

Sweet returned the teeth to his mouth: impeccable; you could swear—

Reinhart went on: "If I lost my hair I would just go bald. I admire the way you fight back."

Bob took off his glasses. "My vision is OK. If my eyes needed correction I would wear contacts. That's my style. These are window glass. The frames give strength to my face." And the champagne seemed to have made him strangely urgent. This was new; still too early to call it a weakness. Not that Reinhart wished to. The bold disclosure of the physical inadequacies of course was evidence of moral force.

Streckfuss at that moment cried, *"Merde!"* and swept a rack of test tubes to the floor. Perhaps he had been influenced by the other breakages. He leaped into the air and landed silently on his rubber soles. From behind he looked like a spring-wound toy.

Sweet said: "I have created myself, Carl, out of very little in the way of raw material. I was born a bastard, you know."

"No, I didn't." Reinhart moved beyond ape's arm-length to the other end of the stainless-steel table on which the cage rested, and sat gingerly on the ham-grooving edge.

"I doubt that my real parents were in the top drawer of society," Bob continued. "I was squirted as a drop of scum out of one tube into another, grew into a blob of humanity, was pulled out, struck, and began to breathe, and was abandoned soon thereafter. I spent my first three years in a public orphanage. The Sweets then adopted me."

"I never knew that in the old days."

"Neither did I, for years. And when I did find out, I

can't tell you how exhilarated I was. Robert Sweet, Senior, was the original Weak Willie. He actually sang in the Methodist choir. He used to listen to the radio and laugh on the in-breaths. His wife was always knitting. I never wore anything woolen that had been bought in a store. She had a brother who raised chickens, so we never had a turkey at Thanksgiving. I studied the clarinet for a while. I can still taste the reed." Sweet was saying this in an in-indignant tone that was gathering momentum to become furious. "Every Saturday morning the two of them would vacuum the *basement!*"

Reinhart said, mollifyingly: "Routine people, with all their little rituals, are what makes the world go round."

"No, they are not," Sweet said decisively. "They don't *make* anything do anything. They *are made*. They accept, they endure. I can't tell you how happy I was to learn that I did not owe life to the Sweets. I could afford to ignore rather than hate them."

Reinhart found this a desolating point of view. He protested: "But that's not all there is to families. My dad was a pretty mediocre guy, too, and my mother has always been something of a crank without an aim, so far as I can see. Not everybody cares about power. It's probably a basic difference in taste. Most people want merely to live. Or anyway they used to. Nowadays you are assaulted from every direction by people who want to do something with or to you. They foist all kinds of responsibilities on you while disclaiming their own. My wife is leaving me because I am not a success at business, though she never encouraged me in any of my efforts. My son blames me personally for the war, poverty, and the Negro problem, and yet when I try to discuss these matters with him he reviles me with obscenities. I catch him in a criminal act, and he falsely accuses me of a worse one."

"Let's face it, Carl," Sweet said cruelly. "You have proved my case. It would be better for all concerned if your son were an orphan."

But pride had a will of its own. Without thinking, Reinhart was moved to strike back. "I don't call Eunice the result of a successful fatherhood."

Sweet laughed brutally.

Reinhart said: "I envy your detachment." But he regretted his vengefulness as usual. All unhappy families were no doubt different, as mentioned in the opening lines of *Anna Karenina*. He actually could not picture Genevieve with a lover, as an Anna K. or Emma Bovary. Living persons were never as susceptible of definition as imaginary characters. Sweet for example could shrug off a daughter, and seemed none the worse for it. Perhaps because of this, Reinhart felt no uneasiness at the thought that he had himself been intimate with Eunice; no sense of triumph, either.

Bob said: "The family as an institution will probably have disappeared by the time the frozen are revived, along with war and poverty. The poor may always be with us as statistics, but an impoverished man, as individual, will have centuries in which to improve his lot. Social problems of the kind man has always known will be merely temporary inconveniences. One might be hungry, but no longer can he die from starvation. Wars may still occur, but no longer will anyone be killed in them. They will in fact turn into games."

Reinhart was conscious of a pressure being applied to him, to what end he knew not, but he reacted to it in the form of embarrassment and turned to look at the monkey.

"Six weeks, you say? Shouldn't you call the newspapers and *Life* magazine?"

"Not till we have our man," said Bob. "Not till he has been there and come back and can tell about it. The greatest news story of all time. Think of it, Carl. It will make the hydrogen bomb seem like the bursting of a paper bag."

Reinhart stood erect. "Just a moment, Bob. Aren't you forgetting something? The body will be dead, clinically speaking. Hans will not be dealing with a healthy, living organism like this monkey. Your story will be only that you have taken a corpse and frozen it."

Sweet nodded vigorously. "Go on, Carl. Pursue that line of thinking."

"It is only a theory that the body can be revived in the distant future. The fact is that it is stone dead at the moment, by the orthodox definition. In other words, so what? I think you will find that reaction widespread, Bob. Whereas if you had some kind of proof—" Reinhart glanced towards the shelves where reposed the other cylinders allegedly containing frozen small-animal bodies. "Photographs should have been taken from start to finish. If Hans has more monkeys he should film them while they are still in the frozen state, then when they are thawed. Movies, really, are what you should have."

Sweet said: "I notice you keep saying 'you,' Carl. Are you dissociating yourself from this project?"

"Just a way of talking," Reinhart explained hypocritically. "I feel a bit shy at this point. I am beyond my depth when it comes to science."

"Or anything else," said Sweet. "One might say bluntly that you are redundant in the logistics of life."

For a moment Reinhart was charmed with the felicity of the phrase, and even its justice. The military idiom was appropriate to the rock-bottom residue of his morality: the old Stoic *vivere militare*: to live is to be a soldier.

Then he bridled. "I tender my resignation."

He had never known Sweet to laugh heartily. Bob resembled Genevieve in the trait of humorlessness. It was true of most of the forceful personages Reinhart had come across in four decades. Thus he was struck by the incongruity of Bob's mirth. The man positively howled, with a violence which might have unseated a less precise set of dentures. Reinhart's dad, for example, never guffawed after losing his natural choppers.

Reinhart's indignation surged beyond itself and became self-pity.

"It is shameful," he said, "to use a man's self-criticism against him. That's the technique of women and politicians. How much humiliation do people want of me? I was once a young man, and I had some good ideas. I have never knowingly been mean or false." And of course, Jim Jackson's voice was heard in instant rebuttal: *You meanly cut off Blaine's hair and you consorted with a common prostitute, false to your vows of marriage.*

Reinhart backed against the table edge and secured himself with both hands.

Sweet removed his glasses and cleaned them with a handkerchief, transforming himself into a sort of Dick Tracy villain: Mr. Noface.

"That's a quotation from *David Copperfield*," said Reinhart. "I forget the rest of it—oh yes, 'cruel.' 'Never be false, never be mean, never be cruel.' Davy's aunt told him that."

Respectacled, Sweet said: "Have you really lived by slogans? Carl, you lack authenticity. You are the product of other people's passions and choices. You might one day be killed by someone else's statement to the effect that you do not exist. Is it really the role of a man to be inoffensive?"

Reinhart stared wildly about, then took a purchase of

eye on the point where Streckfuss' neck hair touched the collar of the lab coat.

"I suppose it's preferable to be a Nazi doctor, performing experiments on the inmates of concentration camps."

"There goes your claim to a lack of cruelty," Sweet said in disgust.

Further discretion was pointless. Reinhart said: "The Israelis are looking for him, Bob." Streckfuss had settled down to his apparatus again: he was a monster of coolness.

"Of all things to say." Bob swiveled his head, eyelids lowered. "Hans was a prisoner for years in Buchenwald. He survived only because the SS officers preferred him to their own doctors."

Reinhart knew in the clarity of dread that Sweet was not being ironic. He asked pitifully: "He's a Jew?"

Streckfuss turned then. He said: "No, I tried zat once and it almost got me killed. I disclaim any ethnic, national or political identity."

Reinhart looked between his own shoes. "What can I say?"

"Nussing which would concern me," Streckfuss answered. "I take no interest in morality. I regard even myself as an organism, of which the constituent parts are replaceable. I have no desires, and do not understand anyvun who has. I have spent zuh lahst thirty years in that condition and I prefer it." He put some test tubes into a machine and threw the switch. It whirred.

"Carl," said Bob Sweet. "How about it?"

Reinhart was still treading water in misery. "Me and my big mouth. But it's more than that. There was a time when I thought the best of everybody until proved wrong. I guess I just can't stand reality any more, because it is both commonplace and unexpected, and whichever comes along I am in the mood for the other. When you are young it is no great tragedy to jump at conclusions. If you still do it in middle age you are a clown."

"Carl, nothing would be more convenient than if you took a vacation at full pay."

Mention of money brought Reinhart partway out of his wallow. "I know it's vulgar of me, in view of all this, but I am down to my small change. I do have to pay that room rent soon."

"There you are," Sweet said. "Living at the YMCA at your age. Why didn't you book a suite at the Shade-Milton Hotel and charge it to the firm? They have a heated pool and a sun club. You could have met girls there."

Reinhart inhaled. "Look, Bob, I want to say I have acted like a gentleman with Eunice. I wouldn't want you to think I took liberties with your daughter."

"My daughter?" Again Bob laughed heartily. "That idiot? If she was my daughter I would freeze her. Her father's Barker Munsing, that psychoanalyst at the end of our office hall. Anyway, Carl, you are a liar. You have been fucking her night and day." Suddenly Sweet lost his good humor, if indeed it had been such. "You must be sick. Would I tell you my daughter was a nympho?"

Reinhart shook his head violently, but not at the question. "I suppose there would be no pain?"

"Absolutely none," said Bob. "That's an assurance you could not get if you were to jump off the Bloor Building." He knew everything.

"There *was* a guy who came looking for Professor Streckfuss," Reinhart said.

"A dealer in laboratory equipment," Bob said. "He had our office address. He delivered that new centrifuge that Hans is using right now."

"You see how I am," said Reinhart. "I ignored the fellow who turned out to be the sniper, and thought this guy an Israeli undercover agent. But those photographers— who were they? My father-in-law disclaims all knowledge of that stunt. Of course he could be lying."

"Eunice has a pretty scummy crew of friends," Bob said negligently. "What did they do, want to sell you some pornographic snapshots?"

"No," said Reinhart. "They depicted me in some." He found this admission almost painless.

"There's a lot you would be escaping," Bob said, "and that's putting it at the worst. At the best there is international celebrity." He gestured. "There's What's-his-name, the South African dentist with the heart transplant, formerly anonymous, now a household word. And for the book and magazine people you could write your own ticket, not to mention the movies."

"Yes," said Reinhart, " 'that undiscovered bourne from which no traveler returns ...' " The freezer program would nullify all of Shakespearean tragedy: maudlin slop from the unenlightened time when men lay down and died.

"Let me ask you one question," he said to Bob. "Was this your plan for me from the beginning?"

Sweet frowned. "Not really. When I saw you at Gino's what I remember thinking of immediately was a vengeful ambition I had as a boy. I always swore I would get you back for that bullying."

"Goddammit, Bob!" Reinhart struck the table behind him, forgetting about the monkey, who made a sputtering sound. "I am guilty of many things, but that's not one of them, I tell you." But in a malignant vision he saw himself as a large boy of sixteen, shoving the frail Sweetie away from the drinking fountain, getting him back from Paul Jeckel's push, then sending him again across the circle like a medicine ball. It had been a mindless amusement, innocent of deliberate malice. When Reinhart himself had been very small, a big girl had beaten him up. He doubted that she would remember. Death might be on its last legs, but envy, spite, and vengeance would still make the world go around.

Bob was smiling generously. "Carl, Carl, do you seriously think I have nothing better to do than hold a childish grudge? You are probably right: it was two other guys—"

"I don't know what you'd do," said Reinhart. "I don't know how you made your money or even where you live. You couldn't prove by me that you own anything but that Bentley."

"Nor that," Sweet said pleasantly. "I hire it, in fact, at a hundred dollars a day. I live at the Shade-Milton. I own very little, and lease what I need because of the tax advantages. I speculate in commodity futures."

The lingo of investors had always been Greek to Reinhart. He had picked up the occasional paperback on how to play the market and ritualistically read the financial page on Sundays but he really understood only the taking of gain from wages or small personal businesses, and of course the simple direct crimes such as pilfering and burglary, not embezzlement.

"That's what I was doing yesterday in Berne. I lease storage facilities there."

"I see," said Reinhart, who did not. But it didn't really matter now.

"Cocoa," said Bob.

Reinhart rallied for a moment, on the strength of suspicion. "I thought you had withdrawn from active participation in the world of finance. I thought you said you had committed yourself wholly to this project, and put your money into the Cryon Foundation. And whether

or not you were in Switzerland yesterday, or have extensive deposits in Swiss banks, as Eunice, who is not your
daughter, claims, you did meet Professor Streckfuss there,
as you yourself assert. And whether or not he is a hero
instead of the villain I so foolishly thought for a while,
without any evidence, he is not licensed to practice medicine in this country."

"What are you getting at?" asked Sweet.

Reinhart stood up. His right buttock was asleep.
"Merely," he said, socking it, "that my life exists in all-too
precise detail. I am a very literal guy. Are you proposing
that I sell you my soul?"

"On the contrary, you are a romantic, Carl," Bob said.
He went to the monkey's cage and began to unfasten the
door. Its lock proved much more complicated than had
been supposed by Reinhart when he groped at it in a
mischievous intent to free the animal. Bob's comment was
to the point. "Otto has a certain sense of mechanics. He
can open simple bolts and levers, and he is a good mimic
of motions. He just struck himself on the behind, imitat-
ing you. But a series of fastenings, moving in different
axes, bores him. Don't they, Otto, you little moron?"

Otto bared a pink mouth with its circumference of
many little teeth, spread-eagled his hairy body across the
front of the cage, and plucked at Sweet's fingers with his
own leathery digits. But Bob persisted.

Reinhart said: "He's going to be a son of a bitch to
catch if he gets out."

Sweet poked the monkey's pink belly. Otto grabbed
himself, and Bob swung the door open. Otto extended his
long arm, hooked a finger into the bars, and slammed it
shut.

Sweet said: "Come on, Otto. Be free."

The monkey chittered at him.

"He's mad," said Reinhart, meaning both "angry" and
also referring to the "craziness" imputed to the smaller of
the nonhuman primates. Whereas a gorilla was never
thought to be nuts in the funny way, probably because he
might kill if he went off his rocker. Size really was an
important criterion among the whole ape family.

"I'll bet you're the kind of guy who feels sorry for
animals in zoos," Sweet said. "Look: he's fighting to stay
inside."

Otto and Bob were playing a finger game in which each
tried to pry the other's hand off the door.

"I'll tell you why I prefer animals to a lot of people," Reinhart started to say.

"Oh, I know why," Bob answered. "Because animals act by instinct. That seems healthy, morally clean, nature's way, as opposed to the corrupt practices of human beings."

"Let me put it to Hans," Reinhart said, speaking towards the scientist's back. "Name me the animal that operates a concentration camp."

Streckfuss was taking the test tubes from the centrifuge. *"Les fourmis,"* he said.

"What?" Reinhart applied to Sweet.

"Ants." Bob had the door open again. The monkey cowered against the back bars.

"I want to prove something," said Bob. He plunged his arm in and seized Otto by the neck. The monkey grasped the bars with one paw and with the other tore at the stranglehold.

"This is disgusting!" Reinhart shouted. "Let it alone, for Christ sake. It is a poor helpless creature. It has just been frozen and thawed. Isn't that enough?"

Sweet seemed to be enjoying himself. "I've got a tiger by the tail," he said from a tight jaw. "It's a standoff at this point. If I let him go now he'll bite me. Otto, you are no Patrick Henry."

"It's a completely false situation," Reinhart protested. "He's scared of this lab. Be different if we were in a jungle."

"Otto's never seen a jungle. He was born in captivity. Metal and concrete are as familiar to him as to us, and human speech. Yet he could not build the crudest shelter, nor say a one-syllabled word. He has the hands and the vocal chords, but he doesn't have the will for it, Carl. He does not sow and therefore cannot reap." Bob's arm trembled with the monkey's efforts to dislodge it. His shoulder-cap was braced against his chin.

Reinhart remembered some old Army jujitsu for use against an assailant who went for the throat: you peeled his fingers back one by one and broke them. If taken from behind you reached back and applied excruciating pain to his genitals. Why did he identify with the monkey?

With a sudden effort Sweet ripped Otto off the bars and brought him out. "There you go, Carl," he shouted. Then he hurled the monkey at him.

Otto embraced Reinhart with his hairy limbs. He threw his head back and pushed his features forward. There was a little dark vee of hair between his tiny mad eyes. He smacked his lips rapidly.

Reinhart wondered where the bite would come, tip of nose or deep into the jugular. He was helpless against animal irrationality, and the ape could tell, as a dog or horse could smell fear. That is the ethic of the beast: sheer opportunism, the old power play, kill or knuckle under.

But Otto scrambled up Reinhart's chest and began to pluck at his crew cut.

"He's grooming you," said a chuckling Sweet. "That is a form of placation. He is acknowledging you as the superior animal, Carl."

Reinhart loved it when the barber massaged his head with fingers or, better, the vibrator, to get the old circulation going, to stimulate the natural oils. Way back in time, Maw used to wash his hair for him, and hold his skull in the rinse until he almost drowned.

"Ouch!" The monkey too vigorously had pulled a hair. Actually, it felt good. He cradled Otto's skinny behind, which seemed to be mainly pointed bones, in one hand, and patted the hairy back with the other.

"As you see," said Bob, "he's a fine, healthy fellow."

Otto had a strong but not repellent stench. He inserted a skinny finger in Reinhart's left earhole.

"He will get after all your fleas," Sweet added.

Reinhart recoiled from the tickle. Perhaps he should have gone into zoology, of which he had taken one course to satisfy the freshman requirement in science, dissecting a huge bullfrog. Its circulatory system was injected with pigment. His partner in lab was a girl named Jackie Heath, who thought the frog's arteries were naturally colored yellow. She had a cast in her eye, was otherwise bodily perfect. While he deliberated on whether or not to take her to a movie, a lecturer in speech got her pregnant, was fired, and she left school—in the last week before exams, because the frog came at the end of the course.

"Maybe I should have gone into a profession that dealt with animals," he said to Bob. Otto clasped his neck affectionately, reminiscent of Winona as an infant. "Contrary to what you might think, what I like about them is their selfishness."

"Better watch yourself, Carl," said Sweet, adjusting the sleeves of his jacket. "Otto is not yet full grown. I doubt he's housebroken."

Reinhart chortled bitterly. "Oh, everybody shits on—"

"Don't say it!" Bob ordered. "As to when I formulated a plan for you, I did not. I loathe people whose demand for sympathy conceals their wish to be exploited. I will choose my own prey, thank you. I do not feed on the decaying carcass of someone else's kill, like a hyena, who is also noted for its laugh. If you are offering yourself to be frozen, it must be your decision alone. You must sign a legal waiver. We will make no promises whatever. Your blood will be drained and replaced with glycerol, your body will be suspended in liquid nitrogen at minus one hundred and ninety-seven degrees Centigrade, or about three hundred and eighty-six below zero Fahrenheit. You will be dead to the world."

Reinhart dandled Otto in his arms. The monkey put its face into his neck below the ear.

Bob said: "But do you have any better offers?"

Reinhart did not find the question cruel. It was justified, and literal. He approved of its morally realistic tone. He no longer thought of Bob and Hans as sinister. They were merely doing a job, something he had never been able to manage because he had always been obsessed with the existence of other people. For the first time in his life he accepted the commonplace yet terrifying truth that everybody would still be here when he was gone.

"It's tougher than I thought," he said. "I guess in my heart I had always assumed I would be overpowered. It's true I have toyed with thoughts of suicide, but I actually never went so far as climbing up the barrier on the Bloor Tower. I mean, I could have done that and still been a fake—you know, the way a guy will walk out on a ledge and let some cop talk him in. Meanwhile he has attracted a crowd, who yell: 'Jump!' That is always deplored in the papers, with the same sort of bullshit they produce after an assassination. Whom are they addressing? Everybody and thus nobody."

Otto made happy little grunts.

"A crowd can't be indicted for anything," said Reinhart. "Even in an outright lynch mob there are only a half-dozen persons who touch the victim, and no one was ever killed by yells, however hateful." He stroked Otto's hair. "I have been alone most of my life, even or especially when accompanied. I have often made that observation. I doubt that it is original. When I was young I had all sorts of exciting ideas about morality, government, business, love. In time I discovered that if they were any good I had plagiarized them from some great thinker. If genuinely original they didn't work."

Otto gave him a kind of kiss on the earlobe. Were there queer monkeys?

"In fact," Reinhart went on nihilistically, "they didn't even seem to work when they were the intellectual property of the great philosophers. Socrates was poisoned, if you recall, and Nietzsche lost his mind."

He wanted to put Otto back in the cage, but the monkey clung to him.

"Otto is an interesting name," he said. "It's spelled the same in both directions." He tried to pry him off. "Funny how he likes me all of a sudden. He began by hitting me with that cork. What becomes of him now, Bob? Will you keep him as a pet?"

Sweet grabbed the monkey from behind, and between them they got him back inside the bars. Bob said: "Hans has to run a number of tests on him, not only physical but psychological, to determine whether the freezing has left any effects." He squinted at Reinhart. "Not only ill effects. Perhaps there are improvements. Who knows? That's what science is, a search for knowledge."

"And that's what knowledge is," said Reinhart. "Both good and bad. It seems to come out even in the end. 'The unexamined life,' said Socrates, 'is not worth living.' But what is the price of the examined one, if they poison you in the end? After Otto is finished with the colored blocks, etc., Hans will dissect him and look at his brain tissue through the microscope."

Streckfuss had come up silently on his rubber soles, a fact of which Reinhart had the first inkling when Otto shrank and whimpered.

"Mister Reinhart." Streckfuss had never used the name before; he pronounced it in the authentic, uvular, Central European style. "No doubt you can sink of many ironies on the subject of monkeys, but they are not actually men. If you prick a monkey he vill bleed, and so on, but they have no potential. Me, I do not deny that Otto was named for an SS officer of my acquaintance twenty-five years in the past, but it may astonish you if I say he was not one of the most bestial: rather, human all-too human, in the vords of the crazy Nietzsche."

This seemed a paradox, if Reinhart heard it correctly. He said: "I'm sorry I got this crazy idea you might be a Nazi scientist."

"Your regret is misplaced," Streckfuss said. "Vot does it

matter to me unless you have some serious criticism of my experimental method? Science is not ethical but quantitative. The poison of the *Latrodectus* spider is among the most virulent, but seldom kills an organism as large as a man, becows of the difference in size. Dinosaurs, on the ozzer hand, were too big to lahst. A *baleine*"—he snapped his fingers.

"Whale," said Bob Sweet.

"A whale must be aquatic, you see, for the water supports his great weight. A land animal cannot be much larger than an elephant and survive, owing to gravity. There *are* natural laws, and zey give us a form and a scale for tings. Nature has worked out its principles slowly, making mistakes of course. One must never sink there is an end to possibility. The moon, for example, with its lesser gravity, would be a sympathetic terrain for the dinosaur and larger, but for the kinds of animals we know now, the atmosphere is wrong."

Reinhart briefly experienced the splendor of Streckfuss' scope, as if he were watching Cinerama: the thrill without the danger, the satisfaction one derives, in simulation, from the risky ambitions of other people. During the era of 3-D, elephants trampled you in your seat.

"As a philosopher," Streckfuss said, "you must know Aristotle: 'No one can understand nature fully nor miss it altogether, but as each makes his contribution there arises a structure that has a certain grandeur.' "

"OK," said Reinhart, who had been brought up on the cocky heroes of the silver screen and now found courage in the echo of their idiom. Perhaps vulgarity was fundamental to all heroism. He would have been scared to say, *Yes, you may freeze me.* "OK. You got your boy."

– 16 –

In his moment of bravado Reinhart had been ready to climb into the freezer capsule immediately, as the movie pilot leaps into the cockpit and, the point of view necessarily switching from participant to spectator, is soon thereafter seen diving down the smokestack of a Japanese battleship.

But reality, however fantastic, consists in specificities, seen from one perspective only. For example, Streckfuss had on hand insufficient liquid nitrogen to freeze a mouse. An order was long overdue, owing, said Bob, to a slowdown of the deliverymen's union, perhaps preparatory to an outright strike.

With the new energy derived from his decision to give up, Reinhart seized the phone and called the supplier's number.

"Listen here," he said, "this is a scientific institution—"

"And we are a business," said the spokesman on the other end. "If you will pay for your last shipment, we might consider making another."

Sweet received this information laconically.

"Jesus Christ," said Reinhart. "I just don't understand you, Bob."

"I've had to put up some cash margins," said Sweet. "No cause for alarm. I can get a loan on the warehouse receipts for my storage at Berne." He dialed a number and began a conversation that might have been in Urdu or Tagalog, so far as Reinhart could fathom.

Streckfuss shook his head. "Leave zese tings to Bopp. I want that in the next fortnight you do not overly excite your nervous system, also that you avoid all ordinary foodstuffs, take no medicines or drugs, exercise moderately but not to the point of fatigue, and sleep as much as possible."

"Two weeks?"

Streckfuss said: "In fact, you must reside in this place.

We will make a bett for you here. Mine, indeed. You may use it. I seldom sleep."

Bob hung up the phone and said: "That's settled, then. I'm leaving now to dispose of these matters. I'll check you out of the Midtown Y, Carl, and bring back your effects. We'll get the papers drawn up. Take my advice and do not inform your family. You would have certain rights as a missing person. They won't be able to get into your safe-deposit box."

Streckfuss produced a stethoscope from the pocket of his lab coat and said: "Remove your clozing."

Now, whereas Reinhart had been ready a few moments before to plunge into the quick-freeze, he balked.

"Just a minute," he cried. "I can't stay here just like this. I've got things to do."

"What?" Sweet asked coldly. "What things? You would hardly have volunteered if that were so. And you did volunteer, didn't you, Carl? Nobody tricked you or used pressure of any kind, isn't that true? You will have to swear to that, you know. Or we can forget the whole thing."

"There's no question, Bob, and you know it. But this is a bit abrupt, on the one hand, and long-drawn-out on the other."

"Like life itself," said Sweet.

"I'm glad you mentioned that. It's mine, isn't it? My own damned life."

Sweet threw his arms up and made his mouth into an O of mock horror. "Far be it from me, Carl . . ."

"I don't intend to live in this mausoleum for what may be the last two weeks of it, either," Reinhart announced. "I'm going to call you on that offer of a suite in the Shade-Milton, and I also want a good car." He stopped to catch his breath. His heartbeat was racing—the sort of thing that did not matter now.

To Streckfuss he said: "I intend to eat rich foods and drink expensive wines. The effects are your problem. You can flush me out when I am unconscious."

"Ah," muttered the little scientist, elevating his shoulders to the level of his ears. "Ah, ah." He put away the stethoscope.

Sweet's neck had gone rigid. "Anything you say, Carl. You're the boss."

The word had a lovely, brutal sound. In his various business ventures Reinhart had employed a few persons, yet never had he felt superior to them in power, perhaps because he had not possessed anything they really wanted: they invariably went to better jobs when his enterprises failed.

"Can your tailor make up some clothes for me within a couple of days?" he asked Sweet. "In all my life I have never owned a suit that really fitted. I have always felt like a bundle somebody wrapped up for the Salvation Army."

He walked to the door. "So long, Hans." His joviality made metallic and crystalline echoes throughout the lab. Streckfuss was a small, old, almost forlorn figure when seen in perspective. "See you in the funny papers!" That sounded cheap. He must take care not to satiate himself too soon.

In the Bentley's back seat Reinhart said: "I'll need some spending money, Robert."

Sweet's energy seemed to have flagged. "Sure, Carl. But you can put the car and hotel on the company, and I have accounts at several restaurants."

"No," said Reinhart. "I don't want that. I will pay as I go. I'm sick of bills, installment plans, pay-now-fly-later, credit cards, and all the rest of that shit. I want genuine, hard cash, such as you hardly ever see any more. I want to crumple a twenty-dollar bill and throw it at some insolent headwaiter and have him kiss my ass. I want to overtip the embittered hoodlums who work in parking lots and hear them thank me. I want to be stopped for speeding and bribe the cop and get saluted. And most of all, I'd like to stop some bitch of a teen-ager with legs that are bare up to the cheeks of her behind and naked tits inside a see-through shirt, and ask her price: you name it, five hundred, a thousand—"

"Sure, Carl, sure."

"—and when I reached it, give her the money and leave her untouched. I'd also like to send Captain Storm a sizable sum for the Black Assassins. Anonymously, huh? What do you think of that? That punk, in his idiotic uniform and phony name, while Splendor lies dying." A gratuitous slur, in view of the boy's manifest concern for his father, but Reinhart tended to project his own son into Storm's jackboots, and vice versa. In time the race problem would vanish, but there would always be failing fathers and succeeding sons.

Call him mad, now that he had guaranteed to be put on ice, but he saw the answer to youth. It was Yes. Press on, full speed ahead. Here, spend this on dynamite and drugs. Blow yourself up while out of your skull. Splendid. Anything you want. Utter acquiescence to the demands of all persons who apply, but applicants are urged to act promptly during the fortnight's amnesty. After which, I personally shall cool it.

"Hey!" Eunice shouted again, gathering herself into the seat and reinforcing the safety belt with crossed arms.

"What's the matter?" Reinhart asked idly. He controlled the car with his left hand, and with his right felt her thigh, which was rather flabby if the truth be known. "Let's live a little," said he.

She pinched her eyes shut. They were overtaking a three-car spread on a tri-laned highway. However, it was one-way and separated from the southbound side by a generous strip of grass defined by concrete curbing, rounded and quite too low to burst Reinhart's tires as he shot over it, getting nicely past the trio of collateral dolts and cutting back down on the pavement without the use of brakes or the loss of rpms.

"You see," he said. "No cause for alarm. Fast driving is not necessarily reckless. The great Stirling Moss, who has won many a Grand Prix for England, will go ninety on glare ice and yet maintain more control than a little old lady in her wheelchair. Precision is the answer, Eunice."

Corrupt politicians, in the pocket of local businessmen, had no doubt been responsible for the battery of traffic lights ahead, which were inexcusable on a superhighway, contradicting its purpose as a high-speed thoroughfare. But a rotten shopping center festered nearby, with entrances and exits at the crossroads. A line of station wagons, full of commodities and spoiled children, eyeglassed fathers at the wheels, smug wives alongside, waited to go in or out. An interminable orange light slowed down the pack of cars at the head of which Reinhart charged. The exiting herd began to edge forward. Reinhart kept his foot to the floor, his left palm on the horn, and blasted through.

A standing cop, in white summer cap and orange Day-Glo weskit, seemed to give him a blurred smile. Reinhart was watching Eunice, who was utterly silent. He poked her.

"I used to be one of those jerks," he said. "With an open Kleenex box, sliding across the back shelf whenever I turned a corner."

Surly bitch. She failed to respond. Looking back at the

road, Reinhart pretended he was a competitor in the
Annual Memorial Day Classic at Indianapolis, that his
pea-green Edwardian jacket was a suit of fireproof cover-
alls. Buster Watkins, Jr., an illiterate but engaging Southern daredevil, had just spun out, hit the wall, and was
incinerated. One down. That's racing.

He poked Eunice again and heard her groan.

"Jesus," he said, "but you are a drag today." He shot
by a marked police car, the uniformed driver of which
touched a finger to the brim of his cap.

People could tell when you were beyond their power.
Reinhart had already noticed that when he bought his
clothes at Outrageous Foppery, a male boutique. He had
the young, lithe, snotty sort of salesman who would have
spat upon him but last week, that new species who com-
peted with the customers in attire and lorded it over them
in manner, muttonchop sideburns meeting over his
mouth, paddlebladed tie, cerise shirt. On his side Reinhart
would have detested this half-assed phony. Now he saw
him as quite a decent sort, with helpful, amusing ideas. If
we must dress, then why not with verve?

Bob had waited in the Bentley. He had been glum ever
since Reinhart had agreed to be frozen—which went to
show you something about getting what you wanted.
Reinhart chose a purple shirt to match the bell-bottom
velveteen trousers, and a scarf of swirling colors instead
of a proper tie, and rather than knot it, drew the silken
ends through his wedding ring and thus added a smear of
verdigris to the psychedelic mélange.

His old-style crew cut was incongruous in the mirror,
all the more so in that the Edwardian jacket, with its high
neck, tended to squeeze him towards the top. Underneath, a plastic belt, wide as a corset, went through the
loops of his low-rise pants, cincturing him below the belly
button, above which the excess meat was hidden by the
jacket's flaring skirt. Reinhart discovered to his pleasure
that he was made for the styles of the moment.

The tight jacket took fifty pounds off him. The slacks
had been troublesome. The largest available waist had
missed closure by a good six inches, but the resident tailor
had so to speak jumped into the breach, inserting a big
vee of extra material in the ass. Also velveteen, but white.
It would be hidden by the jacket's long tail. But the
salesman, and several other customers, bearded youths,
cheered at the effect and one boy demanded his own
trousers be altered in accord, with not only the rear

panel, but another in front giving the effect of a diaper worn over long pants.

Reinhart paid cash for his gear and left everybody in a good mood, indeed almost hysterically agreeable, shouting 'Man!' at him. Not all the young were vicious.

But it was the first time Reinhart had ever seen Bob Sweet look startled. When he got into the car, Bob said: "Are you sure about that, Carl?"

"Never more so, Bob. From this perspective the whole new thing in men's clothes looks different to me. And I hope you don't mind me saying that you seem a bit square."

"No, I don't mind. Far from it." Bob yawned suddenly. "Back to the hotel?"

"You go," Reinhart said, "if you want a nap or something, but there is still one jarring note in my ensemble. This outmoded crew cut. I look like a militarist. I'm going to that place that advertises in the paper, Lasagna's Virile Crests, the people who specialize in hairpieces and false moustaches. I don't have time to let my own crop grow out." He felt a twinge as the sensitive tooth of his soul came down on the adamant seed of this reality. But Bob's awesome look was some compensation. Reinhart enjoyed his chance to show off, perhaps all the more so in view of the price he would pay for it.

At Lasagna's, foremost of the male beauty parlors in the city, Reinhart was fitted into a full wig, with sideburns which plunged an inch below his ears. He chose a rich hue of brown, having not had much fun as a lifelong blond, whatever that ad said. The thought of being frozen did not seem so ugly when he saw his first bewigged reflection. For many years he had had the same general visage, though inevitably aging. Not since '41 when for a semester he had let his scalp grow out, had he seen his locks longer than an inch and a half. Suddenly he had as much hair as Winona, though better groomed.

The barber or fitter deftly swept a comb through it, producing a crackle of static electricity. "Top quality Sicilian," said he, a small man whose fingers danced with energy. "Bring it in once a month for dry cleaning, otherwise forget it and wear it with pleasure."

Bob said nothing when Reinhart rejoined him this time.

Reinhart asked: "Do you sleep in your toupee?" Bob curled his lip. Reinhart said: "Of course the situation is not exactly the same. I have real hair underneath. Mine is anchored down by the sideburns." He tugged at one. "This tape is terrific. That what you use?"

"Fuck off, Carl," Bob said.

Sports Cars Unlimited occupied the suburban site of Psycho Sam's used-car business of the early postwar era when vehicles were scarce. Reinhart had once had dealings with Psycho, a rude, rapacious man.

The current salesman was dressed in a smart linen jacket, navy-blue knitted shirt, and paisley cravat.

"Jagyouar have got it sorted out by now," he said. "The E-Type will satisfy for high-speed motoring, and this is an exceptionally well-kept exahmple."

It occurred to Reinhart that the accent could be fake, but the car soon distracted him. The white XKE looked as though it exceeded the speed limit while lying at rest.

"Actually, I was thinking of a convertible."

The salesman winced. "The drophead? We have an ayolder one, but I'm afraid it has the ayolder three-point-eight liter engine as well. I shouldn't think it would please as much as the four-point-two. And the aerodynamics of the drophead are not nearly as favorable as those of the fixed-head coupé."

Reinhart was trying to act knowledgeable, but apparently, as with any other discipline, trade, or indulgence, there was a unique vocabulary for sports cars.

The salesman sneered at the hood. "Let me just open the bonnet." He thrust his skinny trunk through the driver's open window, then went around the other side and repeated his act. The entire snout tilted up at the wrong end, while Reinhart waited in front. The car seemed to be broken in half. The salesman waggled a finger at him.

Reinhart walked around and looked into an engine compartment filled with gleaming chromium parts. "I'll take it," he said, before having to listen to more imported jargon. His own, from the gas station days, was all-American, and his mechanical expertise was limited to simple procedures like screwing in a new set of plugs and changing the windshield wipers. For any serious trouble he had sent his customers to Joe Laidlaw's All-in-One Service, losing them forever.

Bob Sweet had opted out of this expedition, lending Reinhart the Bentley. Reinhart now awakened the old chauffeur and sent him back to the Shade-Milton with it, and called Bob on the office phone of Sports Cars Unlimited.

"Forty-five hundred dollars!" Sweet wailed.

"I'm saving you money. I would have had to plank down almost seven grand for a new one, but I'd be frozen before it would be broken in. And the car has value. It will still be here when I'm gone." He laughed boisterously. "I'll need more money soon. That makes five I've gone through already, and the day is far from over."

"Carl, if you are going to smash yourself up, the deal is off."

"I know that," said Reinhart. "You'd be surprised how concerned I am for self-preservation. Being liberated is different from being reckless, Bob. I have this sense that for two weeks I can do anything. You see, my nightmare has been faced and conquered. I realize that my trouble has been essentially a fear of death." He hung up abruptly. Sweet had deposited ten thousand dollars in his account. Reinhart was amused and exhilarated to see how quickly it went.

After getting his license plates, usually a vile experience with lazy and insolent public employees, but today a flawless episode—a motherly vehicles clerk smiled and wished him good motoring—Reinhart decided to fetch Eunice and embark on a tour of pleasure. They would drive somewhere at high speed, dine luxuriously, screw under the stars in some redolent meadow, breakfast at dawn in a robust truckers' café to the amazed envy of the unshaven interstate drivers at the sight of a man of their own age with young girl and Jaguar.

The car was an ecstasy, the steering so responsive that a cough could send you off the road, the engine guttural in voice and ferociously potent, ten mph to every pound of weight, more spacecraft than automobile. A bastard for a man of Reinhart's size to enter, but once encapsulated behind the wheel, you lived that dream of infinite power without vulnerability, sealed in a bullet. The low roof cleared his head by an inch, the leather bucket was so integrated with his hams that he could have survived a roll without being dumped. He was *with* car, or vice versa, as a pregnant woman is with child. No, he *was* car. He had a long metal snout, four chromium wire wheels, and his time from zero to sixty was less than six seconds. He, who even before he turned fat was a sluggish runner, left the gaudy Detroit Fireballs and Flamethrowers sitting turdlike at every change of light all the way downtown.

Entering the office he jokingly inquired for Doctor Streckfuss.

"I'm sorry," Eunice began mechanically, while looking him full in the face, "we are not permitted—Carl! What's—Why—"

"How are you making it, baby?" Reinhart said.

Today of all days Eunice was out of it, wearing a pleated blue linen skirt and tailored blouse. Underneath the latter an old-fashioned uplift bra elevated and petrified her breasts. Her hair was pulled tight.

She still gawked at Reinhart. Finally she said: "All right, Carl, *ver*-ry *fun*-nee."

"No," he said. "That's what I used to be. Now I am Where It Is." He reached over and pulled the plug, stunning her electric typewriter. "Come on, let's split."

She put her hands on her hips. Something librarianlike about her today. "All right," she said, looking mock-stern. "Joke over."

"No," Reinhart said again. "It's just beginning, Miss Munsing. How's your dad the shrink?"

"He's playing golf again today. Usually we spend the whole month of August at the lake, but he just started to break ninety for the first time and doesn't want to interrupt his run of luck. He's a Gemini. I'm Aries. These are adverse days for me." She picked up a little book and read: " 'If you do a favor for a friend, you may pay heavily. Be thoughtful and see where hidden dangers lie. The celestial pendulum swings its broad arc, bringing a planetary warning to lay a heavy hand on caution.' "

"And your mother is well, I trust?"

"She sneezes a lot, and it is still a couple of weeks before true hay-fever time. She is full of antihistamines, which make her drowsy. When she really gets going, the bridge of her nose swells—"

Reinhart seized Eunice's wrist and pulled her up from the chair.

Her eyes were not made up. She seemed to be fading out.

"Carl," she said in a frightened voice, "your parody is extremely clever. I think it's yum-yum. I really like it."

"And I admire yours, Eunice, I really do."

"Well then . . ." She smiled placatingly. "Let's just calm down."

He pulled her to the door and into the corridor.

"It's not five o'clock yet," she said in the Down car.

"Eunice, *I* am all that the Cryon Foundation has going for it. When you are with me, you are still at work."

"Yes, sir." There was no content in the gaze of her pale eyes.

"Why," he asked as they descended to the lobby, "why in the world did you tell me Bob Sweet was your father? And that preposterous story about your mother defecting behind the Iron Curtain."

"It seemed like the thing to say at the time."

At the curb Reinhart opened the door of the Jag.

Eunice balked. "Carl," she said. "Please don't do anything you'll be sorry for. They'll catch you before you have driven a block."

He pushed her inside. "This car is my property."

"But I don't know how to get in!"

"Face out, sit down on the seat, then swing your legs around." She did as ordered, but her knees would still not clear the frame, so Reinhart grabbed whatever he could and crammed her in like a bag of laundry.

"For Christ's sake," he said when he was behind the wheel, "you've been half-naked every other day, switched-on to the hilt, but now, in an XKE, you look like a kindergarten teacher."

Her skirt hardly cleared her knees.

"I want onlookers to see your creamy white thighs," he said, pulling up the hem. But the idiot was wearing an outmoded panty girdle, with legs as long as Bermuda shorts.

Reinhart revved up and blasted out with a scream of rubber, snapping Eunice's head against the padded rest. "Sue me for whiplash," he said.

On the way in to the city he had learned the shift points, and with the four forward gears he made monkeys of the jerks in their routine automatics, not braking as he approached the lights but going down through the box, double-clutching, keeping the rpms high as the speed diminished, then gunning away on the green. Only twice in the downtown area, with signals at every corner, did he have to come to a full stop. He had learned this technique in ten minutes' reading of a paperback called *Competition Driving*, while waiting for the bill of sale to be drawn up at Sports Cars Unlimited.

A mile or so beyond the shopping center Reinhart got clear of all interference and a wide, empty straightaway lay supinely inviting his assault.

"Eunice," said he. She was still quiet, and he considered calling her a drag again, but actually it worked out to his uses that she retired in the degree to which he was assertive. "Eunice, you are perfectly safe in this car and in my hands. It is a most advanced piece of machinery of monocoque construction, aerodynamic design, and disk brakes on all four wheels. Tuned for racing, its maximum speed is a hundred and fifty miles per hour. Independent suspension and Koni shock absorbers. It holds the road as if in the grip of a giant hand. You are safer here at speed than at forty mph in one of those swollen American baby buggies with spongy springing. Let's have a go flat-out."

His big right foot grew heavier. The engine's hoarse roar climbed in pitch through howl to scream, the oncoming road became a continuum of immaterial substance, smoke or mist or utter illusion. Only the steering wheel was actual, immediate and hard, intractable, vibrating through his arms and down the spinal column to tingling coccyx. His skull cemented to the headrest, he saw tiny phenomena of horizon swell gigantic, pass in blur, and swoop into the nullity of a rear-vision mirror agitated so rapidly it seemed at rest.

One hundred, threefourfivefifteen. Bugs exploded in white and yellow bursts of liquid shrapnel against the windshield. At the next flick of Reinhart's lashes he saw the bawdy red finger of speed upon the very prick of 125. He had not breathed since 115, but that had been only a millisecond earlier.

An infinity remained between his shoe and the floor, or else his foot had gone right through, his toe would soon touch the carborundum of the road, be instantly ground to a stub: 130. One hundred thirty fucking miles an hour. At the speed of light would one black out? 135. Faster than a speeding bullet, Carlo Kent, mild-mannered reporter for a metropolitan newspaper, is actually Superman.

Reinhart did not have these thoughts—one does not think at high speed, he unthinkingly discovered—but rather embodied them, realized them, *was* them as well as being the car, with grease so hot it was thin as blood, his taut metallic belly-skin seared by the heat of the roadway an inch below, his bearings a blur of joyful fury, his nose cone incandescent. 140.

The accelerator at last touched bottom. He had reached a maximum in enterprise, but not yet in effect. The windshield was translucent with the milk and pus of many small deaths. He rocketed through a void, weightless, silent among the spheres, at a speed so exhausting reason it was one with stasis. He had finally outrun the physical laws, reversed time, and become a baby, serene in the womb.

The sapped speedometer limply fell to zero. The steering wheel was insensate. They glided in orbit.

Eunice opened the door and swung her legs out into rushing space.

He clawed at her, but she eluded him and ran down the highway. The car was quite at rest in the center of the road. Reinhart piled out and saw a steaming pool of water underneath the hood, with replenishment still falling. He broke the body in half, as demonstrated by the salesman, and learned that the fabric-clad rubber hose between radiator and cylinder block had burst. The sparkplug wells were brimming.

Two young guys in a Mustang passed and shouted to the effect that he could copulate with himself. Up ahead, Eunice tried to hitch a ride with them, but a misogynistic, perhaps deviate, spite claims young American males in cars, even if they are quite straight while afoot, and they hooted derision at her and speeded up.

This called Reinhart to sense. He chased her along the barren shoulder, down the drainage furrow full of beer cans, and into a field of fuzzy-topped weeds. She ran on the toes of high-heeled shoes, wobbly but evasive. Though he overtook her soon enough, he could not for some distance put a hand on her, and eventually there was nothing for it but to launch a flying tackle, at the conclusion of which their two large bodies lay prone upon sufficient crushed weeds to bed a heifer.

Reinhart sat up and addressed her back.

"Aren't you the silly one."

She shivered against the ground.

"There was no danger at all," he said. "The car is made for that kind of speed." He grasped her under the arms and got her up to sitting, limp and very heavy.

She whispered: "I blacked out at the intersection. I came to at a hundred and forty." She suddenly sagged badly. Reinhart struggled around, knee-walking, and smartly slapped her gray face.

"I thought you were a swinger," he said in sympathetic remonstrance.

A large blue eye opened, rimmed with wild red.

"Are you going to beat me now?" she asked, still whispering.

He stood up. "I don't get you at all, Eunice. You are a young chick, with your life ahead of you. It is a perfect

summer afternoon, and I have a fantastic car and a
pocketful of bread. This is the kind of thing I thought
would turn you on. We can drive to Shawnee Lake. They
have a peace-rock-love festival there for the whole
month, with the top groups. We can buy all the grass we
want and stay stoned all weekend, or organize an orgy or
something—anything you want, doll." He looked down at
her, over the silken ends of his scarf. "I'm not square any
more."

Fearfully she peeped up. "I don't feel so good," she
said. Reinhart helped her to her feet. Within thirty yards
his arm was cramped by her almost inanimate weight,
and when he altered his hold, she fell again. In the
drainage ditch she vomited. On the shoulder she shuddered and sneezed.

Reinhart had begun to find her a big pain in the ass.

He said: "Now you're not catching cold when it's
ninety-two degrees."

She whimpered. "I'm allergic to weeds."

He looked up to see an old Cadillac, traveling at about
seventy, strike the Jaguar in the back bumper, run it
ahead for a hundred yards, and finally shunt it off into the
drainage ditch. It tumbled onto its back, with an indecent
show of steel genitalia. The Cadillac kept on going.

Reinhart found this one of the funniest episodes he had
ever witnessed. He let Eunice collapse and sat down
beside her in his Edwardian suit and laughed till his eyes
ran. Two great semicircles of sweat showed beneath his
tight armpits. The belt was cutting him into two swollen
bags. Yet never had he felt so free of care.

A bald old man stopped a new car and asked through the
passenger's window: "Can I get you to a hospital or
should I send back an ambulance?"

"A lift would be fine," Reinhart said. "She's just sick to
the stomach. Nothing serious." He got Eunice into the
back seat and stretched her out.

He said to the man's old profile, pointed nose and little
sagging chin: "You're sure taking a chance. We could be
faking it, you know. Once inside we draw our guns, take
you as hostage, and cut a swath of murder and mayhem
through six states until the cops ambush us in a blood-
bath. How do you know we're not Bonnie and Clyde?"

The old man smiled. "I saw Johnnie Dillinger's father
once. He went around in vaudeville, giving lectures. Made
a lot of money. And who would he of been without John
being an outlaw? Did you ever think of that?"

"Actually, I have," said Reinhart. "What would police-men work at if there was no crime, and doctors if there were no disease?"

"Name is Ray Harper," said the man, who looked about seventy. "Would shake your hand if I wasn't driving. Been driving since '26 and never had a bangup nor got a ticket and mean to keep it that way. Put sixty-seven thousand miles on this buggy and you can't tell it."

"It looks and even smells new," said Reinhart. "I thought it was right out of the showroom."

"You sure did." Harper cackled. "I keep it washed and polished and I drive out every day and look at all the fools. I been retired for fifteen years and some say you don't have anything to do, but they are wrong. There is always plenty of fools to look at. I wish I seen that crackup." They were just passing the overturned Jag.

"Looks like it was a doozer," said Reinhart. He glanced back at Eunice, who was breathing through her mouth and staring glassily at the dome light.

"You eloping?" asked Harper. "I buried my old woman last year. We was married for thirty-seven years." He wore a short-sleeved sports shirt, buttoned all the way up to his turkey neck. "If I ain't out in this machine, I'm home watching the fools on color TV. I never eat nothing but canned stuff. I haven't had a banana since 1916, and I call salads rabbit food. I still got most of my teeth. I'm going to take the next exit onto 203."

"Sounds like you've got everything under control," said Reinhart.

"Call me anything but late for breakfast," Harper said, turning carefully into the curving one-lane egress, which within fifty yards debouched onto a state road of blacktop flanked with motel and restaurant ads. "Sometimes," he said, "I will stay the night in a tourist cabin and dirty every towel. I paid for them, didn't I?" While resting at the stop sign he turned and winked. "Where would you like to be dropped, son?"

Reinhart scanned the several route signs. Rabb was 2½ miles to the left, Rumpelstiltskin to the right at 3, and, at 5, of all places, Berne.

"Berne," said Reinhart. "Miss Munsing and I are asso-ciated with the Robert Sweet firm, with warehouses here."

"That's my neck of the woods," said Harper. "I used to own and operate the grain-and-feed store there. I sold it

to a Hebrew gentleman in 1954, but he turned out to be a
real nice fellow. I don't want to call you on it, but I never
heard of any Sweet being thereabouts. Them old warehouses is on a railroad siding, but they closed down the
Mount Whipple spur in '56 and there isn't no trains
coming through town any more. You want a train, you
drive to Babson."

"Well then, you can drop us any place we can rent a
car."

"How'd you get way out where I picked you up without
one?" Harper asked, tooling along at thirty.

"That was it in the ditch."

"You just leaving it there?"

"Sure," Reinhart said. "It is just so much useless metal
if it doesn't work. I have contempt for useless gadgets."

Harper was impressed. He said: "Now, is that
right?"

"You see," said Reinhart, "no criticism of a man like
you, who takes good care of things, but it really does my
heart good to discard a seven-thousand-dollar car when
the water hose breaks."

Harper gave a thin whistle. "Look here," he said, "if
you ain't got anything better to do, I'd be proud if you
would come and have supper with me. It won't be like
when the old woman was living, but I can fill your
gut."

This touched Reinhart, and attracted him, but with as
little time as he had left for warmblooded experience, he
stuck to the idea of gaudier pleasures, and declined with
thanks.

"Well then," said Harper, bobbing his parchment skull
at the windshield, "we can do it when you bring the
machine back."

"Huh?"

"I'm loaning you this here automobile. It won't do you
a thing to decline. There ain't noplace in the whole
township where they will rent you one."

Reinhart asked in amazement: "You would lend your
car, which you have maintained so perfectly, to a man
who just wrecked and abandoned another?"

"I'm insured," Harper said. "Anyway, all my life I've
worked on hunches. I had a hunch a yellow-haired young
girl would work out for a wife and I married her and lived
with her for thirty-seven years. We fought all the time
but that was all right. I had six boys. One died when he
was little, and another deserted from the Army in the war

and stole a tank and was put in prison. The second one
become a shyster lawyer. Alfred was some kind of moron
and is in a home—you couldn't put up with him, except
at holidays like Halloween, where he would stand all day
at the gate holding a little jack-o-lantern. What's that
leave?" He counted on his fingers, still clutching the
steering wheel: raised the nails one by one. "There's
Henry, he sells combines upstate. And then Wallace, he
become a cop in San Diego, California. I got eight grand-
children. Anyway, I got a hunch about you, and I don't
even know your name. You got spirit. I like that. I never
all my life knew a man who would discard a machine,
unless it was an old junker, but even then they would strip
off the usable parts."

"They do the same nowadays with human beings,"
Reinhart said, modestly steering the conversation away
from the subject of his expansive, and expensive, gesture.
It was of course nothing compared to his decision to be
frozen.

Harper said: "Your girl is mighty quiet."

Reinhart looked into the back seat. "She's sleeping, I
think. Hey, Eunice." She was not dead, her chest moved
regularly. He said: "I might throw her away, too."

The old man chortled. "Yes sir, you are something."

"I guess you think I'm pretty ruthless," said Reinhart.
"I am. I am your typical thrill-seeker. I run through
fantastic adventures while other people put in their normal, dull days. I observe no responsibilities towards anyone or -thing. I have no principles. I take women at my
pleasure, use them, destroy them, toss them aside. I have
a family somewhere, whom I abandoned years ago when
my children were babies. At age twenty-one I beat up my
sick old dad, robbed my mom's purse, and left forever."

Harper loved this account. Reinhart elaborated on it
during the ride to Berne, which turned out to be the
typical little rural-American village of pizzeria, Cantonese
restaurant, Maserati showroom, cat hospital, and stereo
center in the business district, before reaching which you
passed a Rose Bowl-sized football field with a million
dollars' worth of illumination for night games.

Harper kept going through all of this, with many stops
because of the sophisticated traffic-control system of a
half-dozen types of electrical signals, painted lanes, and
zebra crosswalks, and at length they reached a residential
area where sunlight filtered through the sycamores and

old houses were skirted in green latticework below their spacious verandas.

Reinhart abruptly forsook his lies to peer in joy. As a child he had visited someone's great-aunt or third cousin in such a house, with even a stone cistern in back. A neighbor kid had tried to push him in it.

However, Harper continued into a tract of beastly ranch houses beyond and Reinhart made the usual cynical reflections to himself. His new power was fading again. This looked like the kind of place Gen had forced him to live for years. He knew from the outside where the toilets were situated, the door into the garage, and the garbage cans.

"You see," he resumed, gesturing at a flabby man on his knees trimming the edges of the lawn while several benuded teen-agers lounged nearby with a transistor radio, "that's the sort of thing, the sort of people, I run roughshod over. Possession-collectors, the imagination-deprived, the little frightened rump-kissers whose opinions are molded by the military-industrial complex."

"Big defense plant in Babson," said Harper.

"I happen to be a leftist," Reinhart said. He was saying whatever came into his head, like one of those new, extemporaneous comedians who get audience suggestions and wing it.

"Figure you was from the way you're got up," Harper said, chuckling.

"I'd love to see everything burned down to the ground," Reinhart stated. "That's the only way you will eradicate racism and poverty and war and sex hangups."

"They sell a lot of filth now in the drugstore," Harper said. "You mentioned Bonnie and Clyde. They got a paperback with a pair of young fellows on the cover who look like girls: call it *Donnie and Claude*. Couple of Percies."

Reinhart forgot himself for a moment of nostalgia. "God, I haven't heard that word in years."

"Cover shows 'em kissing each other on the mouth." Harper shook his old head, but he didn't seem to be seriously bothered.

They were approaching a park full of trailers, except the term was no longer used: "mobile homes" was the current designation when, like these, the containers were static and mounted on foundations of cinderblock and, often, surrounded by little picket fences enclosing growing plants, even birdbaths, iron animals, and mirrored balls.

Harper turned in there and drove the car into a slot beside a sort of refrigerator car of glistening aluminum. The next trailer, a pea-green affair with turquoise awnings over the airplane-type windows, was so close that Reinhart feared he would not be able to open the door sufficiently wide for his bulk. But it cleared. Indeed, there was yet space enough for a four-year-old girl in a bikini bottom to stand and write her name on the wall of her home. If her name was FUCK, that is. Reinhart took the crayon away from her and made it BOOK, an old device of his from the days when Blaine was a dwarf with a foul pencil.

He decided not to wake Eunice, and followed Harper up the little stair. The air-conditioning had been left at idle, and the interior was quite cool. Reinhart successfully resisted the clichéd urge to observe how much larger it looked inside than out.

"I got nineteen thousand five hundred for the old place when the wife died," Harper said. "And then they ripped it down, built a prefab, and sold it for forty-seven. Figure they cleared fifteen. I got a flush toilet here, in case you have to take a trot on the china horse." He went back the aisle, opened a metal door, reached in, and soon a recognizable gush was heard. "Filgas range," he said, and going to the appropriate area, produced a blue flame. "Running water." He filled a kettle at a little stainless-steel sink and put it on to boil. "Anything you want: hot coffee, tea, or ice-cold Fresca. I was put onto that by the commercials where it snows." He opened a small half-refrigerator and revealed several shelvesful of cold cuts mummified in tight-wrapped plastic. "Now for this stew of mine, I slice up baloney, take a can of White Rose creamed corn—"

"It sounds great," Reinhart said, "but coffee will be fine. I'm anxious to hit the road again. Listen, while the water is heating I'll just nip out and find a public phone—there must be one here—and call a cab."

"Not on your life," the old man insisted. "I told you to take my car. I don't need it till you bring it back, with the story of all the adventures you have in it. You are a real interesting fellow, make other youngsters look like frozen fish fillets."

They drank freeze-dried Maxwell House, yellowed with non-dairy Pream. Harper then pressed the car keys and registration on Reinhart, and having switched on an enormous color TV which filled most of the trailer's back end, lay down on one of the built-in bunks to watch it.

"Bring it back when convenient," he said, watching a late-afternoon kids' cartoon show in which a rickety little clerk turns into a monster at the utterance of a magic word. "Or if you wreck it and throw it away, take me a photo first."

Eunice was gone or had dissolved into the dark stain of moisture on the back seat cover.

The moppet from the trailer next door had grown into a long-haired sylph of sixteen and packed her pectoral abundance into a ribbon an inch wide.

"Hey," said Reinhart. "Did you see a girl leave this car?"

"Yeah. She hitched a ride a couple minutes ago."

"What kind of car?"

"A panel truck."

Reinhart pursed his lips. "Thanks."

She wrinkled her little sun-kissed nose, lifting her upper lip so as to reveal only the very tips of the incisors.

"You wanna?"

Reinhart's return expression was of the same genre. Then he shrugged slowly and said: "No thanks."

"Chicken."

Well, why not take Harper's car? The old man relied on him. He got in.

The teen-ager looked through the other window.

"Fag," she said.

She seemed about the age of the next-door Julie, whom he was falsely accused of having ravished. He now recognized his old platonic lust for teen-agers as having been pure and simple fear. Girls old enough to be fully sexed but so young as not to die for decades—he now saw the sentimentality of his old obsession. This maiden, for example, might at any hour be run down in the street or drown in a public pool. She was no more eternal than he, he who had in independent volition offered himself to ice.

"Go tell your mother she wants you," he said and backed out. Anyway, he was not much interested in sex at this juncture, nor in food. A man whose time was precious should have more exalted aims than emptying and filling himself. The high-speed travel had however been profoundly rewarding, disclosing to him truths beyond the range of verbal or pictorial expression in a universe in which the velocity of light is 186,000 miles per second. Yet there are stars whose sparkle takes countless years to reach our planet. And he had moved at a mere hundred and forty mph.

Well, that was done. Harper's car, a 1964 Plymouth, seemed to be inhibited from exceeding fifty: the old guy probably had installed a governor to protect his property against the mechanics who serviced it. Reinhart motored serenely along the back roads, avoiding the big highway when astride such weak horses. It was obvious that Eunice preferred him square. The same thing might well be true of Blaine, and of Gen as well. He was now provoking, no longer provokable. He should go home and terrorize them.

He bumped over some grass-grown railway tracks. To the right were several long sheds, sheathed in undulating panels of iron that had lost its galvanization to orange rust, moss-green stains, purple corrosions: nature's psychedelic turn-on of man-made materials. He drove in on a truck road of dust and stopped below a loading platform.

The warehouse doors were hasp-locked. This was where Bob Sweet kept his cocoa beans. Reinhart had been through the whole of Berne: this was the only place. He worked for Bob. Were Bob along, Reinhart would ask him: OK if I take a look at your cocoa beans? I have eaten a lot of chocolate in my life and never seen what it's made from. That's one of the things I'd like to do before I check out, strange as it may sound. I am gratifying whims nowadays.

And Bob would produce a key.

So Reinhart went to the car, opened the trunk, and found a jack handle. He inserted it between jamb and hasp and ripped the latter off with a scattering of screws. Surely enough, loaded gunnysacks filled the dusky interior. Reinhart withdrew his little pocketknife-nail file and slashed one bag. A stream of pebblelike particles clattered onto the wooden floor. Reinhart picked one up, rolled it between thumb and forefinger, took it out to the platform and appraised it in the light of the sinking sun. It was indeed a pebble.

With the whiskbroom of his left hand he gathered a right palmload of cocoa beans, took it outside for assaying, and saw a handful of gravel.

There could be no mistake. Bob had definitely said cocoa. The words were not similar. "Gravel," Reinhart said aloud and pitched it onto the tin roof, for the childish pleasure of the sound.

Were he a scientist, he would of course have had to examine more than one sack. Streckfuss had frozen a

variety of small organisms before he was ready for a
man. Or had he? One monkey. There were others in the
capsules. Only one had been thawed. When the doctor
tested you for allergies, he made several scratches with as
many substances, but always left one untreated, as "control": the physical abrasion alone might evoke a bump.

But another thing from which Reinhart was now liberated was the law of probability in its literal sense, the
code of the professional seeker-for-knowledge. And it had
not been the truth that made him free.

Sweet had lied. Every sack, in all three sheds, contained not cocoa beans but gravel: Reinhart was convinced of that. It could further be assumed that this fact
was substantive to some sort of swindle. Bob had spoken
of a loan for which the contents of these warehouses were
security. You could not say gravel was cocoa in this age
of computers and wiretapping and hidden tape recorders,
electric eyes, and omniscient professional and private busybodies.

Even secret Mafia meetings were bugged and the minutes disseminated nationwide. Reinhart himself, for example, knew that Luigi Malefice, alias Pat O'Toole, suffered
from hemorrhoids, subsidized a Little League team, kept
a henna-haired mistress in Alpine, New Jersey, and chan-
neled his illicit earnings through a quite legal restaurant-
laundry business.

A queer on the very staff of the White House had been
publicly exposed. Everybody knew everything if it was
shameful, and almost everything seemed to be, under its
rind. Yet to take the Mafia alone, its activities seemed to
be, openly, more profitable every year, its leaders, known,
farther than ever from jail. If the whole FBI and the
combined police departments of the nation could not nail
Malefice, why could not Bob Sweet pass off three warehouses full of gravel as cocoa beans to some Midwestern
bank?

On the other hand, Reinhart had been scandalously
wrong in his easy assessment of Streckfuss as an old Nazi.
There were better things to do with life than getting the
goods on other people.

The precedent represented by Otto was useless for
Reinhart's purposes because the monkey could not speak.
But Streckfuss had also injected goat-liver cells into the
moribund Splendor Mainwaring.

Reinhart drove Harper's car in the direction of his old
homestead.

"So," Reinhart said to Splendor, with reference to his own activities during the twenty years since they had last had a real talk, "I guess you could say I have survived, though I haven't prevailed, to allude to the Nobel Prize speech of the late William Faulkner."

"I have read some of his literary works, but frankly found them to miss the point," Splendor said. "You know, my own immediate origins are in the South. Did you ever see that contemporaneous caricature of the first Negro-American members of a Southern legislature during Reconstruction days, feet up on desks, cigars between teeth, making a mockery of the institution?"

Reinhart shook his head. "Well, rotten lies like that are being discredited nowadays. . . ."

Splendor made his grisly smile on the blanched pillow. "I am convinced it was a literal rendering. What would be more natural behavior for ex-slaves suddenly transformed into legislators?"

"Of course," Reinhart said. "But it was the implication—"

"A disorderly lot of cheeky apes," said Splendor, making his eyes wondrous. "Defecating on the democratic process, the origins of which were in ancient Greece and which had descended through centuries of rationalism. A magnificent progress, the fruit of European civilization, and so on."

Reinhart threw up his hands. "I know. Pretty shabby, behind all the pretensions."

"But then," said Splendor. "What isn't?"

"I started to say that when I think of Negro history I feel you would have a perfect right to destroy this country."

"Me?" asked Splendor in amazement. "I certainly have more important things to do than that."

"I have stayed too long," said Reinhart, taking a new

tack. "You need your rest. Forgive me, but it's been many years since we've had a good talk." Splendor looked worse than he had several days ago, if that was possible. Reinhart told himself this in defense against the cruel illusion that his friend actually looked subtly better: he was of course merely getting used to the sight. But Splendor certainly spoke with much of the old vigor. It was typical of him not to notice, or at least not to mention, Reinhart's new garb and wig. He had always been beyond the personal peculiarities of others.

"Not at all," Splendor said. "You scarcely got here. Do you remember our talks of old? These kids today think they have discovered mind-expansion, but we could tell them a thing or two. We had our guru. Remember the correspondence course from Doctor Goodykuntz's Universal College of Metaphysical Knowledge? My diploma is still around somewhere. It seems ridiculous now, but these things have their function in developing maturity. That's why I say, let's not despair about our children. They may seem foolish at times, but, believe me, they'll turn out to be fine businessmen one day."

"Businessmen?" asked Reinhart.

"Why, don't tell me you have forgotten our youthful peccadilloes." Splendor waggled a schoolteacher's finger. "We were once on the wrong side of the bars, old boy."

Anyway, Splendor himself had been arrested while in possession of a modicum of heroin and the means of injecting it into his circulatory system. Reinhart had visited him in jail. It was interesting that in Splendor's memory Reinhart was a fellow felon: in his current mood Reinhart wished ardently that he had been.

"Don't tell me," Splendor went on from the pillow, "that you are too old to recall our series of experiments to check out the assumption on which this republic operates?"

Reinhart nodded his acceptance of this revision of history.

"Each generation must establish these truths for themselves." Splendor went on. "My son Raymond is not content to sit and listen how I was once incarcerated for carrying a pinch of talcum powder and a hypodermic needle without a plunger. Not him. He must strap to his waist a plastic water pistol molded in the form of a German Luger, and go through the daily experience of being disarmed by the constabulary at the muzzle of a genuine Police Special at the trigger of which trembles the nervous digit of a patrolman."

Reinhart asked: "You mean—?"

"I don't know how you could forget that priceless moment, one night in 1946," said Splendor, "when you came to the jail, and we put on the police force. There I was, supposedly raving on heroin, and you were pretending to be shocked and enraged by my antics. I have often thought, Carlo, that you and I had sufficient talent to have had a go at show business."

Until this moment Reinhart had subscribed to an utterly different version of this incident, but he was free now. He patted the crown of his wig and laughed in a fashion that exposed all his teeth, mimicking Otto's imitation of human mirth.

"That cop Hasek blew his mind," said he.

Splendor said: "Do you happen to recall a small person on the West Side who called himself the Maker? He was a pusher and was generally himself under the influence."

"Didn't he also have his own one-car taxi company? I believe I rode in it once."

"Of course he did," Splendor soberly replied. "That was one of his many covers. Another was prostitution."

"But that's illegal too."

"Ah, yes, but unless a public nuisance is created, sidewalks obstructed, or of course unless an organization of respectable ladies brings pressure on the politicians at election time, a pander who is careful with his payoffs rarely comes to grief."

"Splendor, I always thought of you as quite the Puritan," said Reinhart.

"I have mellowed to a degree. As one ages he looks more tolerantly, I have found, on the vanity of human wishes. It was quite true that when young I had a blue nose. Now I am willing to admit that many men find it necessary periodically to succumb to base impulses. And sex is a good deal less deleterious, if hygienic procedures are observed, than smoking, drinking, and even overeating."

In his new role Reinhart had not taken any food all day, so if he knew sensitivity now, it was in retrospect.

"Narcotics, though, are something else. I put the Maker in prison." Splendor's eyes were feverish with pride.

"You became a cop?"

"Not at all. I sent the police chief and the mayor

carbon copies of a letter I wrote to the state narcotics
bureau."

"The Honorable Bob J. Gibbon and his brother, Chief
C. Roy," said Reinhart. "Wait a minute! It comes back to
me now. That was the beginning of a series of investigations—dope traffic on the West Side, then all the rest of
it, contractor's kickbacks on public projects, the disappearance of municipal funds, and so on. Bob J. blew his
brains out, and C. Roy vanished. Well, you and I were
involved in the building of a sewer, or nonbuilding, as it
turned out."

"The subject of a letter of mine to the state attorney-
general," said Splendor.

"I certainly thought it was strange that a series of
manholes would not have any pipes under them," Reinhart
said, reminiscently. ". . . What?"

"Anonymous, naturally. I sought no personal ac-
claim."

Even in his new character, Reinhart found himself
nettled by this smugness.

"The whole cleanup resulted from a couple of unsigned
letters?"

Splendor said: "Naming names and specifying details.
The right word in the right ear. You'd be surprised,
Carlo. Democracy works, but the correct techniques are
required. The nay-sayers to the contrary notwithstanding,
precision is always the answer."

Reinhart's eyebrows ascended almost to touch the low
brow of his wig, then fell towards peevishing eyes. It had
lately become commonplace for him to hear of remarkable accomplishments which he must accept on faith.
Streckfuss' thawed monkey, Splendor's puissant muckrak-
ing, neither presented with a shred of proof.

"You don't suppose," said Splendor, "that I would have
got far by inscribing my own name and address?"

True enough. Publicity, supposedly so gross a medium,
was actually a subtle discipline. Reinhart could appreciate
that. And like so many things, it was conditioned by time.
Today Splendor might well be given an audience with the
governor as a "black leader," having outlasted an era in
which he was a nothing nigger with a narcotics record.

"Claude Humbold," said Reinhart, referring to his old
realtor boss who had been the prime mover in the sewer
swindle, "Claude got away scot-free, though, didn't he? I
hear he has the biggest used-car dealership in Southern
California."

"Nothing could have been easier than dealing with Claude," Splendor said. "If you recall, when we were blasting for the long-delayed sewer excavation on my home street, Mohawk, a little too much dynamite was employed and we lost half the block. Well, of course, Claude personally owned these houses and did not do badly in his rents, persons of color not having a great deal of choice in their abodes in those days. It was either the West Side or hit the road." Splendor waved his spiderweb hand. "I'm not sniveling, as you well know. I never laid around with a pint of Thunderbird in a paper bag, collecting my relief payments and sourly spitting into the gutter." He cleared his throat and, writhing up against the white-pipe headrail, reached for a glass upon the bedside table.

"Here," said Reinhart. "Let me."

Splendor waved him off. "You don't know what a satisfaction it is after all these weeks to have the strength again to attend to simple functions." Not only did he grasp the tumbler. He managed to fill it from a pitcher heavy with a good four inches of water, though his strained tan arm looked like a working model of stark radius and ulna.

Reinhart had not come here to dig up old dirt. He was thrilled by Splendor's implication.

He asked: "You feel results after only a couple of days?"

Splendor displayed, as a skeleton might, how man drinks. Reinhart followed the progress of the water down through the hollow between the clavicles. His friend then breathed for a while.

At last Splendor said: "Indubitably. I can almost feel those fresh cells putting the malignant ones to rout. Vitality, Carlo, will always win. We tend to forget that, with our easy emphasis on morbidity, but it is the law of life."

"Easy?"

"Lazy," said Splendor. "Dying is hardly a positive procedure. Contrary to the old myths, death is an absence and not a presence, not a hooded figure hacking you down with a scythe—actually an attractive image: were Death an antagonistic personage, intent on imposing his will, we would have known how to defeat him long since. It is nothing, the void at the end of a long incline of passivity, the goal of a negative momentum, a state unknown to any living thing but man."

Reinhart frowned. His earlier peevishness had not evaporated before it was replenished.

"All things die."

"Only man *knows* he will, in the words of the sage."

"Oh." It was one of those semantic sleights-of-hand. You're not unhappy, you just think you are. He hasn't died but gone on to a better life.

Reinhart forced a grin and said heartily: "It's good news that you feel better."

"You don't believe it," said Splendor, with more amusement than reproach. "You think Professor Streckfuss is either a charlatan or a maniac."

Reinhart was embarrassed. "Hell," he began, "hell," petered out. He started all over. "I never said that. I don't know what to think. But when you get into a corner you will take any exit that is offered. He might turn out to be the greatest genius in the history of medicine."

"He has my vote," Splendor stated decisively.

Reinhart would not be such a swine as to point out that it was technically impossible for new cells to do more than swim around in the tissue for the first few days. Even the antihistamines he had once taken for an allergic reaction to a cough medicine showed no results for forty-eight hours, and they were soluble in water, absorbable by the blood. The goat cells were the material, palpable, concrete stuff of life, flesh indeed, alien—far more alien than a heart transplanted from one human being to another, and most of the cardiac recipients had died.

He wondered whether he should tell Splendor of his decision to be frozen. Decided not to: the poor devil might feel jealous.

"Why," asked Splendor, "do you continue to work with him if you distrust him?"

"I had no choice," Reinhart answered in a change of tense.

Splendor flowed back down into a supine position with a serpentine ease that contrasted with his prior efforts to rise.

Reinhart was now ready to hear more scandal. "You were speaking of Claude Humbold?"

"Yes. The way it worked out was that Claude transferred that West Side property to me."

"That was nice. But if I know Claude, he had some cunning motive. He probably ended up with more money than if he had kept it."

"Let me just say this." Splendor's tongue made a big

boil in his cheek. "His name was never found on any kind of document."

"That figures."

"And neither was yours."

Reinhart studied the meaning in Splendor's lowered eyelids.

Splendor went on: "You were titular president of Cosmopolitan Sewers, the dummy firm hiding Claude and the Gibbon Boys."

"And you were vice-president and chief engineer, as I remember."

"You," said Splendor, "signed the contracts and subcontracts, the invoices and bills and the rest of the blizzard of paper. Before leaving for California, Claude burned all of that."

"That was nice of him. Claude wasn't the worst man in the world." Reinhart had never wondered why he himself was not investigated. At the time of the probe he was operating the television shop and doing so badly as to be totally distracted by his losses. He had not known at the outset, when Claude maneuvered him into being front man, that the sewer project was a swindle. When he caught on, he and Splendor had made a serious effort to build a usable facility, ending with the blast that excavated most of Mohawk Street.

"Wait a minute," Reinhart said now. "We picked up your son at your old house the other day—"

Anticipating him, Splendor said: "I restored the area long since. What do you think of that apartment house?"

"I didn't see it." Sweet's car had come from the other direction. Reinhart had also been so apprehensive about entering a Negro neighborhood in this day and age that he might have overlooked the landing of a flying saucer.

Splendor frowned. "About all that's left in its original form over there is our old plantation. Call me sentimental but whatever the cost in dollars and cents I couldn't raze the old home where I used to listen to *Amos 'n' Andy*."

That had a bitter ring, but when Reinhart stared at him, Splendor was looking into the past. "I refused for years to believe the simulators were Caucasian. And the back yard, site of many a Western gunfight and once, with a cast of at least six or seven children, Custer's Last Stand. I was armed with a cavalry saber made from a length of trellis lath. Many years later I read a debunking, derisive sort of book which stated that Custer did not possess his saber at the Little Big Horn, contrary to the depiction in the famous painting." Splendor said reproachfully: "Why must they destroy all the great old images?"

Reinhart shook his head. In his new way of looking at things he did not want to dwell on this.

"There are even those," said Splendor, "who would have you believe that Julius Caesar, that magnificent tragic figure, was a homosexual."

"Frankly, I don't care one way or the other," Reinhart said bluntly. "I am having myself frozen."

There, it was out, and no doubt sounded so outlandish that Splendor would ignore it.

And he did. He said: "Claude did not obliterate those incriminating materials out of the goodness of his heart. That was part of the deal, along with the deeding to me of the West Side property. We had a little ceremony around my charcoal grill: he burned the documents and I in turn threw in the tape recordings made from the tap on his phone." Splendor chuckled. "My cousin," he said, "was a serviceman with the telephone company."

All at once Reinhart had the conviction that Splendor would recover.

He said: "Your son told me he bought this house for you, but I'll bet you paid cash."

"Raymond will say almost anything. He has discovered the technique of bold assertion, in which the content is almost irrelevant. He is American to the core: to *say* is to *be*. You and I make a distinction between rhetoric and reality. Perhaps we are essentially foreigners, Carlo."

Reinhart said: "Yes, I have had the same thought about my boy."

"I put my trust in land," said Splendor. "As soon as I get back on my feet I am going to begin to acquire this whole neighborhood."

Reinhart asked soberly, but not sadly: "And make it all black?"

"Blue, green, or polka dot," Splendor cried. "I'm going to make it all money." Which had also been Claude Humbold's bedrock democratic principle, and it was actually anything but mean.

Reinhart stood up. "I must be running along, old friend."

"Surely not before you get the grand tour," Splendor said. "I have done some remodeling of your old abode, Carlo. A second bathroom, and the basement is pine-paneled and floored with that impervious synthetic carpeting." He shouted: "Grace!"

For an instant Reinhart believed this cry some kind of religious invocation. But soon the plump nurse appeared from the hallway.

"I indulged myself, Carlo," said Splendor. "I also installed a sauna, but I have not yet been able to use it." He gestured at the nurse. "Did you meet the other day? Or did I forget the amenities in a concern with my then incipient mortality? My wife, Grace—Carlo Reinhart, an old, dear friend. You have heard me speak of him on many occasions."

She had a generous smile. Reinhart was reminded of Splendor's sister, years ago. Why were Negro smiles especially gratifying? Suggested the good things, the forgiving materials: leather, wood, copper; or the luxurious tastes, like chocolate. Or merely relieved you of the dark apprehensions, with a show of white.

While he looked at her teeth, Grace said: "You and Sylvester must have been quite the scamps."

Reinhart shook her soft strong hand, and turned to Splendor.

"Now tell me the truth," Splendor said, beating him out again. "Does Sylvester Gordon Mainwaring sound like me? So I changed it to Splendor Gallant. At least I kept the family name. Raymond has become Captain Storm. We Mainwarings are all self-invented."

"What ever became of your sister Loretta?" asked Reinhart, referring to the most beautiful girl he had ever seen on earth. He had never heard her before.

"Married, with three children, and she is as saucy as ever," said Splendor. "In a few weeks we'll all get together for dinner. I miss real food. The Professor's chemical potions are not exactly tournedos Rossini. Grace, I think Carlo would like a look-around."

Reinhart was suddenly desperate. "No, I really don't have time today. Another time. We'll have a good time." He was stuck on the word. Hastily he shook hands with Splendor and then again with Grace, and fled to the door.

"Don't stay away twenty years again," Splendor said.

"I won't," Reinhart lied, and went out.

The Black Assassins' car was parked next to his outside, and Captain Storm was just getting out. Night had now settled in, and Reinhart could not be sure of Storm's expression, with the young man's back to the street lamp.

"Hi," Reinhart said.

"Do I know you?"

Reinhart had forgotten his wig and new shape. He identified himself.

Storm said: "That is hardly thrilling information."

"Look here," said Reinhart. "You got no quarrel with me. I am merely being civil. Why don't you come off this shit?"

"Of course you are. Civility is white, and so are you. But I am black, as you can see, or perhaps you cannot: it is after dark. I happen to believe that it is degrading and evil to pretend to be what you are not."

"Then how do *you* greet one another?"

"It's no concern of yours, whatever," Storm said. "Am I in violation of some city ordinance? Is there a law requiring all citizens to say 'Hi' on passing in the night?"

Reinhart stood quietly.

"Is it illegal to walk around with a black face after the darkness has fallen?" Storm went on.

"Aren't you being childish?"

"I am obsessed by legality," said Storm. "I never break the law. I won't even step off the curb, downtown, until the green 'Walk' sign is fully lighted. And when I buy a pillow I wouldn't think of ripping off that cloth tag that says it is against the law to remove it. I never put turpentine in an old whiskey bottle because, as is embossed on the base, it must not be reused on pain of violating the law."

Reinhart said: "Oh, those things don't apply—"

"You're never going to get me on anything," said Storm. "I am a conformist. I *comply,* man! I pay cash for everything, and the draft board has the cardiogram, made by a member of the AMA in good standing, on which my heart murmur is registered. I am a lecturer in black studies at the municipal university, and deductions from my salary are duly made according to income-tax and social-security regulations, health plan, insurance, and all of it."

"OK," said Reinhart.

"You will look all your life to find a better citizen than I," said Storm. "And now, unless you can cite authority for obstructing the public sidewalk, I will pass across it and go into a private house on a personal mission."

"Vaya con Dios," Reinhart said and stepped aside. He had at last got a clue to Captain Storm, née Raymond

Mainwaring. And if he still found it difficult to like him, he saw no reason why he should. He did not dislike him and he did not fear him and he did not pity him. Which should be enough for anybody, especially nowadays.

In those movies about doomed men there is never enough time. Yet by late afternoon of the first day Reinhart had satisfied all his true appetites by encapsulating them in the E-Type Jag, taking them down the highway at a hundred and forty mph, and abandoning the wreck. And by mid-evening had disposed of such obligations as could be said to apply to a man whom nobody wanted, by visiting Splendor and finding him prosperous and, probably, in the process of recovery. If a Negro could, while pretending to be shiftless and perhaps even mentally defective, outwit Claude Humbold and amass a tidy fortune in real estate, he could no doubt whip cancer. With the help of an unlikely Swiss-German-Jew who chopped up goats and froze monkeys, financed by a man whose money was tied up in cocoa beans which were actually gravel.

Reinhart found himself nostalgic for routine realism, a rarity perhaps no longer available anywhere. Nowadays Midwestern Protestants orbited the moon. Negro militants in foreign uniforms lectured at universities. Girls who smoked marijuana and fucked at the drop of a hat were frightened by fast driving. A cautious old man lent his car to a total stranger upon receiving evidence of the latter's recklessness.

Women were the traditional repository of good sense, representatives of the mundane commonplace: you had to be to carry and deliver new life, and in between bleed every month for years. Thus their universal complaint was constipation, and they were natural masochists. So went the theory. It had to be twisted out of recognition to fit Maw and Gen, neither of whom he intended to check with before entering the freezer.

He could of course go to a bar, take a stool, and leer around at the unattached females, who, if they had not changed since he had given up that practice decades ago, were either professionals or those dreary amateur specimens who drank too much, threw up in the car, and passed out when you got to your destination. They also invariably smelled sweaty. Pros were preferable, drinking unspiked Seven-Up and being obsessive about cleanliness. But Reinhart did not want a piece: he now knew none of the anxiety to dissipate which had been his sole need for seeking sex in recent years. If your pencil will soon be frozen there is little reason to worry about its supply of lead.

He wanted to talk to some stark realist, the implications of whose statements did not apply to him in a personal way. Gloria came to mind. If for twenty-five dollars Gloria would hire out one or a series of her apertures for as long as it took a client to empty himself, surely for a hundred she would converse for an hour.

Reinhart found an outdoor telephone and called her.

Gloria gave her languorous hello.

"Biggie here," said Reinhart.

"Oh, hi, Big. Did you get over your summer cold?" The little personal detail as usual was wrong.

"Actually, my name is Carlo Reinhart."

"I don't want to know it!" Gloria howled and hung up.

Reinhart spent another dime.

"Sorry about that," he said when she came back on. "It's just that I'm on a fearless-truth kick. I forgot it would work both ways. Look, Gloria, I want to come over, and, this will blow your mind—"

"Well, that's a new one," she said. "I thought I knew them all."

"What I want to do is just talk a while. Now don't hang up! You can name your price."

"I don't know, Big. I've never been much for the freaky stuff. I got another client who might come over in a little while and if he don't I promised my sister I would baby sit for her so she and her old man can see *Planet of the Apes.*"

"How's a hundred sound, Gloria? For whatever conversation we can get in between the customers who make you work hard for twenty-five bucks a throw?"

"I don't stand for dirty talk. You know that, Biggie."

"I promise to honor all your scruples and niceties."

"You got to leave when he buzzes."

"Agreed."

Reaching Gloria's house, he parked Harper's car before a fireplug and went upstairs.

Gloria generally walked around in a pink peignoir over black lace underwear, but tonight she wore a linen suit rather like Gen's at the lunch, though Gloria's was oyster white and sported two brooches, one a frog, with protuberant eyes of garnet, the other a cluster of golden grapes.

"C'mon," she said as soon as Reinhart had stepped in from the hall, and led him into the bedroom.

Gloria turned her lacquered bouffant. She also wore earrings, which he noticed now as she pulled them off. She put her practiced hands at the top of his zipper.

"A quick Frenchy. OK?" she asked, running the tab down the track-teeth. "Damn if I want to get dressed again."

Reinhart pushed away and closed himself. "I wasn't kidding about wanting to talk."

She narrowed her burnt-hole eyes. "Biggie, don't think you can shake me down. I pay plenty for protection. You just get in touch with a certain captain at Ninth Precinct. The last one who tried that was a crooked lawyer, and he never got the sweat off my ass."

"Blaine Raven, right?" He saw he had hit the mark. Gloria glared fiercely for a moment, and then twin channels of water coursed over her pancake makeup. She fell onto the bed and wept.

"Come on," he said in rough tenderness.

She wailed: "How much more do they want? My rent is past due, and I got dentist bills in the thousands. My kid is in Girl Scout camp, and that costs money, but I can't let her go to public swimming pools full of child-molesters, can I?"

"I'm not a detective," said Reinhart.

"Your teeth go bad in the life," Gloria said, weeping. "It dissolves the enamel. I had to have them all capped, and that cost three thousand dollars."

"If your daughter is a Scout," Reinhart said, "I wouldn't let her go on their trips to the Bloor Tower."

She patted her eyes with a Kleenex from the handy bedside box, next to which lay a neat rubber circlet of condom. She blew her nose. "You're telling the truth?"

"I'm no cop, for Christ sake."

"Why are you wearing a disguise, Biggie?"

"I decided to get with it, wear mod clothes and have fashionable hair. We only live once, you know."

"You look a little old-fashioned. You know what I go for? Sharkskin suits, Italian cut. Now you've got something."

"Those went out some years ago, I believe," said Reinhart. "This gear is part of the revolution that has taken place in style, in living. We are no longer chained to the shibboleths of the past, worshipping false idols, tolerating the money-changers in the temple—" He was now doing what he had come for, to talk more or less irresponsibly to someone to whom it would not matter.

"And the sex revolution," he went on. "We are emerging from the Dark Ages of hypocritical hangups and cynicism. Sex-repression is another of the techniques by which we have maintained the subservience of women, the kids, and the blacks. Now the orgasm is available to everybody, and we are telling it like it is."

Gloria dabbed her cheeks with the Kleenex, being very careful, but still defacing the outmoded makeup. She was as out of it as, at the other end of the spectrum, Winona. Gloria still wore smeary lipstick and had to blot it off before she went to work, and kept handy a supply of Trojans. Eunice would not have known what a rubber was.

She said: "Yeah, I don't know what the world is coming to. The filthy paperbacks they sell in drugstores now. The other day I bought me a love story to read and when I brought it home it turned out to be about a young widow who was getting it from a big stud nigger, a dykey practical nurse, and even her pet Dalmatian. I tell you it was the most disgusting thing I ever looked at, Big. I tore it into little pieces and flushed it down the john. The Commies are spreading that stuff over the country to break down our spirit."

Reinhart remembered from bits and pieces of Gloria's past statements that she was to the right of the late William Howard Taft.

"And the jigs," she said. "The more they get, the more they want. You know I won't open the door for anybody but a regular client. You can't always tell by the voice. Somebody'll call on the phone and say, Gloria, I'm so-and-so's friend who gave me your number. Well, I look through the peephole in the door when they knock. And more than once I have seen a great big coon face black as the ace of spades." She grimaced. "I'm clean, Biggie. I have a thing about dirt and germs, you know? And then if you read the Bible you will find God never intended the races to mix. That would end up with everybody being muddy-looking. Democracy is all well and good in moderation, but some religion never hurt anybody."

She rose and crouched to look in the triptych mirror of her pink-skirted vanity table.

"Oh, damn!" she said. "My face has to be done all over." She sat down on the matching stool, the legs of which were also concealed with baby-pink pleats.

Reinhart took a seat on the bed. "How do you feel about legalizing prostitution, Gloria? Isn't it a rotten thing that a girl can be harassed for practicing an age-old trade for which there is always a need?"

"I'm against it," said she, scrubbing orange-colored muck into her streaked cheeks. "It represents a breakdown in morality, Big, as I see it. And it's hard enough to come out even nowadays, what with all the freebies on the streets. Of course that's what the Commies want. No, Biggie, the old world has turned a long time and while it isn't perfect by a long shot, you can't give it back to the animals."

"You are pretty well satisfied with the status quo, then?"

"I could use a few more hundred-dollar tricks," she said. "You know, I'm in the life only till my little girl gets through college. Then I'm going to get married and settle down in the country someplace."

"How old is she now?"

"Eleven. Here." Gloria took a snapshot from a series stuck into the mirror frame, and handed it back over her shoulder.

Reinhart saw the image of a little blurry-faced girl in a white frock.

"She was seven there. That's my favorite. She's a dead ringer for me at that age."

Reinhart made a favorable response and returned the photo. He took Gloria for about thirty-five. She might very well realize her plan, which seemed a strange one in view of the fact that she would marry only after her daughter grew up. However, that was one way to avoid the mess of family. Maybe whores did have wisdom in certain matters.

"I have heard that a prostitute gets many proposals of marriage," Reinhart said.

"Biggie, you wouldn't believe it. Hardly a week goes by." Though her original layer of lipstick had not been affected by the tears, she was at work with the little gold tube, kissing at her reflection. "I could have my pick, lawyers, well-to-do businessmen, and doctors with every specialty under the sun. That's who you will have to leave for, any minute: a psychiatrist. You might just pay up so there won't be any delay."

But the old guilt that used to make him hasty with his wallet no longer was efficacious. On former visits he put the folded bills into Gloria's hand before loosening his belt buckle. Often this transfer would have been enough for him, and the subsequent ejaculation was anticlimactic.

"A psychiatrist. Is that right?"

Gloria stood up, modestly tugging at her girdle through the skirt.

"An analyst," said she. "Mine, to be exact."

It figured now that, as Eunice had said, Freud was out, Gloria would be in psychoanalysis. Twenty years earlier she would have been a Catholic.

"I always thought of you as the soul of normality," said Reinhart, "as those things go. You must not have much trouble with sex repression."

"Nothing to do with sex," said Gloria with a certain defiance. "It's money. I got a funny attitude towards money. I lose it. I don't even spend it. I drop it everyplace. I get up in my sleep and burn ten-dollar bills without waking up. I shred money in the Dispose-All. I send clothes to the cleaner's full of money, and tuck it into the coffee grounds and eggshells in the garbage and put it in the incinerator. Which reminds me, I think you said a hundred just for talking, isn't that right, Biggie? That's what made me suspicious, because time and again in the past you tried to jew me down from twenty-five for turning a trick. You got it, haven't you, baby?"

She sat down heavily next to him and again groped at his fly. "Lay back, sweetie, and Gloria will make you happy. We got time. You are always quick."

Reinhart stood up. "I don't expect you to understand, but I reached a turning point recently—"

"Hell," she said. "It happens to the best of them, Big. That's what friends are for. Trust little Gloria. I'll get you up."

"No," Reinhart said. "That all seems superficial now. I had a girl of twenty-two who would give me all I wanted. But man does not live by pussy alone, with all respect to your career. I'm making a big change, Gloria, preparing myself for a long journey."

"Don't do it, Big. Don't turn fag. Take my word for it, it's only worse trouble." Gloria shook her lacquered head. "They're always fighting like cats, scratching and clawing, and bitchier than any woman, and when they get old they commit suicide."

A raucous buzzer sounded.

"Oh Jesus, there he is," she said in consternation. She ran out through the living room to the entryway intercom.

She was answered by an electronic splutter, and pressed the button.

Infected by her nervousness, Reinhart had come along behind. "I'm gone," he said, pressing a sheaf of one hundred dollars into her hand of many rings.

Its delivery put her in a new mood. "You're all right, Biggie, I had you all wrong. Listen, sometimes peeping will help your problem, watching somebody else's troubles. Because they all have them, everybody who comes here." She grinned in a mixture of generosity and pride he had never seen her show before.

"Biggie, if you want to watch, go over behind that Chinese screen in the corner and slide the picture aside and you'll be looking through the back of a two-way mirror into the bedroom. I'll take him right in. When you have seen enough, tiptoe and let yourself out quietlike." She lightly squeezed his testicles. "For free, on the house, and don't say Gloria never gave you nothing."

Why not? He repaired behind the tripartite barrier, which he had noticed the first time he had ever visited Gloria, then fearing it contained her partner in the old badger game, who when he was stripped and defenseless would burst into the bedroom and, claiming to be her husband, demand a payoff.

He now wondered whether on some or all of his engagements it had instead concealed a voyeur, and if so, whether the man had been amused by a performance he had himself invariably found depressing.

With such speculations and sitting on a worn red hassock segmented with white piping, he listened patiently to the routine sounds of arrival, which did not include speech, and when the soft flat footfalls, making a sort of Morse with the sharp reports of Gloria's high-fashion heels of a decade past, reached the bedroom, he stood up and quietly lifted from its hook the Kodachrome enlargement of Old Faithful in hourly eruption: a bit gross but perhaps inspiriting to the impotent peeper for whom this nook was styled.

If one had expected a neatly crafted spyhole, with mitered moldings, he would have been dejected at the sordid reality: the opening seemed to have been rammed through with the end of a baseball bat, jagged plaster margins and broken lath within. And the glass on the other side was a bit filmy, far from the crystal-clear scene available to FBI agents in movie and TV stakeouts.

Still, it sufficed. The client was a tall, comely man,

haired in much the fashion of Reinhart's wig, bronze-
tanned, with robust shoulders, yet narrow hips and sleek
behind. The fitted shirt swooped into his waistband without a ripple in the telltale region. He balanced on one
foot while taking the cordovan loafer off the other, and
did not visibly trim to meet the subtle challenges of
shifting gravity-centers. Reinhart could never do this even
as a slip of a boy.

When the guy was down to his shorts Reinhart had had
quite enough. He had no motive in the world for
watching a sexual junction, which, it struck him suddenly,
was the most banal of human exchanges, confined as it
was necessarily to one ending, no matter what the elaboration in getting there: the meat-and-potatoes truth which
had kept him from ever being a pervert.

He lifted Old Faithful. He had never been to any of
Our National Parks. Perhaps a trip to Yellowstone might
not be the worst way to fill his remaining time among the
quick and warm. Geysers and bears: they had been there
before man arrived to lose children and discard paper
plates. For every prospect pleases, and only man is vile,
and the Bloor Tower guard went on to exemplify the
verse.

The only trouble was that, for good or ill, people were
all that interested Reinhart. Vile they might well be, but it
happens that vileness is fascinating—to a degree, of
course. For example, he said to himself now, you will
never find a transvestite bear.

Gloria's client was in the process of putting on her
brassiere: slack cups but straining backband. Her girdle
was a better fit, and when he had got into her linen suit his
height modernized, minimized, the skirt a good five inches. The little frog's garnet eyes winked redly on the
jacket.

Reinhart dropped Old Faithful, but it neither broke nor
made much noise on the wall-to-wall. Gloria was in the
client's shirt. Owing to the breadth of his chest her own
depth could cope. She did a bad job on the knot of the
foulard tie. The olive-green jacket was too long in the
sleeves, and of course the trouser cuffs gave her funny big
paddlefeet. All in all, he did better by her clothes than she
with his. He was a tall, svelte lady of the type who often
occupy executive positions in the communications media,
while she resembled a stocky United Parcels driver
dressed for Parents Night at the public school.

Never too fine, Gloria's features were coarsened in the

context of this garb, her head a sort of blunt instrument. His lineaments were already softened in contour, and when, with a graceful ballet turn he had gained the vanity table, sunk upon the stool, and applied, with swan-hand, the false eyelashes, Reinhart stared, through the back of the mirror, at the face of Eunice Munsing.

For a moment Reinhart believed it was indeed she, at some extremity of imposture, a double transsex hoax. But, having been made privy to her body on two occasions—though, true enough, once in the dark and once while Alvis, overhead, was wreaking wholesale mayhem: a cunning arrangement of foam rubber was not out of the question, then or now—his entertainment of the outlandish supposition was short-lived. He was quite a literal fellow, even in a life contemporaneous with which other people had invented the atomic bomb and might even abolish death.

Gloria shuffled over and embraced her client from behind, her ardent hands on his imaginary breasts. He threw back his head to take her male mouthings, his dangle earrings two little plumb bobs maintaining true perpendicular. He had a mild case of five-o'clock shadow.

Reinhart quietly replaced Old Faithful, heel-and-toed silently across the living room, and let himself out. Then turned, banged on the door, shouted, "Police!" and projected himself within.

In the bedroom Gloria had a briar pipe halfway to her lips from the jacket pocket where she had found it.

She said, with no astonishment: "I finally get a big spender, and he turns out to be a cop. That's the story of my life. Gloria the born loser."

"Gloria," said Reinhart, "you will oblige me by canning the self-pity. I'm not after you. Sit down and have a quiet pipeful." He turned to the client, who sat looking bitchy, hand on hip. "Are you Dr. Barker Munsing, with offices in the Bloor Building, and father of a young woman named Eunice?"

"Officer," replied the man, incongruously not in falsetto but in a virile baritone, "I could have your badge for this intrusion on a private session of therapy. You must know that patient-doctor relations are sacrosanct, unless the police state has at last come to be instituted." He crossed his legs, matted hair under the nylon. "But for my part I am aware of the pressures you must be under these days, yourselves as a class upwardly mobile, threatened by the ferment in the inner cities, in the colleges. You find yourself reviled for doing your duty. You're Irish, are you not? Once yourself a member of a despised minority, you—"

"Knock off the crap, you weirdo," Reinhart cried. "Are you or are you not Eunice's father?"

"She is a free personality," Dr. Munsing smugly replied, toying with an earring. "She is the biological issue of her mother and me, but if you seek to establish some oppressive relationship thereby, some owner-chattel implication, an image of me in spurred boots as a totalitarian colossus astride—"

"That's all I wanted to know," said Reinhart. "I'm making an arrest."

– 18 –

Gloria began to cry. Munsing shook his head, the earrings swinging. "It is I," he said, "who could have you jailed. But I am a healer, not an enforcer. You are sick. For God's sake, man, accept that, admit it, and you will have taken the first giant step."

Reinhart grimaced. "Look who's wearing the woman's clothes."

"Have you seen yourself?" Munsing rose from the stool and gestured at the mirror. "Sit down here, take a good look, and then ask yourself if your costume is appropriate to a man of your age. Is it not rather a disguise, a mask behind which to conceal yourself from a world you find increasingly hostile, increasingly remote, one you never made but which resulted from your failures to eliminate war, poverty, and hatred? You feel guilt, you fear the revenge of the youth who have shaken off the bonds in which you confined them." Munsing gave him a keen stare of professional sympathy. "But you have no place to hide."

"That's what you think," said Reinhart. "But we're not going to talk about me. People have been doing that all my life, and seldom helpfully. . . . Here you are, dressed like a girl. And Eunice is wandering around someplace, taking drugs and practicing nymphomania."

Munsing said sharply, to Gloria: "In the lower left pocket of my jacket you will find a vial of tablets. Give it to me, and fetch a glass of water." To Reinhart, while she was groping: "A mild sedative." Back to Gloria: "And if you have an empty paper bag in the kitchen." Again to Reinhart, Munsing's head moving as if it were seated at net-end at a tennis match: "You must breathe into it. You are in danger of hyperventilating."

When she brought the bag Reinhart blew it up and popped it with his palm. Munsing narrowed his eyes, still in the false lashes, and swallowed two tablets himself. He

closed his eyes while he gulped water. Then he shook
himself and resumed energetically.

"God knows what you might do in your present condition. Violence is never the answer."

"On the contrary," said Reinhart. "I can't think of an
instance in recorded history when it hasn't worked. But I
don't intend to employ it now, if that's your worry, and I
don't know why it should be anyway, when you are as big
as I and in a lot better shape."

Munsing took this as flattery. His muscular trunk
strained within Gloria's jacket as he rather sneeringly said:
"Thank you. But the paranoid fear of being assaulted in
the streets has been inseminated into a naïve populace by
those at the top of the power structure, for obvious
reasons. People naturally love one another unless their
minds are poisoned. The true purpose of the space program is to abolish the orgasm, to cow the individual into
impotence. How can he match the great, roaring, flaming
ejaculation of the Saturn rocket?"

"Which comes out of the wrong end," said Reinhart.

"Going to the moon is a classic homosexual fantasy,"
Munsing said. "Men without women, in a barren landscape, an anti-paradise where nothing flowers."

Going on the errand for water had soothed Gloria.
Briar in the corner of her mouth, she said: "Hey, Doc,
whaduhyuh think of me inna spacesuit?"

Munsing poured out at least a half dozen tablets and
handed them to her, along with what was left of the
water. "Take these at once."

"What I don't understand," Reinhart confessed, "is what
you two were going to do when rudely interrupted. When
you got down to the nitty-gritty, what then? Or did you
bring along those artificial organs Eunice told me about? I
read once that that's what Jean Harlow's husband had, a
rubber dildo, but it didn't work and she went out and
picked up truckdrivers in all-night cafés to fill her void.
Women are receptacles. Nature decided that, and not the
military-industrial complex."

Munsing peered at him. "Truckdrivers. . . . Interesting
how that example springs to your mind: brawny, coarse,
sweating manipulators of mighty engines. As this taste
grows it becomes more sophisticated, until finally the
astronaut is your love object, clean, hairless, aseptic, he
does not drive but is driven through the heavens, leaving
women behind at a speed of twenty-five thousand miles
per hour, the invert's dream of glory."

Gloria said woozily: "I feel funny." Her enervate lips let the pipe bounce on the chenille bedspread.

Reinhart sat down alongside her. He said to Munsing: "I'm going to wait until you have run out of bullshit, and then I'm going to propose a deal."

Munsing's tan face blanched, as if exuding a white powder. He seized the water glass from Gloria's failing hand and swallowed several more pills.

He sank onto the vanity stool and said, with no confidence: "Blackmail, is it? I have nothing to hide."

Gloria keeled over backwards.

Reinhart said: "You seem to have done a pretty good job with your dong."

Munsing made a desperate try: "Do you have the authority to question my therapeutic techniques? Prostitution is a serious symptom."

"I thought it was a thing-in-itself."

Munsing groaned in cavernous melancholy. "You are wrong if you think Eunice was ever neglected. No doors were ever closed to her, including those of our bedroom and toilet. She was often present when my wife and I had relations, and never put a question that was not answered or demonstrated. That sex should be discreet and that privacy is a good are fascist lies inculcated in children by generations of fools and/or scoundrels." He brightened suddenly. "In fact she used to climb in with us. I suppose that shocks you. The capacity to be shocked is a symptom—"

"Do you know something, Munsing?" Reinhart asked. "If you took wing and flew out the window I wouldn't bat an eye. I walked right past that sniper on the Bloor Tower and said 'Hi' to him, then went downstairs and screwed a girl." Reinhart never spoke a lady's name in low places.

"Lloyd Alvis was a patient of mine," Munsing said proudly. "In the municipal clinic. You know, we are often criticized for our fees, but it is not generally known how much time we donate to public facilities. He is a disturbed personality. I wrote a paper on him, in fact. I like to think it was instrumental in bringing about the self-regulation of the horror-comic industry."

Reinhart considered the implications. "So when you took away his comic books he got himself a gun."

"You oversimplify," Munsing said. "Always the tendency of the layman. It is healthier to possess a real gun of one's own than to relate to violence passively, symbolically, in fantasy. Alvis has made astonishing progress. When he first came to me, he interpreted my welcoming hand-shake as an aggressive gesture, fell to all fours, and whined like an obsequious dog. On top of the Bloor Building he at least coped, if in a minimal way."

Munsing had regained his rhythm now. He was a quick-change artist in more ways than one. "Gloria," he continued, "is on an identity-quest. At puberty she was faced with this overwhelming question: 'My body tells me I am a woman, but my self cannot accept that. What am I *really?*' Reality-doubts are rife at adolescence, and then a curious experience she had at age thirteen rein-forced the confusion. She was molested by a *younger* boy, much smaller than she, a lad of ten. Of course this may have been a fantasy. The important thing is that she *believes* it. It seems they were coasting down a hill on a red wagon and ran into a tree. Pretending to be checking on whether she had been hurt, he pulled her panties down and said: 'Gee, you're hurt bad. Your peepee has been knocked off and you are bleeding!' It was of course her first menses, for which her mother, an ignorant woman, a maniacal puritan in fact, had not prepared her."

Reinhart glanced sideways at Gloria. She was out cold. He leaned over and loosened the knot of her tie, opened the top button of Munsing's shirt.

Munsing said: "Memories of wagons often appear in childhood reminiscences. It is significant that they are always colored red."

"Just as in real life," said Reinhart.

"I thought as much," Munsing said sagely. "Yes, I thought I recognized you as the red-wagon type. Give my receptionist a call in the morning. We'll fit you in some-how." He poured out some more tablets. "These will get you through the night. Try to remember your dreams. Keep a notepad at bedside and jot them down as soon as you wake up in the morning."

"I haven't had more than a half dozen bad dreams in forty-four years. The rest have all been simple wish-fulfillment: laying a movie star, inheriting a million dol-lars, or outgunning the Ringo Kid."

"You repress the horrors, then," said Munsing, in eager arrogance. "We'll bring them back in no time." He was thrusting the tablets at Reinhart.

"No thanks," Reinhart said. "If I got away once, I don't need a replay. I am not here to discuss my uncon-scious, such as it is. When I was young I toyed with the

idea of going into psychiatry because it seemed to be a
guaranteed way of getting one-up on other human beings
without running the danger of being proved wrong. You
can't ever prove anything one way or the other in your
racket. For all I know you're right about Alvis—"

"Certainly I am," Munsing said. "Had he not directed
his aggression outward he might have committed some
self-damage, and his victims, one must not forget, were
employees of the Consolidated Electrical Company, a
so-called public utility which is in reality a monopolistic
tentacle of the Establishment octopus. Alvis may have
been misguided in his choice of means, overromantic, im-
pulsive, a bit of a grandstander, but in his own way he is
a revolutionary. It all begins in the hearts of individual
men, you know, with the question: 'Do I really want to
be no more than a tiny transistor in one big IBM machine?' "

"I was crapping you before," said Reinhart, "with the
stuff about Eunice. I couldn't care less what she is or what
your responsibility, because if I did, I would have to
question my own association with her. Whatever, I suspect she will live out her life without any major disasters.
Most people do, even nowadays with the hydrogen bomb,
snipers, assassins, mobs, crime in the streets, the everlasting war, etc., because on the other hand the bubonic
plague is a distant memory as well as most of the other
diseases which used to keep the death rate up. In fact, as
you know, the life-expectancy rate is at an all-time high,
and the long-range problem is overpopulation. Ecolog-
ically—the word is, I think—there aren't enough wars
and lethal maladies. People in the depressed areas of the
world keep on fucking madly without contraception and,
understandably, do not realize their obligation to compensate by holding their quaint old annual famines. Now
there is even a scheme afoot to freeze a corpse at the
moment of clinical death and preserve it for eventual
reviving."

"Bob Sweet's Cryon Foundation, you mean?"

Reinhart had forgotten that Eunice worked for the
firm.

"Bob is a former patient of mine," Munsing went on.
"You should have seen him when I first got hold of him.
He was totally impotent for one. He was just like Jean
Harlow's husband."

Reinhart was of course interested to hear this, but he

was also indignant. "I understood that you were not supposed to talk about your patients."

Munsing lifted an arm in Gloria's linen suit. "Another of the misconceptions regarding psychiatry. What would I otherwise have to talk about over cocktails and din-din? My work is my life. Does not a lawyer, a salesman, a plumber discuss the events of his day? I play golf with a priest and we deride our respective patients and confessees for eighteen holes. You'd go crazy if you didn't, in our game. It isn't easy to listen to that garbage day after day. Patients are the dregs of humanity. If I had my way, I'd treat them with a machine gun."

Munsing gulped more of the pills that had laid Gloria low but seemed to have no effect on him.

Reinhart said: "About this deal: I work for Cryon, and we are ready to perform a major experiment. Are you an M.D.?"

"That's a laugh," Munsing said, crossing his legs again and swinging a high-heeled shoe. He had small feet for his height and Gloria conveniently had large ones. "I am barely able to peel the protective paper off a Band-Aid. I could not tell one end of a stethoscope from the other, let alone perform an abortion. But let me put you onto the man Eunice uses, Charlie Wilhelm. He's in the book: Northdale, I think."

"Could you sign a death certificate?"

"Frankly, I don't know," said Munsing. "I burnt my AMA card at that last convention. Symbolically, that is: what I actually touched a match to was a Charge-a-Plate for Eisenstein's department store. It was celluloid and stunk. But it got me on TV, if you remember."

"You don't mean, after I've gone through all this, that you're useless to me?" Reinhart asked in disgust.

"I put you onto Wilhelm," said Munsing self-righteously. "If you are a cop you can go and bust him. I can also put the finger on Chuck Makelovenotwar." Pronounced as a last name, it sounded rather Hawaiian. "You can call off your toilet stakeouts. He's a patient of mine, a professional football player. You've seen his beefy face on television, endorsing a shave cream. Actually his obsessive-compulsive urge to scribble on the walls above urinals is not homosexually motivated. He hates fags, as it happens. Writes that invitation and if it is accepted, by the subsequent entry of a penciled phone number, he calls the subject, sets up a date, and beats the daylights out of him. He claims to have so persuaded a number of inverts to go straight. No, Chuck's problem is that he wants to compete with me, thinks of himself as a therapist. That is a symptom of—"

"If I were a policeman, I would have arrested myself long ago," said Reinhart. "Wilhelm, you say, in Northdale?"

"Say I referred you." Munsing began to hum a tune.

"OK, I'm splitting," said Reinhart. "Proceed with your treatment."

"Gloria has made real progress. She now has been brought up to an acceptance of herself as a human being, if of the wrong sex. She will cross over by degrees, little details but each of massive importance: the exchange of her necktie for a string of pearls, say. That alone might take a month."

"Then I don't have time."

"You'd be surprised that such simple truths as you and I would never question are precisely what the sick reject."

In the doorway Reinhart paused to ask: "Such as?"

"Being," said Munsing. "Existence." In a strong baritone he began to voice the lyrics of the song he had been humming: "Baby, won't you light my fire? . . ."

Reinhart had been serious enough when telling Munsing that he was not concerned about Eunice's upbringing or the lack thereof. Look at what he himself had made of Blaine. Having sentenced himself to death—which was the only practical interpretation of what he had done— rising above life, he was gradually jettisoning the ballast of moral judgment. He had been burdened with it, made lead-footed, hunchbacked, his life long.

It would have been typical of his former self to brood on Munsing's daughter, symbol of a social malaise, symptom of the *maladie du temps,* etc., and forget about his own very real, very fat girl named Winona. Eunice after all survived efficiently as long as she kept out of fast cars. She was liberated from what Reinhart believed must be the fundamental fear of women: rape.

Winona was embarrassed by movie love-scenes. Only last year she had reported to Reinhart that a pack of "mad dogs" had chased her from the back yard. He looked out and saw a gang of mongrels howling after a bitch in heat. She might have believed that mammals renewed their race by the wafting of pollen, did he not know that one of those Mr. Penis-Mrs. Vagina courses in sex instruction were incorporated into the high-school curriculum.

Though he had long since cashed in the war bonds he had bought on the Army payroll plan, Reinhart had hung onto his service life insurance. When he got married in 1946 he replaced Maw with Gen as beneficiary.

As an employee of Switched-On Boutiques, Inc., Gen had a full insurance package, and Blaine was heir to its benefits. "If anything happens to me," she had told Reinhart, "he will take care of you." Followed by her malignant snort and: "In a pig's ass."

The point was that Blaine was taken care of, and it would be ludicrous to leave anything to Maw, with her bundle. To approach the situation negatively, this left Winona.

Winona. What would become of her? The trouble with Winona was that she was pitiful. Unfortunately, Winona was a bore. Alas, being tormented by Blaine had been interesting. Even a Jew would sooner pick up *Mein Kampf* than the memoirs of Cal Coolidge, a good man. As a child Winona would smile when playfellows took her toys away. Her plight was serious. To make Winona the beneficiary of his GI insurance would be easy enough. To arrange the payoff required only a licensed physician to certify that the pulse reading of the insured was nil. Ergo, Winona received ten thousand dollars, the widowed Gen could marry immediately, and if Blaine ran afoul of the law he had so far evaded, the judge would take into account the suicide of his father that sent him off the rails.

Nor would it scotch the plans of Sweet & Streckfuss, that firm of organic stockbrokers. If he were willing to call it death, Bob and Hans would be under no pressure to bring him back according to an arbitrary schedule. Could take their time, Bob drumming up new corpses. "Look, he tried it. Why not you? You are dying anyway." Nobody wanted to be first, strangely enough. The national audience had soon forgotten Sweet's appearance on the *Alp Show*. No more requests for information were coming in. Not even eternal life stuck long on the magic slate of the popular mind.

Winona with ten thousand dollars. A heartwarming thought, unless one went into the details of how she might spend it: a stack of pizzas high as the Bloor Building, spaghetti Westerns every night. Why didn't they make more films like *Born Free?* Winona had seen that five times. She should buy some pet too husky to kill with love. Funny about Winona, she even liked serpents. Had once mothered a garter snake she found in the yard. The constricting snakes made good house pets, he had read, were notoriously placid and sometimes even dimly affectionate. He might do worse than suggest Winona's acquisition of a python. Worn around her neck, it would protect her from the slithering, poison-fanged people who prowled the world.

He was seated at a rosewood writing desk in his suite at the Shade-Milton Hotel. The sheet of stationery that lay before him was covered for its top third with a letterhead extolling the merits of the hotel chain. You would not choose such foolscap for your farewell note.

Reinhart picked up the phone, an instrument of ruthlessly modern design he had seen in one or two movies. It resembled an erected penis.

"Look," he said, "at a hundred twenty-five a day I should get a piece of clean writing paper without your ad-crap at the top."

The answer was obsequious, and soon a flunky-buzz was heard at the door, which Reinhart was enjoying the luxury of keeping unlocked, his lifelong fear of burglary now well out of mind.

A bellboy entered, carrying a ream of high-rag bond: so said the box. Reinhart tendered him a piece of currency without looking at the denomination. The lackey's face told him it was exorbitant.

"I suppose you're too young to have heard of 'Calling Philip Morris,' " Reinhart said. "They used to hire midgets for your job and make them wear pillbox caps. I wonder what became of all the midgets?"

"Yeah," said the young man, with an insinuating smile. "You wouldn't be lonely, would you?"

"No," said Reinhart. "I don't want to bugger you or have you get me a call girl, whichever you are offering."

The bellboy was not offended, as Reinhart knew he would not indeed be. You could figure people pretty well when you stopped competing with them.

Reinhart began to write with his ballpoint pen. "Dear Winona . . ." He had not written anything in ages, his Army pals having fallen out of communication long ago. Last year Jimmy Marsala's widow had sent him a Merry Xmas card, telling of Jimmy's death at the end of a long illness ten months before. Wild old, good old Jim: you guinea bastard, why didn't you tell me you were sick? I'll look you up in hell and kick your ass. Jimmy had gone from the service into the Mafia. Reinhart kept watching for him to turn up before the Government hearings, but he was probably not that big. "Our eldest daughter Teresa is now a sister," his wife had scribbled. Only gangsters still had normal families.

Dead Jimmy. There had been a great life in him, and three ineluctable principles: A friend could do no wrong. Anybody not a friend was an enemy. An enemy was to be destroyed.

"Dear Winona ..." Reinhart used to be a great letter-writer, especially to girls. Kid them along, that's what they liked, and then swoop in for the kill: "But seriously, sometimes I think I'll die of longing for you."

An officer in his outfit who censored mail had told him one of his letters, to a girl named Dianne Cooley, was the funniest thing he had ever read: laughed out loud. Reinhart remembered that that one was all-solemn, as it happened. Dianne was considering a reconciliation with her husband, another soldier also on European duty, so this could not take place until after the war. Dianne loved to ruminate on such hypothetical fodder. Reinhart had known Dianne for a year before she left the States. He was in love *with* her without ever having made love *to* her. A familiar situation of his youth, when he repeatedly lost his heart to girls he never knew in the flesh and went to bed with tramps.

"Dear Winona ..." Once in composing a note to his father he had suffered a slip of the pen, writing "Dead Dad" for "Dear," which, in his then naïve orientation, had caused him some agony. Blaine, the playboy of the Western world, had candidly, guiltlessly, returned the favor twenty years later: "Why don't you die?"

Reinhart seized a fresh sheet of paper and wrote:

Dear Blaine,

I am taking your advice. But the Freudian cliché, reflected in the old school of literature, Dostoevski and Synge, is Out. Only squares still believe that the father-figure embodies the threat of emasculation.

I suppose that as the young fogey you are, you will do the right, the right-wing, thing by the girl next door, unless the whole business was a put-on. If you want to cop out, however, there is a Dr. Wilhelm in Northdale who can handle it. Mention the name of Dr. Barker Munsing. The latter, by the

way, is a specialist in sex-identity problems, if you
ever have need of one.

I mention this without irony, because if I ever
knew anyone who accepted his maleness, it is you.
You fearlessly wear your hair and clothes in a fashion which cannot be distinguished from the female
style, yet you are securely masculine in what counts.
You have proved that clothing is the product of social convention. There is no fundamental reason,
under the aspect of eternity, why a man should wear
a suit and a woman a frock.

As to your political views, which have so often
clashed with mine—

Reinhart had begun bitterly, but having lied to the effect
that he did not write in irony, he found himself inadver-
tently going straight on the force of the assertion.

—it would be false for me to announce my sudden
conversion. And grotesque. There is a genuine and
natural difference between the opinions of a man of
forty-four and a twenty-one-year-old. Were there
not, there would be little point in continuing to
age. The joy of life and also the sorrow—taken together they constitute the *interest*—come in and
through the accumulation of moments. In middle age
one looks back on as many as he looks forward to.
The teetertotter is in perfect balance. At the next
step it begins its downward tilt, the back end rising
commensurately. The *saw* outranks the *see*: there is
ever more of it towering behind. But you are still
confronted by a fascinating, challenging incline,
which rewards your every movement by a loss in the
acuteness of its angle.

One should feel his efforts have effect. You should
be gratified that your opposition to the war, to outmoded sexual attitudes, to social injustice has made
its discernible mark on events. If you persist in a
belief that the times they are a-changin', they will
indeed change. The whole of life, as we know it, is a
construct of mind, perhaps of language. We hardly
share anything, any more, with the dumb animals.
Maybe human beings will even abolish death. If so,
we will have removed ourselves from the evolution-
ary process altogether, from the status of creatures.
In the oldest morality, the aim was not to be a beast.

Then, with the development of machines, came subtlety. Immanuel Kant, I think it was, who made the useful distinction between men and *things*. Obviously, this would no longer apply if we were no longer mortal and could, as with cars, replace our vital parts when they failed.

One of the old arguments brought by the devout against atheism was that if there were no God, there would be no good and evil. And armed with that principle the true believers committed every known crime. They were succeeded by the secularists, for whom supernaturalism was the opium with which the masses were drugged to accept slavery, and I suppose in the statistical sweepstakes so popular in our time, social-totalitarianism has run up quite a score in corpses after a much shorter engagement than Christianity or Islam.

But the new composite immortal might get the brain of a sex maniac, the heart of a nun, the gonads of a cost accountant. A standoff. And the brain donor might have been a psychopath only because of a derangement in his endocrine glands: his gray matter, wired into another system, perhaps will not exude poison.

With your quick mind you will have seen the apparent fault in my example: the sex fiend, the nun, and the accountant, three persons, are lost to maintain one. Not true. Their incomplete cadavers will be frozen until mechanical devices have been developed to perform the function of the missing organs.

Neither your morality, as I understand it, nor mine will obtain in this state of affairs. They are separated by only a couple of decades, mine being a product—to put it in the terms which you, a child of the TV era, prefer—of the "generation" which came to majority in the forties. Your epoch has come along only twenty years after.

This new world will be timeless and make obsolescence itself obsolete. No more ripening and no more rot. After a few eons, no part of the father or son will be the original. The old man will have ever-renewed endurance and potency. Both will be immortal. The noble old institutions of put-on and -down, cop-out, sell-out, will have joined the divine right of kings in oblivion.

Even as you and I, for you are not all that young.
It always takes a while to iron the bugs out of a new
process. When the space program began they had
difficulty in getting the rockets off the ground. And
the physical sciences have centuries of sophistication
over medicine. The trip to the moon might well have
become an afternoon excursion before eternal life is
a serious possibility.

By that time you will be old, at best, and low on
the list of candidates for renewal, for surely if
precedent is meaningful, and even though the aged
or ill should obviously get first crack, men will not
have changed in their partiality for vigorous youth.
This will probably be all the more marked if the
whole concept of youth is in danger of vanishing:
man is a persistent innovator, but he also clings to
old sentimentalities.

In short, you will have time to die. I used to think
a lot about death when I was your age, without ever
feeling it. In melancholy moments I was wont to
craft farewell speeches. They were generally characterized by what I would call a noble bitterness. I had
read *The Mayor of Casterbridge* and was much impressed by the hero's valedictory wish to be buried in
an unmarked grave. I had not yet done anything
from which an untimely death could have resulted,
except by pure chance—and I limited the opportunities of fate by never sitting beneath a tree in a
lightning storm, by treating cuts promptly, by keeping
my life jacket nearby during travel on water.

Yet I was ready in fantasy. But when I got into a
lethal situation, with the Army in Berlin, I did not
recognize it as such. My friend and I got into a fight
with some black marketers. Before I knew it he was
knifed to death. I apparently killed one of them,
suffocated him or broke his spine—I don't quite
remember and don't want to. It seemed so long ago
only a few days later. I have never been a man of
action, even when in action, though I was strong in
those days as a result of weight-lifting I had done
while in high school. You have hated sports. I never
cared for the group ones. I have always been a
loner, in a lifetime of preparation for a lonely death—
and now I shall not die one.

You will not understand that statement, and you
would not care one way or another if you did. It is

even likely that you will not have read this far in the letter. Which is OK by me, because I am not writing it to you. Maybe you have seen the TV rerun of the old Marx Bros. picture in which Groucho, asking Chico to sign a contract, gives him a pen without ink. But that's OK, because Chico cannot write anyway.

But they agree: "We've got a contract!"

So have you and I.

YOUR LOVING FATHER

Reinhart found a matchbook imprinted with the name of the hotel. He watched the letter go up in smoke in one of the supersized ashtrays with which the suite was furished.

– 19 –

Dear Genevieve,
   When you receive this I will be not only gone but
dead. You may proceed with your plans without
hindrance. I am changing beneficiaries from you to
Winona, not out of revenge, but because you can
take care of yourself.

                              Faithfully,
                              CARLO REINHART

He would not burn this one, but mail it on the last
day.
   Which left Maw, as well as Winona. But there was
nothing to tell your mother when you were rearranging
fate's schedule and dying before her. She would be jealous
enough without his aggravating it by mail.
   He seized the phone book instead and looked up Dr.
Wilhelm, who was there all right, with a Northdale number.
   "When will he be in?" he asked the answering service.
   "You can't ever reach him directly. He has to call you
back."
   Having nothing to do while he waited, Reinhart decided to eat. He had unintentionally fasted all day.
   "Room service?" the operator cried in disbelief. "It's
now one A.M. They close the kitchen at ten."
   "Look at your board," said Reinhart. "This is the suite
where Eisenhower stayed overnight in 1956. I too am a
veteran, and I am paying one twenty-five a day."
   It now amazed him that he had got the writing paper
so easily; perhaps there was some sort of cutoff of services at midnight. She switched on the night manager,
who sniveled about unions, but eventually Reinhart was
delivered a ham-and-Swiss on rye and a bottle of That
Bud, That's Beer. But he was not hungry. As a boy he

had never eaten Swiss cheese. Another kid told him the
holes were made by worms, keeping him off it for a good
five years. He took the piece out of the sandwich before
him and looked through the orifices at the wall of golden
fiberglass drapery, behind which were presumably windows giving onto a night-lit city under a sky of a thousand stars.

Baloney, he should have ordered. Baloney on seeded rye
with a combination of horseradish and catsup. Or bacon
and peanut butter. Or a wiener, split and covered with
melted cheese and chili sauce. You had to make your
favorite sandwiches, you could never buy them. But once
or twice in a lifetime you might by chance, in a strange
section of town, have an unprecedented taste thrill, a
hamburger on a toasted English muffin, anointed with
some vermilion relish you would afterwards try to reproduce, or look for in the stores, and fail. A unique experience. Neither could you ever find the lunch counter
again, or if you did, they had gone back to buns and
mustard and denied all memory of their former practice,
angrily if you insisted.

In sex it was much the same: the memorable moments
could neither be forecast nor repeated. Reinhart was
about to relive certain of the happier memories—he had
two weeks in which his life could pass leisurely before his
eyes; it was not like jumping off the Bloor Tower and
having to pack it all into a few seconds' descent—when the
phone jangled.

He answered. It was Dr. Wilhelm.

"I'd like to come see you tomorrow," Reinhart said.
"Referral is by Dr. Barker Munsing."

"Munsing is on vacation now at Swan Lake," said
Wilhelm. "I'm afraid I don't have an open appointment
for three weeks, and then I'm going to Valparaiso, Chile,
where their winter is in progress."

"You ain't going nowhere, noplace, notime," Reinhart
said in Hollywood gangster style.

Wilhelm had a dispassionate, professional voice, the
kind that issued from beneath a graying moustache.

"Why don't you check that out with Captain Reynolds
of the Fifth Precinct?" he asked.

"All right," said Reinhart, "so like everybody else you
pay off the police. What does that prove? I know a black
militant whom the city bribes not to start a riot, but he
might do it anyway. Munsing is a transvestite, behind the
mask of his profession. I know a man who raises money

on cocoa beans that are actually gravel, and my son is talking of assassinating the Democratic Presidential nominee. I couldn't care less."

"I am afraid I do not offer the sort of treatment you seem to need," responded Wilhelm. Yet he did not hang up.

"You are speaking to a robust man," Reinhart said. "Yet I expect to die suddenly. I am toying with the idea that life is the disease, and death the cure. This is in accord with Christian theory."

"Dr. Munsing must have given you a number to call if you needed help while he was away."

"Yes, yours. But you still don't understand. I am not a patient of his, but a colleague."

"A physician?" asked Dr. Wilhelm. "Why didn't you say so? I'm a busy man, Dr. Reinhart, and it is one thirty in the morning. We G.P.'s don't keep the banker's hours of you fellows."

"And we can't cure a soul with an aspirin," said Reinhart. "But I suppose you have had your failures too, and buried them. I'd like to consult with you on a professional matter tomorrow."

"How would eleven o'clock be, at my office?" He gave Reinhart the address.

"Thank you, Doctor."

"Thank you, Doctor."

"And," said Reinhart, "I don't want to split the fee. It's all yours." He put down the funny prick-phone, which action, depressing a button underneath, broke the connection.

He went into the bedroom where Eisenhower had slept in '56. It was furnished with twin king-sized beds, the blue counterpanes of which were embroidered with five stars in a circle. Gilded eagles surmounted the posts, claws sunk in the finial balls. A colored, framed blowup hung on the pale blue wall above the near bed: Herd of Black Angus Cattle, Gettysburg, Penna. Reinhart fell onto the spread and stared at the Presidential seal in the middle of the ceiling. Suddenly and unaccountably he was horny, after all, as if in reaction against the decor, which managed to recapture that certain *je ne sais quoi* that had made the Fifties so deadly.

Reinhart pawed for the telephone, a Princess model this time, atop a white-and-gilt night table made in the form of a military trap drum, and asked for the bellhop who had earlier fetched the writing paper.

Since it was even later now, the operator was even more impudent. She said: "Bellman." Though of course it made sense.

"Hi," said the servitor when he appeared. "Change your mind, guy?"

"Let me tell you something," said Reinhart, sitting up in bed. "If you are a bellman, I am 'sir.' If I am 'guy,' you are back to bellboy. I am spending my money for luxury accommodations. I don't expect obsequiousness, but I do demand courtesy."

"I got my rights, too. I am human, you know."

"That's exactly what I am saying, am I not? This is the Age of Science. For every action there is an equivalent reaction."

The individual grimaced. "You're the boss. You got the money."

"By living fifteen years or so longer than you have, and by dying sooner."

The man's collar was open, and his hair as long as that of Reinhart's wig. He whined: "We got to pay income tax on our estimated tips."

"I doubt you report the kickbacks you get from hookers."

The guy smiled and twiddled a loose uniform button with two dirty fingernails. "I thought you'd come around. I can always tell. You learn a lot about people, in this job."

"I doubt it," said Reinhart.

"Listen, I could tell you—"

"Yeah, what apparently respectable and even distinguished personages do behind closed doors, and what male singer, famous for his virility, is privately a roaring faggot, and which venerable actress, who plays Mother Superiors and Queens of England, was stinking drunk in this suite and tore your fly open."

The bellman grinned. "Oh, I told you already?"

"No," said Reinhart. "I can see through the deceptive veil men call reality."

"She'll be here sometime during the next half hour." He put his hand out.

"Blonde, brunette, or carrot-topped?" asked Reinhart.

"Whoever they send. It's an answer service. But they're all women, and they'll do anything you want, so you won't have no beef. Just relax, and leave it to me."

"No, I won't," said Reinhart. "If I get no choice, I'd

rather play with myself. Is this the way it's always worked?"

"Brother, if you got to pay for it, then you can't call your shots. Me, I never have to buy it. I don't even have to ask for it. I get it ladled to me on a silver spoon. There is this rich cunt, see—"

"I am aware that many superior women go for greasy, rude, arrogant, ruthless cretins," said Reinhart, who was not surprised to see the sneer of self-approval survive this statement: the bellhop's egocentric glaze was impermeable. "Not that wealth implies superiority, either. Gloria has several rich clients who, according to her, have trouble getting one up."

He took a twenty-dollar bill from his wallet and ripped it in two. "Here. You get the other half when you get me what I want."

The bellboy took it with his habitual confidence, but then looked doubtful.

Reinhart said: "Dark meat."

The bellboy shook his unkempt head. "The house dick won't let a spade in the elevator at this hour. See, if it was earlier she might be a guest, and you can't keep 'em out nowadays. But this late it would have to be a hooker, and the police have got a cleanup campaign on because of the Presbyterian convention next week—"

"Bullshit," Reinhart said. "You know fucking well that you always pay off the house detective every time you get a girl for anybody, and he goes around and collects from guys who bring in underage girls and from people who have orgies and smoke pot and from anybody who does anything he suspects of being illegal and is always right about."

"Hey," asked the hop. "You a bull?"

"I always get asked that. You can use my phone."

"And show you the number? In a pig's ass."

"All right," said Reinhart. "I'll go shake the dew off my water lily." He went into the bathroom.

When he emerged the bellboy said: "All set. One dark cloud on her way." He looked as if he were going to add some coarse irony, but Reinhart gave him the remainder of the twenty and pointed to the door.

Reinhart had never had a woman of another race. It seemed a good time to fill in this gap. He had lived through several eras, cultural levels, and whatnot, each with a different attitude towards Negro sexuality. They were hotter-blooded than Caucasians, to begin with. Then you became literate and were apprised of the great universal truth of the sameness of people the world around: a Jew also bleeds, a Chinese vulva does not run crosswise, colored people do it just like you and me. But when he reached middle age the best authorities, namely his son and other black-power propagandists, who, admiring or being Negroes, should know, had gone back to where he started. Blaine had displayed to him an underground newspaper with a story entitled: "Honkies Don't Know How to Fuck."

Which might be true enough, for all he knew in his limited experience. "A black woman wants to satisfy her man," the article had said. "Whitey, dead himself, rubs bellies with another corpse." How a man could be certain of this without changing his own race was puzzling, but then Reinhart's idea of the privacy of sexual relations, his old delight in the then unquestionable fact that nobody, except your partner, could possibly be privy to what you did between the sheets, was obsolete. No doubt everyone shared comparisons nowadays. Gang shags, once the abhorred sport of criminal motorcycle clubs, were the routine pleasure of the now generation.

She was a chocolate doll—what else, without being cloying, could you say of a package ordered by phone?— a brown bonbon, sepia sweetmeat, wearing a summer-weight white jersey dress, white shoes, white brassiere and underpants. When this apparel had been doffed, shaken, smoothed, and folded over the winged chairback or quilted seat, Reinhart was led to the bathroom, where quick, efficient, but never rough or painful hands invaded his privacy, soaped, rinsed, and, in a fleecy white Shade-Milton towel, tumbled it dry.

He followed the high, burnished buttocks to the bed he had rumpled earlier. She lifted the superior margins of five-star spread, underlying blanket and sheet, drew them to the footboard, and, with a supple sleight of wrist, made them ripple and fall folded upon themselves like a closing accordion. She stepped into the bed as an athlete walks upon the field, and was much darker against the blanch of sheet than within the half-lighted air of room.

She asked Reinhart what he wished, naming the usual options.

He posed on the axis of shoulder, hip, side of knee, blade-edge of foot, and addressed the amber hub of her wheel-eye, which radiated spokes of lashes.

"I would like to kiss you."

A large brown lid descended serenely, then slowly opened on a bluish white glazed with moisture. But like a Caucasian whore she would put her mouth anywhere but on a client's lips.

"May I ask why?" said Reinhart.

"I save that for my boyfriend." She sat up, and her breasts, with nipples and aureolas of purple-black, regained their fullness. Her hair was in a bouffant stiff and coarse as Gloria's though glossier of lacquer. Her lips were deep, yet not as full as he would have thought. She wore a scent reminiscent of Genevieve's.

"Roll over, and I will rub your back."

"No," Reinhart said. "I don't like that."

"You want me to dominate?"

"No."

"You want me to kiss it?"

"No thanks," he said. "And you don't have to say anything else, if you don't want to. I know the dialogue by heart." He ran through some of it: "Have you got protection? . . . Leave a little slack at the end or it'll break. . . . Higher. . . . Wait a minute, I'll put a pillow under me." Etc.

Expressionless, she asked: "You want to *make* or have fun?"

"For me it has always been an obligation," Reinhart said, "to prove something. Or a treatment to relieve a kind of strain, like going to the toilet. That's it, fun. I guess I never had any in this way. You people do it for fun, don't you?"

His fears that this might be taken the wrong way—as racial patronization—were allayed when she indeed misinterpreted it, but as applying to prostitutes.

"We do it for money," she said.

"You too are supporting a child or putting yourself through night school."

"No, I am buying a Lincoln Continental and a closetful of clothes for my boyfriend."

"You like to do that?"

"No question of liking," she said firmly. "I love him. It is my life, and I can do as I please with it. Now if you want to do something, I have to get to work. That's what I'm getting paid for, I *think*."

So they had fun, or anyway, he did.

Afterward, as they exchanged quizzical but friendly looks, she said: "A penny for your thoughts."

"Do you believe your whole life passes before your eyes when you are dying?"

"I hope not."

"Maybe if it does, it appears as a series of jokes," he said, "which are not necessarily funny-haha. I remember another one: What would you order if it was your last meal on earth?"

Mention of food reminded him of his weight, and rolling aside, he took it off her.

"That's not funny, either. I had a brother who went to the electric chair."

In his old situation Reinhart would have thrilled right down to the tailbone at his proximity to a person with such news.

Now he asked calmly: "What did he eat?"

"It's a lie that they give you anything you want," she said. "You get what *they* want, same as always. Fish, which he hated all the time. Baked apple for dessert. He never ate a bite."

"He was a murderer?"

"I don't know about that. All I can remember is he was black."

"Well," said Reinhart. "How about you? What would you have?"

"I'm going to tell you!" she cried, turning to look into his face. "Lobster. Cold, boiled lobster with mayonnaise, and potato chips, and sliced tomatoes-and-onions on the side."

"You got it," Reinhart said as he reached for the phone on the trap-drum table.

"Why, you going to kill me?" She had a pretty smile, was definitely a pretty girl.

He put his right hand on her warm brown belly. "You drop a peeled peach into a glass of champagne. You drink the champagne with your meal, and eat the peach for dessert. I read that in a story once."

He asked the operator for the night manager again, and getting him, began to lay down the law.

After the feast, which was light and did not weigh one down, they had some more fun, and by dawn Reinhart found himself owing her, at the established piece rate of fifty per, two hundred dollars. Another thing he had never done, a staple of the licentious novel, was taking-a-shower-with-a-girl, mutual soaping and so on. The white foam did look well against her skin, which seemed flawless. Bruises and blemishes, if such there were, enjoyed protective coloration, like the green insect sitting on a leaf. And do you get pimples and how do they look? he did not ask, but wondered about, as well as sunburn, dandruff, and scabs.

She was careful to keep her hair out of the spray, because otherwise he would liable for beauty-shop costs, but sportively he pulled her under and they mock-tusseled and squirted the cake of Cashmere Bouquet back and forth.

The towelwork also amused. Her hair was now a cap of gleaming licorice.

"Leave it like that a while. It's pretty," said Reinhart, though of course refunding the price of the hairset.

But, grimacing, she found a blue scarf in her purse and with it covered her damp head in a sort of African tie.

"My jungle princess," Reinhart said affectionately. But never had he had such a luxurious, sophisticated revel. And with, taking her all in all, such an overcivilized companion.

Reinhart took her to the door. With the turning of the knob he saw come down over her features the same mask she had worn on entry, hours earlier. Through the eyeholes she looked disinterestedly at him.

"If you want to see me again next time you come to town, tell Larry—you know, the bellboy? Ask for Sybil. Now, take care."

He watched her white-clad behind dance to the turn of the corridor. He was glad she had come, but not sorry to see her go. A human relationship is successful if confined between these brackets.

To keep up a front, Dr. Wilhelm apparently found it necessary to accept patients with the usual run of maladies. Either that, or the old man, staring rheumily at his spotted knuckles capped upon a cane, and the twelve-year-old with his ankle in plaster, and the shriveled spinster who climbed up the opposite sofa arm as Reinhart sat down at the other end—all these unfortunates required help with their illegal pregnancies or represented someone who did. Or having contracted to be frozen by an unlicensed fanatic, needed an unscrupulous member of the AMA for certification of death.

The magazines strewn upon a table against the windows also were a surprise: *Wine & Food, The American Rifleman, Black Belt,* and *Mad.* Reinhart also found a copy of *Road & Track,* containing a road-test report on the Jaguar XKE. Standing at the table he perused it. He was conscious he had not got all he could have out of his model before discard.

He dropped the magazine, gazed idly out the window, saw a fat girl deboarding from a bus, and was reminded of Winona. After Sybil's departure he had slept only three hours. He was among the earlycomers at the Veterans Administration downtown: ex-servicemen of many conflicts, one wheelchaired codger, bald and desiccated, might have charged up San Juan Hill with Teddy Roosevelt. Others had been maimed at twenty in seek-and-destroy missions, just last year. Escalation, defoliation, and body counts. Wretched jargon, whereas that of World War II had been popular with everybody: Kilroy, short-snorter bills, flak, dive-bombing.

Time was, the guys who worked at the VA were themselves war mutilates. You were handed a pen by an aluminum arm terminating in a sort of C-clamp. The employees were now mostly dim-witted females of indeterminate age. One such took care of his change of beneficiaries.

He still had not written the letter to Winona. For all his alteration of personality, now in its second day, he expected to wait until the last evening, as he had with college themes, spend all night on it, and go red-eyed and coffee-bilious into a bed of ice in the morning.

The fat girl turned in the doctor's walk and came up it wearily but also inexorably, putting one foot ahead of the other as if plodding through knee-high surf.

Reinhart was reminded of Winona because it was she, had been she since the descent from the bus. He had recognized her instantly because she had been his daughter for sixteen years, but it had always been his habit when seeing Winona at a distance to assume, until she reached his immediate vicinity, that she was someone else—no, that she would *turn* into someone else, be transformed by a sudden miracle, pumpkin into golden coach.

Ah, Winona, why must you choose this doctor for your scratchy throat, sinus congestion, chafing-rash, or gas pains? Old Doc Perse, five blocks from home, can meet the needs of your hypochondria, as he always has before, with the usual dietary recommendations which you never follow, the pills you cannot tolerate, the tinctures you never apply because they burn.

Why can't you let me alone? Reinhart was thrust back into his old bitterness at Winona's lone pursuit while all others retreated. Followed by the old guilt. Perhaps she was truly ill for once, childhood cancer, spinal meningitis, muscular dystrophy, leukemia. Had terrible symptoms with which Doc Perse, senile eccentric, could not cope: lumps that would not go away, strange bleeding, persistent pain.

But a new jealousy ensued. You will die before me, is that your game? Even that will be taken away from me? And by you, Winona. How could you? You who, uniquely, never caused me trouble. How dare you? A fat little simpleminded girl.

His daughter. You could still love someone for whom you felt contempt. Else you were stuck with those who were contemptuous of you. The world was accessible to such divisions: young or old, black or white, masochist or sadist, those you wanted or those who wanted you.

Winona halted halfway up the walk, as if by the force of his silent speech. Go home, dear; go elsewhere; go eat. For the love of God, Winona, I am leaving you ten thousand dollars. What more do you want of me?

This turned her around. Her dress was one solid bag of flesh. He could see, from the plastering of her skirt to her rear, that she had got a seat on the bus; and from the great circle of damp, that the vehicle had not been air-conditioned.

You don't want to see me, Winona. I've been rolling with a whore all night. I am not a fit father, never have been, and will be a nullity soon. Quit while you're ahead.

This started her walking towards the street, eyes downcast to paddle shoes. Unless she watched where she went, Winona was liable to severe stubs of the toe; in winter, flops on icy patches; in spring-swollen gutters, ankle-deep immersion. Once she had lost a shoe to mud, and left it there.

I tried to teach you things, Winona. Both you and Blaine, but he was too clever to believe them and you were too stupid. Now look up, Winona, before you step off into the street, make sure no cars are coming, then look down again to see whether the usual public enemy has pitched the usual beer can or throwaway pop bottle below the curb. Step over, not upon, it.

That warning she heeded, reaching the asphalt roadway without misadventure, but her head was still down.

Neck straight now, Winona. Chin high, eyes right and left. With a smart, rapid stride you have plenty of time to cross to the opposite bus stop, boarding station for the return home, the means to get well out of my hair, before that oncoming truck gets anywhere near.

No, you had better run, Winona. Either across or back will do. Plenty of time, no panic. But please look up. *And don't, of all things, stop dead!*

He punched both fists through the window of this controlled-climate room.

Winona turned at his shout. The truck lifted her as though, despite her bulk, she was weightless.

— 20 —

Both Reinhart's hands were cut but not seriously. The emergency reception at St. Bartholomew Hospital made short work of these matters: a student nurse swabbed his hurts and circumnavigated them with a giant roll of gauze.

Winona's blanket-covered stretcher claimed the journeyman personnel. They disappeared with it behind a white door. Reinhart's efforts to follow had been frustrated, and for a number of reasons, most of them arising like noxious vapors from the cesspool of his weakness, he could not persist.

But he stayed and drank the proffered coffee, declined the bed, later on refused the meal, still later was mostly mute with the kindly priest except to say they were not Catholic, information he had already provided for the nun who filled out the admission card and which indeed was not asked now, but he had no one else to apologize to. Three of the Reinharts had no religion. Blaine of course saw God as the "face of mankind." Gen used to pretend to be Episcopalian for snob reasons, but wouldn't have known where to find the church. Reinhart had been raised on Presbyterian sermons on themes taken from the *Reader's Digest* by a stout preacher whose sport was bowling. But because her gang of inimical girl friends were Methodist, Winona padded off weekly to that Sunday school and sometimes as well to fun-filled Young People's Group get-togethers, at which the boys ignored and the girls derided her.

The priest said it didn't matter, smiled cryptically, and went away. Reinhart sat on the bench for three hours more, endlessly contemplating his exchange of suicide for murder, commission for omission, father for daughter. He also tried many times to reach Genevieve, but no one answered the phone at the boutique. This must be the one day in summer midweek they were closed. Neither was anyone home, nor at the Raven household. He must take it in the classic condition of the nightmare: alone. And no one was more deserving.

In the frenzy of his entrance, he had however managed to notice one doctor, a short man in a crew cut. Later on, reliving the whirl of images, he remembered him, remembered his own obscene wig, snatched it off with some difficulty owing to the bandaged hands, and thrust it down the throat of a swing-lid wastecan. The catastrophe had turned him back into the old Reinhart. And in his old style he sat there, a fly of soul imprisoned in the amber of existence.

It must have been evening when through his stupor he recognized the crew-cut intern leaving by the door to the emergency driveway. All over, then. The man could not face him. Reinhart felt sorry for the doctor: to have worked so long and hard. He pursued the white jacket, caught up with him on the asphalt outside.

"Doctor," he said, panting in the torrid evening air, "I want to thank you for all you've done. I don't want you to think I—" He lost his thought in tears.

"Now, now," said the intern. He patted towards Reinhart's arm, missing it. "You go see Father Horgan."

Between the sobs Reinhart said: "I'm not Catholic."

"Well then, the receptionist will call your clergyman." He was kind, but seemed anxious to go, probably to supper; they worked long hours for little money and their meals were catch-as-can. Reinhart remembered *Dr. Kildare:* the original films, to which the TV version could not compare, for the simple reason that Reinhart had been a youth when the former came out.

"I don't want to detain you after a backbreaking day," Reinhart said, trying to get a handkerchief out of the pocket of those indecent, tight pants. "It must be as terrible for you. I don't know how you—"

"In fact, it wasn't one of the worst ones," the intern confessed. "Not a single cut throat or gunshot wound of the abdomen—some of them can be real dillies. But I've got to run to catch the first show."

The coldblooded skunk! Let a little girl die, and then, calling it a good day, go to a movie. Reinhart tried to ball his bandaged fist. Then it came to him, awfully, that even in death Winona was overlooked in the distractions of spite, as she had always been at home.

"I'm sorry," he said, opening the hand and offering it to

the doctor. "I know you tried. Did she ever regain consciousness?"

"Who?"

"The child, the little girl, who was hit by the truck. My—" Reinhart broke down again.

"Nobody like that showed up today. Some big fat woman was brought in in late morning. I don't know what hit her, but whatever it was it probably got the worst of it. Wow, some adipose tissue! She got off with a few fractures and bruises."

Winona's right leg, encased in plaster and attached to a rope-and-pulley arrangement, pointed to the ceiling. Reinhart could see her round face, unmarred and rosy, through these obstructions. He came around from the foot of the bed.

"Dear . . ."

"Hi, Daddy," she said as of old. "Well, I did it again, I guess! If you told me once, you told me five thousand times not to cross in the middle of the block. So I got what was coming to me."

"Ah, Winona." Reinhart bent to kiss her wide forehead.

"But I guess it just wasn't time for my number to come up." No doubt she was quoting a line from some war movie. Her wry grin dimpled one cheek, over a squared jaw.

"Darling, what matters is that you're alive," Reinhart said. He pulled up a chair. He had done that to someone else's bed recently—oh yes, Splendor's. It was difficult in one episode to remember or believe in another.

"I would have been in *really* bad shape if I hadn't heard the sound of smashing glass a split-second earlier, and turned to look, you know: well, because of that, the bumper caught me on the bottom, where, if you have to get hit, it's the best place, especially on me. I guess I am all green and purple there. You know how I bruise so easy anyway. They got an air cushion underneath, shaped like a doughnut. Which reminds me: Do you think you have to go all evening without anything else to eat after having supper at five thirty?"

"It was a miracle, Winona." Reinhart searched for her near hand, which was under the sheet. "What's this, dear?"

She pulled out another plastered part. "That's the funny thing, Daddy. I only broke bones when I landed. My leg got twisted and my wrist and a couple fingers. If there had been a soft place to land, like a pile of tires or a pond full of water—"

It was hard to show affection to a cast. Reinhart withdrew his hand. Winona saw his own bandages.

"Oh, you got hurt too! Did you burn yourself?"

"A minor mishap, dear. Very routine in the kind of life I lead."

"I thought about that, Daddy. I thought about how you went through the war, getting shot at and bombed and never got a scratch. And then hanging around with the Mafia, and your other adventures. And here I can't cross Northdale Avenue."

Reinhart realized he had exaggerated somewhat in disclosing his history to Winona. He had been in the rear-echelon Army and he had known Jimmy Marsala, who later on seemed to have become a gangster.

"Too much can be made of that sort of thing, darling. Comparisons are invidious, as they say. You are a young girl and I am an old man. Naturally we will have different experiences."

"Not old, Dad. You're in the prime of life. That's where I wish I was, in my forties. So I didn't have all that stuff to go through yet."

"What stuff, dear?" Though he thought he knew what she meant.

She grimaced. "Maybe I wouldn't mind being a mother after it was all over and I could change the baby and rock him and so on. But you got to go through a lot of unpleasant things before that."

"Not nowadays, Winona. They give you pills and shots and it is relatively painless. You are thinking of the olden times, when a woman had to bite on a bullet. Anyhow, that is still many years in the future. And last time we talked you didn't think you wanted to get married at all, if you remember."

"I sure haven't changed my mind about that."

Reinhart looked around the room. "Not bad here, TV set and all. I would get you some flowers if you weren't allergic to them."

"I told them my father was *very* well-to-do," said Winona, showing a new smugness. "I hope that was OK. I didn't want to go into a ward. Course I would if you said so—"

"Don't be foolish, Winona, certainly you shall keep this lovely private room. The best is none too good."

"Daddy, I hope you were not called away from one of your important business meetings for this stupid accident of mine. I told them not to bother you, and anyway I didn't know where you could be gotten ahold of anyway, now you don't live at home any more. I never expected to see you this soon."

"I was here right along, dear, as it happened. I was sitting down there in emergency reception all day and nobody bothered to tell me. I thought you might have died."

"Poor Daddy, how rotten for you." Winona's eyes watered. "I bet you didn't get anything to eat, either."

"Don't you worry about that, darling." Reinhart saw the crucifix above the bed. "I guess these Catholics are treating you pretty well."

"Oh this is a neat place," said Winona with enthusiasm. "You know, they don't have nurses but nuns. Isn't that neat?"

"Yes, it is," Reinhart said, "and I am happy to see they still wear the good old-fashioned habit and don't belong to one of those modernized orders who wear civilian-looking outfits. That takes away the whole idea, if you ask me, even though I'm not Catholic."

She gave him a searching look. "What about, Daddy, if I became a nurse-nun? Would you just hate me for that?"

It was the perfect solution, in fact. Reinhart said: "You might think quite seriously about that, dear. I have always thought that when it comes to religion, the only genuine one, all wool and a yard wide, is the Catholic Church. It is a magnificent institution and responsible for most of the culture of Europe. If I had it to do all over again I might very well become a priest or monk, myself."

Winona's face was a sun upon the pillow. "Then that does it!" she cried. "I always wanted to help people, to be as nice as I could, even when it hurts—and it sure does hurt sometimes, and you wonder whether you have done the right thing, but you are repaid by the knowledge that you relieved somebody's distress."

Reinhart felt his eyebrows coming together. "That's right, that's right," he said vaguely, then collected himself. "Of course, you can't live only for other people, though. If, being human, they deserve help, so, being human yourself, do you. I mean, your own self is sacred too. That's why, I think, the Church calls suicide as great a sin as murder."

Winona also frowned. "But if someone wants you to do

something they cannot do for themself. and it has to be done or they will go crazy, well, don't you have to be pretty nasty not to help them out?"

A nun entered the room at this point. She was a young woman, healthily colored within the white coif. Reinhart had always found them female yet sexless, and stayed away from those obscene movies in which voluptuous actresses, negligeed or bikinied in their last feature, wore the habit.

"Hi!" she said, breezing up to the bed. "How's the girl? This your dads? Groovy gear you're wearing, man!"

"This is Sister Mary Margaret, Daddy," said Winona. "She is my friend."

"You know it." She put her hand at Reinhart. He shook it. "I'm going off now, and came to say good night." She smiled brazenly into Reinhart's eyes. "I'm glad I did."

He opened his hand but did not succeed in getting rid of hers. He said: "I want to thank you for taking care of my little girl."

"Oh, that's my specialty," said Sister Mary Margaret, twisting her trunk in such a way that her breasts made themselves known. "I take care of everybody."

Reinhart blushed. She still had his hand. He mumbled: "Winona was just telling me she might like to become a sister."

"It can be pretty dreary," said Mary Margaret, hooking her free hand into her waist rope and arching her hip, "but thank God, not what it used to be. I mean, we have to wear this sheet at work, because it is more practical than even a nurse's uniform when the blood and pus are flying, but when you're off you can go back to the barracks and get into something human." She leered at Reinhart. "You should see the clear plastic miniskirt I got the other day at Switched-On. You really should."

Winona said excitedly: "That's my mother's shop."

The nun ignored her. "But," she said, "not tonight. I'm spoken for." She pinched Reinhart's palm. "Hey, wait a minute. We're going to the Gastrointestinal System. He'll probably get stoned after an hour. So if you want to come around later—you know the Funky Broadway? You look like a mean dancer."

Reinhart said: "Sorry, I'm all tied up."

"That figures." She ran a hand across his crew cut. "Sexy. I thought they were out." She turned to Winona: "Keep it cool, baby." And left, like a sloop in a gale.

"Isn't she nice?" asked Winona. "She told me to call her Marge."

"Really a terrific person," Reinhart said, "and full of pep."

"So everything's just fine now, Daddy. I was pretty worried for a while, because though, well, you weren't around to talk to, and you know how Mother is, working her fingers to the bone, poor thing, and I don't like to bother her, and Blaine, he would just make fun—"

Reinhart said, not listening: "It is certainly something to think about, dear, being a nun. But you might check into the various orders. Sister Mary Margaret is an excellent type, no doubt, but not everybody has the same personality, Winona. You might find you prefer the serenity of some secluded convent. You do see a lot of ugly sights around a hospital."

"I don't mean that, Daddy." She giggled. "It's kind of embarrassing, really. But at first he reminded me of you—you know how sometimes when you have worked terribly hard and all sorts of big business deals are on your mind, you look so sad? Well, so did he, standing there in the lobby last night, looking at the stills for the coming attractions. I waited about twenty minutes for the girls to come out of the ladies', before I realized they had slipped out the back exit."

Reinhart sat there quietly while a great hairy beast slouched towards him.

Winona said: "He saw me looking at my watch, and he looked at his, and he said: 'Well, I guess we both have been stood up. We are the kind of people to whom other people do that, aren't we?' So terribly sad. I remembered what you told me once. I said, 'I guess so, but you shouldn't ever give up. Something really fabulous might happen at any time.' 'You give me hope,' he said. 'And that's what a woman's for, all in all.' He had the nicest boyish voice, like yours, you know, Daddy, and was about the same age. He said, 'I trust you won't think me forward, miss, but if you don't have anything better to do, I would call it a fabulous event right now if I could buy you a milk shake. Do you know Alfie's, where they make 'em so thick a spoon will stand up?' "

Winona was at pains to be accurate: "I think it was Alfie's, but it might have been Ralphie's. Anyhow, I never heard of either one and in fact I don't really like the double-thick ones, which are almost solid ice cream and stick in the straw. But I could tell by looking at his sad

face that he thought they were fabulous and I wouldn't
have wanted to disappoint him when he had already been
ditched by whoever he was waiting for. So I said, 'If you
could wait a minute while I check the ladies' lounge and
see if my friends are there.' But he said, 'I have such a
fear that if you leave me I will never see you again.'

"Well, Daddy, I guess you have never had the experience, but when somebody else in the world makes you
feel useless, and then suddenly somebody seems to require
you for an important purpose. . . ."

Reinhart nodded in his rigidity. Control, control must
be imposed. Inevitable as this fantasy seemed, it could be
rewritten: *Nevertheless, I said I had to check on the
ladies' and as it turned out my friends were still there and
when we came out he was gone.*

Winona responded to this silent direction, just as she
had done on the sidewalk outside Dr. Wilhelm's office.

"But still I had to make sure my friends were not
looking for me after all, to be fair, you know, and I went
there, but they were gone, and I came back and said, 'It
would be a pleasure.'" She carried obedience only so far:
had turned away from the doctor's office but lost direction at the curb.

"'Is it close enough to walk there or should we get a
bus?' I asked him. 'Little princess,' he said, he said that,
I'm not making it up, and he seemed so happy all of a
sudden, he smiled when I came back, you should have
seen how happy he was, Daddy, and he clasped me by the
hand."

The beast had now reached Reinhart. He could feel the
sinking heat of its breath.

"He had a beautiful car, but we had a hard time
finding it because everybody else was parked there for the
second show, rank after rank, but it was fun looking for
it, because he kept calling me nice things I never heard
outside of movies and every time I giggled at them he
would squeeze my hand, and when we found it he gave
me the keys and said, 'Would you like to drive, my
treasure?' 'I have trouble operating a bicycle,' I said. He
said, 'Nonsense, dearest! You just never have had the
right instruction. Remember this: you can do anything
you want to, if you tell yourself you can.'"

Winona looked at her suspended leg. "He had your
manner, Daddy. You know, the kind of confidence that
won't take no for an answer, like when the fuses kept
blowing at home?"

At last Reinhart had caught Blaine under the hair dryer, air-conditioner on full blast, and a hot iron propped on the dresser-top. Blaine ironed his hair in hot weather, else it developed a slight curl.

"But what bothered me was that you never had suggested I learn to drive. He said, 'Your Dad is too busy for that.' 'You know him?' 'I certainly do. He's one of the people I admire most,' he said. 'I've even tried to model myself after him, but that's not easy. He's one great guy. Of course he's told me a lot about you, how beautiful and smart you are, but I don't mean any disrespect when I say that not even his extravagant statements did justice to you.'"

"You got his name then," Reinhart tried to say nonchalantly.

"Sure," said Winona. "It rhymed: Gordon Horton. 'Remember me to your Dad when you get home,' he said. 'Gordon Horton.'"

There was a telephone on the bedside table, and a metropolitan-area book on a shelf below. Reinhart seized the latter and looked for this diabolically impossible name.

"Yes," he said, "old Army pal. Here he is, Howard J. Horton. Good old Howie." He peered at his daughter through pinpoint eyes.

"No," said Winona, "Gordon, because he told me to call him Gordie, and he doesn't live here but in Delaware, I think he said, which is why he hasn't seen you for a while. I saw the license plate and it said 'Delaware.'"

"Happen to get the number?"

"I'm hopeless at numbers, Daddy."

True. Winona had to look up their home phone when she was out.

"Wait a minute. I think the Delaware plate was on the car ahead. I saw it when I put on the headlights. I think he said Iowa was where he lived now. I put on the lights when I was trying to start the motor and pulling the different knobs, but he told me where to put the key and how to move the lever to 'Drive' and what to do with your feet, and we *moved!* I tell you it was a thrill, Daddy. We moved out of the slot and across the aisle, real slow, and we almost banged the Delaware car, but Gordie put his foot across and braked just in time. And then we backed into the slot. And that was all there was to it. We never did go for the milk shake."

Winona's grin was resplendent. The monster clutching

Reinhart turned out to be one of those amusement-park illusions, 3-D fakery, luminescent paint.

"That was all?" he cried triumphantly.

"Absolutely," said Winona. "I sure didn't want to wreck his nice car, a nice man like that, and maybe you won't believe it, but for once I wasn't interested in treating my sweet tooth. So then he turned off the motor and the lights and said, 'Let's just sit here for a while and talk. I seldom get the chance to talk to a beautiful and intelligent girl. Girls have always made a fool of me. I give them everything they want and yet the more I do, the more contempt I get in return. I sometimes think I am under an evil curse.' The poor man, he began to cry then, the way you did when Granpa died and I'll never forget that as long as I live. 'I have *never* been loved,' he said, 'never in my life. A lovely creature like you can't understand that, but it is terrible to always want and never be wanted in return. You feel you don't exist.'

"I said I couldn't understand that, big and handsome as he was, with a new car. 'It's something about me, I guess,' he said. 'Some sort of radiation that other people feel. It tells them that I mean well, that I am good, that they have nothing to fear. People don't like you unless they fear you. The way to succeed is to be mean.' "

"No, no, no," Reinhart shouted, shutting his eyes as the beast returned gnashingly to life. "You told me that was all, Winona. After the little driving lesson, that was all. You said good-bye and walked to the bus stop."

"That was all of the *driving*," she said. "But it wasn't all of our friendship. I gave him my handkerchief. I carry two in this hot weather, one to wipe the sweat off my face. He buried his face in it and said, 'What is this heavenly fragrance?' 'Only Fab with enzyme-active borax, I think,' I said. Isn't that the soap you use in the wash machine, Daddy?"

"New blue Cheer," said Reinhart. Precision could save your soul.

"Then I was wrong."

"Well, not very. I might have used Fab once or twice, when there was a special on it. A penny here and a penny there, you know." He had a desperate urge to keep this trivia going forever.

"I guess it really doesn't matter."

"Oh, it does, Winona! It matters awfully." She got a stricken look, and Reinhart shouted horribly: "No, it doesn't! Go on."

"I only want to get it right, Daddy. About your friend."

The chimera was sniffing around Reinhart's large body, seeking a vital part for its fangs.

Winona said: "Well, nobody had been that nice to me in all my life. I mean, nobody but you of course. I knew he was just being kind. I'm not beautiful for gosh sakes, and I am anything but brilliant, that's for sure. I am fat and I am stupid. I can't get a date, and I flunked geometry and barely squeaked through social studies."

There is a kind of pain that can be exquisitely pleasurable, gratifying the thrill-seeker who through surfeit has become immune to simple amusements. But that was not the kind which Reinhart now experienced.

"I know I can get by only if somebody shows me what they need," Winona said. "Those girls *need* someone to ditch. If I wasn't good for that, they wouldn't ask me to come with them. They would get somebody else, and I would not have anyplace to go. You see, the way I have figured it out, I actually am popular."

Reinhart nodded. Winning and losing were relative states of being, perhaps only matters of definition.

"So when he asked me, I said OK, if that's what would make him happy."

Reinhart instinctively found a means of survival, like certain living things in a drought: they burrow.

"You're a good person, Winona," he said as the cool, moist earthworks rose around him. "And the really good are—" As the surface grew more remote he might have said, since like all philosophy it did not matter now, "even more frightening than the really evil, for we cannot punish them."

But Winona said quickly: "No, I'm not Daddy. I didn't like it. It hurt. And I got to thinking—" Her face wrinkled, smoothed, blushed. "I got to hating—you, Daddy, you of all people. He was your friend, you see. You were both men. Oh, I was pretty rotten, and it's not easy to confess this, but if you love someone you can hate him temporarily, can't you, if in the end you come back to loving him? I mean, it would be bad only if it was permanent, wouldn't it?"

Winona distressfully awaited an answer. Damn her, he was just ready to pull his hole in after him.

"Yes, dear."

She breathed heavily. "That's a weight off my conscience. I try to do the right thing, but it isn't always easy

to tell what it is. Like today. I thought I ought to go and
get an abortion, where Blaine sent Julie, because I heard
him telling her in his room last week, but when I got
there I couldn't go in. Some voice inside just told me not
to, told me I should have the baby and love it, not have it
murdered before it was even born just because it would
be painful. So it was thinking about that, that I got hit by
the truck. And that brought on my period, anyway. So
there's no problem now." She grinned and said again:
"So everything's just fine now."

Reinhart's chair sagged somewhat on the right. Looking
down, he saw he had bent the metal leg he had not been
aware he was clutching. His bandages had unraveled. He
still had the great strength of yore. Once he had killed a
man with it, broken his back. He would never do it again.
He would not locate this newfound friend and destroy
him, because though it could be managed, it could not be
rightly done without publicity. Stealthy poison would not
serve, nor a silenced weapon. Sheer brutality was called
for, flesh-tearing, bone-breaking, head-crushing, the making of a man into a heap of offal, and doing it so that the
object would, till the end, feel the how and know the
why.

Revenge, pure and beautiful in its orgy. For Winona,
who was quite happy now, had no interests to represent.
Indeed she would be damaged when the news got out:
you could not beat a man to death in seclusion nowadays;
there were no private, soundproof places. Providing you
could even find him. You could not ask Winona for
identifying features of *your friend,* whose name you already possessed. So you killed him and revealed him, to
her, as a statutory rapist, in submitting to whom she had
not done the "right thing." But then you also killed
Winona.

"It is, isn't it, Daddy?" she asked. "Just let things take
their course, and they will come out all right, like you
have always said. Only, I wish you still lived at home."
Her sweet smile became reflective. "I guess you are still
the only person I can talk to."

Reinhart caught sight again of the breech-clouted
Christ, hanging on the plastic cross. Whether He, or he,
had been fake or freak or real McCoy, winner or loser,
was largely another matter of definition.

"How would you like to live with me until you go off to
the nunnery?" he asked. "In the Presidential suite of the

Shade-Milton for a few days until we can find a nice little apartment?"

"I wouldn't get in your way, Daddy. If you had business to discuss I would go to my room." Her fat cheeks swelled as her lower lip oozed out. It was Winona's expression for brain-scouring thought. "You could even watch TV after I went to bed, and I wouldn't complain next morning."

"Darling, that's the best offer I have ever had."

He could also tell her some of the things he had never got around to, such as that a pregnancy does not necessarily develop overnight.

"Carl!" Bob Sweet shouted at him as he entered the lab. "I've been trying to get hold of you all day. We've—"

"I'm looking for you, too," said Reinhart. "The phone number here is unlisted, and I didn't have it."

Sweet began to speak, but Reinhart stopped him. "I'll get right to the point. The deal is off, Bob. It turns out that I am worth more alive than frozen."

"Carl—" Sweet was agitated, as Reinhart had expected.

"It's no use, Bob. I know about the sacks of gravel. If you told me they were cocoa beans, it figures you have allowed other people to assume the same thing. Like the bank that gives you loans on them. It might seem impossible that a professional financial institution would not carefully inspect the collateral, but then I remember a couple of years ago some guy in the salad-oil business filled his storage tanks with water and bilked half of Wall Street, including the First National City Bank of New York and the American Express Company. I guess all it takes is nerve."

"Carl, that doesn't matter now," Sweet snapped, in his urgent style that no longer stirred Reinhart.

"Right. I am disaffiliating. I don't want to be frozen, at least not for some years and not then unless you get somebody who seems more reliable than a Swiss-German fanatic. Even though he was in a concentration camp."

Bob seized Reinhart's lapels, but the big man broke the hold with a jujitsu thing he had learned in the Army.

"And, furthermore, there's no such thing as a black belt in kung fu," Reinhart said. "That was another of your alterations of truth. If I pushed you around in high school, I'm sorry. But, Jesus Christ, that was in 1939 or '40. How long can you hold a grudge?"

"Carl, Carl!"

"No, Bob, I won't listen to any more of your cunning. Also, I don't intend to return what is left of the money after buying the Jag and a few other things, and I'm going to stay at the Shade-Milton on the company account until I can find another place to live. My daughter is going to join me there. I'll have them open up the door to the bedroom next door where the Secret Service men slept when Eisenhower stayed there."

Now it was Reinhart who grabbed Sweet, pulling him up close and looking down as if he were a child. And like a child who finds himself being lectured, Bob hung his head between his shoulders.

"Do you know," Reinhart said, really oblivious to Sweet, "all this while I thought the big problems were my wife and son. Not so: nasty people are easily handled. I mean, it may not be easy to accept the fact that your wife of twenty-two years is and has always been a bitch—not under the aspect of eternity, or anything like that, but simply vis-à-vis me, who am all I can speak for. And the reason she is has largely, I am certain, to do with my own character. To Harlan Flan she may very well be a yielding, receptive sort of woman."

Bob was struggling. Reinhart had him imprisoned, a big bandaged hand on each of Sweet's slender arms.

"And Blaine," said Reinhart. "The way it has worked out is a total standoff: we each defy absolutely the other's idea of what we should be. Something clean and perfect about that. We are such total enemies that if either of us did not exist, the other would have to invent him. We may be, in fact, figments of each other's imagination as is. Everybody needs a red herring to throw pursuers off his trail."

Bob broke away from Reinhart's right hand and threw an ineffectual left that grazed Reinhart's temple. Reinhart knocked him to the lab floor with a blow to the solar plexus.

While Sweet was doubled up, gasping, Reinhart bent over and continued, tightening the loose bandage.

"So both of them, Gen and Blaine, are seen as taking their place as figures in the rich tapestry, as the fellow says. Life would not have been the same without them, but can be lived in their absence. Does that sound heartless?"

Bob made grunting noises.

"It is. It is virtually impossible to be absolutely generous to someone you love: the time will always come when their interest is served only at the cost of yours. If you acquiesce in it, they will have contempt for you. The old power play. The world is made up not of winners and losers, but of followers and leaders. The divine right of kings is a much more natural principle than that all men are equal."

Understandably enough, Sweet was still totally occupied with himself.

"The really sinister person is the saint," said Reinhart. "With whom every association insures your being further damned. If you think I pity Winona, you are wrong. She is utterly devoid of a sense of evil. I don't know how she got that way. Gen and I are both masters of malice. She scares me. She makes me feel more inadequate than Blaine ever did. She will stumble through life, corrupting many a soul with her goodness, mine first of all. I expect eventually to burn in hell, so it would be copping out to begin it at this point, deal or no deal." Reinhart laughed. "You see, already, because of her I am welshing on my word, my Dad's idea of the worst sin a man could commit, but then, unlike me, he was a man of honor."

Reinhart helped Bob to his feet.

"Sorry about that. You might be a crook, but I know you are serious about the freezer program, the end of which may indeed justify the means: some do. I don't question your good faith. I'll tell you what I'll do: I'll make up a will by which my body will be donated to you when I die a natural death. If I don't outlast you, that is. But now I need Winona. She doesn't need me, make no mistake about that. In a profound way she is invulnerable."

Bob was bent over. In that position he said: "We got . . . our man." He breathed carefully several times, and gingerly straightened up. "Mainwaring. . . . He didn't make it. Gone too far before the cell therapy."

It came to Reinhart that this was final. Splendor, his old friend, had died, for all the bold talk.

Sweet said: "But it works! If Hans had got to him a few weeks earlier, maybe only days, he would have brought him around. The large intestine, you see—"

"He was dying anyway," said Reinhart. He looked at Bob. "You did no harm. You tried."

Sweet was gaining energy. "No time to stand around and snivel, Carl. His head is packed with ice cubes from the refrigerator now, and they are rapidly melting. We need dry ice. I came back here to find Hans's supply has evaporated. Otto apparently let himself out of his cage and broke open the insulated crates."

"He needed a hammer or crowbar for that," Reinhart said wondrously. "Imagine, he can use tools!" He looked around for the animal.

"All the dealers are closed at this hour. I've been calling everywhere. The head is at present wrapped in a plastic laundry bag full of ice cubes."

Reinhart did not want to think of poor Splendor, beyond hope. He was still searching for the remarkable Otto.

Bob struck his arm. "Carl, we need your aid. Unless that brain is frozen while it's still vital, we've lost. Hans has a portable iron heart going, to maintain blood circulation. But all that water ice can do is a slight cooling. The head must be packed in dry ice before we can bring the body over here. Those Black Assassins aren't helping any, either. They're holding Hans a virtual prisoner, a hostage, with the corpse."

Reinhart saw Splendor as he had been twenty years before: healthy, handsome, quixotic. A man dies when he becomes effective. Then he saw helpless Bob Sweet, whose toupee had got off register in the fall to the floor.

"Look," Reinhart said. "You know who'd have a whole truckful of dry ice? It's still early evening. There may still be some ice-cream vendors making their rounds. There's your answer: send the Assassins out to hijack a Mr. Softee truck."

Bob thought for an instant. Then he said: "Carl, you have proved your worth to this organization." He pointed to the wall telephone. "Would you mind? They might listen to you."

"Splendor was my friend," said Reinhart. "You know he never mentioned the pain, not once. It must have been indescribable. I never knew him as well as I should have."

Bob's exigent finger stabbed the air. "Then get going," he cried. "You can make up for it in the next century, when you are both thawed out."

"But that," said Reinhart, "may be more than a century from now. Meanwhile, we won't know if it works. Also, it supposes that I too will be successfully revived. But what if I live another forty-four years, am then frozen, and—"

"Carl, there are times when you can be petty." Sweet

changed color in exasperation. "This is a serious matter, and when did you ever know anything serious that was absolutely certain?"

Reinhart reflected on this interesting question while he dialed the number.